FAULT LINES

Cover background: Composite image of the Fractal Flame series by Jon Zander/CC-BY-SA-2.5 (http://creativecommons.org/licenses/by/2.5/)

"Fault Lines," by Douglas Clark. ISBN 978-1-62137-570-8 (Softcover); 978-1-62137-571-5 (Hardcover); 978-1-62137-572-2 (eBook).

Library of Congress Control Number: 2014914235

To Josie

Also by Douglas Clark

FAULT LINES

A Novel

Douglas Clark

Life is a tragedy wherein we sit as spectators for a while and then act our part in it.

Jonathan Swift

PROLOGUE

Carlos Perez and Patricia Reyes drove into the United States from Tijuana. They had been in line for two hours at the San Ysidro port of entry south of San Diego. Their black SUV had U.S. license plates. Both spoke English and showed U.S passports to Immigration. The passports held their photographs but not their real names.

Periodically they entered the United States under these same false identities. They were Salvadoran citizens. The real passport holders were also Salvadorans but with U.S. citizenship. Under threat of violence the naturalized husband and wife immigrants were forced to submit passport renewal applications in their names with photographs of Perez and Reyes. Perez and Reyes had sufficiently prepared their photographic appearances so as not to raise questions if the State Department compared to the original file photos of the real passport holders.

Perez was a high ranking leader in the ultra-violent Mara Salvatrucha, or MS-13 gang of El Salvador immigrants. The gang had its origins in Los Angeles with Salvadoran refugees fleeing the civil war there during the eighties. MS-13 invoked fear among the Central American immigrant community with the violence in support of their subcultural moral code of vengeance.

Years previously, both Perez and Reyes had been actively involved with the Salvadoran civil war, fighting with the rebels until the declared truce in 1992. Still under threat of arrest in El Salvador, Perez illegally went to the United States after an uneasy peace came to the country. The rebel insurgency turned to politics. Perez turned to a continued life of violence becoming involved with MS-13 in its formative years in Los Angeles. He was intelligent but with a violent character. Turning to the violence of the criminal gang was a preferred option to menial work as an illegal immigrant in the United States, or imprisonment back in El Salvador. He already spoke fluent English. His military experience with the Salvadoran rebels gave him immediate stature among the Los Angeles Salvadoran gang members.

Deported back to El Salvador after four years in the United States, Perez continued to rise within MS-13, eventually becoming their principle liaison to the Mexican Sinaloa drug cartel. The Sinaloa cartel was fighting the rival Los Zetas cartel. The Zetas, made up of Mexican ex-military elite forces, were highly organized and characterized by their extreme violence. MS-13 was equally as violent making them the perfect subcontracted muscle for the rival Sinaloa cartel.

This trip was a meeting with several MS-13 cell leaders, first in Los Angeles then in San Francisco. The local MS-13 gangs were mostly made up of young men in their twenties. Most were distinguished by excessive tattoo displays often including the neck and face. Their sole existence was directed toward violence to rival gangs. Prison was a natural part of their usually abbreviated lives. Prison acted as a course in advanced education.

Perez was now a senior leader, old by MS-13 standards at age forty-seven. He had tattoos but not visible. He could move about without instantly being recognized as a gangster. The MS-13 movement was becoming more organized and starting to compete with other ethnic gangs to move drugs in the United States. They had established a presence in several other U.S. cities. But unrestricted violence at the local cell level brought unwarranted police countermeasures. Counterproductive to drug trafficking, but also posing an increased threat to the leadership both in the United States and El Salvador. Low level members arrested for murders were giving up names to those higher up the food chain. That resulted in increased retaliatory murders within the membership ranks. Arrests and convictions for conspiracy and racketeering were increasing. Perez was in the United States to try to put a lid on this unsanctioned violence.

The Salvadoran community in Los Angeles was concentrated in the Pico-Union area just west of the Harbor Freeway. It was a poor high-crime area only a short distance from the sports and entertainment center of downtown Los Angeles east of the same freeway. Central American immigrants settled here in the seventies and eighties to flee the political violence in their home countries. Pico-Union gave birth to Mara Salvatrucha. It was still a tough place.

Perez knew the area well from the years he spent here in the early nineties. He and Reyes checked into a motel on Alvarado. A meeting was scheduled for that night at a Salvadoran restaurant in the area. Reyes would wait in the motel. Tomorrow they would drive to San Francisco. Flying would invite using their false identities unnecessarily. Their cover was best for the real passport holders, residents of Los Angeles, to limit their record of travel only to periodic crossings into nearby Mexico by car, raising no red flags in this age of NSA data-mining into electronic records.

Reyes expected Perez to be gone for several hours. Perhaps they could still make love tonight when he returned. After all, that's why he liked her to accompany him on his trips to Mexico and the United States. Reyes ordered pizza for delivery. At least she could watch U.S. television for a couple of hours.

Her pizza was long since finished. The television shows were boring. Stupid gringo comedies or police solving crimes with complex improbable forensics. Flipping channels she landed on local news with a breaking bulletin.

We are interrupting our regular programming to bring you breaking coverage of what appears to be a major police-involved incident in the Pico-Union district. Gunfire was exchanged less than thirty minutes ago outside a Salvadoran restaurant. We have no official comments from law enforcement yet, but several witnesses said there appear to be casualties as evidenced by bodies covered on the sidewalk. As you can see from our helicopter coverage, there is heavy police presence at the scene. We're standing perhaps a block from the apparent scene behind police barricades which have cordoned off the entire block. Multiple law enforcement agencies appear to be involved, including LAPD, LA Sheriff's Department, FBI, ATF, and DEA as evidenced by vehicle and officer markings.

Unconfirmed reports suggest this may have been a gang-related police raid that turned violent. Again there are still no reports of victims or law enforcement casualties. We are waiting for some official announcement from law enforcement to provide more details on this incident. We will stay on the scene throughout the evening as this story continues to develop. Now back to our .....

Reyes starred at the scene in disbelief. The location scrolling at the bottom of the screen identified the street and restaurant name Carlos had mentioned. He had made no contingency plan for her for such an eventuality. Was he killed or captured? Maybe he had gotten away. Carlos was smart. What was she to do? Wait of course. He would call on his cell phone if he had escaped. Both had cheap pre-paid cell phones for emergency use only. They knew of the U.S. government's ability for monitoring cell phone traffic and the GPS tracking capability. She held her own phone in her hand for thirty minutes ready to answer immediately. No call came. She repacked her small suitcase.

Instinctively she decided not to wait inside the motel room. There was only one way out, the front door. The widow in the bathroom was barred. She needed escape options. Grabbing her suitcase and Carlos' duffle bag, she cautiously opened the door. Looking to make sure there was no one outside, she walked down the stairs and found an outside hallway area with vending machines off the motel lobby. It was a good vantage point to watch the parking lot out front. She was on street-level with an exit out the back of the motel, down from her room's location by a hundred feet.

The precautions proved fortuitous. After only minutes standing in the dim recess of the vending machine area, three police cars drove up, no sirens or lights. The officers drew their weapons and headed up the external stairs to the second floor. They positioned themselves outside her room. She heard her name called out shortly before the door was kicked in.

Reyes walked quickly out the back of the motel. From the alley she crossed the street to another dark alley. She needed to gain distance away from the motel. Along the way she threw the duffle bag into a dumpster. She needed to leave the area quickly. This was a mean neighborhood. Not safe for a lone woman, even one carrying a 9mm semi-automatic.

PART ONE

El Salvador
1989

CHAPTER 1

The street of expensive homes could have been an exclusive neighborhood in any sunny part of the world. Block walls or wrought iron fences surrounded many of the homes. Lush landscaping on large lots secluded each house from its neighbors. All were set well back from the street. It was seven-thirty on a Tuesday morning in early May, eighty-five degrees already and sunny. Another monotonous repetition of every other day for the last three weeks.

A much abused and rusted stake truck pulled into a driveway entrance to a large estate surrounded by a ten foot stucco wall. The wall was topped with coiled razor wire. Security here was more important than aesthetics. The truck was stopped at the heavy steel gates by two soldiers armed with American M-16 assault weapons. An officer approached from a guard house concealed around the corner of the wall. The affluent tranquility was just a veneer in this Central American police state. This was El Salvador.

The guards were not relaxed. Both had brought their weapons to their shoulders. Even the officer had drawn his sidearm.

These were violent times with the continuing civil war now ten years old.

"Out of the truck, now! Everyone!" the officer shouted.

The two men in the front opened the doors and stepped down.

"You in the back. Get out of the truck. Hands on your head. What is your business here?"

The driver answered, "We're here to work on the grounds, Señor."

"You're not the regular crew."

"That is correct, Señor. Señor Mendez said we were to come here today because Colonel Solorgano has complained about the work. My crew is the best. All our customers ....."

"Shutup." The officer was in no mood to listen to the prattle of this idiot.

"Face down in the grass," he ordered.

All four laid face down in the grass next to the driveway. The officer returned to the guard house while the two soldiers trained their weapons on the four workers. He called to the house and spoke with the duty officer. After giving the information he was ordered to stand by and the duty officer would get back to him.

The duty officer then called the maintenance company to verify the identity of the gardening crew. Eduardo Mendez, the owner, assured him the men were reliable and would do better work than the previous crew. The officer took down the names of the workers from Mendez and hung up.

The officer called his subordinate at the gate and told him to verify their names and papers, and then search the truck thoroughly. If everything was in order, he was to let them pass into the grounds.

"You did well Mendez. In a short while we will leave you." The stranger said. He was still holding the barrel of the gun behind Mendez's ear.

A man and a woman had broken into Mendez's office through a rear window early in the morning before Mendez arrived. As they heard him unlocking the door, they pulled nylon stockings over their heads. It was important to not have their faces seen by Mendez otherwise he would have to be killed. As it was, Mendez' life would later be in danger even with his story of being held at gunpoint.

After examining the identity papers of the crew, one of the soldiers searched the truck thoroughly, including the undercarriage. The truck was allowed to pass through the gate. The driver pulled up behind a jeep with a mounted 30 caliber machine gun parked in the circular driveway in front of the house. In front of the jeep was a black Mercedes sedan. The gardener's truck was able to park in such a way as to conceal any activity in the rear of the truck from either the house or the gate.

All four workers began unloading their tools. The driver put on gloves that reached to his forearms. Two fifty-five gallon drums stood at the back, filled with cow manure for fertilizer. They had made sure it was fresh in order to discourage too close a scrutiny. One nose full in the hot sun had been enough to divert the soldier from probing further.

Reaching down in the still moist manure, the driver pulled out several plastic bags from each drum. While two of the men kept a lookout as they arranged shovels, hoes, and rakes, the driver and the other man laid out the bags on the bed of the truck.

The contents of the bags consisted of four Israeli made Uzi machine guns, four Soviet 9mm Makarov pistols, eight U.S. fragment grenades, several pieces of steel wire cut in two foot lengths, and four black commando balaclava hoods. The hoods would offer sufficient disguise of identity for contact with anyone after getting by the gate guards. More importantly, they added a romantic flavor of terror the leader liked.

Unfortunately, the knit masks were not only hot, but the plastic had not effectively insulated out the odor.

"Mother of God, I can't wear this." The other man in the truck said as he pulled the hood on then quickly removed it.

"Carlos, put it back on. The smell will pass." The driver said.

Reluctantly Carlos did as he was told without further comment. The driver was not only the leader, but obviously commanded a special respect. Even dressed as a laborer with a stained shirt, old denims, and work boots, he generated authority. He was average height, physically fit, in his late thirties. Older than the others. His black hair was stylishly cut although uncombed for his present disguise. He had near-black eyes that fixed intently on whoever he was speaking to. A black, close-trimmed beard and moustache. Dark Latin complexion.

The leader and the other three put on their balaclavas. All of them took an Uzi and stuck a Makarov 9mm pistol in their belts. Into their pockets, each put two grenades and several coils of the steel wire.

"Now," ordered the leader.

All four men ran in a crouch to the side door. The line of sight from the guards at the gate was obstructed by the stake truck. There were no perimeter guards visible from this end of the house. The leader carefully looked through the window of the door. The quick glance revealed at least two people in what appeared to be the kitchen. He held up two fingers signaling to the door. Stepping back he nodded to Carlos who pulled open the door. The leader took two steps into the kitchen.

"Quiet. Don't move," he said in a loud whisper to the two startled occupants of the kitchen. One was a young soldier in uniform, the other an older man in an apron, probably the cook.

The leader pushed the barrel of his Uzi under the chin of the terrified soldier. Carlos coming in right behind him did the same to the cook. The other two assailants quickly took positions to cover the door leading to the rest of the house.

"Where is the colonel?" the leader asked the soldier. The soldier said nothing, not so much from resistance as from sheer terror.

The leader pulled a hunting knife from his boot, and substituted it for the Uzi at the soldier's throat. "I will not ask again. Now tell me where the colonel is."

The leader's manner was calm and pragmatic. He had every intention of ramming the broad blade knife into the throat of the soldier if he didn't give him the information. That would certainly make an impression on the cook.

"Straight down the hall .....at the end .....his office .....I think ....." The soldier was stumbling over his words.

"Slow down. At the end of the hall?" the leader asked.

"Yes."

"Right or left side?"

"Left. Facing out to the rear of the house."

"Who else is in the house?"

"Three ....no, four other soldiers and an officer."

"Where are they now?"

"They're in the room next to the colonel's office, at least the soldiers are. I don't know where the captain is. Maybe with the colonel."

"Anyone else?'

"No."

The leader ordered both the soldier and the cook to get down on their knees on the floor. Carlos quickly wrapped the wrists of both men with the steel wire. The wire cut sharply into the flesh and the older man started to whimper from pain and fear.

"Shut up old man. Be glad you will live. The pig will not," Carlos Perez said. The leader gave Perez a sharp glance of rebuke and told him to hurry. Perez pulled the bandanna from his neck and used it as a gag on the old man. One of the other attackers offered up his for Perez to use on the soldier.

Both men were pushed face down on the floor. Perez finished by tying their ankles with wire. Only two minutes had passed since they had entered the house.

Using none of his group's names, the leader pointed to one and said, "Stay here in the kitchen. If there is shooting, prevent any of the soldiers outside from entering." To the other two, "You and you take the guards down the hall. I'll take the colonel. If there is trouble, kill everyone. No more prisoners. And make sure you destroy any radios and telephones."

The leader cautiously opened the swinging door leading to the rest of the house. He saw no one. To the left was a large formal dining area. The polished mahogany dining table could easily seat fourteen. To the right was a large sunken living area with striking cream colored furniture, contrasting with the dark gray slate tile floor. Beyond was a hallway leading presumably to the guards and their target.

Hearing voices, they stopped outside the doorway to what served as the guard contingent operations room. All three assailants were sweating profusely. They would either bloody the enemy today or die in the next few minutes. They would become a force to be reckoned with, or just a few more, unremembered martyrs.

The leader nodded to Perez and the other man named Rafael. The two burst into the room with Perez in the lead covering to the right and Rafael covering to the left. Three soldiers were sitting at a table playing cards and smoking. Their assault rifles were propped against the wall.

The room was approximately twenty feet square with two large windows facing the back yard. To the left was a door which was closed. On a table on the right hand wall, stood a field communications radio and three telephones.

"Hands on your head!" Perez ordered in a load whisper. All three soldiers obeyed immediately. The black hooded figures made a terrifying impression. A cigarette dropped from one soldier's mouth. Another's bladder involuntarily let go.

"Where is the other one?" Perez said. Before any of the three could answer, the door to the left opened apparently from a bathroom. The fourth soldier immediately pulled his sidearm and fired at Rafael. The first shot missed, but the next two caught Rafael in the chest. He went down without firing his own weapon. Perez turned and emptied a burst from his Uzi in a wide arc, mostly as a reflex action. The three soldiers sitting at the table scrabbled to get down on the floor. One attempted to pull his own sidearm. His eyes locked with Perez's for a fraction of a second. He knew he was dead.

Perez emptied a sustained burst into the three men now on the floor. At this close a range, the damage was substantial, particularly those rounds that struck the head. Turning to the left, he hit the door with a short burst to pin the attacker who retreated back inside the bathroom. Perez then backed out into the hallway for cover.

Perez turned quickly to the right in the direction to the door to the colonel's office. No one was in the hallway. Several more shots came from the soldier behind the bathroom door. Perez pulled a grenade from his pocket. He pulled the retaining pin ring, waited a couple of seconds, and threw it like a baseball at the partially closed door shielding the fourth soldier. The grenade dropped to the floor with the door partially open. Probably recognizing what was happening, the soldier slammed the door shut a second before the grenade exploded.

Perez had never exploded a grenade before. Inside the house, the noise was awesome as it reverberated off the walls, blowing out the windows. He pulled a second grenade, tossed it underhand where the door had been, and held his ears. The second grenade made sure the fourth soldier was no longer a threat.

Simultaneous with Perez and Rafael rushing the guards, the leader kicked open the door to the adjacent room, the room presumed to be the colonel's office. Two men were standing in the middle of the room. One had the shoulder board insignia of a full colonel on his beige uniform blouse, the other a captain dressed in camouflage fatigues. Both put their hands up in response to the gesture from the Uzi.

"On your knees, hands behind your heads," the leader said.

"You'll never get away with this you filthy son-of-a-bitch," the colonel said, as he quickly got down on his knees.

"You're the fucking ......"

"Yes, we're the gardeners, idiot," the leader finished the sentence for the captain, whose face was reddening, maybe more from anger than from fear.

As the two officers got down on the floor, automatic fire broke out in the next room. Preparing for the worse, the leader got behind the two kneeling men in order to watch the door. If he was to die, at least he would take the colonel with him.

It seemed like minutes, but only a few seconds had passed before the first grenade exploded, closely followed by the second explosion. With the grenades, he at least knew that his men had inflicted damage.

Perez quickly but cautiously shot a glance into the office. Seeing the situation, he entered and reported to the leader. "Rafael is dead. The four guards are dead."

"The telephones and radio?" the leader asked.

"I ....I don't know. I'll take care of it." He turned to leave, but the leader halted him.

"Wait. First tie their wrists. The colonel first."

Perez took a coil of wire from his pocket and tied the colonel's wrists. Putting a hefty twist to the wire, he was rewarded with a sharp grunt of pain from Colonel Javier Solorgano.

While Perez was tying the colonel, the leader stepped behind the captain. As soon as Perez finished, the leader fired a single round into the back of the captain's head. The entire head appeared to explode. Blood and tissue sprayed in a wide pattern across the room. The colonel was splattered with blood on his left cheek. Perez was surprised but he was used to such carnage from fighting with the rebel insurgency.

Colonel Solorgano could not control the effect on his stomach as he retched and vomited.

The leader moved to the door and looked down the hall. Roberto Salas had opened the door from the kitchen at the sound of the gunfire. He was trying to maintain a position to cover an attack from the outside while trying to understand what was happening inside down the hall.

"Roberto, what's happening outside?" the leader asked.

"One man is approaching the kitchen door cautiously. From the picture window I can see at least two approaching the front."

"Where are the keys to the car?" the leader asked the colonel.

"In my desk drawer," the colonel answered weakly.

"Carlos, quickly. And rip that phone out."

Perez located the keys then tore the phone loose from the line. The ornate glass case displaying a collection of pistols and revolvers became a likely target for the disconnected phone. He pulled the colonel to his feet and pushed him into the hallway. As they moved down the hall, a phone was ringing from the guards' operations room. The leader picked up the receiver. "Yes?"

"Who is this?" the voice demanded.

"Listen. We have Colonel Solorgano. Who are you?"

"This is Lieutenant Aviles at the gate. I demand to know what is going on."

The leader smiled as he realized this was an internal line. "Listen to me, Lieutenant. You will order your men to pull back from the house immediately. If you attack we will kill Colonel Solorgano. You can't get to us without killing Solorgano. In one minute we will leave the house and get into the Mercedes. Do not attempt to stop us."

The leader disconnected the call by yanking the cord from the wall. He did the same to the other phones, and smashed the radio with the butt of his Uzi.

All three assailants moved quickly down the hallway. Looking outside through the large window in the living area, they could see two soldiers on the front lawn in prone firing positions with rifles trained on the house.

"Roberto, come with us, we're leaving now. They know we have Solorgano. They won't shoot," the leader said.

The leader moved down the two steps into the sunken living area and across to the foyer and front door. Behind him, Perez dragged the colonel with Salas following.

"Roberto, get two grenades ready," the leader said, as he also pulled a grenade from his own pocket.

Opening the front door a few inches, he yelled, "We are coming out. If you shoot, the colonel dies. We have grenades. Even if you were to kill us, Solorgano still dies."

"Okay, ready?" the leader looked at his two men.

Each nodded.

"Carlos, you hold Solorgano's arm tightly. I'll be on his other side. Roberto, stay behind us."

The leader opened the door and edged out with Carlos Perez pushing Solorgano ahead of him. He held the grenade in his left hand with the Uzi in his right. Holding the grenade up, he hooked a finger in the ring, and pulled the pin. Holding the spring loaded handle from releasing, the grenade was now live. It would explode within seconds after releasing the handle.

Ramming the grenade under Solorgano's chin he told him, "Tell them."

"Don't shoot! Don't shoot!" Solorgano shouted.

The Mercedes was only fifty feet from the front door. The leader opened the back door and Perez pushed Solorgano in.

Salas moved in right behind. Perez opened the front door and got behind the wheel. The leader surveyed the scene. Two soldiers were still lying on the lawn maybe a hundred feet away. He could see at least one more behind a tree to the left. The gates were closed. Someone was standing in the guard house, presumably the lieutenant.

The leader got in the back on the right side of Solorgano. "Let's go, Carlos."

"The gate? What do we do?" Perez asked as he turned the key in the ignition.

"He'll open it, or we will."

Perez eased the car around the circular drive toward the gate. The lieutenant clearly did not know what to do. As the Mercedes moved closer, he retreated back from the guard house and gate. Perez brought the car to within ten feet of the still closed gate. The leader got out slowly. He moved to the gate still holding the live grenade in his left hand, the Uzi in his right. He released the latch and pulled the inward opening gate open.

Perez eased the car forward. Before jumping into the car, the leader threw the grenade in the direction of the officer. Salas tossed another grenade into the guard house as Perez hit the accelerator, gravel flying with the spinning tires.

As the car sped down the street, sirens could be heard in the distance. Perez jerked the Mercedes through a series of turns as he worked his way through the residential area. He had familiarized himself with all of the streets for the past several weeks and knew exactly where he was going. Minutes later, the Mercedes slowed and turned onto a main street, assuming a moderate speed equivalent to the sparse traffic.

At 7:50AM a call was received at the Salvadoran Treasury Police, Policia de Hacienda headquarters. The caller identified himself as a Sergeant Moreno. The state of the sergeant's agitation brought the duty officer to the line.

"This is Captain Jimenez. Identify yourself."

"Sergeant Moreno. At the colonel's house."

"Colonel who?"

"Colonel Solorgano."

"What's the problem, Sergeant?"

"He's been taken. They killed five men."

"Taken? Who's been taken?"

"Colonel Solorgano."

"Taken by who?"

"I don't know. There were four men. Well armed. Disguised as gardeners." The words were tumbling out.

"Standby, Sergeant," the captain said.

Turning to the other staff in the communications room he said to a sergeant, "You, take this call. Get all the information you can from this fool. Lieutenant Flores, gather a squad of men immediately and go to Colonel Solorgano's residence."

"What's going on, sir?" the lieutenant asked.

"Now lieutenant, move it!" the captain ordered without further explanation.

The news of the attack spread quickly through the chain of command. The duty captain informed the deputy commander of the Treasury Police, Major Jaime Rivera, second in command to Colonel Solorgano. Rivera in turn placed a call to national military headquarters reaching a Captain Ramirez, aide to Colonel Francisco Benavides. Benavides was deputy chief of staff, the third highest ranking military officer in the country.

Captain Ramirez walked down the hall and stopped in front of Colonel Benavides' closed door. He knocked and opened the door without waiting for a reply to enter.

"Captain?" Benavides said, slightly perturbed at the intrusion.

"Sir, we have a report that Colonel Solorgano's residence has been attacked and the colonel taken."

"Taken? What do you mean taken?" Benavides stood up abruptly from his chair behind his desk.

"Apparently abducted, Sir. They took heavy casualties. There is not much information yet. Major Rivera is investigating."

"Investigating? What the hell does that mean? Does he know what happened or not?"

Before the captain could answer, Benavides said, "Get Rivera on the line, I want to talk with him."

The captain came to the side of the desk and picked up the colonel's telephone. He ordered the operator to get Rivera on the line immediately.

While the captain was attempting to contact Major Rivera, Benavides considered his next steps, assuming that Colonel Solorgano had in fact been kidnapped. The initial shock of the news had passed. He started to consider the potential opportunities this presented. Benavides' career had been built on accurately assessing situations and determining how best to personally profit. Benavides was a skilled strategist and politician as well as a creative opportunist.

The rebels had never attempted this bold an incursion into the capital. Benavides was most concerned about the negative implications of an apparently successful attack on the military, not about the well-being of Colonel Solorgano. Solorgano was an embarrassment anyway. A sadistic pig. Benavides had no moral compunctions about the use of torture to extract information, but Solorgano liked torture for its own sake. He was a stupid thug.

As a brother officer of the same *tanda*, one's graduating class from the military academy, Benavides was constrained by tradition from doing much about Solorgano's excesses. With increasing frequency, he had to explain away those excesses to the Americans. As the American military attaché would repeatedly point out, it was increasingly difficult for Washington to justify military aid when these *incidents* appeared in the foreign press.

Benavides detested having to *explain* anything to the Americans, especially making excuses for someone like Solorgano. If he could gain command then he could overhaul the structure of the Treasury Police. Remove the thuggish tactics while enhancing the intelligence collecting effectiveness.

He contemplated this new situation. The army chief of staff would want immediate recommendations. Did they kidnap Solorgano to simply facilitate their escape, or was he the target? To use for bargaining? Possibly as an exchange for rebel prisoners? Not likely. He could not imagine them ever releasing Solorgano, not with his reputation. Clearly, they would kill him, probably after making some ridiculous demands. Solorgano was publicity. Maybe he was dead already. The thought brought a subtle smile to Benavides' face.

Benavides contacted his superior, Army Chief of Staff, General Arnulfo Garcia, in the office of the minister of finance. After a summary of the events, Benavides recommended a course of action to exploit the situation.

Increase security for all senior officers. Place all barracks on alert. He himself would assume temporary command of the Treasury Police. Make immediate arrests of suspected dissidents. Wait for demands from the rebels if any are forthcoming. But take a hard line, non-negotiation response. Write Solorgano off. Take the opportunity to make changes in the Treasury Police command. General Garcia also thought Solorgano was a liability.

The unsaid part to the last action was for Benavides to gain personal control over the Treasury Police permanently. Benavides still had unfulfilled career ambitions. Control over the Treasury Police would add tremendous personal power.

The Salvadoran military was organized into two groupings. The first consists of the army proper with a few hundred in the navy and air force. The second and smaller group was comprised of several command organizations responsible for internal security. These security forces consisted of the National

Guard, National Police, and Treasury Police. The National Police handled typical police duties in the urban areas, while the National Guard performed a similar function in the rural areas.

The Treasury Police was a bland name for a secret police force rivaling the most brutal and repressive in the world. Their function was ostensibly intelligence. Their real mission was to do the dirty work to support the military's hold on power through fear. Their techniques of torture were learned from the U.S. CIA and U.S. Army Green Beret Special Forces. Acquiring command, even temporarily, would provide Benavides exceptional advantages.

Benavides was essentially the number three ranking military officer in the country. His immediate superior was the army chief of staff, who in turn reported to the minister of defense. Currently, with a civilian president, the minister was the highest ranking military officer.

With control of the Treasury Police, Benavides would have access to highly sensitive files. Some of this information would not even be known by his boss, General Garcia, since Colonel Solorgano reported directly to the Minister of Defense, General Ruiz.

After relaying the news to national command headquarters, Major Rivera made straight for the communications room with Captain Jimenez close behind. A sergeant on a telephone saw the Major Rivera come into the room and said, "Sir, I've got a Sergeant Moreno on the line from Colonel Solorgano's residence. He reports they were attacked and the colonel abducted. They have casualties. Do you wish to speak to him?"

"I've already dispatched a squad under Lieutenant Flores to investigate, sir," the captain reported.

"Very well, Captain, tell the sergeant help is on the way," Major Rivera said. "I've notified National Command. I want road blocks at all exits from the city. Call the commander at the Alvarado Barracks for additional manpower for the road blocks.

Order all our off duty personnel to report back to duty immediately. Order all staff personnel to my office in thirty minutes."

"Yes, sir," the captain responded. He immediately started issuing instructions to the communications personnel in the room.

The Mercedes left the city and moved north on the Inter-American highway. Ten miles out of the city it turned onto an unpaved rural road. After a couple of miles, it pulled to a stop behind a sixty's-vintage Ford station wagon with the hood raised. All three men got out. Colonel Solorgano was removed roughly by Perez.

The young man under the hood of the station wagon closed the hood and opened the tailgate of the station wagon. Perez pushed the colonel into the back and covered him with a blanket. All four got into the car without a word. The driver swung the station wagon around and returned to the main highway. They continued away from San Salvador and eventually turned onto another road which led deep into the hills. Bumping along the rutted dirt road, they eventually arrived at a small rundown tenant farmer's house secluded on a remote coffee plantation. It was a little over two hours since they had attacked Solorgano's estate.

"Miguel, the binoculars," the leader said to the driver. "Carlos, get him into the house," he said referring to Solorgano.

Miguel Cortina got the binoculars from the front seat of the car and ran back to the leader. "Santiago, you got him," Cortina said excitedly. "Where's Rafael?"

"Rafael was killed." Santiago Molina said with no particular emotion. His thoughts were focused on the next step. Rafael was a casualty. On balance, his loss was well worth the gain. The attack was an unqualified success. After surveying the area, Molina went inside the dilapidated house. He gave the binoculars to

Cortina who immediately took up an observation position out-side. The interrogation of Solorgano should not take long.

Solorgano was sitting on the earth floor against the wall. He looked up with renewed terror in his eyes. He was a small man, no more than five-six, stocky, out of shape, probably in his early fifties. He had a round, squat head with a broad nose. His hair was sparse on top and streaked with grey at the temples. Right now he was sweating profusely. He smelled like an animal. By any assessment, Solorgano was ugly.

"Who are you?" Solorgano asked. He received no answer.

"My wrists ..... please."

The wire had cut deeply into the flesh. Dried blood covered his hands. The swollen flesh over the embedded wire had turned black-purple.

"I will ask you questions, Colonel. I expect answers. I have little time, and even less patience. We will inflict even greater pain than you now feel. In fact, you will lose your hands unless the wire is removed soon. We will remove the wire only after you have told us all we want to know. You of all people know the effects of torture. Eventually everyone talks. You don't look the type to have a high threshold for pain."

"You're going to kill me aren't you?"

"Of course, Colonel. But how you die depends on you. Tell us what we want to know and you die like a soldier. A drink of alcohol, a cigarette, a quick painless bullet in the back of the head. The alternative is to die screaming in agony for hours."

Solorgano wailed like an old woman for several minutes, pleading not to be killed. Eventually he regained some measure of control.

"Give me water, please. I'll tell you what you want to know. My wrists? Please?"

"Water now, the wrists after you answer some questions."

Perez retrieved a plastic jug of water from the car. After tending to Solorgano, he sat down at the rough hewn table along with Salas. Salas had writing materials to take notes. Santiago Molina began the questioning. He paced about the small room as one answer prompted the next question.

The interrogation lasted almost three hours. Somewhere during that time, the wire binding Solorgano's wrists was removed. This turned out to be a mistake. The surge of blood through the damaged wrists caused Solorgano to almost faint with the pain. Trying to improve the situation by giving Solorgano some bread only worsened matters by his choking and vomiting. After a delay of thirty minutes, they bond his wrists loosely with a cloth rag.

By half past noon all three men were showing fatigue from the stress. Salas had filled a notebook with information that poured out of Solorgano. Solorgano had gone into such detail that Molina had to frequently cut him short and go on to new questions. The only thing you could respect about Solorgano was his memory for detail.

Molina eventually exhausted all his questions. Solorgano had even volunteered a wealth of additional useful information.

"Well, Solorgano, you have cooperated. However, it is now time."

Molina motioned to Perez and Salas. They got up and pulled Solorgano to his feet.

"No, please!" he whimpered. Tears ran down his face and his legs buckled. Perez and Salas half carried, half dragged him from the farm house.

"Solorgano. I promised you a cigarette," Molina said. Solorgano only stared blankly. Molina lit a cigarette and stuck it in Solorgano's mouth. The cigarette bobbed up and down with the trembling of his lips. Solorgano coughed. Tears ran down his cheeks.

"And a drink. I almost forgot. Some Mexican tequila? A moment please."

Molina walked behind Solorgano who was being held up-right by Perez and Salas. He drew the Makarov pistol from his waist, put it within an inch of Solorgano's back, and fired three times in rapid succession.

All three shots tore through the heart and exited the chest in what appeared to be one massive wound.

Perez and Salas were expecting the execution, but not in this manner. They released their grip on the arms of the now lifeless body as if it was contaminated. It pitched forward into the dust.

"Carlos, bring me the machete," Molina said.

Perez now understood what Molina was planning to do. Clearly their leader embraced the use of violence without any hesitation.

Perez returned with the machete. Molina pointed to the body and nodded to Perez, "You know what to do, Carlos."

The other two watched with the fascination of horror as Perez decapitated the head from Solorgano's body with two strokes of the machete. Salas stood numb. Cortina turned away and vomited.

"The information he gave us will damage the fascists. His head will send a special message to the military high command. The colonels do not get this close to killing. This will remind them they are vulnerable," Molina said. "Carlos, get a container for that," pointing to the head. "We're leaving."

Solorgano's body was dragged into the house. No need to have it spotted from the air. His head was placed in a wicker basket in the back of the station wagon. Two hours later they re-entered the capital, San Salvador. Road blocks had been estab-lished, but only for vehicles apparently leaving the city and its suburbs.

Shortly after entering San Salvador they pulled into an alley behind what had been a restaurant in a poor section of the city. The street was unpaved. The neighborhood was a collection of small, single story buildings housing mostly small shops. Many of the buildings were boarded up. The former restaurant was one such building. There were few people to be seen about. Safer to remain indoors. All four men got out of the station wagon.

The alley ran behind a string of shops at the rear of which were gutted hulks of old automobiles and lines of hanging laundry. Most of the merchants lived in the rear of their businesses. Four small boys could be seen at the end of the alley a block away. They were engrossed in their game of kicking a soccer ball. Cortina took a tire iron from under the seat. He used the iron to pry off the boards securing the door. It took little effort since the boards were secured with only a couple of small nails to facilitate easy removal. Perez opened the rear of the station wagon and took out the basket.

Molina, Perez, and Salas entered the building and closed the door after them. Cortina quietly replaced the boards over the door by using the same nail holes. He then went to the car and raised the hood to the engine. Under the guise of working on the engine, he took up his duties as lookout.

The three men were inside the old restaurant less than ten minutes. Molina opened the door carefully until Cortina signaled all clear. Behind him, Perez pushed an ice cream vendor's cart. Molina had noticed the abandoned cart in the back of the restaurant when they had checked it out as a safe house. Perez had also donned a large hat and poncho.

"Good luck, Carlos'" Molina said.

Perez nodded and left the alley pushing the cart. After re-securing the boards across the door, the other men drove off in the car.

Colonel Benavides had taken personal command of the search. Road blocks had sealed the city. The security forces had units raiding known gathering places of those who opposed the government. Benavides did not expect any real results from these actions but it would satisfy those expectations for an immediate response. At a brief meeting with the Defense Minister and the Army Chief of Staff, he was assigned the task of devising an operations plan to deal with the incident. He had scheduled a meeting that afternoon with selected senior officers.

Benavides was making notes for the upcoming meeting when Captain Ramirez opened the door abruptly.

"Sir, they found Colonel Solorgano's car."

"Where?"

"On a back road, off the Inter-American highway west of the city. No sign of the colonel. There were tracks of another automobile nearby. The officer at the site says they are recent tracks."

"Very well, Captain. Pass the information on to the necessary commands."

"Since we found the car, sir, do you want to issue any new orders?"

"Not yet, Captain. We'll take the question up at the meeting."

The crisis meeting convened in the conference room of the Army National Command headquarters. In addition to Colonel Benavides, there were two other full colonels and two lieutenant colonels from brigade commands and the National Guard, the commandant of the military academy, Major Rivera from the Treasury Police, and Captain Ramirez, Benavides' aide. Benavides had selected this particular group since they shared generally the same political position. All but Rivera could be counted on to support Benavides proposals.

Benavides opened the meeting by updating them on the discovery of the car. Captain Ramirez presented the details of the attack on Solorgano's residence assembled from the witness accounts at the scene. He reported that they had not yet identified the terrorist that was killed at the scene. After reviewing the security measures that had been put in place, and paying lip service to concerns over the fate of his brother officer, Benavides got down to his real purpose for the meeting. This was to explore ways to exploit the situation. Before getting very far, the meeting was interrupted.

Bursting into the office, which caused one startled colonel to come out of his chair, a junior officer excitedly reported, "They found Colonel Solorgano! At least ...."

"Where?" a colonel asked, cutting off the rest of the young officer's words.

"It's his head sir!"

"Lieutenant, slow down," Captain Ramirez ordered.

"Sir, they found Colonel Solorgano's head."

After the initial furor had subsided in the room, the lieutenant reported the details of this latest development.

"At approximately 1850 hours, the headquarters for the 8th National Police Brigade received a call instructing them to examine an abandoned ice cream vendor cart across the street. Fearing a bomb, it took over thirty minutes before they were able to open the lid. Colonel Solorgano's head was found in the cart. In the mouth was a type written note. The note is on its way over here right now."

The note arrived fifteen minutes later at Army National Command Headquarters. It read:

To all military officers:
The head of the butcher Solorgano is only the first.
All military officers will be considered legitimate
targets. The blood of thousands of your countrymen
is on your hands and those of your predecessors.
Only the destruction of the military can atone for
these atrocities. We demand only your death.
La Mano de Justicia

CHAPTER 2

It was an extraordinarily hot day in May. Summer comes early to Southern California, but typically not ninety degrees in the last week of the month. The hills surrounding the campus of the California State Polytechnic Institute in Pomona, California were still green from the winter rains. The semester had ended and Victor Castell had completed the requisite number of courses to obtain his bachelor's of science degree in electrical engineering.

Graduation ceremonies were two weeks away, but he had no plans to attend. In two days he had a flight to San Salvador. He was going home. Sort of. At least to Central America. He was to spend the summer with his mother in Santa Ana, El Salvador. Although an American citizen born in California, home for most of his childhood had been Panama City, Panama. Only for the last four years of college had he returned to Southern California.

Castell had lived in Panama City, Panama since he was nine. Three months ago his mother called to tell him that she and his father were separating. She told him she would be returning to her homeland, El Salvador, and wanted him to come spend the summer with her.

His father called the next day from Panama. It was only a five minute conversation. He told him much the same thing as his mother except in briefer terms. In fact, it sounded like a business briefing. His father also informed him that he was leaving his executive position with the Canal Authority and returning to California. Interestingly, his mother had made no mention of this.

Like most things his father did, he assumed this too was well planned. His father had held the post of Deputy Administrator for the Panama Canal for the last four years of his thirteen years at the Canal. With the operation of the Canal reverting to Panama within ten years, the next administrator would undoubtedly be Panamanian. With this in mind, his father had secured an executive position with Bechtel Corporation, the large engineering and construction firm headquartered in San Francisco.

The circumstances of the separation were only vaguely explained in the conversations with both his parents. He suspected that his father had seized not only the opportunity at Bechtel, but also the opportunity to leave his mother. He wasn't sure he really cared what the truth was. Castell wondered if his father actually even liked him. He knew he didn't love him. At best his father was apathetic. Or was it the other way around? Castell had never been able to determine what he in return felt for his father. As for his mother, that was more complicated. Sometimes she seemed more of a name than a person. His detachment was not something he could explain, much less understand.

He frequently thought about his past. Those thoughts seemed always to be just images. It was difficult to evoke emotions. Castell's past was one of privilege, but emotionally sterile. Was he just genetically self-absorbed or did his familial circumstances make him that way? It had ceased to trouble him as he grew older. It was just the ways things were.

His father, Richard Castell, was a standard story of a bright young man from a prosperous family, making his way up through the levels of business. He had all of the right things and did all of the right things. His ancestors had come to California from the Catalan region in Spain in the late eighteenth century. They had secured substantial land holdings in Southern California from the Spanish crown.

For most of the nineteenth century the land was devoted to cattle ranching. Into the early twentieth century, oil and land development broke up the great ranching estates of old California. For Castell's grandfather, the land was his link with tradition. He had managed to retain considerable real estate holdings, valued in the tens of millions. His son Richard did not share this sense of tradition. To him, retaining much of that real estate was simply poor management of assets.

By the sixties, Richard Castell had graduated from UCLA with a degree in civil engineering. When he entered college his aspirations were to become an architect. He soon discovered that neither his talents nor inclinations ran to the creative artistic side of architecture. Civil engineering was a natural alternative direction. With the building and population explosion in Southern California, the opportunities in land development eventually proved more enticing than building roads and bridges. With ample financing from the family, he enrolled at Stanford to pursue an MBA.

Richard had been an exceptional student at UCLA. Literally tall, dark, and handsome, he attracted girls easily. Although a little too serious, girls found him intelligent, and of course he had money. No problem getting girls into his bed.

One of those girls was a magnificent beauty, Alicia Portillo, also a student at UCLA. A foreign student from a wealthy El Salvador agrarian family. She was tall with long black hair. Her figure was striking with large breasts and long legs which she dressed to show off. No sandals, sweatshirts, or flower child look for her. She tended toward tight skirts and sweaters from the best shops. She walked with the confidence of not only a beautiful woman, but a woman who thought herself superior. She was snobbish and arrogant. As many men remarked, *a beautiful bitch*.

Richard and Alicia met at a beach party in Malibu. With the liquor and marijuana, they eventually found themselves in bed together at a friend's beach house. A year later they were married in a large ceremony in El Salvador.

In Richard, Alicia had apparently found a suitable mate. He was good looking, smart, and apparently going places. They shared a similar background of the landed aristocracy of Spanish ancestry, him from California, her from Central America.

Alicia Portillo was born in El Salvador to one of the original *fourteen families* that grew out of the consolidation of lands into the great agricultural estates in the latter part of the nineteenth century. These great estates, mostly coffee plantations, became the core of the emerging El Salvador oligarchy. Her father had been a powerful landowner that wielded considerable clout in the political affairs of El Salvador. Her sense of superiority was that bred of old money.

The separation of Castell's parents was the culmination of several events coinciding. In truth, his father had tired of the Canal, and for that matter Panama. Richard Castell had no interest to aspire to the top post. Panama had taken on a decidedly different tone under the rule of the narco-dictator, Manuel Noriega. Relations with the United States had deteriorated during the last couple of years. By treaty, the Canal was scheduled to revert to Panamanian control within ten years. Richard Castell needed to seek a new professional opportunity. That meant a return to the United States. Panama had become a foreign backwater.

On the other hand, Alicia was the grand hostess of what served as the social circle in Panama City. This circle included the wealthy of Panama City, the *rabiblancos*, or *white-tails*, those of European decent that dominated Panamanian politics and economics. Augmenting the *locals*, were diplomatic officials from various countries. For her, Noriega's ascendancy to power changed more than the ruling political group over the past years. There was a growing populist movement that was demanding increased power from the wealthy elite. Even if Noriega was removed, the winds of change would continue. At least with Noriega, there was a familiarity with her own El Salvador where the military held power. Even with his populist support, the ugly Noriega still ruled with iron control, leaving the wealthy class alone as long as they offered no political threat. Like her husband, she now wished to leave Panama, albeit for different reasons.

The military was necessary to El Salvador. They were the instrument of power for the ruling class, such as the Portillo family in El Salvador. As two dissimilar organisms, the wealthy and the military coexisted in a symbiotic relationship. The military may support a civilian government or try their own hand at governing by junta or dictatorship. Whether the process was elections or coup d'état, there always remained one constant. That constant was the powerful land holders who had built large enterprises upon which the economy rested. They were ultimately the ruling class. It was the same in all Central American countries. It was the same everywhere; wealth and power always ruled.

Increasingly, the ruling military junta in Panama was clashing with the elite Panamanian establishment. Demonstrations were frequent. Openly antagonist press comments suggested a deteriorating relationship with the United States. There were carefully whispered rumors that Noriega was involved with Columbian drug cartels. Alicia Portillo had tired of Panama City with its urban dirt and social unrest.

That was not the only source of her unhappiness. For longer than she cared to remember, Richard had been growing more distant. He seldom accompanied her to her frequent social functions. She had taken to arranging a cadre of eligible escorts. Since her husband had not made love to her in months, she easily drifted into a casual affair with the French ambassador. She was reasonably sure that her husband knew about it. Also reasonably sure he didn't care. She wondered if he too was having an affair.

Alicia was still a striking beauty at forty-six. Her figure had not changed much since her college days. She still weighed the same as she did when she met Richard at UCLA. Her face had few lines that would suggest her age. She was good looking and still liked sex. Life for her revolved around parties and socializing with the right people. She liked to dine at the best restaurants. The role of the aristocrat fit her well. Most of all, she liked herself. She determined that it was time to leave both Panama and Richard and return to her native El Salvador.

She made her announcement one evening just after he arrived home late one evening. She was sitting in the living room with a glass of wine. The cook and maid had left earlier.

"Richard, I've got something I need to tell you," she said just after he walked through the door. They had gradually abandoned even a perfunctory kiss when they met or parted.

He went to the bar to pour a scotch. "And what do you have to tell me, Alicia?"

"I'm leaving and going back to El Salvador."

Richard twirled the scotch around the ice in his glass. No surprise or anger registered in his expression. He stood next to the bar across the room from his wife.

"Well can't you say something?" she said.

"What's there to say? Obviously things have been difficult between us for some time."

"Difficult? For some time?" Her voice held the edge of barely concealed anger. "Yes it is difficult living in this miserable city, with a miserable husband who won't make love to me."

"I'm not going to argue with you, Alicia."

"Tell me one thing, Richard. Are you sleeping with someone else?"

"No I'm not sleeping with someone else," he replied with of resignation. He wanted to be through with this as soon as possible.

"I don't know why we have stayed here as long as we have. You could be doing so much more than running that damned Canal. You have never considered other opportunities."

"Other opportunities? What the hell do you know about my position at the Canal? You make it sound like I'm some sort of junior engineer." His voiced rose.

Questioning his marital fidelity was one thing. Disparaging his professional stature was quite another. Richard Castell may be cold, but he had a giant ego.

"I'm responsible for over 5000 people. My staff are senior managers, equivalent to top executives at major companies. My annual budget is in the hundreds of millions of dollars. That doesn't sound insignificant to me."

He was getting more worked up as he continued. "You don't know or care about anything of real importance. You finished school and turned your brain off. When was the last time you read a book? Or for that matter the newspaper? You spend all your time at endless parties or the club. Your friends are a bunch of brainless assholes."

"Wait one goddamn ....," she said, but was cut off. She had hit a nerve and he was not to be denied.

"You talk about opportunities. The only opportunities would be in the States. And we both know you do not want to go north. You couldn't be the grand dame, the nobility up there. You'd be just another middle aged, middle classed, idle bitch with nothing to do but screw the local tennis pro. Here you can screw ambassadors from all over the world. No, you need to stay in a chicken-shit banana republic to be important."

"You sonofabitch. *Eres un pinche gringo pendejo!* You call my friends assholes. Well you don't have any friends. You never go anywhere, and when you do you never talk." She ignored the reference to ambassadors.

"Alicia, let it go. I'm tired and none of this is doing any good. Tell me what it is you want."

"Just like that, drop it. Just another problem to be solved rationally. We can't even fight like husband and wife."

She was right. He couldn't, or didn't want to continue the argument. Just get it over with. The emotions were long gone. Only the logistics remained to be resolved.

"What do you plan to do," he asked.

"I'm leaving in two weeks to go back home. I'll stay with René for a while."

Home of course was the family estate in the western region of El Salvador. René was her older brother who managed the family's vast land holdings and the country's major export company.

"Divorce?" he asked.

"Maybe. I don't know yet." She was calmer now. "I'll call Victor tomorrow."

"Okay. I'll call him myself in a day or two."

Victor Castell did not know what he wanted to do regarding his future. He enjoyed the study of technical subjects and the abstraction of advanced mathematics. The thought of working at a real engineering job was not appealing though. He knew that his first job would have him doing some mundane task, probably not even associated with his training. His father had intimated that he could probably get him into Bechtel.

He had given some thought to eventually teaching at the university level. The drawback to that was getting up in front of people. He recalled the agonies of a speech class in his second year at school. The same fears were still there at the end of the semester. Still, the academic life was a possibility.

Castell had pretty much decided to continue his graduate studies if for no other reason than to postpone making a more specific career decision. His grades had been good enough to get accepted at Caltech in Pasadena. He had decided to depart from electrical engineering and pursue computer science. He was already experimenting with writing computer code. The thought of a new school's environment was something to look forward to. At any rate, working on an advanced degree made sense for whatever career path he took. Computers were the future in all sorts of fields. The fact that he had a source of money which allowed him to choose among options was something he thought about infrequently. His father confirmed he would fund his continuation of school during their brief conversation. In fact, there was the impression that it was a way of appeasement for his father, that this at least was something he could do for his only son.

Victor agreed to spend the summer with his mother in El Salvador. It was something different and there weren't too many alternatives. Besides, it would be a good environment to do work on some programming ideas he had. Working on his computer was one of his few passions. The family estate would be a good environment, provided his mother would leave him alone.

It had been almost nine months since he had seen his mother. He had spent a week with his parents in Panama City the previous summer. For Christmas, to avoid going back, he lied by saying he was invited to a friend's for the holidays. At best, Castell was ambivalent about his feelings for his mother. At worst, she was to be tolerated by ignoring her. That was the extent of the range of emotion. Maybe it would be different on the plantation. No one else, of course, called it a plantation, but that's how he thought of it. It reminded him of the great estates of the antebellum South in the United States. Not necessarily in appearance, but in practice. Castell had no particularly refined sense of politics or social equality, but the parallels were obvious.

He would enjoy seeing his uncle René again. He might also be able to talk with his other uncle, Augustin. Since Uncle Augustin was a professor of economics at the university in San Salvador, it might be interesting to talk to him about an academic career.

Castell had not seen Uncle Augustin since his grandmother's funeral, seven years ago. He would have to find a subterfuge in order to see him. If his mother found out, she would have a fit followed by a lecture. If his uncle René found out, he would fly into a rage. Uncle Augustin was the leftist outcast of a politically ultra-right family. The Portillo clan fought their own personal civil war. It would be interesting to see why Augustin provoked such intense political controversy in his mother's family.

Goodbyes were not difficult when he left California. He simply didn't say goodbye to anyone. His last night was spent at a hotel near the Los Angeles International Airport in order to avoid the traffic to catch his morning flight. After a long layover in Mexico City, he arrived that evening at Comalapa International Airport outside the capital city, San Salvador.

Castell was wearing jeans, tennis shoes, and a polo shirt. He was carrying a duffel bag and his laptop computer. He was of average height and build, with moderate, though undistinguished, good looks. The short, dark young man had no problem recognizing him as he exited immigration control. Castell looked around as he walked into the terminal, trying to spot a familiar face there to meet him. The young man approached him and announced his name was Juan and that he worked for his uncle, Señor Portillo. He had been sent to drive him to the family estate. Juan took Castell's baggage claim stub and his carry-on bag.

After collecting the luggage and clearing customs, Juan lead him to a silver Mercedes parked at the curb and opened the rear door for Castell. As they left the airport, Juan told him it would take about ninety minutes to get to the house. Juan said little af-

2

8

ter that since his English was only marginal. Castell did not tell
him he spoke Spanish fluently. This way he could relax and not
feel compelled to talk.

It had been four years since Castell had last been to El Salvador. That was just before going to college in California. On appearance, nothing had seemed to change. You could still feel the tension of the unrelenting civil war. A sense of detachment swept over him as they drove to his mother's family estate seventy miles away to the west of San Salvador. The streets of San Salvador were semi-deserted with few cars and the occasional military vehicle. Few people were out on foot. The dark Inter-American highway leading out of the city was even less populated. Driven by someone he did not know, the impression was less than welcoming.

He wondered if things were the same with the continuing civil war. He didn't read the newspapers, but the news had recently mentioned that the Salvadoran military was waging an aggressive campaign against the leftist movement. Apparently this was in response to the murder of a high ranking military officer. The report had even speculated about whether this might lead to a return to the extraordinary violence of the early eighties. Arriving at the family estate, the Mercedes pulled up behind a military jeep parked in the manicured gravel drive. Two soldiers armed with assault weapons stood alongside. Why had he come here?

Maybe he was critical about everything else in El Salvador, but his uncle's house was truly impressive. The house sat three miles off the main highway. The last quarter mile wound through beautifully landscaped lawns. Trees set off the several manicured acres that immediately surrounded the house, secluding it from the other working buildings of the estate. The house itself was immense. The exterior was a graceful blend of stone and wood with a veranda running the entire front and one side. He had early childhood memories of parties on the veranda with what must have been a couple of hundred people.

As they drove up to the front of the house, the driver blew the horn.

"We're here, Señor Victor."

As Castell got out of the car, he saw his mother come down the veranda steps, followed by his uncle.

"Victor, Victor!" she yelled.

"Hello mother," he responded, with not the same exuberance. His mother hugged him and kissed him on the cheek.

"*Mijo*," his uncle greeted him, repeating the hug. "It's been so long, Victor since I've seen you. It is good to have you here."

René Dominguez was on the short side, only an inch taller than his sister. Nevertheless, he was a strikingly handsome man of fifty-one. His black hair was heavily streaked with grey on the sides. He wore a close cropped mustache which offset a narrow, straight nose. He was of average build, but in obviously good condition with no hint of a middle age belly. Good looks ran in the Portillo family.

Castell walked up the steps to the great house with his uncle's arm around his shoulder. A servant joined the driver in unloading his bags from the trunk of the Mercedes. He was ushered into the large living room. A young man in his late twenties got up from his chair, excusing himself from a conversation with two other men.

"Victor, it's been years," his cousin Hector greeted him then embraced him. Hector was René's only son. He too had his father's good looks and the added advantage of being six feet tall. "Let me introduce you to our guests."

The two men Hector had been talking to rose from their chairs.

"Colonel, this is my cousin, Victor Castell. Victor, this is Lieutenant Colonel Andres Osario, the commander of the local National Guard regiment."

"It is a pleasure, Señor Castell," the Colonel said in Spanish as he shook Castell's hand. "We have been enjoying the company of your charming mother."

"And this is Guillermo Valdez, our manager," his cousin said, introducing the other man. Since this was a coffee plantation, Castell was reminded of the coffee commercial seen on American television. The handsome Juan Valdez of the commercial was lean and aristocratic. Guillermo was short, stocky, and swarthy.

"Victor!" the pretty middle-aged woman in a peasant dress said as she came into the room.

"Hello, Aunt Maria." He obligingly hugged her and kissed her cheek.

"Sit down everyone. You have time for one more glass of wine before dinner is served," his aunt said.

At dinner, there was the usual round of exchange of family information. Not that he cared, but he was informed that his three other cousins, René's three daughters, had all married since his last visit. His aunt was proud to point out that they had all married well, meaning into the right economic circumstances. He was asked the usual questions about school. What were his future plans? Was there a special girl? The prospects of marriage?

His uncle and the colonel were interested in how the American public felt about the civil war. Of course, they did not use the term civil war. To them it was the problem of the Communist insurgency, backed by outside countries such as Cuba. A Communist-based insurrection fueled by the same sources as elsewhere in Central and South America. El Salvador could not be allowed to fall to a leftist takeover like the Sandinistas accomplished in neighboring Nicaragua.

Castell said he didn't think that most Americans even knew about the conflict in El Salvador. Like others his age, he did not typically read the newspapers. It had to make TV news if anyone was to know about something. He did mention that he had heard about the army officer that had been killed. The one with his head cut off. Colonel Osario quickly pointed out that it was murder. An act of terrorism by the Communist FMLN rebels. He told Castell that the Army and the National Guard had the upper hand and would shortly eliminate the rebels. The murder of Colonel Solorgano was an isolated attack. It was two weeks since the killing of Solorgano and no further attacks had taken place. Osario said this proved the weakened state of the rebels as unable to sustain such publicity charged terrorist attacks.

The political conversation was interrupted by his mother suggesting he accompany her on a trip into San Salvador the next morning. Fortunately, his uncle insisted that the boy be allowed a day or so to relax. His uncle suggested that Alicia and Victor wait and return to San Salvador with Hector. Hector was staying a couple of days before returning to his office in San Salvador. Apparently his wife and daughter were currently out of the city. He was using the time to discuss various business issues with his father. Besides, his uncle pointed out, it would give him the opportunity to get reacquainted with his nephew. When René Portillo spoke, it had the ring of an order. Even Alicia rarely argued, much less ever challenged her brother.

Later, Castell lay in bed listening to the gentle whir of the ceiling fan, finding sleep difficult even with the fatigue of the trip. Even though this was family, he was still a stranger. He did not share the sense of heritage that his mother and uncle did. The talk of Central American politics at dinner held no personal connection. It held no frame of reference for him. The business of growing and exporting coffee was equally foreign.

Victor Castell was keenly aware of his feelings of detachment. He did not necessarily feel comforted by it, but it also did not disturb him. He understood that he was somewhat different. He was neither happy nor unhappy. The only major problem in his life seemed to be about career directions.

It was not that he was actually self-centered, but more that he was not people centered. He was typically polite and courteous. Quiet, but not shy. What people mistook for introspection was usually preoccupation with something other than the immediate activity or conversation. Castell had no personal relationships of any depth. He was generally ambivalent about people. Only concepts and ideas held his interest.

Electronics held a particular interest. It held for him the beauty of a pragmatic discipline, yet with no defined or rigid boundaries. It allowed for creativity and held rich opportunities for scientific elegance. In his studies, he gravitated more to electronics rather than such things as power distribution and devices like motors. Electronics held the ability to control things. Computer electronics took that to a level of infinite prospects.

So different from his cousin, Hector. Hector too had been educated in the United States, returning to El Salvador to manage the family's export business. He had inherited not only the good looks of his father, but also the charm. He was married and already had a young daughter.

Hector had invited him to visit his home in San Salvador when he returned there in a couple of days. His wife, Esperanza, would love to meet him. She would also like the excuse to dine out and party he added jokingly. Castell had let the offer pass without making a commitment.

The next couple of days were spent relaxing and horseback riding through the hills of the vast estate. Castell was wondering if he had made a mistake coming to El Salvador for the summer. Reprising past childhood summer vacations in El Salvador was not to be. He had been here only two days and was already feeling bored. He had seen about all there was to see of the beauty of the estate. Growing coffee was not very exciting. He found himself trying to steal as much time as possible reading in his room.

His mother was particularly irritating with her obsessive manner of constantly talking. He was rarely interested, tuning her out as much as possible. Her latest topic concerned arrangements to purchase a suitable house in San Salvador. She liked the family estate, but it was too *quiet* for her. Too rural. That translated as too remote for an active involvement in social affairs. The nearby city of Santa Ana was too provincial for her tastes. She was still an attractive woman that cultivated male attention. Her sister-in-law would likewise also welcome the return to quieter times in her own house with Alicia in the capital city, San Salvador.

The prospects of at least diversions in San Salvador prompted Castell to accept his cousin Hector's offer to spend a few days at their home just outside the city. It would also afford a good opportunity to slip away and see if he could contact his Uncle Augustin at the university.

The following day, he and his mother drove to San Salvador with Hector. Alicia wanted to do some shopping and look up old acquaintances. Hector's wife was to return that evening, so they all spent the morning showing Castell the city. Over lunch Castell casually asked if his Uncle Augustin was still at the university. Alicia stiffened at the mention of Augustin's name.

"Yes, I suppose he is. At least as far as I know. I haven't talked with him in quite some time. Augustin does not think like the rest of the family," she said.

"That's putting it very mildly, Aunt Alicia," Hector said. "How long has it been since you saw him, Victor?"

"I don't know. I guess I was maybe sixteen."

"Well I can tell you he has gotten worse since then."

"Worse? Is he sick?"

"Only in his politics. The sonofabitch is a traitor. He would give up the land to the illiterates and turn the country into another Cuba," Hector said angrily. "I'm sorry about my language, Aunt Alicia."

"That's all right Hector, we all know about Augustin."

"You make it sound like he's a criminal," Castell said.

"He is. The worst kind. Spreading his Marxist political garbage to students. Rumor has it that he has ties to the FLMN. The only reason he hasn't been arrested is because of the family name. Father cannot even talk about him without becoming upset. He is an embarrassment to the family. Worse than that, he's dangerous." Hector's voice still rose with emotion. Vigorously gesturing with his hands, he tipped over his wine glass. Alicia touched his arm lightly in a gesture conveying for him to take it more quietly.

"Listen, Victor, El Salvador is a poor country. We know that. But breaking up the large agricultural estates is not the answer. That would only reduce productivity. That in turn would reduce exports. The economy would be destroyed. We would have disastrous inflation. Believe me that kind of so-called land reform never works. Augustin and his kind would turn all that we have built into socialistic ruin."

"What about the military and the death squads?" The question was more from curiosity rather than argumentative.

"That's all bullshit. Excuse my language again, Aunt Alicia," Hector said. "That nonsense about death squads is a tactic by the leftists and supported by the left-wing press of the United States. There is no such thing. Never has been. All those pictures of bodies are from rebel guerrillas killed in attacks. The numbers quoted in the newspapers are even ridiculous.

"The rebels themselves killed many of those shown in the mass graves. These were reprisals against peasants for lack of support. It also made good propaganda. Simply bring in some sympathetic reporters and tell them so called death squads had murdered these people.

"Besides, that is all in the past now. Look at the progress that has been made in the last five years. The violence of the early eighties has been brought under control. We have a civilian government now. We have a strong army but they don't run things.

We have successfully prosecuted and removed from power those elements that have abused their power in the past."

"What about the killing of that army officer a few weeks ago?"

"That's what I mean. Look at what the Communists do. They commit a heinous act of torturing and beheading a man and call it war. Harsh action by the government is labelled repression and violation of human rights by foreign liberals. The FMLN has lost popular support and is now resorting to crude terrorism."

"No more politics you two," Alicia said. "It's too nice a day to deal with those unpleasantries."

"You're right, Aunt Alicia."

The conversation did not return to the subject of Augustin Portillo. No matter. Castell was now even more interested in contacting his uncle. It had been a long time since he found himself interested in meeting someone.

CHAPTER 3

The day after the killing of Colonel Solorgano, Colonel Benavides held a press conference at the National Military Command Headquarters. Folding chairs had been arranged for the reporters who were milling around talking. The major wire services and international broadcast networks were in attendance.

"Gentlemen, please sit down," Benavides said as he walked to the lectern. "As some of you may know, the commander of the Treasury Police, Colonel Javier Solorgano, was kidnapped yesterday during an attack on his residence. Colonel Solorgano's adjutant, a Captain Mendez was murdered execution style by a shot to the back of the head. Four other soldiers were murdered and two others were wounded in the attack. One of the terrorists was killed.

"Late yesterday we discovered that Colonel Solorgano had also been brutally murdered." Benavides paused for effect and turned to an aide who was placing a covered easel next to the lectern. "This was delivered outside the National Guard Headquarters."

Benavides lifted the cover from the easel. A large blowup of a photograph of Solorgano's severed head resting on a hospital gurney was displayed.

Several exclamations came from the group of reporters. Flashes started going off as the photographers crowded to get pictures. The video cameramen pushed their way to the front realizing a good visual story for that evening's broadcasts throughout the world.

"Gentlemen, please be seated," Benavides said, directing his comments to the crowding photographers. "Photo enlargements will be made available to you at the end of the press conference along with a press release of the facts as we know them."

One cynical journalist commented to a colleague next to him, that Solorgano was certainly an ugly fucker. Rather impertinently, he then shouted a question asking Benavides if they had found the rest of body.

"No, we have not found the colonel's body. If you'll be patient, gentlemen, I have a statement then I will answer questions.

"It is unfortunate that the Communist insurgents have resorted to acts of terrorism in the wake of defeats in the field. It is a clear attack on the institutions of El Salvador, intended to cause fear and disorder. These same people that pay lip service to calls for political reform and human dignity have resorted to acts of barbarism. These people are common criminals, terrorists. They cannot be considered soldiers, certainly not patriots.

"The government of El Salvador will not be intimidated by such acts from the FMLN. Security has been increased for all senior government officials and military officers. We are particularly concerned about the families of these officials. Fortunately Colonel Solorgano had no family at his home when the attack occurred. We are conducting an intense investigation to identify the perpetrators. To preclude any unnecessary incidents of violence, the police have imposed a temporary curfew from 7:00PM to 5:00AM. For those who are sympathetic to the insurgents, these murders should be a warning as to their true colors. Now, I will take your questions."

"Colonel, have you identified the perpetrators as being from the FMLN?" the CNN correspondent asked.

"Yes we have. The one attacker that was killed has been identified. He had a known affiliation with the FMLN."

This was of course not true. The dead attacker had not even been identified. When and if he was identified, it would be found that he did not have any known affiliation with the rebel FMLN, the acronym for the Farabundo Marti Liberation Front.

The FMLN was the leftist dominated military arm of the Democratic Revolutionary Front, or FDR, opposing the government and the right-wing military junta controlling El Salvador. It took its name from the 1930's communist peasant leader, Augustin Farabundo Marti killed in the great *matanza*, or massacre of 1932. To crush the political opposition and a budding rebellion lead by Marti, El Salvador's first modern military dictator, General Maximiliano Hernández Martinez, ordered the slaughter of 30,000 people, or four percent of the population at that time. That seminal event would usher in a succession of repressive governments for most of the remaining century.

The FMLN was formed in 1980 in the wake of the instability of a reformist bloodless military coup that deposed the unpopular dictator General Carlos Romero in October, 1979. The U.S. backed the coup with promises of military aid. The Carter Administration feared the worse alternative of a leftist insurrection like the leftist Sandinistas deposing of the Nicaraguan dictator, Somoza. Several different ruling juntas attempted to run El Salvador during 1980. Helping to fuel the fires of dissention was the Defense Minister, General Tomas Garcia. Garcia was the most powerful member of the junta and as far right politically as the deposed Romero. The vacuum left after the ousting of Romero unleashed the polarized elements of the extreme right and left. Full scale civil war resulted. It was a perfect example of the United States meddling in the affairs of other countries with resultant unintended consequences.

"Do you expect more bloodshed in the form of reprisals by the military?" Another foreign reporter asked.

Benavides glared at the reporter. "The government does not resort to what you call reprisals. The military will conduct its investigation in accordance with the law and the constitution. The government will not use terror to counter terror."

"Can you confirm reports that the army has stalled in its offensive north of San Miguel, even with the increased use of aircraft?" the Associated Press correspondent asked.

"Gentlemen, I must insist that you restrict your questions to the issue of Colonel Solorgano's murder," Benavides said.

Since Benavides would not reply to general questions, the press conference concluded after another fifteen minutes. As the press filed out, they picked up the promised press release and the 5x7 photo of Solorgano's severed head.

"A fucking monster. I've been down here a year and I can tell you that this asshole Solorgano got what he deserved," the same reporter who asked about the body said to his companion. "He was a chief organizer of the paramilitary death squads years ago. He was a major at the time and second in command of the Treasury Police. He took over the command three years ago. Rumor has it that he still kept his old habits. Might have been a victim's relative that got him. Maybe it was even ordered by some of his more moderate brother officers. He was an embarrassment. I'll bet that Benavides is as happy as a pig in shit. Look at this. Giving out pictures. Wants to make sure he gets good play in the press. I bet the sonofabitch would autograph one for you if you asked him," the reporter said as he picked up a photo.

The so-called investigation was proceeding as Benavides planned. Although Solorgano's deputy, Major Rivera did not like Benavides' direct involvement, he was obeying orders by keeping his men in check. Rivera was not as blatantly sadistic as Solorgano, but he was just as extreme in his political views. Eventually he would have to be removed.

Benavides had amended the list of people to be arrested for questioning to include a troublesome freelance journalist and a young Guatemalan professor at the university. The journalist was held in too much favor by the guerrillas. He was allowed photographs and interviews not assessable to most others. His work was reported frequently in the western press. Reporting from war zones was dangerous. His disappearance would cause minimal repercussions.

The politically active, anti-military professor presented a somewhat more delicate situation. He was articulate and charismatic with a growing following among university students. He was a colleague of the popular leftist Professor Augustin Portillo, sure to capitalize on any action by the security forces. Benavides sensed the future threat of the outspoken young man with a gift for oratory. Portillo might be out of his reach but the younger foreign academic did not yet enjoy the same international stature. However Benavides did not want to make the young academic a martyr. Since the professor was a Guatemalan citizen, Benavides would justify the government's actions based upon the threat of foreign subversive activities.

Benavides gave Rivera these two names, plus the gardening contractor whose truck was used in the attack on Solorgano. They were to be intensely *interrogated*. Rivera was ordered to use no extreme measures on any other new detainee, and to review arrest lists with Benavides. Additionally, Rivera was to have his men re-interrogate known FMLN prisoners. Here he was free to employ whatever means necessary. Benavides wanted no further embarrassing public excesses from the Treasury Police.

Two days after the killing an anonymous call led to the discovery of Solorgano's Mercedes. The following day a group of young boys had been attracted to an old abandoned farm house by the barking of a pack of feral dogs. After chasing the dogs off, they discovered Solorgano's fly encrusted decomposing body.

A day after the story broke in the newspapers and appeared on international network newscasts, the press was contacted by several FDR-FMLN senior officials. All disclaimed any responsibility for the killing.

Benavides was trying to determine what the killing of Solorgano meant. It was well planned, well executed, not a desperate reactionary move. He wondered who had the capability among the guerrillas to execute this kind of bold attack behind enemy lines so to speak. Which faction of the opposition movement? What was the FDR-FMLN trying to accomplish by disclaiming credit? Was it possible that a new unaligned group had surfaced? The best guess at the moment was that this was a counterattack for high visibility. Support for the guerrillas had been flagging in the wake of recent military setbacks. But then why not claim credit?

If the purpose was publicity, Benavides would oblige them. More could to be served by holding up evidence of the barbarism of the left. Colonel Taylor, the U.S. military attaché at the embassy, called after the press conference. Taylor complimented Benavides on the way he *handled* the situation. *An unfortunate occurrence but one that that still offered useful possibilities.*

Taylor was a hawk on the embassy staff. He had been on Benavides back to curtail the more extreme elements and the effects in the American press. After all, 1.4 million dollars a day in aid was at stake. There was always unrelenting opposition from the liberals in the U.S. Congress.

Like Benavides, Taylor could see advantages to the removal of Solorgano if the Treasury Police could be brought under control. The sadistic Solorgano had been chief among the most extreme elements in the military. His demise could only prove helpful to Taylor's liaison mission. As added benefit, the spectacular barbarity of Solorgano's killing was damaging to international sympathy for the leftist insurgency.

Benavides expected few results from any new arrests and interrogations. It was to serve primarily as visible activity. With this success he expected the guerrillas to strike again. That could only be helpful to bolster the Salvadoran position for continued U.S. aid.

Jose Aguilar sat hunched over an old manual typewriter. He was transcribing the information obtained from Solorgano as Roberto Salas read from his notes. They had been at it for several hours. Solorgano had told all sorts of things in a torrent of words. Aguilar's first task had been to organize the information into categories. Killings and who committed them. Which officers aligned with whom? Corruption. Who was on the take and how? Sexual proclivities and deviance at the top. Key information concerning relations with Washington, and some interesting insights into certain U.S. officials. Aguilar punctuated his work with an occasional verbal obscenity.

"How's it coming along?" Molina asked.

"Another hour or so. I tell you, hearing it was bad enough, but reading from my notes is difficult," Salas said.

"A fucking monster. Trying to organizing this .....well .....it's unbelievable .....it sickens me," Aguilar said.

"I know. But we will put it to good use. The intelligence we learned about these degenerate pigs will help to damage them in many ways," Molina said.

They were in an apartment over a restaurant in a commercial section of San Salvador. The restaurant was owned by a friend of Molina. The man was totally reliable. One son had been killed by the death squads in the early eighties. Another son disappeared just in the last year. The restaurant was frequently patronized by the military and therefore felt to be secure from any unexpected raids.

Molina had not completely decided what he would do with all the information obtained from Solorgano. He had not expected the quantity or scope of the intelligence. Some of the information would be leaked to selective elements of the press. Some would be given to the FDR-FMLN. Professor Portillo at the university could help with the details. One piece of information, however, would have immediate use.

He had constructed the essentials of his next operation even before the raid on Solorgano's house. He knew the killing of just one colonel would not prompt the kind of reaction he was looking for. Death was all too common in this country. Another incident would be required, and even that would have to be followed with yet another.

Molina viewed El Salvador's problems for the last fifty years to be a direct result of the economic power of the large land owners, backed by the military, in turn supported by the United States. The reasons might be varied, but the results were always the same. The military and other far right elements always retained political power. They maintained that power through military aid from the U.S. If the U.S. discontinued aid, the whole cancerous structure could not sustain itself.

That was the goal. Get the United States out of El Salvador. Stop the military aid. How to force that was the question? It did not seem to matter what particular administration was in office in the U.S. Foreign policy relative to Latin America did not vary. All the way from Roosevelt in the thirties to the new President, George H. W. Bush. The only close call the ruling elements of the right had was in 1980 when then President Carter suspended aid after the rape and murder of four Catholic nuns by the National Guard. Suspended for less than two weeks. Reinstated after a new junta was formed with the weakling puppet president, José Duarte.

The elements in the U.S. government that controlled the foreign policy in Latin America were just as right wing as the worst in El Salvador. The State Department, Pentagon, and CIA were always able to continue and even increase the support to whatever government was in power at the moment. The more liberal Congress and the sometimes liberal White House were always seduced by the argument of a Communist threat in the Americas. All the hawks had to do was wave the hammer and sickle red flag and military aid funds poured in. As long as the current dictator or ruling oligarchy restrained from the worst of excesses, the pipeline of money was not jeopardized. Restraint itself was not always necessary, only the ability to keep it out of the American press.

From the repercussions of the murder of the church women in 1980, and the earlier Vietnam scenario, Molina formed his strategy. The strategy was built on certain basic premises. The central premise was founded on Molina's interpretation of the mechanisms that drive change in United States policy. The key was the press. If it pushed the right buttons, enough bad press led to change.

The vast majority of people in the U.S. did not demonstrate, write their elected officials, or join activist organizations. Only half the citizenry voted. When they did vote, there were only the same two party choices. An issue had life only if the media gave it play. They gave it play based on interest value. Scandal, horror, good visuals had the highest interest value. Policy debates were boring. A sex scandal of an evangelist was first rate news. The environment was not news. Blood always was. Things changed in the U.S. as a result of the extent of media play. Congressmen and senators choose their positions and crusades from the news headlines.

The military in El Salvador could be counted on to react violently to any direct threat. They had held the ultimate power in the country for over sixty years. As a body, they were not sensitive to public opinion. Few officers had any understanding of the broader political implications related to the exercise of their power. Operations against the rebels had been going well lately. The old ways of disappearances, torture, and murder had correspondingly subsided. Given the right stimulus, Molina felt sure they would revert to the time of the death squads.

Molina intended to give the American press frequent doses of blood. He intended to make El Salvador the country of front-page attention. He intended ultimately to kill Americans. Make America sick of El Salvador. Another Vietnam. And if they would not let go their hold, he would continue to kill Americans, on their own soil if necessary.

Molina had developed the essentials of another assassination plan immediately after the Solorgano killing. The target had been chosen even before Solorgano's death. The idea being to move up to an even higher-value target after Solorgano. With a new piece of information acquired from Solorgano, he would alter the tactical plan for the assassination of General Martin Ruiz, Minister of Defense.

Solorgano was not only the head of the equivalent to a secret police organization, but the whoring buddy of the Defense Minister. The Defense Minister was five years senior to Solorgano. He was smoother, more polished than Solorgano, but with the same base appetites. Solorgano enjoyed his position largely due to his association with the highest ranking military officer of the country.

The assassination of General Ruiz was set for a Saturday night, two days from now. Molina had assembled the attack group to finalize the last of the details. The group consisted of Carlos Perez and Roberto Salas from the Solorgano operation. Miguel Cortina as a driver. Jose Aguilar who held the gardening contractor under threat. And a girl, Patricia Reyes, a student and new recruit. She had assisted Aguilar proving her mettle. All were young. All felt a fierce loyalty bordering on reverence to Santiago Molina.

Solorgano had revealed that a party had been planned by General Ruiz for the upcoming Saturday night. According to Solorgano, Ruiz was celebrating a deal he had made with a Columbian. Apparently the deal involved drugs. Ruiz wouldn't give him any details. He told him that he was expecting this Columbian on the fifteenth and he wanted to consummate the deal with something special. Ruiz told Solorgano that there were some new girls at the club. He had arranged for six girls, two each, for the entire night.

The Gato Afortunado was a well known exclusive night spot. The club catered to the rich and powerful. Drugs and girls could be had for the price. Given notice, the club would arrange any form of debauchery. Well-appointed rooms upstairs were available. The place was perfect for an illicit rendezvous. You could buy what you wanted, or bring your own. Security was tight.

"Let's go over the plan as it now stands," Molina said. "At approximately seven-thirty, Patricia and I will arrive at the club. I have rented a Mercedes for the evening. Miguel will act as driver. I have reservations under the name Betancourt and a Mexican passport under the same name. My cover is that of a Mexican export company executive.

"The party for Ruiz is scheduled for eight o'clock in a private dining room. Knowing Ruiz's sexual appetites, we expect him to go upstairs within a couple of hours. Patricia and I will go upstairs around ten o'clock."

This drew smiles from the men and a light comment from the youngest, Miguel Cortina, "Isn't Patricia a little young for you, Santiago?"

She blushed and glared at Cortina.

Molina smiled. "Since we know there are women for hire upstairs, I will offer the maitre d' a substantial tip to arrange for a so-called ménage a trois."

"A what?" Cortina asked.

"Three people having sex," Molina said. All but Reyes smiled.

"Patricia and I will incapacitate the woman and locate Ruiz. I will use a silenced .22 caliber weapon. Patricia and I will then leave. Carlos, you, Roberto, and Jose will be outside in a car across the street. In the event that there is trouble as we're leaving, you will do what you can to help us. Carlos, you're in charge. You are not to do anything foolish. Expect the General to be accompanied by a squad of soldiers after what happened to Solorgano. If the situation is hopeless, you're to leave. Is that understood?"

"I don't like it, Santiago," Carlos Perez said. "You should let me do it. No offense, but I am better at such things."

"I know you are, Carlos, but, you don't look the part." Molina said. Carlos Perez looked like an athlete. He was six feet tall, a hundred and ninety pounds, well-muscled. His hair was cut very short and he looked even younger than his twenty-five years.

"Let's say you just don't look the mature degenerate type."

"What if Ruiz cancels the party. Especially since Solorgano was killed?" Cortina asked.

"That's a possibility. But I think Ruiz will go ahead. He likes his fun too much and we can only assume the business with the Columbian is important. But he'll be well protected. At any rate, if Ruiz does not show, Patricia and I will just leave."

Molina turned to her, "How do you feel about doing this, Patricia?"

"Ok. Well ....I'm nervous."

Patricia Reyes was twenty-two, five-six, with a slim figure. With her shapely breasts and long legs she turned heads. She was perfect for the role of escort to a wealthy business man. Right now she was more than a little nervous. She sat forward on the chair listening intently to Molina, biting the knuckle on her hand. She had never done anything like this before. They were going to kill someone. She might even be expected to kill. Could she?

"I'll pick up the car late in the afternoon. Everyone meet here by five o'clock Saturday. Any questions?" Molina asked.

As everyone left the apartment, Molina said, "Patricia, wait a moment." He closed the door after everyone had left.

"Are you really all right, Patricia?"

"Yes. I'll be fine, Santiago."

"You know you may have to kill don't you?"

"Yes."

"Can you? Will you?"

"Yes. I'm sure I can."

"Very good. You will buy a dress and shoes tomorrow. I know your long hair is naturally beautiful, but I want you to go to a salon and have it styled. Have your makeup done at the salon. Even though you wear little makeup, in this case I want quite a bit. You need to not only look the part, but it should act as a disguise to some extent. A look of money and arrogance. The dress should be revealing." Molina pointed to his own chest. "You know what I mean?"

Reyes blushed again. She had known Santiago Molina for six months. When she first met him, she had romantic fantasies about him. It was the intensity of his dark eyes. However, Molina never seemed to encourage anything sexual in their relationship. She did not make any bold advances, or even any overt flirtatious acts. Not that she was shy, only that something about Santiago Molina seemed to discourage such frivolity.

Molina gave Reyes enough money to buy an expensive dress at the best shop in San Salvador. After giving her a chaste kiss on the cheek, she left the apartment.

At five-thirty, Molina knocked on the apartment door and identified himself. Perez let him in. Everyone was there.

Molina was dressed in a cream-colored double breasted silk suit. A light blue shirt and darker blue tie with matching handkerchief contrasted elegantly. He wore expensive Italian loafers and a gold Rolex watch.

"Where is Patricia?" Molina asked.

"In the bedroom dressing," Perez said.

"Is everything ready?"

"Yes. Miguel stole a car from the airport. He made sure it was from somebody leaving so it would not be reported soon. The weapons are also ready."

"Good."

"Santiago, what are you going to do after this is over? They will know your face."

"I don't think so. People really aren't that observant. At any rate, after this I will shave off my beard and cut my hair shorter. You'd be surprised at the effect. I have another passport with a picture of me that way just for such a need."

"How does Patricia look?"

"Great!" Cortina said with emphasis. "She's beautiful. You wouldn't recognize her." Cortina's boyish enthusiasm helped relieve a little of the tension.

"See what I mean by only superficial changes making a huge difference."

Molina picked up the attaché case he had brought and laid it on the dining table. He extracted two matching Beretta .22 caliber semi-automatic pistols and placed them on the table. Next to these he took out two long, narrow boxes and two smaller ones. All four of his men stood by the table to examine the weapons.

"Jesus, this is beautiful," Perez said as he fondled the weapon. Perez appreciated weapons. "Where did you get these, Santiago?"

"I'm not allowed to divulge that. Part of my agreement with those that are helping us."

Perez did not really expect an answer since Molina did not explain a lot of things. Never a hint as to his source of money. Money never seemed to be a problem. No one ever asked.

"Look at this, Carlos," Molina said. He opened one of the longer boxes and took out a five inch long, one inch diameter metal cylinder and handed it to Perez.

"Czechoslovakian made."

Perez instinctively knew what it was, fitting the cylinder to the barrel of the gun, locking it in place with a quarter turn. It appeared an awkward weapon, eleven inches long with the fitted sound suppressor. Perez sighted the gun assessing the weapon's balance.

"Why the small caliber, Santiago?" Aguilar asked.

"For close in work the smaller caliber is the best, especially for silencing. These are subsonic velocity rounds with hollow-points. The weapon also won't kick off target as you fire, so rapidly fired subsequent shots are more accurate. The expanding aspect of the hollow-point inflicts a greater wound. The .22 caliber is the weapon of choice for Israel's Mossad assassination teams. With this suppressor it is not easily heard through a closed door. Just a muffled-sounding *pop*. The shots will be at close range. They also hold a thirteen round magazine."

"Carlos, will you load these?" Molina asked, referring to the two weapons. "What about your weapons?"

"Roberto and Jose will have the Uzis and the Makarovs. I will have the sound suppressed M16 in case that is necessary. Miguel, of course, will not be armed," Perez said while loading the magazines of the .22 pistols.

Patricia Reyes opened the bedroom door and stood in the doorway. All the men turned. Molina smiled. She looked exactly right for the part. Beautiful with a decidedly sexy edge.

She had selected a simple, powder blue dress that crossed her breasts low in front. As Molina had instructed, her hair was pulled up in a current style. She looked remarkably different with the makeup, particularly the eye shadow with dark eye liner, and rose-colored lipstick. Her nails matched her lipstick. Bare legs, no nylons as Molina instructed. Three-inch-heel white pumps completed the outfit.

"You look beautiful, Patricia," Molina said. He went to her and air-kissed her cheek, careful not to disturb her makeup. "You will need these." He reached into his coat pocket and took out a double strand of pearls.

"Oh my god! They're beautiful, Santiago. Are they real?"

"Of course."

He went behind her and connected the clasp.

"There's one more thing, Patricia," Molina said as he motioned to Perez to bring him the two .22 caliber pistols. "These." He removed the sound suppressors. "I want you to tape these to the inside of each thigh," Molina said handing the guns and suppressors to her. "It's always possible they might search me. Not likely you in that dress." He took a roll of tape out of his other pocket.

Reyes took the guns and the tape and returned to the bedroom. She would have to be careful not to cross her legs in the short-length dress to accidentally expose the weapons. The Cinderella spell had been broken. The reality of what they were about to do reasserted itself.

At seven o'clock, Cortina retrieved the rented Mercedes parked in a nearby garage. It would have been out of place parked on this neighborhood street. Molina and Reyes met him outside the restaurant, as if being picked up there.

The others would arrive outside the club Gato Afortunado at nine o'clock. They had previously established a location as inconspicuous as possible across the road and down a hundred meters from the entrance to the club.

Molina and Reyes arrived at the club at seven-thirty. The club was a former large mansion. It was situated two miles outside the city on a slight hill. An eight-foot wall surrounded the three acres of grounds.

Aguilar drove the Mercedes up to the ornate wrought iron gates which were open. A man in a white tuxedo walked to the window and asked their names. After checking his clipboard they were allowed to pass. Two soldiers of the National Police, armed with assault weapons, flanked the gates. Molina knew that as many as a dozen police guarded the grounds, in addition to the club's own security inside. On any given night, someone of power or wealth could be found at the club.

Aguilar drove to the front of the building under a large portico. The rear door was opened by a doorman in red livery. Molina and Reyes walked up the steps to again be checked by another employee in a tuxedo. Aguilar drove the car to the parking lot which was populated with a similar class of vehicles with their drivers standing around smoking.

The maître d' greeted them. Molina requested a quiet out of the way table, discreetly passing a U.S. fifty-dollar bill to him. They were escorted to a table for two, partially secluded by potted plants. Molina ordered a good bottle of wine. He lit a cigarette.

"Have some wine, Patricia."

"I'm afraid I won't be able to keep it down. My stomach is in knots."

"Take a sip. It'll relax you. It will be awhile yet. After dinner."

"I know. I'll be all right."

"I need to make arrangements for later. I'll be back in a few minutes."

Molina left the table to find the maître d', returning after only ten minutes.

"It is arranged. I told him sometime after ten o'clock."

"What did you tell him?"

Molina smiled and said, "I told him my companion and I wanted another woman to join us, someone that could please both a man and woman. Preferably black."

Reyes swallowed hard, embarrassed but too stressed to blush.

General Ruiz arrived just before nine o'clock. He was a large man of modest height, probably in his early fifties. His hair was salted with gray and thinning on top. He was forty pounds overweight with a fairly prominent belly. Still, he had the aura of intelligence. He wore his general's uniform.

Accompanying Ruiz was a younger, fitter man in a well tailored, beige suit. He looked around and made a comment to Ruiz. Behind Ruiz was an army lieutenant with a sidearm. As the maître d' led them to a private dining room, Ruiz turned to the lieutenant and said something. The lieutenant left them and took a seat in the bar.

"That is General Ruiz. I assume the lieutenant is his personal bodyguard. There are probably several more outside. Looks like he feels secure in here," Molina whispered to Reyes.

"At ten o'clock I will signal the maître d' that we would like to go upstairs. We will then wait for Ruiz to come upstairs. Remember, Patricia, all you have to do is restrain our companion, just like you did with the gardening contractor. For now, just finish your dinner."

She picked at her food for the sake of appearance. The tension was becoming almost unbearable. She could feel the perspiration under her arms and even on her upper lip. Her breathing was measured. The tape holding the weapons was making her sweat between her legs. Molina on the other hand appeared relaxed although acutely alert.

Eventually Molina said, "It's time, Patricia." He laid two hundred-dollar bills on the table.

They walked over to the maître d' who led them to a staircase. Bowing slightly he said to Molina, "Señor, I have arranged the remainder of your evening as you requested. I think you will find everything to your liking."

Molina nodded and smiled passing another fifty dollar bill discretely into the man's hand. Turning to Reyes, the maître d' acknowledged her with exaggerated formality, "Señorita."

A well built man escorted them up the stairs. Obviously the club's muscle, probably armed. The hallway was papered in red velvet with a gold design. Just what one would expect for a classy whorehouse.

Their escort motioned them to a room halfway down the hall and closed the door behind them without a word.

The room was large with a king size bed. A wet bar with a full stock of liquor and crystal glasses was located against the wall opposite the bed. Two upholstered chairs were located in the corner, separated by a small, round table. One wall was covered with mirror panels, as was the ceiling over the bed. The other walls were papered in the same velvet as the hallway, decorated with paintings of female nudes. A door led to a bathroom.

"Patricia, go into the bathroom. Remove the weapons and assemble the silencers as Carlos demonstrated. Stay in there until I call for you."

Reyes went into the bathroom and closed the door. It was a relief to remove the tape holding the weapons. Her thighs were damp with sweat. Large red welts outlined the weapons on her skin. A few minutes later she heard a gentle knocking at the hallway door.

She heard Molina open the door to the hallway.

"Good evening. My name is Cecelia, Señor," the black girl said in English. The precise, clipped British English of somewhere in the Caribbean. She was wearing a red evening dress with matching colored heels. Her hair was full, but straightened, with no kinky curls. She entered the room and Molina closed the door.

"Good evening, Cecelia. Please come in. Why don't you fix us all a drink? My lady friend is in the bathroom."

Cecelia looked at Molina seductively and said, "My pleasure, Sir. What do you like?"

"Scotch on the rocks. The same for the lady." Molina walked to the bathroom door and said, "Come out when you're ready, dear and meet Cecelia."

Reyes came out within seconds, concealing the pistols behind her. Molina reached around her and took one of the pistols. Cecelia turned from making the drinks at the sound of the bathroom door opening. She dropped the drink she was preparing when she saw Molina pointing the weapon at her.

"What the bloody hell is ...."

"Shut up, Cecelia. Nothing will happen to you if you keep quiet," Molina said sharply. "One sound however and I will kill you."

Molina took the other pistol from Reyes. Tossing a small pocket knife onto the bed, he said, "Take the sheet off the bed and tear it into strips. Tie her hands and legs. Gag her."

It took Reyes several minutes to complete the task of shredding the sheet and securing Cecelia. After the terrified woman was immobilized on the bed, Molina opened the door to the hallway a crack.

"Make us both a drink. We must now wait."

Forty minutes later General Ruiz and his Columbian guest came up the stairs. The maître d' was personally escorting them. He showed them to separate rooms at the end of the hall.

Molina closed the door and said to Reyes, "I know which room. We'll wait thirty minutes. Give me the camera from your purse."

She gave him the small camera with the built in flash which he put into his jacket pocket.

Molina sat down in a chair. He lit another cigarette and sipped at his Scotch. No sound passed in the room for the next thirty minutes. After what felt like an eternity to Reyes, Molina abruptly stood up.

"It's time. I'll go down the hall. It's the last room on the left. It will take less than one minute. After I leave this room, step into the hall and cover me from anyone coming up the stairs. Keep your eyes on that end of the hall leading to the stairway. If anyone appears, and I mean *anyone*, you must shoot them. Say nothing to them. Just take aim and shoot, as many times as necessary to silence them. Do not hesitate for even a second. Do you understand?"

"Yes." Patricia Reyes was breathing rapidly to control her anxiety.

Molina looked out into the hall. Seeing no one, he moved briskly down the hallway and put his ear to the door of Ruiz's room. After a couple of seconds, he turned the door knob and quickly entered the room.

The room was dimly lit, but he could easily see his target. Lying on the bed, General Ruiz was being aptly attended to by two young women. One had his erect penis in her mouth, the other straddled his face. The one girl looked up from her vigorous work on Ruiz's member with an expression of surprise. The other girl had her back to the door. Ruiz saw only the delights of the young woman's pubic area in his face. He did not hear the door.

"Move," Molina said to the girl staring wide eyed at him. She quickly moved back from Ruiz.

"What the fuck?" Ruiz said as he pushed the other girl away. The last thing the General saw was a fleeting glimpse of Molina and several small muzzle flashes.

Molina shot Ruiz four times. The first two shots struck him in the upper abdomen. The next two were to the forehead at a distance of only a couple of inches. The small caliber rounds with the sound suppressor still made a pronounced noise but lacked the sharp crack of the muzzle pressure report of an unsuppressed round. It should not be heard much beyond the room.

Molina then fired two shots into each girl. The second girl was cut off in mid-scream. A final shot to the head of each insured their death. He walked over to the bodies. Making sure they were dead, he moved the lifeless bodies of the two women into a gruesome pose then took out the camera and captured the scene on film.

After snapping all twelve exposures, he put the camera back into his pocket. Stepping close to the bed, he fired one more round into the head of the Minister of Defense before leaving.

Molina opened the door slightly checking the hallway. Patricia Reyes was the only one in the hall, her gun trained on the stairs as instructed. The killings had taken only two minutes.

"Back inside," he said to her as he closed the door to Ruiz's room quietly behind him and motioned her back inside their room. "Get your purse. Let's go. Take a deep breath. Act relaxed." He disconnected the silencer from his weapon and put both the gun and silencer in her purse. "Give me your gun." She still had a full magazine in her weapon.

Reyes left the room first. Before closing the door, Molina turned and fired three shots into the bound black girl on the bed. Reyes turned wide-eyed at the muffled sounds realizing what had just happened but said nothing.

Molina stuck the pistol into his waistband in his back. After descending the stairs, Molina saw the maître d' across the room with his back turned. The opportunity allowed them to walk quickly to the front door without having to offer an explanation for their premature departure. The doorman flagged Cortina to bring their car. All three left the Club Gato Afortunado only minutes after assassinating the Salvadoran Minister of Defense.

CHAPTER 4

All hell broke loose at the National Military Command Headquarters with the news of the Ruiz assassination. The lieutenant accompanying General Ruiz made the call to headquarters a little after midnight. The duty officer dispatched an entire company of troops to the club and then made the necessary notifications. President Cristiani followed by Army Chief of Staff General Garcia, and then Colonel Benavides were the first to be notified.

A crisis meeting was held in the President's office at five o'clock in the morning. After a lot of indignant outbursts and angry recriminations, the meeting broke up with little changed. Security would be further increased for senior officials. Arrests would be increased. That was General Garcia's directive supported by the President. This was over objections by Benavides arguing this was what the terrorists clearly intended; provoke the government into overreaction. Benavides remained in charge of the investigation into these terrorist assassinations, and would continue to temporarily head the Treasury Police. At least he could control the targets of the arrests.

Garcia and Benavides were just as ruthless as the two assassinated officers, only more sophisticated and nuanced in their methods. The killings of the politically crude Ruiz and the sadistic Solorgano were not wholly unwelcome. Their removal opened new opportunities. On the plus side, it would make an easier case for continued military support from the United States. However, the success of the attacks could also add a needed boost to flagging support for the rebels. For General Garcia it was a direct challenge to the military. Both targets were ranking military officers. The perpetrators could have killed any number of public officials or civilians of power, but they choose senior military figures. Even the civilian President would have been an easier target. They chose the more difficult for greater effect. For Garcia it was now as much an exercise in machismo as one of power politics. It was Garcia's order to increase arrests to demonstrate a heavy-handed response. Benavides was ordered to take whatever measures were necessary to identify the killers. He had full authority, but results were expected.

Later that morning Benavides held a meeting at the Treasury Police Headquarters. He informed Major Rivera that he was assuming command of the Treasury Police. He would be occupying Colonel Solorgano's office when he was present at the headquarters.

He also informed Rivera, that Captain Ramirez, Benavides' aide, would be temporarily assigned to the Treasury Police. Rivera offered objections citing Ramirez' inexperience with their operations. Benavides dismissed his objections. Rivera knew what Benavides was doing. He wanted his own man on the scene. To Rivera, Ramirez would be nothing more than a spy for the Colonel.

"Give your report, Major," Benavides said to Rivera.

Assembled at the conference table were Major Rivera, Captain Ramirez, and two other Treasury Police officers of captain rank.

"Yes sir. General Ruiz was killed sometime between 10:00PM and the discovery of the bodies at approximately 12:30AM. He was shot six times, twice in the abdomen, four times in the head. The entry wounds indicate a small caliber weapon. They are performing an autopsy right now. We should have more information later since the bullets did not exit the bodies.

"There were two women in the room with General Ruiz. They were also killed. Appears to be the same type of weapon. Additionally, the body of a black woman was found in another room down the hall. We believe this room was occupied by the killers. She was bound and shot. These bodies are also at the hospital awaiting autopsies. Captain Jimenez conducted the investigation at the club this morning. Captain," Rivera said, turning to Captain Jimenez.

"The maître d' told us that a well dressed man and an attractive young woman had gone upstairs before Ruiz. The man had previously requested the maître d' to arrange for a black woman to join them. He paid the maître d' three hundred American dollars. The man was described as being average height, black hair, black mustache and short-cropped beard, dark eyes, medium build. The woman was younger, attractive, brown hair, medium height. Both were well dressed. The man tipped generously. The maître d' had not seen them before. They arrived in a white Mercedes with a driver. The car has not been located yet. Other staff gave similar descriptions. No one has given us anything conclusive."

Jimenez continued his report, "I personally questioned most of the people at the club. Everyone has been detained. All the guests and military on duty at the time are being held at the club. We are continuing the questioning. All of the employees have been brought here for further questioning. A Colombian by the name of Manuel Orto has been demanding to be released. He was a guest of General Ruiz last night. He was also the one that discovered the bodies. Claims he heard nothing."

"Because he was being professionally fucked by an accomplished whore I assume?" Benavides said.

"Yes, Sir."

"And this Columbian's occupation?"

"He claims to be a business man. Exporter of agricultural products." Benavides took that to mean narcotics products. A drug dealer connected with General Ruiz.

"Never mind the Columbian. What about the gunshots?" Benavides asked.

"Everyone claims they heard no gunshots," the captain said. "If that's true, and it appears it is, that means ...."

"I know what it means, Captain. It means they used sound suppressed weapons. Small caliber. Assassin weapons. It also means sophistication, which means professionals. Not our usual FLMN rebels. Anything else?"

"We're checking on a number of guests that left before the bodies were discovered. Also, employees who were not working that night are being located and brought in."

"How did the killers know Ruiz would be there that night?" Benavides asked.

"We're making investigations at the General's office. Naturally we are being cautious," Major Rivera answered. He did not disclose his knowledge that Solorgano had also frequented the Club Gato Afortunato with the General. Whoring buddies. So the assassins probably learned of the Ruiz schedule from Solorgano before they killed him. Rivera did not need to involve himself or the Treasury Police officers in the investigation for the source of the assassins' intelligence.

"Major, are we assuming that these are the same people that killed Colonel Solorgano?" Benavides asked Rivera.

"Possibly, but we can't be sure yet. There are a lot of differences."

"What about the earlier interrogations after the killing of Colonel Solorgano?"

"We arrested over two hundred people. No one knew anything about a group calling themselves *The Hand of Justice*. Approximately thirty of these people are still being detained. Some, like our French journalist friend, Decartes, are undergoing continued and vigorous interrogation," Rivera said.

Benavides understood the euphemism for torture.

"And the young professor?"

"Yes, he is here also. A lot of pressure coming at us about that one. Apparently his mentor is Professor Portillo. You know the kind of stink he can make with his connections. He even got the Chief Justice to call. I told him, that he would have to discuss the matter with you, Colonel."

"His physical condition?"

"Reasonably good."

"Prepare charges on him that will be sufficient for immediate deportation," Benavides ordered.

"And Descartes?" Rivera asked.

"That's up to you, Major. However, I do not want him released. Nor do I want him to be become a public relations problem. Understood?"

"Understood, Sir."

The following day, the office of President Cristiani of the Republic of El Salvador received an envelope. Inside were three 5x7 color photos of General Martin Ruiz after he had been shot. Ruiz's naked, hairy fat body was flanked by the two dead whores. His penis was prominent in the center of the photograph with the head of one woman next to it on his thigh.

U.S. Ambassador to El Salvador, Lawrence Bennett received the same set of photos. The Washington offices of the Associated Press, United Press International, Washington Post, the Enquirer, the British tabloids, The Sun and the Daily Mail, the French Closer Magazine, and CNN Broadcasting received theirs a few days later.

Three days after the Ruiz assassination the body of Henri
Descartes was buried in a rural area by Treasury Police out of
uniform. The body had suffered much damage before death as
evidenced by burn marks, flayed skin, and a swollen, unrecognizable face. The record of his arrest was expunged. He joined
the ranks of thousands that just disappeared during the civil
war.

The young Guatemalan professor was deported three days
later on charges of drug possession. He required assistance to
board the plane. His feet had been beaten, a favorite method of
torture. It would be months before he could walk again without
pain.

On the third day of his stay in San Salvador, Victor Castell
was able to slip away from his mother and cousin, Hector. He
was using the stay at Hector's house in the city primarily as a
vehicle to clandestinely meet his Uncle Augustin without the
knowledge of the rest of the family.

He arrived at the campus of the University of Central America shortly before noon. After asking directions, he found his way
to the office of his uncle. The office was locked. He decided to
wait in the hallway. After fifteen minutes sitting on a bench, a
slender middle-aged man came down the hall. They looked at
each other for a moment. Both had changed in appearance in the
years since they had seen each other.

"Victor?"

"Uncle Augustin?"

They shook hands and embraced tentatively. Castell did not
know his uncle very well. He had really only seen him briefly a
couple of times.

"Come in. This is a wonderful surprise," his uncle said unlocking his office door. "Sit down, sit down, Victor."

He took a chair. His uncle sat on the corner of his desk. They both felt a little awkward. "I assume you're visiting with your mother?"

"Yes, for the summer. I'm staying at Uncle René's. Mother is here too."

"And how is she?"

"Fine I guess. Did you know that she and father separated? Father went to San Francisco to take a new job. Mother is going to live here."

"I'm sorry to hear that. I didn't know. Of course you know we haven't talked for a long time."

"I understand that you don't talk with your brother René either."

"That's true. And for that reason, Alicia has followed his lead. She always did. It can't be because of the political differences. Your mother is not that interested in politics."

"But Uncle René apparently is."

"We both are, Victor. The problem with René is that he wants to live in the past. He wants to protect what he has, what our father and grandfather built. The trouble with that it was built on the backs of the people and maintained by the army in blood. But enough talk of politics. It's good to see you. Tell me what you've been doing these past years. Last time I saw you was at father's funeral. That was seven years ago."

"I've been in school in the United States. California. I completed my bachelor's in electrical engineering. I'm down here for the summer trying to decide what I want to do."

"Good for you, Victor."

The phone on his desk rang. After a brief conversation, Augustin told the caller, 'ten minutes' and hung up. "Listen, Victor, I have a commitment in a few minutes that I cannot get out of. Tell you what. I am having a few people over to my house tomorrow afternoon. I think you would enjoy them. Some are students. We can also talk more. Can you get away without anyone knowing? Believe me, there would be hell to pay if René found out you saw me."

"I think so, Uncle Augustin. I'm staying at Hector's here in the city for a few days. I can find some excuse."

"Good. Here's the address and phone number." He wrote the information on a slip of paper and handed it to Castell.

He embraced his uncle again and left.

The excuse he gave for staying over another couple of days in the city at Hector's came as a surprise to his mother. He told her he had a date. Someone he met at a shop the previous day. She was a student. There was nothing really odd about her son having a date. She assumed he knew about sex, probably even had some *experiences* when he was at college. It was just something she never discussed with him. And for his part, he never talked about girls. In high school in Panama City she assumed he had dates, but she did not recall him ever mentioning that was where he was going. It seemed uncharacteristically bold for Victor to pick up a girl in what amounted to a foreign country. She always thought him introverted and too bookish, never much for socializing.

He gave the same excuse to his cousin Hector. Hector was more concerned that his cousin would fall into the wrong crowd. University students were a hotbed of leftist politics. Look at Uncle Augustin's following. Be careful. Mind the curfew. These were dangerous times.

Augustin Portillo lived in a modest house in a middle class suburb of San Salvador. Several cars were in the driveway. He could hear voices from the backyard as he walked to the front door.

Castell knocked. A young woman, about his age opened the door. A very attractive young woman.

"Hi, I'm Victor Castell. My Uncle Augustin is expecting me," he said in Spanish.

"So you are Professor Portillo's nephew from the United States. I'm Patricia Reyes." She extended her hand. "Come in. Everyone is in the backyard."

Castell and Reyes walked out under a large covered patio at the rear of the house. Plants abounded. Vines and lush greenery climbed the patio posts. Two large trees provided shade from the oppressive afternoon sun. Plastic chairs were scattered about and a long table displayed a variety of food. There were about fifteen guests.

"Victor," his uncle said. They embraced. "I'm so glad you could come. Any problems? What did you tell them?"

"I told them I had a date."

"Good thinking. Now I want to introduce you to my wife, Claudia."

"How do you do. It's nice to meet you," Castell said to Claudia. She embraced him and kissed him on the cheek.

He turned to his uncle and said, "I didn't know you remarried, Uncle Augustin."

"And that you had a new aunt? We were married four years ago. Claudia teaches high school. I'm sure René and your mother knew. Shows how little they wish to talk about me."

Augustin took him by the arm. "Let me introduce you to everyone. You've met Patricia. Patricia is a student of mine. I'd like to say one of my best students. However, she is too preoccupied with politics to devote the proper time to her economics studies. She is perhaps my prettiest student, though."

"You know neither statement is true, Professor," Reyes said with a smile. You could see that she liked the professor.

Augustin introduced Victor to the other guests. It was an eclectic group; professors, a priest, a lawyer, someone with the Red Cross, a journalist, along with several students. The only other women besides Patricia Reyes and Claudia were the wives of the two professors.

"Wine or beer?" Reyes asked him.

"Oh ..... *cerveza* I guess. Thanks."

"Professor Portillo said you were visiting?"

"Yes, with my mother. We're staying at my other uncle's house outside of Santa Ana. My mother is going to move back here. She and my father are in the process of getting a divorce."

"I see. Where did you grow up? Your accent is not Salvadoran."

"Well, I've been in the United States for the last four years going to school. I'm an American but I lived in Panama City before that. My father worked for the Canal Authority for many years, so I really grew up there. He comes from an old Spanish family in California so with my mother's background, Spanish was always the language we spoke at home."

"So that's why your Spanish is so good. You only have a slight gringo accent," she said teasingly. "What was your major?"

"Electrical engineering. I just got my bachelor's."

"Congratulations. That's great. I've got about another year to go for mine. Economics. I think I want to teach at the university. Means I'll have to go on for my graduate degree. So a few more years I guess."

"Really? I've been thinking about going on for my masters too. I'm interested in computer science."

God, she was pretty. Sexy pretty. Her eyes were large, intent, flirtatious, intelligent. Long, full hair that fell past her shoulders. She was slim with long legs. She wore tight jeans, heeled sandals, and a simple white, cotton blouse that showed off her curves.

Reyes was taken with him as well. He was intelligent, good looking, even if a little shy. Interesting background too. He belonged to one of the *original fourteen families* of El Salvador. The other uncle he mentioned was one of the most powerful men in the country. He had lived in both the United States and Latin America. Professor Portillo even mentioned that he was a U.S.

citizen. The only questions Reyes had were about his politics and how good he might be in bed.

As for him, he was more than attracted to her. Like never before to a girl. Enthralled was more apt. She talked a lot, but not of frivolous topics like his mother. She seemed to say what was on her mind with real intellect. Not the mindless, shallow chatter of the girls at school. This was a real woman. Intelligent, confident, totally engaging. He was instantly smitten.

Augustin Portillo was the kind of man that enjoyed wide respect. He was genuinely likeable, totally sincere, and a persuasive intellectual. As usual, what had started out as light conversation had resulted in Augustin holding forth with what sounded like a lecture. He had been talking intently with a journalist named Harmon from the United States. Soon, everyone had gathered around to listen.

The assassination of the defense minister dominated much of the conversation that afternoon. Given the politically-left leanings of the group, no one was lamenting the death of General Ruiz, much less the hated head of the secret police, Solorgano.

"Whoever this *Hand of Justice* group is, they take provocative photos," John Harmon commented lightly. "You should have seen the ones of the General. We received them in the mail. Unfortunately, we could not print them because of the sexual explicitness. It's okay to print the severed head of that colonel, but no sex. Of course that rag the Enquirer printed a retouched version."

Harmon was a reporter for the Washington Post. He had covered Central and South America for the last ten years. He had known Augustin Portillo for a number of years dating back to the onset of the civil war in the early eighties. Harmon shared the group's collective revulsion of the right-wing military junta that actually ruled El Salvador.

"Any ideas as to who or what they are, Augustin?"

"No. And I wouldn't tell a journalist if I knew," Portillo said jokingly. "But whoever they are, I can't say that I like it."

"Why not? Aren't they killing the enemy?" a student named Jose Aguilar asked.

"Listen, Jose, talk like that is dangerous, even when you're among friends," Portillo warned him. "Look what's happened as a result of these killings. Look at the increased arrests. Look what happened to Enrique." Portillo was referring to his colleague, the young Guatemalan professor that was deported. "He wrote me after he arrived in Guatemala. He is in a hospital there. Let me read part of it to you."

Portillo took the letter from his jacket. Everyone came over to listen.

I was held at the Treasury Police Headquarters for over a week. I was questioned, sometimes roughly, for the first few days. The police ostensibly wanted information on this so called Hand of Justice group. However, most of the questions had to do with the university. Who was saying what? Who was talking to whom? Details of my movements. Which students were active politically? That sort of thing. They wanted to know everything about your movements, Augustin.

After a few days two men took me from my cell. They were not wearing uniforms. Instead of being taken to the room where I was usually questioned, they took me to the basemen down two levels. There was a long corridor with a series of steel, windowless doors. They pushed me into one of the rooms.

I was placed in a heavy wooden chair in one of the rooms. The steel door was closed. My wrists were secured to the arms of the chair by leather straps. One man simply told me that I was not cooperating. I was asked no questions. Another chair was placed in front of me. My legs were lifted onto the chair with my feet hanging over. The larger of the two men held my ankles. The other used a hard rubber truncheon on the bottoms of my feet.

This first session lasted thirty minutes. It is impossible to describe the pain, Augustin. I vomited. I wet myself. Afterwards, I was taken to a different cell in the basement. No bed. No blanket. No toilet. Only a bucket.

The next day it started again. This time for longer. First in the morning then they came again for me later in the afternoon. Still no questions. Only the torment. I passed out this time and woke in my cell. I woke screaming. Screams and crying could be heard from other cells. I realized that this block of cells was for prisoners undergoing torture. Prisoners were dragged from their cells. Some like me could not walk. Many cried. Some vomited just at the thought of what was coming. I swear, Augustin, if I would have had the means I would have killed myself. This was something out of a vision of hell. I did not reveal anything to endanger you or others. But eventually I would have told them everything had the torture continued, Augustin. Anything to stop the torment. But there were no more questions. It was only about inflicting pain.

On the third day, they tried a variation on the same theme. They tied my wrists with the palms up. This afforded access to strike the muscles of the forearms. They still worked on my feet.

On the fourth day, I was given an injection. They told me it was a stimulant to keep me from passing out. My heart beat wildly. I don't know if from fear or the drug. They were correct, I didn't pass out. I actually started to hallucinate under the pain. If I would have been there another day, my mind would have snapped.

The next day, with no explanation, I was ordered to clean myself from a bucket of water. Clean clothing was provided. Around noon I was taken from the prison and driven to the airport. An officer of the Treasury Police read a ridiculous official statement informing me that I was being deported as an undesirable alien.

I cannot walk yet, or flex my fingers. The doctor says I will recover but there will be some long term damage. He meant of course my body. As to my mind, there will be everlasting terrible damage.

Portillo finished the letter. "That's what I mean. Killing on both sides just fosters greater acts of barbarity. Look what they did to him. This sort of thing had stopped years ago. The assassinations have simply given an excuse for the military to revert to the old excesses. It plays directly into the hands of the security forces.

"Look at the situation we have now. Curfew, more secret arrests, torture. Rumors of killings. Rumor of the resurrection of the death squads. It hasn't done the rebel cause any good. The FDR-FMLN has even disclaimed responsibility for the assassinations. The death of Ruiz and Solorgano only satisfies a primal feeling. I'm afraid that the extremists on the right will seize this as an opportunity to escalate their repression. That is always the outcome of acts of terrorism."

"Still, I'm glad that the bastards ....," Aguilar said, but was interrupted by Reyes lightly touching his arm. Her look suggested that he not be so vocal.

Augustin Portillo was intimate with several leaders in both the Democratic Revolutionary Front (FDR) and the Farabundo Marti Liberation Front (FMLN). He served a role of an eminently respected figure with ties to people of influence in other countries, including the United States. The FDR-FMLN's international associations were principally limited to leftist regimes such as Cuba, Nicaragua, and the Soviet Union. Portillo had ties to academics and journalists in the United States and Western Europe. He was a frequent correspondent with Pope John Paul II.

"Is El Salvador doomed to eternal violence? What do you see as the future, Professor?" the priest asked. He was a Jesuit, posted as the assistant to the Vatican representative in El Salvador.

The Central American University in El Salvador was a Roman Catholic university run by the Jesuit order. As a distinguished professor and scholar, Augustin Portillo therefore had close associations with the Roman Catholic clergy in the course of his work. Because the school was operated by the Church, Portillo enjoyed a good deal of latitude in his political criticism of the ruling regime. For some time, the Church had been critical of the brutal excesses of the military, yet remained too powerful to come under direct attack.

"I don't know what the future is, but I do feel it totally hinges on the United States," Portillo said. "I'm not naive enough to believe that if the United States ceased military aid that democratic processes would come to El Salvador. But it is a prerequisite to anything for the better happening."

One of the men, apparently an American working with United Nations relief said, "I can never understand us. As a nation, we abhor hate groups like our own white supremacists, we impeach officials for what would be minor corruption anywhere else, we vigorously prosecute white collar crimes, we let killers go free for fear of convicting someone innocent, yet we prop up brutal dictators around the world. All because of an unreasoning fear of Communism, especially in the Americas."

"I think the explanation is quite simple," Portillo said. "The United States simply has the best system of law and government when viewed domestically. Best from the standpoint of the rights of the individual. Best if you live in the United States. Externally, those in power are not fettered by that same system of law. The United States is only unique in social rights when viewed internally. Externally, it acts like any other country. Everything in the context of its own interests. The United States and the Soviet Union have never contested over ideological differences. The issue is always power."

Portillo looked around and noticed that everyone was listening intently. "Enough lecturing. Don't you get enough of that in my classroom, Jose? Let's eat."

Castell listened intently to his uncle. He realized how little he knew of history and current political events. And almost nothing of events in El Salvador. The letter his uncle read of his tortured colleague deeply affected him. It gave substance to the daily horrors in this country. This was someone close to his uncle. It put an evil specter on the military that he now saw in evidence everywhere.

Reyes guided Castell to the food and another beer. They sat next to a professor of mathematics from the university. Castell found a kindred spirit in his fascination with mathematics and its application in computer science. At an opportune time, she dragged Castell away from the highly technical conversation.

"I'm very impressed, Victor. I thought I was fairly proficient in mathematics but I couldn't follow anything you two were discussing."

He smiled at the compliment.

"Where are you staying for the summer?" she said.

"Right now I'm staying with my cousin here in the city. I'll be going back to my other uncle's place in a couple of days."

"That's your uncle, René Portillo?"

"Yes. Do you know him?"

"You're joking of course. I know of him. He's Professor Portillo's brother. Head of the Frente Unido Cafetalero, the coffee plantation owner's association. He's one of the most powerful men in the country. Tell me, which side do you favor?"

"Favor? Side? What do you mean?"

"Both of your uncles are powerful men, but they're on totally opposing sides politically. I'd like to know where you stand, Victor."

"I've only been to El Salvador a few times since I was a kid. Then only for short visits. I'm not political. I'm an engineer. Up until the last couple of days, I had no idea what was going on down here. All I knew was that just another civil war was going on. I don't even read the newspapers."

"Just another civil war? Is that the way you gringos see it? People have been slaughtered in this country for over fifty years by government sponsored terrorism. And it's the American government that has given the military the means. You fucking Americans just pay for whatever you want done."

He was hurt by her verbal attack. "Listen, I'm not part of that. I don't want to see people killed and tortured. I ….. never mind, just forget it."

After glancing at his watch, he said, "It's getting late. I should get going."

"Please, Victor, I'm so sorry," she said placing her hand on his arm. "I shouldn't have said those things. It wasn't fair. I can't blame you just because you're an American. Please forgive me?" Do you really have to be going? I'd like you to stay."

Castell succumbed easily to Reyes' charms. Her eyes had softened looking intently into his eyes.

"Ok. But I'll probably have to leave soon though. I've got to go all the way across the city and there's the curfew. Do you think I can still get a taxi?"

"Tell you what. Jose and I came in a car we borrowed. We'll take you home."

After the usual back and forth about the inconvenience, he agreed. An hour later Castell said his goodbyes and told his uncle he would like to see him again soon. Castell, Reyes, and Jose Aguilar left at five-thirty in an old beat-up Volkswagen beetle. Everyone would be leaving shortly because of the curfew.

At the end of the street they were stopped by a group of four soldiers of the National Police with their vehicle blocking half the street. Both the National Police and the National Guard discharged policing functions. The Treasury Police was the more sinister secret police command. All were full military organizations that come under the same military command structure.

The police leveled assault weapons at the car and ordered everyone out. The sergeant in charge was greasy looking with dirt under his fingernails. He took their identification papers.

"What were you doing at the Portillo house?" the sergeant said.

"He's my uncle," Castell answered.

"Your uncle? Your passport says you are American and your name is Castell."

"He's my mother's brother."

"And you two are students? Is that right?"

Reyes and Aguilar answered yes in a slightly defiant tone.

"And what were you doing? Listening to the good professor preach Communism? Preaching the overthrow of the government perhaps? "

"It was just a party sergeant, not a political rally," Reyes said.

The sergeant moved close to her. She winced at the smell of his breath. "Maybe you had sex at the party?" He cupped Reyes' breasts hard with both hands. "You're a skinny bitch but you have nice tits." All four soldiers laughed.

"Maybe you're going to go party some more? Maybe you're going to fuck both of them," the sergeant said gesturing to Castell and Aguilar. "Maybe you want a real man?" He dropped one hand from her breast and cupped his genitals. This prompted more raucous laughter from the other soldiers.

She realized the sergeant was just trying to provoke them into reacting. They would already have been arrested if that was their intention. Castell did not have the same comprehension of what was going on.

"Leave her alone," Castell said sharply to the sergeant.

"What did you say?" the sergeant said. Leaving Reyes he pushed Castell against the car. He drew a revolver from his holster and stuck the barrel under Castell's chin. "Shut your fucking mouth, gringo."

Castell could smell the stink of the sergeant. He didn't move or say anything. After an anxious silence that seemed forever, the sergeant backed away. He looked at Castell as if debating what to do next.

"Get in your car now."

All three obeyed without comment. After getting in, they were unsure if they were meant to drive away. The sergeant leaned on the open door.

"Get off the streets by curfew time. If you're caught after seven o'clock you'll be arrested. Things can happen when you're arrested."

The sergeant backed away from the car and motioned to his men to let them pass. Aguilar put the car in gear and drove off slowly.

Aguilar pounded the steering wheel in frustration. "Those fucking pigs. We'll kill more ....."

"Jose, just shut up," Reyes said sharply.

"What the fuck was that all about?" Castell said. He was breathing heavily. His face was covered with sweat.

"That was El Salvador," she said. "That's what life's all about here."

Outside of giving Aguilar the address to his cousin Hector's house, no one spoke further. It took thirty minutes to get there.

"You have rich relatives, Victor. You've got nothing to worry about. The military doesn't arrest people who live in this neighborhood," Aguilar said sarcastically.

"Quit being an asshole, Jose," Reyes said.

Castell got out of the car without comment. Reyes also got out.

"I'd like to see you again, Victor. Talk some more. Would you like to see me again?"

Flustered, he swallowed hard. "Sure. I mean, yes of course I'd like to see you again."

"Next Saturday we're having a party. Mostly students from the university. Starts around noon because of the curfew. Here, I'll give you the address."

She took a matchbook out of her purse and wrote the address on the cover.

"Will you come?"

"Yes I'll come. I'd like that very much."

"Good. See you next week, Victor."

She kissed him on the cheek and got into the car before he could say anything. A couple of days later, Castell returned to the plantation with his mother.

On Saturday morning, he borrowed one of the plantation's jeeps to drive to San Salvador. His Uncle René had admonished him to be careful. The military was very nervous because of the assassinations. He stressed that *mistakes* could be made. In case of any trouble, Victor was to be sure to say that he was René Portillo' nephew. His mother did not want him to go. She relented only after he told her if he had to be kept prisoner on the estate, he would return to the United States.

He had a map of San Salvador. The address Reyes had given was in an area not too far from his cousin Hector's home. Although not as large and well-appointed as Hector's, it nonetheless was still middle class.

He rang the doorbell. A handsome man in his late thirties with dark hair answered the door.

"Yes?"

"My name is Victor Castell. Patricia Reyes invited me."

"Certainly. Patricia told me about you. Please come in." Extending his hand, the man said, "I am Santiago Molina."

Before Molina could introduce him to the other guests, Reyes came out of the kitchen. "Victor!" She came over and kissed him, this time on the lips. He blushed with a wide smile.

"I'll introduce him to everyone, Santiago," she said taking his arm.

Many of the guests were students. There was also a doctor and three teachers, all young and recently graduated. The only face he knew, other than Patricia Reyes, was Jose Aguilar. Everyone was drinking beer or wine. Two women were fixing food in the kitchen.

Castell quickly became the center of attention having lived in the United States. Especially after Reyes told everyone that Augustin Portillo was his uncle. They questioned him on what school was like in the United States. What did the students do for fun? Did everyone have money? Castell felt himself warming to them. He found himself wanting to talk, be a part of the group. Maybe it was the influence of being around Patricia Reyes.

A young engineering student named Ramon was particularly interested in Castell's talk about computers. He told Castell that there were only a few terminals at the university, and the mainframe computer was slow. There were no personal computers. Castell invited him to see his personal laptop computer at his uncle's where he was staying. He told Ramon he would drive him out to Santa Ana sometime. Reyes clarified the puzzled expression on Ramon's face at the mention of Santa Ana since he knew Professor Augustin Portillo lived in San Salvador.

"He lives with his other uncle, René Portillo," she said.

Everyone was suddenly silent. Everyone knew of René Portillo. Not that he was notorious, but he was wealthy and a powerful political force aligned with the government. This meant he was aligned with the military. He represented the true ruling class of El Salvador. The ruling class that got their wealth by owning the land and keeping it by force.

"He can't help it if he has a wealthy relative. You can't hold that against him. You certainly don't condemn Professor Portillo because his brother is René," Molina said. He had been following the conversation from the kitchen. "Besides, if Patricia likes him, he must be all right."

"Shit, you mean you're inviting me to go to the house of Señor René Portillo?" Ramon said delighted with the prospect.

That broke the ice. After teasing Ramon, the conversation resumed. Castell felt accepted. He even felt somewhat liked. Patricia Reyes sitting on the arm of his chair helped.

"Santiago, what do you think will happen as a result of these assassinations?" someone asked.

"You're seeing some of it right now. The military is doing what could be expected. The curfew, increased arrests. It's starting to look like how things were years ago," Molina said. "I think there are very bad times ahead."

"Yeah, but at least those two pigs are gone," someone else commented.

"There are too many to kill," Molina said. "Those just as bad as Ruiz and Solorgano will take their place. The real problem is the United States. Without the aid, the military would have no power base. The government has no popular support. They hold power only by force. This country gets over a half billion U.S. dollars in military aid a year. The military are nothing more than mercenaries. The United States pays them to protect their interests. El Salvador is one of the last of the United States' colonies."

"But what interests could the United States have in El Salvador," a young man said. "There's no return on their investment. There is nothing here of economic importance to the Americans. Is it all because of a fear that the country would go Communist if they didn't give military aid?"

"Partly, but that is an over simplification," Molina said. "Most of it comes from the fact that those in the United States that make policy are just as right wing and militaristic as those in power here in El Salvador. They use the scare tactic of a Communist threat to maintain the status quo. When we talk about *them* in the United States we're talking about the military, the CIA, the State Department, and the suppliers of military goods. Their idea of a return on the investment is measured in different terms than profits alone."

"Military goods are a huge business. Think about it. El Salvador and countries like it can't afford these kinds of military expenditures. The United States can. But the American Congress needs a reason. That reason is the threat of Communism. That is the economics involved.

"The other reason is that the United States does not want to give up influence, which means power. They have dominated Central America throughout the twentieth century. The United States has been taking from Latin America for a long time. No one likes to give back what they have gained. Things are changing, but the United States is resisting."

Santiago Molina concealed his even greater antagonism toward the United States. Only to his immediate group would he give vent to his hatred. He hated American self-righteous hypocrisy as justifications for their self-interest. It was the heel of the United States that kept the dictators in power, the wealthy controlling all the land, and the people living in disease and poverty. There was no hope of change without the removal of the United States from Latin American affairs.

"The problem is that most Americans have no idea what their government does beyond their own borders," Molina said. Personally, he felt that they wouldn't care anyway. "Most Americans know nothing of history. Most know nothing of Latin America. Most don't care.

"Since the turn of the twentieth century, U.S. imperialism has been the dominant political factor in Central America. And it looks to be no different at the turn of the next.

"The United States first discovered its power when it appropriated their states of California, Arizona, and New Mexico from Mexico in the 1840's. In 1898, they ordered Spain out of Cuba. They forced Cuba into a virtual colony. Cuba was coerced to sell or lease land to the U.S. They forced the Cuban constitution to carry a provision to allow U.S. intervention if law and order was threatened. In effect a threat to U.S. interests. They still occupy the Guantanamo area based on their original right of seizure.

"Next, they architected Panama's secession from Columbia so they could build a canal. Then they leased the Canal from

Panama for almost nothing. U.S. imperialism truly started there at the turn of the twentieth century. "

Everyone was listening to Molina's impromptu lecture. Castell felt a similar interest in listening to Molina as he did for his Uncle Augustin. The difference lay in the intensity and magnetism of Molina. Whereas his uncle evoked a sense of wisdom and reasoned logic, Molina provoked the emotions. Santiago Molina had the gift of an accomplished orator. His dark eyes flashed with his passion.

"About fifteen to twenty years before the United States built the Canal, a French consortium had tried. They gave up after ten years of work because of engineering problems and the diseases of the jungle. The United States was very interested in a canal. The economic and military advantages were considerable. Reports favored a route through Nicaragua. However, since the French consortium had rights in Panama, they lobbied and bribed the U.S. Congress to vote for a Panamanian route.

"At that time, Panama was a province of Columbia. The Columbians could not agree on terms with the United States. Instead of continuing to negotiate in good faith, the U.S. engineered a rebellion in Panama. They even bribed Columbian officers who were supposed to put down the uprising. As a result, the U.S. forced the newly independent state of Panama to agree to a treaty. That treaty leased a ten mile wide canal zone for ninety-nine years, for a payment of ten million dollars, and only two hundred-fifty thousand dollars a year. The U.S. could also rule the Canal Zone as its own sovereign territory."

"God, I never realized the history behind it, and I lived in Panama most of my life," Castell said.

"And while the theft of Panama was going on, companies like the notorious United Fruit Company were establishing themselves in other parts of Central America. These companies became heavily involved in local politics in order to obtain concessions to land and create monopolies. They bribed local officials and even U.S. officials.

"United Fruit directly engineered the overthrow of a democratically elected Honduran president and reinstated an exiled former dictator. Needless to say, they got every concession they asked for from the new president. That's the origin of the term *banana republic.*"

Molina was warming to his audience. One of the women refilled his wine glass. He was pacing and gesturing as he talked.

"We still have the same thing today. American interests are like a cancer we cannot exorcise. We don't have the blatant behavior of companies like United Fruit anymore, but we do have the blatant behavior of the CIA. The United States has supported every repressive dictator in Central America. General Jorge Ubico in Guatemala from 1930 to 1944, Anastasio Somoza in Nicaragua from 1936 to 1956, Tiburcio Carias Andino in Honduras from 1932 to 1949, and here in El Salvador, our own General Maximiliano Hernandez Martinez from 1932 to 1949. More recently you have Manuel Noriega in Panama." Molina emphasized each name. "Since World War Two, the CIA has become the secret instrument of U.S. subversion in Latin American affairs.

"I only named you the most infamous dictators. Since that time, El Salvador like our sister countries has had dictator after dictator. And behind each dictator is a military junta. The military determines who governs here. And somewhere behind each right-wing Latin American military is U.S. aid.

"I'll bet none of you know that the American CIA is directly responsible for the death squads. In 1953, the CIA helped form the ultra-right-wing organization, Movimiento de Liberación Nacional, or MLN, in Guatemala. The MLN was a U.S.-funded mercenary army that succeeded in overthrowing the reformist president, Jacobo Guzman in 1954. The MLN began a new organization in the sixties called the *Mano Blanca*. In two years the death squads of the Mano Blanca killed as many as eight thousand Guatemalans. When the Guatemalan resistance movement reappeared in the late seventies, the death squads also returned. Each time the death squads appeared in Guatemala, the far-right elements in El Salvador have adopted the same measures."

"So what is the answer? Revolution?" one student asked.

"We already have a revolution, or civil war depending on your point of view. Whatever it is it's stalled. In fact the rebels have been losing ground lately," Molina said.

"Your argument suggests that the fundamental issue is U.S. military aid. If the rebels cannot topple the government, what other strategies are there?" another student asked.

"The question is not so much the strategy as the tactics. The strategy is to find a mechanism for the United States to become disillusioned with sending military aid to El Salvador. If the Americans could be made to feel like they did about Vietnam, they would stop supporting the military and the far-right. The difference is that Americans are not dying in El Salvador. All that seems to move the American public is the death of their own people. They easily accept the death of others."

Molina enjoyed the role of revolutionary teacher and ideological mentor, but he had to be cautious. He didn't need a bunch of wide-eyed disciples quoting him in the wrong places.

"Martha, Lucia, is the food ready yet?" Molina asked the two women in the kitchen.

"Almost. We could use some help. That is if you can pull yourself away from politics," Martha said.

Everyone got up and either arranged the furniture or helped with the food. Castell could not remember a time when he felt so connected in a social environment. For once, he found himself preferring to be with these people rather than alone. Particularly with Patricia Reyes.

They made eye contact frequently. While Molina was talking, she sat next to Castell on the arm of his chair. At one point, she put her hand on his shoulder. The sensation was electric. Castell had been surprised at the kisses, but her touch had signaled something different. A kiss in greeting or goodbye need not be that selective. Placing her hand on his shoulder conveyed intimacy.

After eating, Castell and Reyes walked in the backyard.

"Tell me about Santiago, Patricia. Where did you meet him?"

"Do you like him?"

"Yes. He's very interesting. Very intense. An intellectual like my uncle. I do like him."

"I met Santiago through your Uncle Augustin."

"Really? You mean my uncle knows Santiago?"

"Actually I think they're friends."

"That's great. I mean, that's interesting." He was delighted that these three special people, all new to him, were themselves connected.

Santiago Molina was the most engaging person Castell had ever met. He talked of the world as if he had been everywhere. According to Reyes, he worked for a French firm looking to make investments in Central and South America. Apparently he travelled a lot. He was in El Salvador for a couple of months while he conducted business in Central America. She said he was Salvadoran but grew up in France.

For Castell, the afternoon went by too fast. It was already getting near dusk and the curfew would again cut short the evening. The last thing he wanted to do was leave the party. Especially not to leave Patricia.

"Patricia, it's getting late. Unfortunately I must go soon," he said.

"Oh no. I don't want you to go yet." She had a pouting expression on her face.

"Neither do I, but the curfew. What about you? Where do you live?"

"Me? I live with my brother and his wife. He's a foreman with a produce distribution company. But I have an idea, Victor. Wait here a minute, I'll be right back." She left him and went to say something to Molina.

After a brief exchange, she came back all smiles. "It's all set. You're going to stay here the night. So am I. I asked Santiago and he said he would be delighted. He said this way you two could talk more after everyone else left."

"Well .....I don't know ....."

"What's there to decide? It's settled. Come on, let's get another drink."

CHAPTER 5

Toward the evening, the people started to leave in order to get home before the curfew. The woman called Martha was staying, along with Castell and Reyes. Martha was more than just one of the guests. She owned the house. With the others gone, Martha became quite affectionate with Molina. Remaining slightly aloof, Molina did not return her kisses and touches, but neither did he stop Martha's attentions. They were clearly lovers.

Martha was a real beauty. She was tall with a head-turning figure. Most of the men, including Castell, had found it hard not to stare with her blouse unbuttoned as low as it was. Martha was a schoolteacher. Her manner was confident and assertive. She seemed a match for Molina's intellect.

"Tell me about yourself, Victor," Molina said.

Martha brought more wine and they all settled in the living room.

Castell talked in brief general terms, giving few insights. He made few emotional comments. The issue of his parents' separation was treated matter-of-factly. The only enthusiasm he conveyed related to his technical studies.

"Good Lord, Victor, you make your life sound like *I was born, I grew up, I went to school, I am going to work, and when I'm old I'll die*," Martha said teasingly.

"How do you feel about your family being so politically divided?" Molina asked.

"You mean my two uncles? I don't think my parents have strong political views. My father seldom commented on politics. My mother never does. Around my Uncle René, she frequently tries to change the subject away from politics. As for my uncles, I don't know either of them too well. I hadn't seen Uncle Augustin for seven years."

"Augustin and I are good friends. He's a great man. A great intellectual force. How did you get along with him since you hardly knew each other?" Molina said.

"Oh, it was great. I liked him. I liked him a lot. I'm going to see him as much as I can while I'm here this summer."

"What do your mother and your Uncle René think about that?"

"They don't know I even saw Uncle Augustin. When I mentioned his name, my cousin, Uncle René's son, had a shit- fit."

"I would bet he did. What are your politics, Victor?"

"You mean about El Salvador, or just in general?"

"Oh, general is too broad a topic. Let's say about what's going on right now in El Salvador. For example, Patricia told me about you and Jose being stopped after you left your uncle's house. How did that make you feel?"

"I was scared. I don't mind admitting it. A bunch of soldiers pointing weapons. We hear about things like that even on United States television. But to experience it .....well that was something else. I wanted to kill that fat stinking soldier. He touched Patricia." Castell looked over at her with a pained expression.

"That goes on every day, Victor," Molina said. "Right now there are hundreds of arrests taking place. The fortunate are released after a few hours or a day. Maybe they were threatened, maybe pushed around and slapped. The unfortunate rarely get released, at least alive. Of these, the lucky are killed quickly with a bullet. The unlucky are tortured first, or raped if they're women. The stories told are unbelievably ugly."

"I know. My uncle read a letter from some professor friend who was deported. He was tortured first. It was difficult hearing about his terrible experience in detail."

"The other day when you were stopped, that's how it happens. People are never heard from again. If you would have risen to their provocation, you would have all been arrested. That is after you were beaten. Because your uncle is the powerful René Portillo, you would probably have been released. As for Patricia and Jose, any number of unpleasant things would have happened. That's what has been going on in this country for over two generations."

The rest of the evening passed with more food, more wine, and stimulating conversation. Castell's contribution was about computers. He could become quite animated on the subject. His knowledge of a new field of mathematics referred to as *chaos theory* impressed everyone. He talked at some length about a computer program he was working on, relishing explaining how programming code worked.

Molina looked at Martha and smiled, "I think Martha and I are going to retire. We'll talk more tomorrow, Victor. The bedrooms are at the end of the hall. Goodnight to you both."

Everyone kissed and embraced. Castell thanked both Santiago and Martha for a wonderful day and evening. Santiago walked to the bedroom with his arm around Martha's waist and closed the bedroom door.

Castell was still standing when Reyes reached up and touched his cheek. She kissed him slowly but ardently as she pressed against him.

"Victor, let's go to bed," she said pulling back and looking into his eyes. She grabbed his hand and led him down the hall. It was dark but the moonlight shown through the light fabric curtains. Reyes guided him to the bed. He sat on the edge and removed his shoes and socks. She kicked off her sandals then removed her blouse.

Castell removed his jeans and shirt. He could not take his eyes off of her.

"Do you like what you see, Victor?"

"Oh yes. You're beautiful, Patricia." He made an attempt to reach out to her.

"Not yet. Look at me first," she said as she unfastened her bra and let it fall away. Her eyes fixed intently on him. She pulled off her panties. He was breathing deeply, aroused beyond anytime he could remember.

Reyes moved to him and touched a hand to his chest. "Lie back." She hooked her fingers in his shorts and slipped them over his legs.

She gripped his erect penis in her hand. He groaned.

"You have a beautiful cock, Victor. And it's nice and hard. Do you want me?"

"Yes I want you." It came out raspy. He started to sit up.

"Not yet. First I want you."

She took just the head of his penis in her mouth. He made a sound of exquisite pleasure. Her mouth moved in a circular motion. The head of his cock glistened with her saliva.

After teasing his erection, she plunged the entire length of the shaft into her mouth. He came bolt upright, his eyes clinched shut. He had never experience fellatio before.

She could taste his wetness as she worked up and down.

"Like that? I do. You taste sweet, Victor."

Castell was writhing with every movement of her mouth. He was exceedingly hard and her lips were pulling the taunt skin. Sensing an eminent eruption, she eased her efforts. With his erection still in her mouth, she maneuvered herself over his face. She could feel her own wetness between her legs.

"I'm really wet, Victor. Lick me."

He plunged his lips and tongue into her opening. He could taste her. The sensation was indescribable. He had never made love to a woman in this way before. In fact he only had a couple of sexual experiences, all hurried, and none memorable.

"Easy, Victor. Take my lips in your lips. Work me with your tongue. Gently. Oh, that's the way."

She suspected that he had never made love this way before. He was much too rough initially but was acquiring a reasonably good technique with her help.

Periodically she eased the pressure of her mouth on his erection to sustain him longer. Her teeth gently clamped his cock when she sensed he might let go. Even so, he could not last too much longer.

"Inside me, Victor. Quickly."

Turning around, she stayed on top, guiding him inside of her with her hand.

She was pleasingly amazed that he had sustained himself from coming this long. This guy was a pretty good lover. As his erection grew even harder, she could feel his release building. She increased her rocking motion to a vigorous tempo. He held her hips and moved himself even deeper into her.

To her surprise, she came first. The muscles of her abdomen distended with the intensity of her mounting orgasm. As she contracted around his cock, he released along with her. She could feel him pouring hotly into her. He arched his hips off the bed to feel the full depth of her. She came in a long sequence of repeated orgasmic peaks.

Minutes later, she rolled off him and collapsed in exhaustion. They both laid there for some time without saying anything.

"Patricia?"

"Yes?"

"That was …..," he didn't know what words to use.

"I know, Victor. It was for me too."

They kissed. Each could taste the other's excretions on their lips. In a few minutes they were both asleep.

They awoke to the warm sun coming in the window. Neither had moved from the positions where they had fallen asleep the night before. There was a faint aroma of brewing coffee wafting into the bedroom.

"Good morning," Reyes said. She kissed him. "Sleep well?"

"I slept very well, thank you. That was some sleeping pill. It was beautiful last night."

He had never spent an entire night with a woman much less experienced anything approaching that range of sexual delight.

She smiled and kissed him again. "I thought so too."

They dressed and joined Molina and Martha in the kitchen. Martha grinned knowingly. After the *good mornings* and coffee, Castell asked Molina what sort of business he was in.

"Well actually I'm an attorney. International trade laws are my specialty. I run a European investment firm. We represent corporations looking to make investments in Central and South America. My job is to locate opportunities and help negotiate the details."

"Sounds interesting."

"It can be, but mostly it's just a lot of travel and paperwork. I'll be in El Salvador for a couple of months and then I'll probably go to Brazil. Normally I'm here for only a week or two about every other month. Actually, I'm probably wasting my time here in El Salvador. I just don't see much investment opportunity for my clients with the continued violence here. But I am Salvadoran so I have a personal interest."

"What do you mean?" Martha said. "There are lots of opportunities here. You've just got to look harder."

"I met Martha at your uncle's about six months ago. Ever since she found out what I do, she and some of her friends are continually coming up with investment ideas. I agree that's what

El Salvador needs. Martha forgets though that I have to first find a company interested then convince them that it is a good investment. The political situation here makes any investor wary."

"What about the United States? Do they invest here?" Castell asked.

"Not really. The aid I was talking about yesterday, other than military aid, comes in the form of surplus food, medicine, that sort of thing. No real investment either by the U.S. government, or U.S. private corporations. Our political climate is so bad not even the companies willing to pay bribes want to come here."

"Being Salvadoran how was it that you wound up in Europe?"

"My father sent me to school in France when I was about twelve. It was about a year after my mother died from cancer. My father owned a prosperous import brokerage firm so he had the means to send me abroad to school. I think he also wanted to get me away from the influence of the constant unrest in El Salvador."

"I went to boarding school. My father had a business acquaintance in France who looked after me."

"Where is your father now?"

"Dead. Killed in 1980. Like so many others, he was an early victim of the death squads."

"Jesus. What did he do to get himself killed?"

"Not necessarily anything. That's the horror of what went on and still goes on. It could happen just like you getting stopped by that patrol the other day. Actually, I suspect it was probably because of some acquaintance of his. My father was not political, but many of his friends were.

"At any rate I decided to stay in France and go to the university there. With the money I received from the sale of my father's business I had modest financial means. My only other family was an older sister and some aunts and uncles. No one close. My sister was married. So France seemed like a good idea. After all, I'd lived there for the last six years. Spoke French. Except being too cold in the winter, what's not to like about Paris? It was now more of a home to me than El Salvador."

What Molina told Castell was partly true. He did go to France when he was twelve. His father was killed in 1980. He was an investment broker. The unsaid events of his background made for an entirely different history however.

His father was killed by the Treasury Police for smuggling guns to the rebels. The business acquaintance in France that Molina mentioned was an expatriate Salvadoran and a dedicated Communist. He had close ties with the oldest guerrilla group in El Salvador, the Fuerzas Populares de Liberacion, or FPL. The group was formed in 1970 from the radical wing of the Communist party. His father's friend also had close ties with Cuba.

Molina's father was never a Communist himself. He became *political* only after the military's manipulations and frauds of the 1970 and 1972 elections. His politics were bread of nationalism more than ideology.

Molina lived with his father's friend while attending the University of Paris. This exposed him to not only the political left, but radical elements bent on change through subversion throughout sensitive places in the world. He was part of the violent student demonstrations in Paris in 1968. With the murder of his father years later, personal revenge now fueled his already militant ideology. Thus began his association with Cuban Intelligence. The Cubans would ultimately provide him training and funding.

By the time he graduated from the university he had set a course. He found politics impotent, but violence seductive. He trained one summer at Camp Matanzas, a guerrilla warfare school run by the Cuban DGI near Havana. The Cubans had maintained the camp to train an international group of terrorists in subversive methods and guerrilla tactics. For the first time he was exposed to the sensual feel of weapons and the seduction of violence.

He met Antonio Bouvier at the camp. Bouvier was Ecuadorian and had taught the infamous international terrorist Ilich Ramírez Sánchez, who became known as Carlos the Jackal, guerrilla tactics at the camp a number of years earlier. Ultimately, the Jackal was to plan the hijacking of Air France flight 139 from Athens in 1976. The passengers were rescued of course by the Israelis with their famous raid on Entebbe, Uganda. The only terrorist to escape that raid was Bouvier.

Molina envisioned himself another Che Guevara. The enemies were the right-wing militaries of Latin America supported by the United States. He had fixed on the United States as the key element to the salvation of Latin America. The heel of U.S. imperialistic oppression was never more blatant then in his homeland El Salvador. While Che Quevara rejected terrorism, Molina did not.

To Molina, acts of terrorism represented the means for small, committed groups to make significant impact against a seemingly overpowering enemy. It was a political weapon that could bend the enemy to respond in desired ways. Like for many at Camp Matanzas, Communism held no particular appeal. What was shared most with the Cubans was a hatred for Americans.

His father's friend, now his mentor, was an investment broker. He developed deals primarily for European investment in South and Central America. After graduating from the university, Molina set up his own firm. The business provided a cover to travel widely, and provide a conduit for funds from the Cubans. His mentor would also provide covering support by sending commissions his way. He rented a small office in the same building in Paris.

"So tell me, what do you and this pretty woman have planned for today?" Molina said.

"Victor, you are going to stay the day aren't you?" Reyes asked.

"You bet. Oh shit!" he said loudly. "I forgot to call my cousin Hector yesterday and tell them I was going to be here last night. I better call them now."

Castell called Hector's office. His cousin was at first relieved and then angry. He was curious as to where he had been. After Castell intimated it involved a girl, Hector didn't pursue the matter. Castell listened to his cousin's admonishments to be careful, telling him he would be back at the house before curfew that evening.

After a large breakfast, he and Reyes left in the jeep. It was a sunny, cloudless day, perfect for a drive in the countryside. He had never felt happier. They did nothing special, just talked and enjoyed each other's company. At a roadside stand they lunched on chicken and tortillas.

Neither wanted the day to end. It was Sunday, and Reyes had classes tomorrow.

"Victor, let's call your uncle and ask Claudia and him to have dinner with us."

"You really like my uncle."

"I adore the Professor. Let's call him."

Augustin was delighted when they called. After a brief discussion with his wife, he suggested instead that they have dinner at his house. With the curfew, they would again have to cut short their evening. Castell agreed on the condition that he and Patricia would bring all the food. Augustin suggested that he and Patricia plan to spend the night to avoid any problems with the curfew. The curfew was becoming quite accommodating.

Castell called his cousin Hector again. He told him that contrary to their earlier conversation, he wouldn't be back again tonight either.

"What the hell is going on Victor?" Hector asked.

"Listen Hector, I met this girl and we've been with her friends. You know how it is."

"Yes, I know how it is. Is she ..... is she that good?" Hector asked sarcastically.

Castell bristled with his cousin's inference, but said only, "It's not what you think, Hector."

"These friends, are they political?"

"What do you mean political?"

"Do they talk politics? Are they Communists? Do they talk against the government? That's what I mean." Hector was more than a little irritated. He felt responsible for his cousin's wellbeing.

"Listen, Hector, we just party that's all. No politics."

"Is there a number I can reach you at?" Hector asked.

"I don't think so. Quit worrying, Hector."

"If your mother calls, what do I tell her?"

"Tell her what I told you. I don't much care what you tell her. Got to go now, Hector." Castell hung up.

Reyes and Castell stopped at her brother's house to get a change of clothes and her books for class tomorrow. No one was home. Reyes left a note saying she would be at a student picnic then spending the night with a friend.

They bought steaks, fresh vegetables, and Chilean wine. Castell insisted on paying for the expensive feast. He would tell Claudia this way she did not have to spend all her time in the kitchen preparing dinner. They would grill steaks just like in California.

Claudia however insisted on making *quesadilla*, the Salvadoran equivalent to a pound cake, for dessert. Reyes helped her in the kitchen, while Augustin and his nephew sipped their wine in the back yard.

"You and Patricia obviously like each other," Augustin said giving his nephew a wry smile. They were sitting in the backyard under the shade of large tree.

"Yeah I do, and I think she does too, Uncle. We're becoming very close," he said, avoiding admitting to the stronger emotional feelings he actually felt.

"Patricia is an exceptional young lady. She's intelligent, assertive, and yet charming and very feminine. She's the daughter I never had. I worry about her though."

"What do you mean?"

"Like I said, she is intelligent and strong willed. Too strong willed perhaps. She sees what goes on in this country. She's educated. She knows what the rest of the world is like. What the Western democracies are like. What El Salvador could be. As with any right-thinking moral person, she's appalled by the abuses of the government and military. Patricia cannot reconcile herself to accepting the nature of these things as inevitable. Unfortunately, she's vocal about her contempt for those in power. She is both impatient and *political*. That can be dangerous in El Salvador."

Reyes came out of the house. She kissed Castell on the cheek. "What are you two talking about so intently?"

"My Uncle was telling me about your big mouth," he said while putting his arm around her waist.

"Oh? In what way, Victor?" she said winking at him. He understood her innuendo. "Professor, is that true?"

"Not exactly the words I chose, but close enough. You know that you are indiscriminate about who you talk to. It's a dangerous time, Patricia."

"You should talk, Professor. You're quoted in the press. You associate with all sorts of people on the military's shit list. In fact, next to known FDR or FMLN members, you have to be high on that list yourself. Look what happened to Professor Ellacuria," she said, making reference to the young Guatemalan professor that was tortured and deported.

"We all worry about your safety, Professor. They picked on Ellacuria only because he was an easier target. And maybe to send you a message. The only reason they don't arrest you is because of your reputation in the international community. They aren't prepared for the heat they would take if anything happened to you. But that could easily change."

Privately she wasn't so sure that Augustin Portillo's stature would serve to protect him. She loved him like her own father. He gave her a love for knowledge and exposure to philosophical concepts.

She had discussed her fears with Molina. He had been empathetic, but told her that the Professor did his part in the struggle and knew the risks. Every revolution needed intellectual inspiration. Augustin Portillo served the cause in this way. But Molina also added that while every revolution needed an ideological foundation, change never happened without violent force breaking the power of the oppressor.

"Are you in danger, Uncle?"

"Essentially everyone in El Salvador is in danger, Victor. But I don't think my situation is necessarily what Patricia depicts it to be. At any rate, one must be lead by his own conscience."

Castell realized his uncle had not really answered his question. His evasions gave concern after hearing Patricia's comments.

After dinner they sat outside. The moon was full and the night air was just the right temperature. It was the first opportunity for Castell to become acquainted with his new aunt, Claudia. Although quiet, she was a perfect companion to his uncle. He thought her high school students must like her a lot. Like his uncle, Claudia was warm and caring. Together, they were the nicest people he had ever known. The concept of family was new to Castell. His father was not close to his siblings and growing up in Panama made interaction with either side of the family infrequent. Already he felt more attachment to his Uncle Augustin and Aunt Claudia than to his own parents.

They all said goodnight at a reasonable hour. Except for Castell, all had to work the next day. Patricia was to sleep in the spare bedroom, he on the sofa.

Patricia gave him more than a perfunctory goodnight kiss. Claudia smiled knowingly.

Castell lay awake thinking about things that had always been foreign. For the first time in his life he genuinely cared for somebody. Not just one somebody, but several. He found the stirrings of the feeling of family in his aunt and uncle. A friend, maybe an older brother figure in Santiago Molina. And of course Patricia. He had never felt this way about a girl before.

It wasn't just the sexual excitement. The night before with Patricia was entirely more profound. His limited prior sexual experiences were just that, nothing more. The first time had been with a Panama City whore. He and two of his classmates from the high school for U.S. personnel in the Canal Zone had gotten their first experience after getting drunk. She was a little chubby and smelled bad. For him it was memorable only to the extent he worried about venereal disease for weeks afterwards.

While in school, he had no real girlfriend. There was a girl that seemed to chase him, but there was something irritating about her. Twice at parties, he found himself with girls eager only for the nearest cock to satisfy them. In one instant the girl was drunk, the other stoned on cocaine.

Starting to dose off, he was startled by Patricia's whisper. "Victor, are you awake?"

"Shit. You scared me."

"Grab your blanket. Let's go outside."

She was wrapped in her own blanket.

They snuck quietly out the back door. The night was still warm. Patricia led him under the large tree that dominated the back yard.

"Lay your blanket on the ground."

Castell did as she asked. He was dressed only in his under-shorts but the tropical night was still warm.

"You won't need those," she said pointing to his under-shorts. She opened the blanket wrapped around her. She was naked.

He stripped his shorts off. She knelt down beside him.

"Tonight you have to be very, very quiet. We don't want the neighbors complaining."

They kissed for a long time until their arousal could no long-er be contained. They kissed again as he climaxed as a means to avoid uttering any sound.

After an early breakfast, everyone departed for their indi-vidual schedules. Patricia kissed Castell. They agreed to meet the following weekend. He gave her both his Uncle René's number and his cousin Hector's number. He was staying at Hector's one more night. Patricia gave him her brother's address, but told him they did not have a telephone. If he had to contact her, he should call his Uncle Augustin.

Castell returned to the plantation on Tuesday. He had decid-ed to work intently on the computer for the rest of the week. Pa-tricia dominated his thoughts and he needed a diversion to get through the week. It didn't work. The allure of the abstractions of mathematics and computer code couldn't compete with the flesh and blood of the beautiful Patricia Reyes.

It was not only Patricia, but his Uncle Augustin, Claudia, Santiago Molina, Martha, and many new friends. He had sud-denly acquired a life full of people. People he cared about. He now felt the isolation at the great plantation house even more keenly.

Castell liked his Uncle René but not with the same feeling as for Uncle Augustin. Uncle René was kind. He took a genuine interest in his nephew. Benevolently paternal was the word he thought to describe René. But the public René Portillo was powerful and wealthy. He was what represented the aristocracy of El Salvador. René was used to giving orders. What sounded like advice was actually a directive. With a different perspective on things here in El Salvador, Castell now saw his uncle in a different light.

Castell was evasive to his mother and uncle when questioned about what he had been doing in San Salvador. He told them he had met some students. Made some friends. Mostly he just drove around the city and stayed at Hector's house. Yes he had kind of a date with a girl. They went to a party with other students. He avoided saying that two nights were not spent at his cousin's house, but not really caring if his mother ever discovered this lie of omission.

The next couple of days passed slowly for Castell. He made little progress on his computer programs, too distracted by thoughts of Patricia. On Thursday evening, the housekeeper told him he was wanted on the telephone.

"Hello?"

"Victor, this is Patricia."

He was delighted to hear her voice. But before he could say anything she said, "It's your Uncle Augustin. He's missing."

"Missing? What do you mean *missing*?"

"I mean he didn't return home after classes today. He didn't call Claudia. She says that's not like him. It's been over six hours now."

"What does this mean?" Castell was genuinely scared.

"Some students remember him leaving in his car. I've checked with several of his colleagues. Nobody knows anything. Victor, I think he might have been arrested."

"Christ, no!" Castell remembered the letter from the Guatemalan professor. "What can we do?"

"You could ask your Uncle René for help. Do you think he would?"

"I don't know. He never speaks of Augustin. Considers him an enemy. But I'll talk to him."

"Will it cause you trouble, Victor?"

"Yes, but it doesn't matter. Where are you?"

"I'm here with Claudia. I'll stay with her."

"I'll call you later."

His mother and Uncle René were having coffee and brandy after dinner. After talking to Patricia, he came back into the room.

"Uncle, I need your help."

"Help? What's the matter?"

"It's Uncle Augustin. I think he might have been arrested."

René came up abruptly out of his chair. "You mean you've been seeing Augustin?" His eyes showed anger at the mention of his brother.

"Is that what you've been doing in San Salvador?" his mother asked. "You know how we feel about Augustin."

"Well I don't feel that way, Mother." His withering look took her aback.

"What makes you think he was arrested?" his uncle asked.

"He left the university but never arrived home. He hasn't called. It's been hours now."

"Who called you?" René asked.

"A friend." He felt uncomfortable giving his uncle any more information. He had a sudden feeling that it was us versus *them*. His emotions had clearly made him to feel part of Uncle Augustin and Patricia.

"Who have you been seeing?" his mother asked angrily. "I don't want you in San Salvador again."

"It's none of your goddamn business who I see, Mother. And I'll go to San Salvador when I please," he shouted at her.

"Victor, I won't have you speaking to your mother that way. Like me, she is only concerned for your well-being and safety. Things here are not like in the States." Gone was René's initial flash of anger. He was back in command playing the family patriarch.

Castell held his feelings in check. He needed his uncle's help.

"Will you help, Uncle René?"

"What can I do? In the first place you don't even know if he was arrested. Secondly, if he was arrested, it may be deserved. His public comments promote the cause of this violent insurgency. His comments represent sedition."

"What the hell do you mean?" Castell said raising his voice again.

"I mean, Victor, that Augustin is an enemy of the government. He does everything possible to aid the cause of the rebels. I'm sure he has contact with the rebel leadership. That makes him a criminal."

"Criminal? The fucking criminals are the government, or I should say the military. They torture and kill people. All Uncle Augustin wants is a just government."

"I will not permit such language in this house, especially in your mother's presence. I can see Augustin and his crowd have persuaded you to their treasonous politics. You didn't feel this way before, Victor. That's the danger of someone like Augustin. Especially at the university where he can preach his socialist ideology."

"I didn't need Uncle Augustin to open my eyes to what is going on here. The last couple of days I experienced it for myself. Will you help? He is your brother."

"There's really nothing I can do."

"Can't or won't?"

"I won't be challenged in my own home, Victor. In the morning I will make some calls to see if he has been arrested. That's all I can or will do."

René turned to Victor's mother, said goodnight, and left the room.

He and his mother stared at each other. Castell was enraged. His mother had never seen him like this.

"You can't talk to your uncle like that, Victor. Long ago your Uncle Augustin turned against René and the family. He took up with the Communists. Augustin wants to destroy all that we have worked for."

"Uncle Augustin is not a Communist. He.....never mind." Deciding there was no point in arguing with his mother, he turned and left the room without saying anything further.

Castell called Patricia. She told him there was no news. He told her that his Uncle René would make calls in the morning, but not to count on any help. He told her he would come to Augustin's house tomorrow morning. Lastly, he told her he loved her.

Over morning coffee, René informed Victor that there was no record of Augustin being arrested by the National Police. He told Victor that he had talked with people at the highest authority. It was his speculation that Augustin had secret business to conduct and had left suddenly to avoid any surveillance.

Castell said nothing in response. If his uncle had been arrested it would be the notorious Treasury Police not the National Police. He chose not to raise that point with his uncle instead asking if he could borrow the jeep again.

"Where are you going, Victor?" René asked.

"I'm going to Uncle Augustin's house. I'll stay with Claudia until we find out what's happened to my uncle."

"Claudia?" His mother asked.

"Yes, Mother, my Aunt Claudia, Uncle Augustin's wife, your sister-in-law," he answered sarcastically.

"Well, Uncle René?"

"I don't want you to go to San Salvador, Victor," his mother said.

Ignoring his sister's protestations, René said, "All right, Victor, you can take the jeep. But you must agree to call us and keep us informed of where you are."

Castell called Patricia and told her he was on his way. There was still no news.

After Victor left, René said to his mother, "Alicia, I think it would be better if Victor were to return to the United States."

CHAPTER 6

Castell arrived at Augustin's house late in the morning. Patricia hugged and kissed him. No news yet. He went to Claudia. She resumed crying quietly. He hugged her. Never had he felt such emotional pain. For the first time since he was a child, tears ran down his cheeks.

Molina called in the afternoon. "How are you holding up, Victor?"

"Okay. Good as can be expected."

"Are you going to stay there with Patricia and Claudia?"

"Of course."

"Listen, Victor. I'm sure your uncle was taken by the police. It's hard to say what will happen. My guess is that your uncle won't be harmed. If he were, it would cause serious international difficulties. The government can't afford that kind of problem right now with the United States. It's probably just a tactic to intimidate others from following Augustin's lead.

"Now listen carefully, Victor. I told Patricia to call me every hour. If the police should come, you be sure to emphasize that you're René Portillo's nephew. Be arrogant about it if you have to. Make sure you have his telephone number written down.

And you're to tell them that Patricia is your girlfriend. Do you understand what I am saying, Victor?"

"Yes, I understand, Santiago. Do you think Patricia is in danger?"

"I don't know, Victor. I told her to leave since you were there, but she refused. She said Augustin was the same as her own family."

Castell had never experienced anything like this. He was scared. Terribly scared. But more than that, he was experiencing feelings for his uncle that he had never felt. Claudia too, yet he hardly knew either of them. But this terror made him realize what it meant to love. And Patricia? Molina had implied danger for her too. He could not bear the thought of anything happening to her.

While Molina liked Augustin Portillo, if he had been arrested that might prove beneficial to Molina's broader strategy. It would be just one more event that would gain the attention of the world press. If Portillo's fate was not known by tomorrow, he knew the people to contact. Among Portillo's acquaintances were two U.S. senators, a congressman on the House Foreign Relations committee, and several prominent academics. Portillo was also a correspondent with former President Jimmy Carter. And of course there was Pope John Paul.

Molina was however displeased with Reyes' insubordination. Her exposure also exposed him. Using the same restaurant as a cutout, he told her to leave a message with the proprietor every two hours. Molina would of course not be there. He in turn would call the proprietor. Molina warned her that if she failed to call, he would assume she too had been arrested.

Molina reminded her that if she was subjected to questioning and the prospects of torture, she should tell all she knew. He had instructed his entire group this way. One could not expect associates to stand up to torture anyway. If they were captured the others would react as if all of their identities and plans were now known. It was basic to security.

He kept in constant contact with his group, issuing a new code word every few days. The code word was actually a word or phrase that required an appropriate response. An incorrect response meant that security had been breached.

Molina also knew each one of his people intimately. He knew the methods the police could employ. In the worst case scenario, his people might be forced to reveal the existence of the correct all clear code. He therefore was tuned to not only the correct all clear response, but the voice inflection. Contingency plans were arranged for the entire group based on a prearranged coded signal.

The waiting was the worst agony Castell had ever experienced. Claudia proved to be a remarkably strong woman. She had occupied herself with calling everyone in Augustin's address book. Unfortunately, if the police were willing to arrest someone of Augustin's stature, it was unlikely that any of his acquaintances could apply any pressure. However, it gave her something of purpose to do. Claudia also warned everyone she called not to come to the house. They would only expose themselves further. As instructed, Patricia called the restaurant every other hour.

Castell called his mother later in the day. The conversation was short and strained. She asked when he would be home. He bluntly answered, when Uncle Augustin was safe. Out of character, his mother told him she loved him. He hung up with no reply. His mother's sudden display of maternal affection was only more troubling. Not once had she asked about how her sister-in-law was holding up.

Friday ended with Molina calling late that night. His sources could not confirm Augustin's arrest but there was little doubt that was what happened. Patricia told him she would call again in the morning. Molina reminded her to continue to contact him through messages to the restaurant since he was not yet returning to Martha's house. He would call her again sometime tomorrow.

Molina was in fact at a safe house. It was the house of an old family friend, unknown to anyone in his group, even his lover Martha. Her house could be compromised if Reyes or Castell were arrested and harshly questioned.

Castell slept fitfully that night. He awoke at first light. Claudia was already in the kitchen. Her eyes were red and puffy. Patricia looked no better.

Saturday passed with no news. Patricia got Claudia to bed at one o'clock in the morning. She then sat down with Castell in the dark living room.

"You know it's possible that your uncle may be dead, Victor."

"Do you think they would dare do such a thing?"

"A few months ago, maybe not. But since the assassinations, things are different. The killings of these high ranking officers have stirred them up like hornets. I talk with other students. A lot of people are being arrested. Others are missing like your uncle."

To Patricia Reyes, a realization of what Molina was unleashing was taking real form. She was part of it. The military was reacting just as he predicted. Would it start by hurting the people she loved?

Molina had warned all of them that things would become more unpleasant. If the military responded as expected, it would mean a return to the bad old days. El Salvador must stay in the news. It took blood to make world news. The more repressive, the more brutal the military, the more it made international headlines, the more difficult for the United States to justify continued aid. Reyes understood, but hoped that Augustin Portillo would not have to be part of the sacrifice.

"We've got to do something, Patricia. We can't just continue to wait," Castell said.

"I know, I feel the same, but there's nothing more to do."

They held each other. Both were exhausted and fell asleep on the sofa.

In the predawn early hours of what was now Sunday morning, Castell and Reyes awoke to car doors closing. They rushed to the front door in seconds. As they opened the door, the car sped away. A figure was slumped on his knees at the edge of the street. Castell ran to his uncle who was struggling to get to his feet.

Augustin looked a mess. His hair was uncombed and he had several days' growth of beard. His shirt was soiled. By his smell, he had not bathed for days. Castell and Reyes helped him into the house. Claudia appeared. She uttered a gasp and rushed to her husband.

"Oh my God! What did they do to you?"

They seated Augustin on a sofa. He asked for water. After the tears subsided, he told them what had happened.

"I left my office at the regular time. A few blocks away, I was forced to a stop by another car. The car was unmarked but the four men wore Treasury Police uniforms. One stayed with my car, the other three took me to Treasury Police headquarters."

"I was put in a cell with no explanation. In the morning, I was taken to an interrogation room. A captain questioned me for several hours. They made me sit on a hard wooden chair all the time. I couldn't go to the toilet. I was given no food or water for that first day since they arrested me."

"What did they want you to tell them?" Reyes said.

"The usual. Names of friends, who I was corresponding with. Things they probably already knew. It was evident that the information itself was not the purpose. No one even took notes. Intimidation and humiliation seemed their intent. My wrists were handcuffed in front ever since that took me. The captain would frequently stand in front of me, his face inches from me. Spittle hit my face. Two men would hold my arms. The impression was that he would strike me. But they never hit me that first day."

"I was taken back to my cell in the afternoon. They gave me water for the first time, but no food."

"Augustin, you mean you haven't eaten since Thursday?" Claudia asked.

"No, dear."

Claudia went to the kitchen to fix food. Reyes got glasses and brandy for all of them.

Augustin took a sip of the brandy. His hand shook. "I was not allowed to sleep. A guard would walk by the cell every ten minutes or so. He would bang on the bars with his baton if it looked like I was falling asleep.

"That afternoon, I was again taken to the interrogation room. Same officer, same line of questions. He told me if I didn't tell them what they wanted, he could have my wife brought in for questioning. I knew what he was trying to do, but the thought of Claudia in this hell still terrified me. This went on for a couple of more hours before I was taken back to my cell.

"There were no windows or natural light in the cell. I lost track of time. I had read about sleep deprivation, but one cannot appreciate its effects unless you've experience it.

"I had no concept of the time. I lost track of the interrogation sessions. It was becoming increasingly difficult to listen to the interrogator. It was difficult to determine if I was falling asleep or hallucinating. Once in a while he would slap me across the face. Actually, that brought me back to reality."

"For some reason, probably because they were going to release me, I was eventually allowed to fall asleep. I fell asleep sitting on the floor propped in the corner of my cell. There was no furniture. Nothing except a slop bucket to relieve yourself. They woke me not too long ago."

"Jesus Christ," Castell said. Tears ran down his cheeks. Augustin hugged his nephew.

Claudia returned to the kitchen and brought back a bowl of soup. As exhausted as Augustin was, she was able to spoon-feed some nourishment into him before helping him into bed. Castell and Reyes fell asleep on the sofa, this time with the exhaustion of emotional relief.

The morning sun again woke Castell. His movement woke Patricia. They got up and made coffee.

After their coffee, they decided to leave Augustin and Claudia a day alone to recover from the ordeal. He would return to the plantation. Reyes to her brother's. She would return to his uncle's house later that evening and call him. She would also call everyone and tell them that Augustin was safe.

Castell and Reyes embraced with a newfound sense of shared experience. This was his family.

When he arrived at the plantation, fortunately his uncle was not at home. He informed his mother that Augustin was home and that he had been arrested then eventually released. He was badly treated but not seriously hurt.

"Uncle René either never called anyone, or he lied," Victor said to his mother.

"You will not say that about your uncle. Do you hear me? And how do you know that he did not intercede to get Augustin released?"

"Don't worry, mother, I won't be staying here that much longer to confront him with that question."

"Where are you going?"

Not answering, he left her and went to his room. If it wasn't for Patricia, he would simply leave El Salvador. To a semi-foreigner, it was a violently dangerous third world country. Things however were no longer that simple. Castell had found something here, something precious.

He had all but made up his mind to enroll at Caltech in Pasadena, California and work on an advanced degree. Now that decision was infinitely more difficult. The thought of leaving Patricia was not something he could deal with right now. He had some money in an account in the States. There was still over two months before the fall semester would start. He could afford to rent an apartment in San Salvador. Tomorrow he would go to a bank and arrange a transfer. Right now, he needed a shower and some sleep.

He was still soundly asleep when his uncle woke him.

"Victor, wake up. You're wanted on the telephone," René said. He was clearly irritated.

"What time is it?" he asked, still groggy. It was dark outside. His uncle had switched on a light.

"It's ten o'clock. Whoever it is will not identify himself. Only that he is a friend."

Castell hurriedly put pants on and went downstairs to take the call.

"Hello?"

"Victor, this is Santiago. Don't repeat my name out loud. I have ......" Molina hesitated before continuing. "I have some very bad news. Your aunt and uncle were killed earlier tonight, Victor."

"No, goddamn it!"

His mother and uncle hurriedly came into the room.

"How?"

"Apparently hand grenades were thrown into the house. Into their bedroom. It happened about an hour ago."

"Patricia, what about Patricia! She was going to be there tonight!" Castell's heart felt suspended between beats.

"Patricia is all right. She was there earlier but left before the attack occurred."

"Where is she? I want to see her."

"She's safe, Victor. She's not at her brother's house. You can see her tomorrow. Write this number down. Come to the city. Once you are in San Salvador, call and tell the person that answers who you are. He'll give you instructions."

Castell found a pen and note pad on the desk.

"We all must be very careful now, Victor. If they could do this to Augustin Portillo, no one is safe. Even you as an American. Don't trust anyone, not your mother, especially not your Uncle René. I'll talk to you tomorrow." Molina abruptly hung up.

Castell put the phone down. Tears filled his eyes. He turned to face his uncle and mother.

"Augustin and Claudia were just murdered. Your fucking military murdered them! I hate this fucking country!"

"Victor, please." His mother began crying.

René Portillo said nothing.

Before his mother could embrace him, he turned and went up to his room. He was determined he would leave in the morning. Only the curfew prevented him leaving that very moment.

Castell was up before daybreak having packed everything. He would not be returning to the house. Taking the jeep, he didn't really care if his uncle objected. His mother would never allow his uncle to take any serious action against him.

The number Molina gave him was the same number the other members of the group called with their safe codes. Castell was told to be at a certain downtown restaurant at noon. He would be contacted.

Colonel Benavides was in a late night meeting with General Garcia, Army Chief of Staff, when the call came through. Benavides took the call in the general's office. He listened without comment, but his eyes narrowed and his jaw clenched. On the other end of the call was his aide, Captain Ramirez. Ramirez just informed him of the killing of Augustin Portillo and his wife. Benavides acknowledged the information and hung up.

Benavides turned to the general, "That sonofabitch Rivera just had Professor Portillo killed."

"What happened, Colonel?" General Garcia asked.

"That fucking Rivera ordered it. I'm sure of it, even if I can't prove it. He's cut from the same mold as Solorgano. That place is a pest-hole of sadistic deviates with no brains. About eight o'clock, somebody threw grenades into the professor's house. Portillo and his wife were killed."

"I don't understand, Colonel. You told me that you were going to have Portillo picked up and detained for a couple of days, then released. What happened?"

"He was detained. I personally ordered Major Rivera to make the arrest. I was explicit to the Major about the extent of the interrogation. I had Portillo released earlier today, in the early morning hours.

"Rivera has resisted all my orders. He especially resents my prior review of all arrest lists before they are executed. Portillo has always been high on his list. When I approved the arrest, he fought me on the constraints I placed on him. So he just circumvented them."

"Can you prove that, Colonel?"

"No," Benavides answered flatly. "But Major Rivera is a threat. He's maybe more dangerous than Solorgano. He doesn't have quite the appetite for sadism that Solorgano had, but in other ways he may be more of a threat. He's an animal that thrives on crude methods. He's smarter and more ambitious than Solorgano. With Solorgano gone, he sees the opportunity of eventually having command of the Treasury Police."

Benavides was feeling the General out. Like organizational politics anywhere, if your superior felt the same way, your freedom of action greatly expanded.

General Garcia was equally politically astute.

"I understand the dangers of control over secret police files. However, Rivera does have support. He's highly respected in his tanda," Garcia said. "So you will have to be careful, Colonel."

The cliquishness of one's graduating military academy class, or tanda, was a foundation of the Salvadoran officer corps. An officer's standing with his former classmates could provide a significant power base. This was the stuff that coups were made of.

The General had just obliquely told Benavides to proceed as he felt necessary, but that he was not condoning any particular course of action. It was Benavides' problem. If there was any trouble, the General could disavow Benavides actions.

"There is also the continuing pressure from the United States regarding so-called human rights abuses. This stupid murder of Professor Portillo only complicates our relations with the United States," Benavides said. "I have a very good relationship with Colonel Taylor, the U.S. military attaché. He tells me that there is renewed pressure brewing in their Congress concerning our military aid. He told me the Washington Post was doing a major series of unfavorable articles. He gave me copies of the first two articles."

Benavides took the copies out of his brief case and placed them in front of Garcia.

"You'll notice the byline; John Harmon."

"And the significance of that?"

"Harmon has been down here until a short time ago. He was well acquainted with Professor Portillo. Also, there is information in the first of the articles about Colonel Solorgano that I didn't know. My guess is that Harmon has access to some very detailed information. It may mean we have someone highly placed feeding information to the leftist American press. Portillo's death assures continued bad press.

"Taylor told me that we still have strong support in the U.S. military, CIA, and the White House. Even the State Department is only responding from the pressure from the U.S. Congress. He worries about the weak Secretary of State, and that prick, Bennett at the embassy."

Lawrence Bennett was the U.S. ambassador to El Salvador. Benavides had had several confrontations with him in the past.

He was not a weak token political-appointment diplomat. Nor was he particularly sympathetic to the present Salvadoran government or the military high command. Taylor had told Benavides to be careful with Bennett. Bennett was shrewd and he had clout in Washington.

"Nothing is more important than keeping the Americans satisfied," General Garcia said. "Nothing can be allowed to affect the aid package. I rely on your outstanding skills to manage the Americans, Colonel,"

It was clear that Garcia was going to cover his ass until the situation became clearer. Benavides left his superior's office and returned to the Treasury Police Headquarters. He asked the duty officer, "Is Major Rivera here?"

"Yes, Sir, he's in his office," the officer answered.

"Get him. I want to see him in my office, immediately."

"Yes, Sir." There was no mistaking the Colonel's mood.

Benavides went to his office. Major Rivera knocked on the door a couple of minutes later.

"Enter."

"Sir, you wanted to see me," Rivera said saluting casually. Benavides could feel Rivera's arrogance.

"I know you ordered the Portillo killing, Major."

"You have no proof of that, Sir."

"Shut the fuck up, Major. I said you ordered the killing. If I could prove it, I'd have you up for court martial for insubordination. Since I can't, I will give you revised orders. They will be confirmed in writing. Those orders will limit your authority severely, Major. In fact, you won't be able to take a shit without my authorization."

"Colonel, I resent ….."

Benavides cut him off. "Shut up, Major. And stand at attention." Rivera came to a relaxed attention.

"Don't contest with me, Major, you'll lose. Now get the fuck out of my office."

Rivera's face was red. He would have killed anyone else that had talked to him like that. But Benavides was powerful. Rivera would have to be careful. At any rate, Benavides reaction was not totally unexpected. It also showed that Benavides' authority had its limits.

Rivera had ordered the killing of Augustin Portillo. He was not sure who actually executed the killing. Plausible deniability. Rivera left those details to Captain Alvarez. Alvarez was the key liaison to several groups of ultra-right military personnel that could be relied on for such work. These groups were more tightly directed than the death squads of the early eighties. Under Solorgano, now Rivera, they were an instrument that allowed the military extremists to operate counter to even the right-wing government's control.

Benavides was too soft on the leftist opposition in Rivera's opinion. Those like Portillo should be removed. There was a war going on and Portillo actively aided the enemy. The military command could not tolerate assassinations of its top officers without a strong counter-response. Besides, Benavides would be the one to take the heat from the weak-willed Americans from the U.S. State Department. They would talk about human rights, but it was all show.

Castell arrived at the designated restaurant at a quarter to twelve. He sat outside as Molina had directed. The restaurant was located in the center of San Salvador. Business men and government officials represented the clientele. It was early for the lunch crowd and only a few tables were occupied. Molina arrived exactly at noon. Actually, he had been across the street for some time watching who entered the restaurant.

"Hello, Victor." Molina grabbed Castell's forearm affectionately and sat down.

"Hello, Santiago."

"Where is Patricia?"

"She's staying with me at the home of some friends. I won't be returning to Martha's house. Patricia also shouldn't go back to her brother's until we're sure about what is going on."

"I want to see her."

"I know. I'll arrange it."

"Jesus Christ, how could they kill him?" Tears ran down Castell's cheeks.

Molina put a hand on his shoulder. "That's the nature of things here. It's now come close to you. Sooner or later, everyone here is touched by death. The victims of the killings and torture are always the innocents, or the best of us."

"Why did they let him go, just to kill him hours later?"

"Hard to say. I suspect his arrest was intended to send a message to others in opposition of the government. He could of course been just made to disappear yet they chose a more measured approach. He was not seriously abused physically during his detention. His murder seems to run counter to all of that. As you point out, why go through the charade if you intend to kill him? It may signal factional differences in the security forces command. May have been different groups working at cross purposes. It does revive the fear of the death squads."

"I'm not going back to my Uncle René's house, Santiago. I'm going to find an apartment here in San Salvador."

"Good. It will also be good for Patricia. Will she live with you?"

Castell hadn't thought that far yet. But, yes, he would ask her to stay with him. The thought made his heart leap.

"I hope so. I will ask her to."

Since Reyes had told him about Castell's background, Molina had been interested in the possibilities that Castell might represent. He had to be attuned to even highly remote possibilities to find people to use for support. Recruitment was a delicate process of selection and cultivation.

Victor Castell was an obvious attraction. His technical background could be a vital asset. The scope of Molina's plans required more than risky individual assassinations. Even though he lost only one man in their first operation, he felt they had been exceptionally lucky in the Solorgano and Ruiz assassinations. Molina did not want to have to rely on luck. His plans called for something much more spectacular.

Castell was also a U.S. citizen as well as Salvadoran, at least partially. There might yet be nationalistic feelings for El Salvador, especially after meeting his Uncle Augustin. On the other hand, the United States may hold no particular emotional bonds. After all, he lived much of his life in Central America. He came from wealth and was educated. He spoke Spanish. His romantic attachment to Patricia Reyes was a powerful snare. Revenge may now be a factor. Molina mentally ticked off the list of potentially favorable circumstances. At the least, there seemed little risk in pursuing the matter further.

Successful recruitment is nothing more than effective selling. The good salesman assesses his customer and takes advantage of opportunities. Augustin's murder was just such an opportunity. Molina would see how far he could exploit Castell's grief.

They finished their wine and a light lunch. Castell hardly touched his food. Molina looked at him and made a decision.

"Victor, do you know why I am being so cautious?"

"I assume because you're afraid the police might now arrest all those associated with my uncle?"

"Partly. But actually it's more than that, Victor." Molina glanced around to determine how close anyone was. "I myself am very active in opposition to the government. Your uncle and I shared more than just a common philosophy. He fought in his way, I in mine. I am committed to the fight for freedom, Victor. I'm committed to my people. My business is essentially a cover that allows me to freely move around without raising suspicion. If I was found out, I would be executed."

"Does Patricia know?"

"Patricia is also part of the resistance against this government and the military."

Castell swallowed hard. Fear came into his eyes. "What exactly are you into, Santiago?"

"I don't want to go into details here, Victor. But I can tell you that our resistance is not passive. We intend to drive a stake in the heart of the military, and their master the United States."

"And Patricia is part of this?"

"Yes, Victor. Patricia is one of my key people."

"Why are you telling me this?"

"Because I understand your feelings for Patricia. I wanted you to know. She would not have told you herself for reasons of security and your own safety. Also, Victor, I can see the hurt and rage within you with the loss of your uncle. I needed to tell you that there are those of us that are fighting these monsters. I've taken a terrible risk by confiding in you, but I feel you can be trusted. We need friends that might someday help. You are a friend, Victor."

"When can I see Patricia?"

"Tonight. I suggest you take a room at the El Presidente Hotel. Patricia will call you there later. I will personally bring her to the hotel, Victor."

"Thank you, Santiago."

Molina's revelations had thrown Castell off balance. He felt like he was sinking into quicksand. Only a few weeks ago he was taking final exams at a university in California. Now this. This was the real world. But right now all he wanted was to see Patricia.

He drove directly to the hotel. Patricia called around five o'clock in the afternoon. She knocked on his door an hour later. Castell pulled her into the room. They kissed with tears running down both their cheeks.

He started to say something, but she placed her fingers on his lips and whispered, "later". She locked the door and led him to the bed. They both undressed in a rush.

They groped each other, savoring the feel and the pleasure they caused the other. She rolled on her back and guided him into her. Castell crushed his mouth against hers. They held each other tightly. He moved slowly within her. She flexed her vaginal muscles, gripping his cock tightly.

After several minutes, he straightened up on his arms. Long, slow thrusts brought groans from her. Her abdomen arched each time to meet his thrusts. He could feel her rising to orgasm. She could feel the wave of foreshocks cursing through her body. Locking her legs around his hips, she came violently.

Some moments later she said, "You liked that didn't you? Making me come like that." She smiled into his smiling face. "Now it's my turn."

She rolled over and got up on all fours, quickly reinserting his cock into her from behind. Finding the optimum angle to enhance the friction, she moved herself against him feeling the depth of his penetration. He gave out a constant, low moan. As he felt his impending release, he increased the rhythm of his thrusts. She sustained the motion throughout his ejaculation, pulling the last drop from him.

They lay in each other's arms for a long while. Patricia eventually said she was hungry, suggesting they order room service. While she showered, he ordered dinner.

Castell joined her in the steaming bathroom. He started to grow hard just looking at her. She soaped and washed him. His cock became erect with her hand pulling firmly as she lathered him. She rinsed him and knelt in front of him. His cock grew to its full erect length with the firm pulling of her mouth. He held her head to him as he came. His release made his legs so weak they trembled.

They ate dinner on the small balcony. Neither said much. Every moment was precious. This was just a temporary escape. Both knew they had serious issues to confront.

"Patricia, what are you and Santiago into?"

She looked at him trying to decide how much to reveal. "We are fighting the government and the military."

"I know. Santiago told me. But how? Are you helping the rebels?"

"Not exactly."

"What then, Patricia? I love you, I need to know. What are you into?"

Reyes decided to essentially tell Castell everything. She and Molina had discussed the possibilities. Her feelings for Castell were genuine, but she was equally committed to the struggle. If she was taking advantage of him, it was justified.

"The recent killings of the military officers. They were our doing. Santiago's group. Our group," she said in a quiet voice, fearing his reaction.

"Jesus Christ! I can't believe that. You and Santiago? What was your part?"

"I just supported the operation. I didn't kill anyone myself. I don't think I could."

"Why in hell would you get into something like this?"

He stood and paced about the room.

"Why? Look around, Victor. This is my home, my people. This is also a fucking war zone. This is Nazi Germany. This is the Klu Klux Klan in your country lynching people. Everybody I know has lost someone. We're in the middle of a running civil war that's been going on for years. I told you my parents died when I was quite young. But I didn't tell you how.

"It was in 1980. I was only twelve years old. Mother and father were attending the funeral of Archbishop Romero. You know about his assassination?"

Somewhat sheepishly he said, "No. I'm afraid not."

"He was archbishop of El Salvador. Beloved by everyone. But just like your Uncle Augustin, he was an outspoken critic of the military junta's repression and brutality directed at the people. He was saying mass at a small church when he was gunned down at the altar."

"Who killed him?"

"No one was ever arrested. But we all know it was ordered by the military. One of their killers. The same people that make up the death squads.

"Anyway, the funeral was enormous. Some say a quarter of million people turned out. Pope John Paul sent a cardinal to speak as his personal delegate. But even with all of that outpouring, the military could not restrain themselves. Smoke bombs exploded in the streets near the cathedral. Who set them off? That was never determined. Gunfire then erupted from the surrounding buildings, including the National Palace. It wasn't rebels firing into the crowd, it was government security forces. Thirty to fifty people were killed either by the gunfire or the stampede of thousands trying to flee."

"And your parents were among those killed?"

Reyes just nodded. "It won't stop by itself. It's been going on for over a hundred years. Can't you feel a little of what I feel, Victor? How does the murder of your uncle make you feel? Don't you want to fight back?" The words spilled out in a torrent.

"Santiago has given us dignity. We've hurt them, and we'll hurt them more. We've just started." There was the zeal of the fanatic in her voice now. "You can help us, Victor. We can be together. I love you and want you with me, Victor."

"How could I help?"

His thoughts ranged wildly through skepticism, curiosity, excitement, and a measure of dread. This was almost too much to comprehend, but her passionate fervor struck responsive cords. No longer an outsider, he felt himself drawn several levels deeper into these alien circumstances.

"I don't know. Lots of ways. You're smart. You have connections within the enemy camp, your mother's family. You speak English. You are an American. You could provide all sorts of information. Be our spy. Lots of things. Santiago trusts you. That is why he told you about our fight. Will you help us, Victor?"

Molina had not told her what role he might want Victor to play. The spying was an assumption on her part.

"I don't know, Patricia. What will I have to do?" The idea of retaliating against the bastards who killed his Uncle Augustin did strike primal feelings of revenge. He felt guilty and frustrated by not being able to do something. He would be leaving El Salvador in a couple of months. Once he left, there would be no opportunity. Could he just do nothing? If he felt this way about Patricia how could he not help? If he refused, would he lose her?

"I don't know, Victor. All I know is that I want you with me. We can talk about it tomorrow with Santiago. He'll have breakfast with us. Now, let's go to bed."

CHAPTER 7

Molina phoned their room from the lobby the next morning. The call woke both Castell and Reyes. Castell mumbled that they would be down in a little while.

Thirty minutes later they located Molina in the dining room and sat down. Castell was somber and said little other than hello to Molina. The waiter served coffee and took their order.

"I told him, Santiago," Reyes said. Molina knew what she meant.

"Are you shocked, Victor?"

"Of course I am. It's stupid. You'll all be killed eventually. You know that, don't you?"

"Maybe. We've already lost one of our people. But you must understand it's a risk that we must take. There are things worth dying for, Victor. I love this country. It can be beautiful and a good place to live. I remember my childhood here. I remember the passion my father felt for El Salvador. What did Patricia tell you?"

In a whispered voice Castell said, "She told me you are responsible for the killing of the defense Minister and that other army officer. I remember the newspaper story. It showed his head cut off. Did you do that?"

The thought of the severed head made Castell shudder, not to mention talking to the person responsible.

"Unpleasant things are necessary in war, Victor. The twentieth century has a long list of atrocities. The severing of the colonel's head was done for a purpose. He was executed humanely before that. The purpose was to gain media attention and to maybe instill some fear in the minds of those that will murder our people. The enemy kills to silence dissent. They torture to satisfy their own sadistic lust."

They were interrupted with the waiter serving their breakfast.

Molina continued once the waiter left. "Look around you, Victor. This is a vicious police state. This is something out of a history book. This is Nazi Germany suppressed by a Gestapo. Enemies of the state are murdered or just disappear. Internationally El Salvador is just a third world backwater. Our plight is ignored. Only spectacular events draw international attention.

"Tell me something, Victor. Did you ever hear about the various resistance organizations during World War Two? The French Maquis, the Yugoslav Partisans, the assassination of the Nazi, Reinhard Heydrich by Czech dissidents?"

"Well, I've heard about the French resistance. I've seen documentaries on TV." He was not a student of history.

"Would you condemn their actions?"

"No," Castell sighed as he answered. He could see where Molina's argument was leading.

"How is our situation different? Is there any question about how the military controls this country in a grip of terror? You can see it yourself and you've only been here a short time.

"Victor, this is a fight for the realities of those things you only read about; justice, liberty, freedom, life itself. It is up to those like us that have the will." Molina looked intently at him for his reaction.

Castell looked at Patricia, then at Molina. Molina's arguments were persuasive. It was the stark reality of it all that was so hard to grasp. A few weeks ago he was studying integrated circuit design in Southern California. Now he was talking to violent revolutionaries, one of which he was in love with. Did he have the courage to become part of this?

"What kind of help do you want from me, Santiago?"

Molina looked around to make sure no one was close by. "I need your technical expertise, Victor. I need your knowledge of electrical circuits. I need you to make me bombs, Victor."

Castell nearly choked as he sipped his coffee.

"You're out of your fucking mind. I don't know anything about bombs. Besides, I'm not going to kill anybody!" he said vehemently in a loud whisper. "Patricia told me about getting information for you. Nothing about bombs."

Reyes was equally shocked at what Molina had just said. She had speculated about the spying. She also had no idea what Molina was planning. On the pretext of security, he did not share such details with any of his group.

"To wage war against those that killed your uncle, we need to use all means. The people have suffered for ten years living in a state of fear from the security forces. It must end. What I ask is not all that much. Only simple control devices. Devices that will allow us to carry out our mission with less risk."

Molina himself had been trained in the use of explosives. What he lacked was the knowledge to construct sophisticated detonating devices that went beyond mere timing devices. He wanted something more than to explode car bombs outside buildings. He needed to have weapons like the device that downed the Pan Am 747 over Scotland. He needed an engineer.

"Our mission, Victor, is to break the chains that have been around the neck of this country ever since the time of the Spanish. That chain has three parts. The wealthy land owners like René Portillo support the military to maintain their hold on power. The military officers are themselves made wealthy by their support of this oligarchy. The third element is the United States who funds the means of oppression with their military aid. The United States is the weakest link in the chain. It is the ceasing of military aid from the U.S. that is our objective."

"Suppose aid is cut off. Then what?"

"Possibilities. New opportunities. There would be a real chance to topple the power structure and create a truly democratic government. With all its resources, the government has not been able to suppress the insurgency. There is too much support from the people. It would take those like your Uncle Augustin to build a new El Salvador. All we want is the opportunity. With the massive U.S. military aid, there are no opportunities."

"Will you help us, Victor?"

"I.…. I don't know. I don't think I can."

Molina's arguments were persuasive. But the thought of making a bomb was just too far beyond him.

Molina did not really expect an affirmative answer. It was enough to plant the seed and counter Castell's initial reaction. The line had not broken. The fish was still held fast.

"Just consider what I've said, Victor. We'll talk again. I have to leave now."

Molina got up, kissed Reyes on the cheek, clutched Castell's shoulder affectionately, and left the restaurant.

Castell looked at her. He was angry and confused. "Did you know what he was going to ask me to do?"

"I swear, I didn't, Victor." She laid her hand over his. "Victor, you're still going to stay in El Salvador for a while aren't you?"

He looked intently into her eyes for some time before answering. "Yes." He paused, wondering what kind of a commitment he might be making. Patricia Reyes entering his life complicated everything. Now this thing with Molina had taken things to a different level. "I need to find some place to rent. I'm not returning to my uncle's."

Patricia looked into his eyes. She too was wondering what complications her emotions would be causing. She was a soldier. A committed revolutionary. Would love get in the way?

They left the hotel restaurant. Molina told Reyes not to return to her classes at the university yet. Therefore, she was free to help him find a place to rent. She kissed him after they got into the jeep. Her exuberance started to change his gloomy mood.

As their jeep left the parking lot, a taxi pulled onto the street behind them. The taxi followed them a block behind. There was no passenger in the taxi.

It took all morning to locate a place suitable to Patricia. She had taken command like a new bride. Castell would have been satisfied with at least two of the previous places they had looked at. The apartment they settled on was one of four created out of an old mansion. In its time, it must have been a grand house. Fully modernized, it offered a pleasant view to a flower garden in the rear. The owner of the house, a retired widower, kept daily care of his flowers. It was located in a modest neighborhood of newer single family homes.

Without any discussion, Patricia confirmed the fact that she was moving in with him. They went first to her brother's house to pick up her things. He sat in the kitchen while she packed, and had an awkward conversation with her sister-in-law. From there they returned to the hotel to get Castell's things. They did not notice the taxi parked a short distance down the street.

"Alicia, I have some troubling news," René Portillo said to his sister. "It appears that Victor has taken an apartment in San Salvador. A girl has moved in with him. Worse yet, it appears this girl was closely connected with Augustin. I am concerned, Alicia. Victor could be getting himself into a dangerous situation. A situation perhaps beyond my influence."

The day after Victor Castell rented the apartment, René Portillo requested the surveillance on his nephew. The National Police were more than willing to accommodate someone of Portillo's prominence.

"What girl? Who is she?" Alicia asked her brother.

"Her name is Patricia Reyes. A university student. As I said, a frequent visitor to Augustin's house. Therefore she must have leftist leanings. Peasant background. Parents are deceased. Lives with her brother and his family."

"Some whore that wants to improve her station in life, maybe even marry into a wealthy family. I won't have Victor getting involved with this ..... this peasant bitch," Victor's mother said. The thought of her son involved with such a girl was unthinkable. "He would be throwing away his future. I'll go see him, talk to him."

"You know that would do no good, Alicia. No, Victor must leave El Salvador. Return to the United States. It's for his own good."

"I suppose you're right. But how is that to be accomplished?"

"I'll find a way. As long as you agree his leaving is for the best. I'll give the problem some thought. I doubt he can be persuaded so you must be prepared that there will be some unpleasantness. "

It had been several days since they had found the apartment. Things were feeling more relaxed, more stable since the funeral. Even though the funeral of Augustin and Claudia Portillo was attended by a sizeable number of mourners, Patricia said it would have been much larger under other circumstances. Many people were understandably afraid to publicly associate themselves with Augustin Portillo. His political leanings were public knowledge. Everyone knew the origin of his murder.

Neither Castell's mother nor his Uncle René attended their own brother's funeral. Other than Castell, no one from the family attended. Mass was said by Archbishop Rivera, prelate of El Salvador.

Castell avoided discussing the subject of Molina's request that he help them. They talked about each other, about all the possibilities of a life together. Patricia also avoided the subject. She too found a relief in talking of things other than politics and death, even if a normal future might be unrealistic.

It was late evening, a week after they had moved in. He and Patricia had just finished dinner. Patricia was an accomplished cook and introduced him to *pupusas*. Pupusas consisted of corn meal filled with ground pork and beans, then fried. For dessert, Patricia prepared flan. Castell raved about how good a cook she was as he helped clear and wash the dishes.

They took their dessert to the living room. Castell had bought a bottle of Mexican brandy to celebrate their first week living together.

There was a knock on the door. Patricia was instantly apprehensive. Knocks on doors at night after curfew in a police state instinctively provoked fear. Castell answered the door, opening it slightly. It was immediately thrust violently aside.

Four uniformed men with weapons pushed into the apartment.

"What the fuck?" he yelled.

"Shut up. Is your name Victor Castell?" the one in charge, a lieutenant by his uniform name tag, said.

"Yes. That's me. I demand to know what this is all about."

The lieutenant looked at Castell with a hard stare. He ordered him to get his passport.

"You are a United States citizen?" the lieutenant said.

"You've got the passport in your hand. Can you read?"

The lieutenant drew his sidearm from the holster and glared at Castell. Using the barrel of the revolver, he slapped him on the cheek lightly, but enough to hurt.

"You will shut your fucking mouth, gringo. Just because you speak Spanish changes nothing. You're still a gringo pig." The revolver remained pointed at Castell's face. "Do you own that jeep outside?"

"No, it's my uncle's, René Portillo. Do you know the name?"

"Oh yes, I know the name. Señor Portillo is a very important man. Now you will come with us. You're under arrest."

"You can't arrest me, I'm an American citizen. I demand to talk with someone at the American embassy." He displayed an arrogance that he no longer felt. The term *under arrest* brought a cold fear.

The lieutenant did not respond. Instead he turned to one of the soldiers and said, "Pack his belongings."

Neither Castell nor Reyes could understand why they were packing his clothing. That was not typical to an arrest. They didn't know if this was a good or bad omen.

"What about her?" Castell said.

"The whore?" the officer said.

"Fuck you, asshole!" Castell screamed at him.

Castell started to take a step towards the lieutenant. He was hit in the shoulder by the butt of a rifle and fell to the floor. The lieutenant restrained the soldier from any further blows.

As Castell went down, Reyes instinctively started to move to him. A fist slammed hard into her face, sending her also to the floor.

The lieutenant went over to where Reyes lay. The blow had almost knocked her unconscious. He turned to Castell and said, "My orders stipulate that you are not to be harmed. I have no such orders regarding your woman."

The lieutenant reached down and gripped the top of Reyes' blouse, ripping the front away, displaying her bare breasts. She wore no bra.

Reyes made an attempt to cover herself with her arms. The lieutenant hit her again over the eye with a vicious backhand. He reached down with both hands and tore away her skirt. Only her panties remained.

Castell attempted to get up but was held on the floor by a rifle pressed to the side of his neck. "Please don't," he said pleadingly. "Don't hurt her, please."

The lieutenant only grinned, returning his attention to Reyes. The soldier throwing Castell's clothes into the suitcases had stopped. All three soldiers looked with wide-eyed stares at her naked breasts. The lieutenant was more angry than sexually aroused.

"Tell me gringo, does your woman fuck good?" The lieutenant looked at Castell and rubbed her breast with his hand.

"Nice big tits. I'll see about her pussy. Teach her what it feels like to have a real man."

"When I'm done, my men will take turns with her."

Castell knew he could do nothing. He clinched his eyes shut and prayed that whatever was going to happen would be over quickly.

The lieutenant reached down and ripped off Reyes's underwear. She mustered all of her reserves and grabbed for the lieutenant's face. He was caught off guard. A fingernail found an eye. Not as a scratch but a forceful direct plunge into the eyeball.

The lieutenant reared back and yelled with pain. One hand covering his injured eye.

"You fucking bitch!" He hit her full in the jaw sending her head to the floor knocking her unconscious. He grabbed her head and brought her to a sitting position. The left side of her face was already swelling from the first blow. The right eye was almost closed.

"Wake up bitch, I'm not through yet." He smashed her face repeatedly with his fists. Patricia Reyes remained mercifully unconscious. The lieutenant let her head fall back. It hit the floor with a loud crack. The lieutenant spent his fury and frustration by kicking her in the abdomen and legs. The abuse went on for minutes until the officer had spent his anger.

Once he had recovered his breath from the exertion, he turned to Castell, "She doesn't look so pretty now does she?" There was blood running down his cheek below his injured eye. "Take a good look. It's the last you'll ever see of her."

Reyes' face was discolored by the blows. The right eye was now swollen shut. By her breathing he could tell she was still alive. He prayed they would not kill her while being hauled to his feet, still restrained by a soldier holding each of his arms. The lieutenant ordered the other soldier to bring the suitcases. Castell was handcuffed and forced toward the door.

"You'll pay for this you fucking pig. My family is very powerful."

"Let me show you what I think of you and your family," the lieutenant said. He released his grip on Castell's throat and walked over to Reyes. He unbuttoned his pants' fly and urinated on her unconscious body.

The two soldiers held Castell. The lieutenant came back over to him, grabbing Castell's face in his hand and bringing it close to his own. Castell took small pleasure in seeing that the lieutenant's eye was clinched shut, oozing an ugly discharge of blood and viscous tissue.

"I don't give a shit about you or your fucking family. Besides, asshole, who do you think ordered this?"

Castell said nothing. The torment of watching Patricia beaten and humiliated while being able to do nothing was almost unbearable. It took several moments for the lieutenant's last comment to register. By then he was being ushered out of the apartment into a waiting sedan.

He looked at the lieutenant. "You're lying. No one in my family would do this to me." The statement was part question. The lieutenant only grinned back.

It took forty-five minutes to get to the airport. Once Castell realized their destination, he asked the lieutenant, "I thought I was under arrest?"

"You are. And you are being deported."

"You can't deport me!" He suddenly understood the meaning of the comment about not seeing Patricia again. He hoped it meant that rather than her death.

The lieutenant made no comment. Gone were the violent emotions provoked at the apartment. Now, he wanted only to have his injured eye attended to.

Castell was taken briskly through the airport. The lieutenant took a ticket from his pocket and gave it to the clerk at the ticket counter. A soldier set down Castell's two suitcases and laptop computer.

After a brief exchange with another officer, the lieutenant gave Castell his passport. He ordered two of the soldiers to stay with him on the aircraft until just before takeoff. Castell was then taken out to an empty Mexicana airliner.

Thirty minutes later, after all passengers had boarded, the handcuffs were removed. The soldiers departed and the door closed immediately after. The aircraft taxied down the tarmac for the two hour flight to Mexico City.

Tears of anger, fear, and frustration welled up in his eyes. All he wanted at that moment was to kill those responsible for hurting Patricia, especially his Uncle René.

The flight was an unrelenting agony. Patricia's fate was uncertain. At least they did not appear to have arrested her since they all left with him. But that also meant she was just left in the apartment. Castell could not gage the extent of her injuries. The officer had kicked her viciously enough to have caused possible internal injuries. His mind played over every detail of the past few hours. It was difficult to think clearly.

The other passengers continued to stare at him as he left the plane in Mexico City. He retrieved his luggage and quickly moved through the relaxed Mexican customs. A barrage of porters converged to carry his luggage. Exhausted with his head throbbing, he gladly accepted the first offer. It was an effort to focus his thoughts. He knew only that he must contact Molina.

He still had the number he had called before. He hoped that he could get a message to Molina. There was no point in trying from the airport. Both the Mexican and Salvadoran telephone systems were abysmal. It could take some time to get a call placed outside the country. He would not be up to standing at a pay phone in the airport waiting for the call to go through. Best to get a room at a hotel and call from there. He also needed a place for Molina to call him back. Gone, was any intention to continue on to the United States.

After a discussion with the cab driver, Castell decided on a hotel. It was difficult to stay awake for the twenty minute ride. The adrenalin overdose had long worn off. An overwhelming fatigue was setting in. Every detail of getting a room was agony. Finally alone, he lay back on the bed, only to sit up suddenly. If he lay down, he would go to sleep immediately. He must call first.

Mercifully, the call went through with little delay. The voice that answered was the same as before. Castell panicked after he told the voice the message was for Santiago Molina. The voice said he knew no one by that name. In truth, the proprietor of the restaurant did not know Molina by his real name.

Castell realized that he was supposed to identify Molina as the *Frenchman*. The voice acknowledged when he made the correction and repeated the message back.

Fifteen minutes later the phone rang. It took several rings to wake him. It was Molina. He spilled out the story of what happened in a disjointed torrent. Molina interrupted him several times. He told Castell he would go to the apartment immediately. Castell was to stay put and Molina would call him as soon as he had word about Patricia. Castell replaced the receiver, and fell back on the bed, asleep almost immediately.

It was close to 2:00AM when the phone rang again. It was Molina.

"Victor, Patricia looks like she'll eventually be alright. She is safe. They didn't arrest her. She is severely injured however. A doctor is with her. She is in a safe place."

"Thank God. How is she? What does the doctor say?"

"She has several broken ribs. A concussion. Some blood in her urine. He can't be sure she didn't sustain any serious internal injuries. Since we don't want to take her to a hospital, he'll just have to watch her carefully for the next few days. A cut over her eye, which needed some stitches. Other than that, she is very badly bruised. In a lot of pain. Her face looks a mess and one eye is closed, but the doctor says there will be no permanent scars. No bones in her face were broken."

"Will she be alright?"

"Yes, she'll eventually fully recover. She was more worried about what had happened to you when we found her. I told her you were safe. I'll talk to her again in the morning to give her more details. The doctor gave her something for the pain. She was asleep when I left her."

"Now tell me again from the beginning, what happen, Victor."

Castell related every detail of the horrifying experience. The exhaustion and the hurt turned to rage by the time he recounted the whole episode.

"I won't let this go, Santiago. I want the fucking bastards to pay for this. I want my fucking uncle to pay for what he did. I want my fucking mother to pay too. They were both behind this. It was because of Patricia. They would get me out of El Salvador and hope I'd eventually forget the whole terrible event. My mother knew, but she would blame it on Uncle Augustin's politics if I ever accused her. They wouldn't know the stupid officer would say too much.

"I mean to have my revenge. If that means killing those bastards running El Salvador, so be it. You want fucking bombs, I'll make your goddamn detonating devices. Tell me what you want, Santiago."

Castell had turned the corner. Life would never be the same again. For that matter, his sheltered existence had ceased the minute he first set foot in El Salvador.

"I know how you feel, Victor. I'll call you in the morning. Right now, get some sleep. Stay at the hotel."

"Santiago"

"Yes?"

"Tell Patricia I love her. Tell her I'll be back."

Molina called again midday. "I saw Patricia this morning, Victor. She's better. Still in a lot of pain though."

"Where is she? I want to talk with her."

"She's safe, Victor. At the house of a friend. Unfortunately, there is no telephone. You'll have to be patient. As soon as she is better I'll arrange a call. About what we talked about last night. Do you still feel the same way?"

"Yes," Castell answered flatly. The rage had turned to a single-minded focus. He knew exactly what he wanted to do.

"Tell you what, Victor. I'll meet you at your hotel there in Mexico City tomorrow. We can discuss details."

"There is a stipulation to my help, Santiago."

Molina was immediately wary. "What is that?"

"I want to see Patricia."

"You will, Victor. Soon."

"No, you don't understand. I want to see her now."

"That's not possible, Victor. She is in no condition to travel. It's also much too dangerous."

Molina could also not afford to lose Reyes. She was vital to his group. Not only was she committed, being a woman was an asset. He had to be careful how he handled these recent events. Reyes was the instrument of Castell's recruitment. Molina did not want to put Reyes' loyalty to the test matched against her feelings for Castell.

"I know that, Santiago. I want you to get me back into El Salvador."

Molina did not respond immediately. Since yesterday, he had been thinking about how to utilize Castell's help in making detonating devices with Castell now out of the country. He assumed Castell would be wary of going underground to return to El Salvador. He shouldn't have underestimated love. Even with the difficulties of getting him back into the country, the benefits were attractive. With Castell in El Salvador, Molina would have control. Living underground, he would be drawn totally into the group. Molina liked the prospects very much.

"It would be difficult. Certainly dangerous for you."

"That doesn't matter. Can it be done?"

"Yes. It will take some planning. I'll call you tomorrow. Do you have money?"

"Some. I have credit cards. I have money in a bank in California."

"Good. Here's what I want you to do. I want you to fly to Tegucigalpa."

"Where?" Castell had never heard of the place.

"Tegucigalpa, the capital of Honduras. I want you to find a hotel and call me at the usual number."

"Why there?" He knew little of Central American geography even though he lived there a good deal of his life. He was only vaguely aware that Honduras bordered El Salvador.

"Because Tegucigalpa is less than a hundred miles from the El Salvador border. I will work on arrangements to smuggle you across the border."

Castell made reservations on the next flight to Tegucigalpa, Honduras leaving Mexico City that evening. The hotel made him a reservation at their sister hotel in Tegucigalpa. He also arranged for a cash advance on a credit card at a Mexico City bank. The rest of the day was spent in agitated brooding.

In a few short weeks, his life had been totally altered. Even in the wake of these terrible events, he now felt an appreciation for life, an emotional passion never before experienced. Patricia Reyes, Uncle Augustin, and Santiago Molina had brought about a range of completely new feelings. All this only to have these newly discovered relationships destroyed or compromised.

The only thing that remained was Patricia. He did not condemn her or Santiago from hiding what they really did. He did not feel deceived, or used. Patricia didn't recruit him. Santiago of course did, but being in El Salvador it is easy to understand. Uncle René and his mother he did condemn. At least his uncle. He hoped his mother was not complicit in what happened to Patricia. Most of all he wanted revenge on the monsters that ran El Salvador. The ones that murdered his uncle and aunt. The ones that beat and were about to rape Patricia. The ones that tortured only to inflict suffering. The ones that murdered thousands to maintain power.

If it took making detonating devices for Santiago in order to be close to Patricia, he would do it. Right now he welcomed the opportunity to kill anyone in the Salvadoran military. Perhaps even his uncle for what he did to Patricia. Most of all, he ached to see Patricia.

The flight from Mexico City to Tegucigalpa, Honduras took only slightly longer than the flight from El Salvador. An hour after landing, he arrived at his hotel. This time his call to El Salvador took longer to go through. He left the same message for the Frenchman.

Two hours later, Molina called. He instructed Castell to buy sturdy boots for hiking. He also told him to purchase shirts and trousers that would make him look like a local. Molina told him that Jose would meet him at the hotel tomorrow. Jose would escort him across the border into El Salvador tomorrow night.

Molina added that Patricia said to tell him she loved him.

That afternoon Castell purchased the required clothing. He discarded much of his old clothing. His belongings were narrowed down to one suitcase and his laptop computer. The second suitcase was packed with the articles he would abandon. It would be discarded after he checked out of the hotel tomorrow. Castell already felt like a fugitive. He was about to become something much worse.

Jose Aguilar knocked on his hotel room door the following morning. Castell opened the door, recognizing Patricia's friend. They stared at each other for several seconds. Both were a little uncertain as to their feelings. They had not hit it off initially. But events had changed things. Molina told Aguilar that Castell would be helping them. Patricia was like an older sister to Aguilar. He had seen Patricia after the beating. He knew how she felt about Castell. If Castell was returning to join them, Aguilar too would accept him. They both embraced awkwardly.

Aguilar told Castell they would leave after dark. It was a sunny day in the Honduran capital. Eating and drinking beer, they even found occasion to laugh. Aguilar outlined the plan for crossing the border. He had traveled all the previous night and they would set out to return to El Salvador that night. It would be a long night's hike. They needed to get some sleep.

While Aguilar slept several hours during the afternoon, Castell couldn't sleep. How could he with what lay before him? He was anxious to get started. Anxious to see Patricia.

It was dark when they checked out of the hotel. The extra suitcase was discarded in a trash bin. Aguilar carefully checked for any possible identification on the discarded articles. They left the city in an old sixty's vintage pickup truck travelling south to the small town of San Antonio del Norte near the border with El Salvador.

Outside the town, Aguilar turned the truck down a tortuous single lane road no better than a cow path. They bumped along for several miles on shock absorbers long since worn out. Jose eventually stopped the truck at a remote farm house. Aguilar explained that the farmer was Salvadoran. The truck was his. He had led Aguilar across the border into Honduras the night before.

They would be walking about twelve miles through the high country. Someone would be waiting to pick them up at a prearranged place once they crossed into El Salvador.

The trek took almost seven hours. It was not easy walking terrain. Once they finally stopped, Castell was exhausted, sleepy, and hungry. The farmer shook their hands and left them. To Castell, it appeared they were still in the middle of nowhere.

Ten minutes later however, Carlos Perez greeted them carrying an assault rifle. He had been watching to insure they were not followed. He told Castell it was only about a mile further to where he had a car waiting.

"Where are we going?"

"To a safe place outside of San Miguel. It is well east of San Salvador. Not far from here."

"Patricia?"

Perez knew what Castell meant. "Patricia is also there. You will see her."

San Miguel was the principle city in the eastern part of El Salvador. The eastern provinces were far less densely populated, and hotly contested by both the government and the rebel guerrillas. Molina had decided to reestablish his new base of operations here in the wake of recent events. The military did not have the same control here as they did in the capital, San Salvador. Anti-government support was easier to find even though Molina was not part of the rebel organization, the FDR-FMLN. He was however an important facilitator of arms shipments to the guerrilla fighters so he had contacts among several ranking leaders.

Molina greeted Castell at a house in a rural area several miles outside of San Miguel. There was a small barn in the back. A couple of pigs, a flock of chickens, a milk cow. No neighboring farms were visible. They hugged. Castell did not have to ask his question. Molina took him straight away to a bedroom. Opening the door quietly, the moonlight fell over Patricia's sleeping face.

Castell audibly gasped at the site of her face. He walked quietly to her bed and knelt on the floor. When he touched her hand she groaned and stirred. Opening her one good eye, she yelled out with pain as she attempted to move toward him.

He gently laid her head back down on the pillow then stroked her forehead. Her upper lip had been split. A kiss would hurt. The hate and rage of that night returned.

"Victor." Speaking hurt. The pain medication also made her groggy.

"Don't say anything, Patricia. I'm here now." He closed the bedroom door and came back to lie down next to her on the bed.

"Go back to sleep. I won't leave you."

Both fell asleep within minutes.

CHAPTER 8

Castell and Reyes were allowed to sleep late into the next morning. Castell awoke first. Looking at her in the full daylight made him shudder. Her bruised body looked so painful. He told himself that she would look her old self soon, hoping that was true. He crept quietly out of the bedroom without waking her.

Molina and Aguilar were having coffee in the kitchen. It was after nine o'clock in the morning. A middle aged woman was stirring a pot of something on the stove.

"Join us, Victor," Molina said. He got up and ushered Castell to his chair. "Victor, this is Isabel Salas. This is her house."

Isabel came over and shook his hand. She smiled shyly and returned to her cooking.

"Isabel is Roberto's mother. Roberto is one of our group. He and another brother take care of their widowed mother although she's pretty self-sufficient. Roberto's father was taken by the police. Suspicioned to be aiding the rebels. That was six years ago." Molina poured Castell a cup of coffee. "He's never been accounted for."

The men drank their coffee. Isabel served them breakfast. Castell was starved, finishing off seconds of eggs and beans wrapped in tortillas. After breakfast, he checked on Patricia. She was just waking. He hugged her carefully.

"Victor, I'm so hungry."

Her words were slightly distorted due to the lopsided swelling of her face. She laughed at the sound of her voice but it hurt. It brought a pained smile to his face.

Castell helped her out of bed and into her robe. Aguilar took her other arm and helped her to a chair in the kitchen. Once Isabel saw Reyes, the older woman took charge, ushering the men outside telling them to give her some peace. Castell kissed her and went outside with Molina and Aguilar.

It was a beautiful sunny morning. Outside, Carlos Perez and Roberto Salas were leaning against the car having a cigarette. Perez appeared to be in his mid-twenties. He was well built with the body of an athlete. Molina introduced Salas who looked a few years older.

"Victor, this is our group. There is one other, Miguel. You'll meet him later. I've told them about you, Victor. We welcome you as one of us." Molina watched Castell's reaction closely.

Castell's jaw was set. He nodded in agreement and looked at the others. Molina also looked to Perez and Salas to assess their reaction. He had explained to them the events and his decision regarding Castell. However, their gut reaction was still important. So much of what he was doing was dependent upon the devotion of his followers. It was Carlos Perez he was most concerned about. Molina knew he was attracted to Reyes. While the others treated her like a sister, Perez wished for something more. Reyes had not totally rejected his advances. Perez was a handsome guy. But that was before Victor Castell entered her life.

Molina guided the conversation around small talk. After a few minutes he suggested Perez and Aguilar go in the house and get something to eat. Salas took up a lookout position.

"I'll tell you what I need, Victor. I need a bomb that will go off at my command. I need to trigger the device from some distance, say as much as a thousand feet. I need a bomb that is absolutely reliable. Can you make such a triggering device?"

"I can make a circuit that can be remotely triggered to activate a switch. It's fairly simple technology to construct a radio frequency device to activate a relay to close a circuit. I assume you will know how to connect this switch to the explosives?" There was little emotion in Castell's voice. He had made his decision. There was no turning back. He was even surprised by his resolve.

"What are you going to bomb, Santiago?" In a way, Castell dreaded the answer but he needed to know. Mentally he had not yet considered himself a violent revolutionary.

"I'd rather not discuss the specifics yet, Victor. It's a matter of security. I'm the only one that knows for the moment." That was not entirely true. Perez and Salas knew the target.

"We must get started, Victor. Let's determine what you need."

Molina got Perez and Aguilar from inside the house. All four walked to the back of the house and sat around a weatherworn wooden outside table.

Molina explained to Castell that the explosive would be concealed in large speakers of the type used by professional musicians. Eighty pounds of a stable, putty-like explosive known as Semtex would be used. Molina explained that this explosive was substantially more powerful than the old plastique. It was remarkably stable, yet with the proper detonator it required only a moderate electrical source to trigger detonation from a blasting cap. Standard dry cell batteries would be sufficient.

"How many individual bombs?"

"Three."

"All triggered simultaneously?"

"No. Two different triggering commands will be required.

"Where will they be located?"

"Two in a building, one in a vehicle."

"The maximum distance?"

"Like I said, one thousand feet."

Castell chewed on his lower lip as he thought about what he was undertaking. Rage was a powerful motivator, yet this was extreme. But to do nothing was not an option. The technical aspects were an intriguing challenge. Constructing a radio transmitter and receiving circuit was within his capabilities.

"If I were in the United States, I could buy the equipment easily. Even model aircraft radio frequency equipment could be used. But in El Salvador that might be more difficult to find."

"Perhaps more dangerous also," Molina said. "The Treasury Police might suspect such technology to have such application."

"Maybe it's better to assemble my own transmitter and receiver from individual components. It will also be more difficult to trace fragment evidence of the receiver circuitry that might be left afterwards. But even obtaining the necessary components in El Salvador probably requires caution in this police state."

Molina nodded with a slight smile. "Very good. And you can do this?"

"Yes. But I'll need to work on the design."

"How soon, Victor?"

"I don't think it will be all that difficult. I'll start work on it today. The problem might be getting the electronic items without raising suspicion."

"Where could the necessary items be purchased, Victor?"

"A commercial electronic supply distributor. Maybe even a radio and television repair shop. A hardware supply for some other items."

"That should be no problem," Molina said.

"I assume the police have informants everywhere. You will need a plausible reason for buying these electronics without raising suspicion."

"You seem made for this secretive work, Victor. Any suggestions?"

"Let me work out the design first and the bill of materials needed. I'll try to think of a cover story. Better too if we can use several sources for buying the components."

"Very good," Molina said. "Victor?"

"Yes?"

"I'm glad you're with us. Patricia is glad too." Molina laid his hand on Castell's shoulder.

Castell was curious about one thing. "Where is the explosive material, Santiago?"

"In San Salvador. I will be bringing it here this evening. Miguel will be bringing the speakers the day after tomorrow." Molina got up from the table. "Carlos and I are leaving now. We'll be back tonight."

Molina had several things to do that day. He had arranged to have lunch with Martha and a friend of Martha's in San Salvador. Other than Molina's political leanings, Martha knew nothing of his activities other than his cover story identity of a businessman. Her friend was a secretary at the United States Embassy.

Martha had introduced her friend to Molina. Molina had previously contacted the secretary and visited the embassy himself a couple of times. Ostensibly he was looking for trade and investment related information for interested American companies. He even had a couple of phony meetings with a low level embassy trade relations officer. Today's lunch was to explore the secretary's efforts to wangle an invitation to a forthcoming embassy party. Like Martha, the secretary saw the benefits of Molina's efforts for U.S. investment in El Salvador.

Molina had kept up the pretext and the contact with the secretary. The embassy had been his ultimate target all along. By now he knew the grounds and a rough idea of the layout of the building with his several visits. He understood the embassy's general security procedures and the manpower strength of its Marine contingent.

By carefully worded comments and questions by Molina, the secretary had revealed other potentially useful information. Molina knew who typically provided services such as maintenance and catering. Several weeks ago, Molina had decided on the date for the attack. It was in the newspaper. The event was the eighteenth birthday of the United States ambassador's daughter. It was a major society event. There would undoubtedly be many high ranking Salvadoran government and military officers in attendance. The primary objective was to kill Americans, but any Salvadoran politicians or military would be a bonus.

Originally, he had wanted to obtain an invitation to gain entry. At that time he had not worked out any specific plan of how to place explosives within the embassy. But access to the ball would open up options. The idea about smuggling the explosives inside the speakers came to him two weeks ago. The press reported that a popular musical group had been invited to perform at the event. The picture in the newspaper showed them on stage with their amplifiers and large speakers.

Lunch that day with Martha and her secretary friend was intended to confirm that this particular musical group would be performing. The secretary enthusiastically said she had typed official correspondence to that effect. She then proudly presented Molina with his invitation. From the invitation, Molina now had the schedule of events for the evening gala.

Molina had a substantial cache of high grade explosive material. It had arrived by a circuitous route from Libya. From Libya, it was smuggled aboard an oil tanker bound for Amsterdam. At the Amsterdam docks, it was concealed in the bottom of a crate disguised as cushioning material for large machine tool parts. The crate left the port of Amsterdam aboard a small freighter bound for Nicaragua. From a Managua customs warehouse it was removed from the crate. It was bundled into four conven-

tional suitcases with the assistance of Cuban intelligence opera-
tives. From there it traveled first into Honduras then took a route
not much different through the backcountry which Castell took
to enter El Salvador.

Molina had determined the means and the date for the
bombing. Before the acquisition of Castell's engineering expertise he had agonized only over how to construct his own triggering device. His training equipped him only to be able to construct simple timing-type mechanisms.

Reyes was still recovering. The pain from the broken ribs and
trauma to her body from the beating left her still in considerable
pain. With the pain pills, she slept most of the time.

Castell crept silently into her bedroom to check on her. She
was sitting on the edge of the bed.

"Ah, you're awake. How are you feeling, Patricia?"

"Better." She attempted to get up but wobbled before he
caught her and set her back on the bed which caused her to cry
out in pain because of the damaged ribs.

"Shit. I'm sorry. Let me check your bandages."

He carefully unbuttoned her blouse to check the bandages
binding her lower abdomen to secure the damaged ribs. It had
only been a few days since the beating. Her entire left side was
purple with massive bruising, even her breast. Below her shorts,
the massive bruising carried down her thigh. But it was her face
that still disturbed him. It was now various shades of colors
from the bruising. One eye remained partially closed with swelling. The stitches still showed ugly.

Castell fed her soup prepared by Roberto's mother.

"Santiago told me you came back to help us."

"I came back for you, Patricia."

"But you are also helping us with our fight?"

"For me it's revenge. Someone must pay for what they have done to you and me. It's personal. I can't say it's political like it is for you, Patricia."

"Perhaps not. But we all fight for our own reasons. For me, it also started with revenge. I eventually found it was something bigger. I'm glad we're together, Victor."

Castell found himself intrigued with the problem of designing a radio frequency control system from scratch. Outside of an hour with Patricia, he spent the entire day working on the schematic. It was challenging without the benefit of reference materials. Calculating the various electronic component values tested his fundamental electrical engineering knowledge. His idea was to use a mobile telephone as the transmitter. He wasn't familiar with mobile telephones, only the general concept. He would reverse engineer it once he had his hands on the device. By the time Molina returned that evening, Castell had worked out the basic design. He had even prepared a parts list.

Molina and Perez each carried two suitcases filled with the explosive material to the table outside in the backyard. Both men swung the heavy suitcases onto the table. Castell, who had gone outside after hearing the car arrive, winced as the suitcases slammed down on the table knowing what they contained.

"Don't worry. The explosive material is essentially inert. It takes a detonator like this to explode it." Molina produced a small pencil-like item with two protruding wires from his pocket. "This detonator can be triggered by a small electrical current from a couple of batteries."

Molina opened one of the cases. Everyone examined the explosive. It was the consistency of stiff modeling clay. Molina explained that it could be molded into any shape. This would allow for convenience in packaging the bomb as well as shaping the charge to achieve maximum blast effect. Everyone poked the material cautiously with their fingers.

"Victor, how are you coming along with the design of the triggering mechanism?"

"I think I have it, Santiago. It's simple, should be very reliable. It will work at the distance required. The more delicate part will be obtaining the electronic components," he said without a twinge of conscience, caught up now by the technical aspects of the challenge.

"Excellent. Let's all go inside and you can tell us about it," Molina said.

They all huddled around the small kitchen table as Castell laid out a diagram of his design.

"Tell us what you've created, Victor."

"It's quite simple, yet elegant. Obviously, we use a radio frequency transmitter. The beautiful part is the transmitter. We use a mobile car phone. It's really just a radio transmitter that connects to the switched telephone network. There are mobile car phones here aren't there?"

Everyone looked at Molina.

"Yes, rare but they exist, at least in limousines," Molina said.

"Someplace in El Salvador should sell them. In your line of work, Santiago you can easily explain such a purchase. I can rig it to do what is required."

Castell hoped the necessary electronic hardware could be obtained. After all, this was El Salvador.

"Assume we can obtain this car telephone. Go on."

"Okay. Actually the beautiful part is not really the transmitter, but rather the receiver. You see, I'll construct a receiver to accept the car phone's radio transmission. In this case the multiple signals that correspond to the numbers being input on the keypad. The receiver is a circuit with a logic program that will activate a relay switch if the proper sequence of signals is received. In other words, you can decide on a code, some sequence of numbers that will activate the relay, and in turn detonate the explosive. It's safe because no stray signal will activate the relay, only the programmed sequence of dialed numbers. You simply drive within range of your target, dial a number, and boom!" Castell threw up his hands to illustrate an explosion. "And since you are already driving, you immediately make your escape."

Molina looked at Castell for several seconds. "You can construct such a device?"

"Yes. Given the right parts it's not even too difficult. Here." He handed Molina the parts list. "We should be able to get these at a radio and TV supply or repair shop."

Molina looked at the list then handed it to Perez. After reviewing the list, Perez said, "I assume Victor is correct about finding these items at a television repair shop. I do not know such things. But buying such a list of all these electronic parts must not be common. What cover story can we use to avoid arousing suspicion?"

"Carlos is correct about not arousing suspicion. Therefore I should be the one to purchase them," Castell said. "I can answer any technical questions. Speak the terminology. I will explain that I am an instructor at the university teaching engineering. These parts are for my engineering lab."

Molina said, "That is too dangerous, Victor. You don't' have papers. There is no way to avoid possible checkpoints."

"Can't you get me papers that make me out to be Salvadoran?"

Molina thought for a moment. "Perhaps. Roberto, is there a radio and TV repair in San Miguel? Assuming I can arrange a Salvadoran identity for Victor, I would prefer not to chance going all of the way to San Salvador. Besides, security is heavier in the capital."

"I don't know. I will find out tomorrow," Roberto said.

Molina nodded his head as he contemplated the plan. "Yes. Very well. I will explore securing a mobile phone. Assuming we are able to purchase these items, how long will this take, Victor?"

"A few days."

"Excellent. Tomorrow we start. Right now, we celebrate. I have brandy. Let's go in the house and include Patricia," Molina said.

The next day, Castell met Miguel Cortina, bringing with him two large speakers as well as a large amplifier. He arrived in a truck not too much better than the dilapidated vehicle Castell and Aguilar used in Honduras.

Salas reported there was a radio and TV repair shop in San Miguel.

That afternoon, Santiago Molina also returned. He handed Castell a couple of documents. "You are now, Emilio Chavez, instructor at the Universidad Tecnológica."

Castell thumbed through the papers. He was amazed with the resources at Molina's disposal that could conjure official papers so quickly.

"There is a real Emilio Chavez. An actual instructor of electrical engineering at the university. But of course that is in San Salvador so you must be careful. Someone at the university was friendly with your Uncle Augustin and agreed to help."

"And the government identity document?"

Molina smiled. "Our cause has those willing to help in unlikely places. But let's hope there is no need to use these documents."

Castell looked at the photo. It wasn't him but a reasonably general likeness. The photo was purposely scuffed on the identification card.

Molina said, "I think it's a good enough likeness. It's not the real Emilio Chavez. Another friend. Talented at forgery. He found a photographic likeness to you that seemed to fit. Altered the photo slightly. Still I hope it will be an unnecessary precaution."

Castell nodded and pocketed the documents. "I will go into San Miguel tomorrow and get what we need. And the mobile telephone?"

"I will take care of that tomorrow also," Molina said.

The foraging trip into San Miguel the next day was uneventful. The police were on less heightened alert than around San Salvador. Perez drove. As they left Isabel Salas' house, Perez removed the 9mm semi-automatic from his waist and placed it under the car seat. But they encountered no checkpoints.

The electronic components were all available at the radio and television repair shop. Castell used the planned excuse of being an engineering instructor at a university to account for the variety of sizes of resistors, capacitors, transistors, inductors, programmable memory, and an electrical meter, along with the costly purchase of a radio frequency oscilloscope. Although he had constructed a schematic calculating the values of the components, he may well have to modify his theoretical design in actual practice by checking actual empirical values of his circuits.

Various tools including soldering gun, hand drill, other hand tools, epoxy cement, fiberglass sheet, and insulated copper wire came from a hardware supply. Lastly, a box of latex surgical gloves was purchased at a farmacia.

"Why the rubber gloves?" Salas asked.

"Fingerprints. After the explosion there will be fragments. We must not leave any fingerprints. Always wear gloves."

Molina purchased the mobile telephone from an auto dealership. From the scratches, he assumed he was purchasing a phone recently *removed* from a vehicle. It was just as well that the phone was probably stolen. Less reason for the auto dealer to raise any questions about such an unusual purchase in El Salvador.

Castell was overly optimistic in his time estimate to create the remote signaling system. It took a full three days and most of two nights to create a working prototype. Aguilar had started out observing what Castell was doing and ended up fully involved in actually helping him construct the devices. Reyes watched with fascination as Castell scribbled changes to his schematic design. Ultimately there was a fair amount of trial and error by changing actual components to refine the circuits. He would take readings with the oscilloscope then make changes to what was an incomprehensible device of connected electronics to Reyes and Aguilar.

"Patricia, don't touch those," He said as she picked up several electronic components. "Fingerprints. When we're done, make sure every item is wiped for fingerprints, Jose. We don't even want the shop keeper's prints."

Castell and his enthusiastic assistant Jose Aguilar eventually tested the finished system several times before announcing completion of their work.

The mobile phone would act as a radio transmitter to communicate directly with the receiving device that would trigger the blasting cap detonator which in turn would detonate the Semtex plastique primary explosive. For this purpose, the phone was not intended to connect with the central telephone switching system since it would be communicating only a code sequence not a recognizable telephone number. There were no physical modifications required on the mobile phone, but a lot of work went into reverse engineering to identify the output transmissions in order to construct the receiver.

The receiver consisted of a small metal electrical junction box to shield the electronics from any electromagnetic interference. An antenna was mounted from the side. Lead wires from a pair of nine-volt dry cell batteries thread through a hole in the side. Two leads with bared ends protruded out of the box. To these a voltmeter was connected for testing the receiver circuit function to close the battery circuit. Everything was mounted on a piece of wood.

It was a warm evening. The sun had just set. Aguilar called everyone together to witness the demonstration. Castell helped

Reyes out of the house and sat her in a chair with a blanket around her shoulders, watched over by Isabel Salas.

With everyone assembled, Castell began explaining. "Ok. Now the device you see on the table will be concealed inside each speaker. The device works on the principle of radio frequency transmitted signals. The mobile telephone connected over here to a car battery acts as the transmitter. For our use, it is not communicating signals to the telephone exchange but instead to our receiving device.

"See these here?" He pointed to the leads connected to the voltmeter. "When the required signal is received, a relay closes activating the circuit that furnishes the electrical current from the dry cell batteries to trigger the blasting cap which will detonate the explosive material. The voltmeter simulates the blasting cap in this test."

"Now Jose will activate a sequence of five numbers on the telephone. 1, 3, 5, 7, and 9. Odd numbers. Easy to remember. Won't be confused with a real telephone number. Little chance of any other mobile telephone in the vicinity accidentally transmitting the same number sequence. Now, watch the voltmeter needle. When it registers a voltage that means it has closed the circuit that will detonate the blasting cap."

He nodded to Aguilar. The voltmeter registered the circuit closing.

"Again."

"Excellent," Molina said with a broad smile. "That's brilliant. And the distance?'

"Yesterday we tested at 500 paces. That's more than the one thousand feet you wanted. Jose, take the phone out further."

Aguilar took the bulky mobile phone in one hand and a car battery rigged with a sling for a handle in the other then walked a distance of a couple of hundred yards into the dark.

After allowing Aguilar time to reach the prearranged spot, Castell said, "Watch." Illuminated by a weak outside light, he waved his arm in the direction of Aguilar. The voltmeter confirmed successful operation.

He repeated the test a couple of more times.

"See this toggle switch and the red LED light? When the light is on, the system is armed. You activate the arming circuit by the toggle switch. So it can be armed at the latest possible moment to avoid any accidents."

Castell flipped the toggle switch to off. He removed the voltmeter then twisted the two leads of a blasting cap to the receiver output wires. With the heel of his boot, he dug a small hole in the ground, placing the blasting cap in the hole which he covered over. A cardboard box was placed over the receiver circuit to protect it from debris.

"Everyone move well back."

He flipped the switch and the LED glowed red. After he stepped back as well, he waved again to Aguilar.

Seconds later the patch of earth erupted with a muffled bang.

"Just to demonstrate that it will detonate a blasting cap, Santiago."

Molina stepped over to Castell and embraced him. "Impressive. It's precisely what we need. Much better than anything I expected, Victor."

Castell grinned with pride. "I've incorporated a slight time delay of about three seconds after the signal is transmitted. This will allow the person triggering the device to seek cover or get further away assuming you are in a moving car."

Reyes smiled and touched his face as he bent to kiss her forehead. It was great triumph. Better to revel in his ingenuity than to think about its intended purpose.

It took another day to construct and test all three receiving devices. Molina had explained that two devices were required for the speakers, and a third for another bomb. The third device was intended to detonate explosives in a separate location. Molina asked if a longer time delay could be rigged for the detonation of the third bomb. Castell told him that could be accomplished with the addition of a timing circuit.

While Castell and Aguilar finished the detonating devices, Molina directed Perez and Salas in the molding of the Semtex explosive material within the speakers. Once that was completed, Castell mounted the toggle switch and LED to the outside of the speaker cases. It would look to be part of the speakers. Everyone used the latex gloves.

The speaker cabinet interiors allowed ample room to place thirty pounds of explosive material in the bottom of each. Molina added an insidious modification. Around the periphery of the explosive material, they imbedded hundreds of ball bearings, approximately an eighth of inch in diameter. The outward direction of the forces when the material exploded would hurl the steel balls like shotgun pellets.

The remaining twenty pounds of explosive would remain in the van rigged into a third speaker. The van was now located in an unused warehouse in San Salvador. This was the vehicle they would use to deliver the musical equipment to the embassy. A shallow concealed array of one-inch PVC pipes, 96 inches long laid side by side had been fitted under a false wooden van floor. Salas and Cortina had constructed Molina's design such that the modification was undetectable by the eye. These PVC pipes were filled with a total of fifty gallons of gasoline and capped at both ends. Along with the existing twenty-five gallon fuel tank, the blast effect would be augmented by setting anything in proximity on fire.

Two days before the embassy party, Molina assembled everyone in the Salas house. Reyes had recovered to the extent that she could move about without severe discomfort. The swelling had gone down from her face, but the deep purple bruises were still vivid.

"This is the plan everyone. Listen carefully. We will attack the day after tomorrow. Our target is the U.S. embassy," Molina said. He looked at Castell for his reaction.

Castell's expression noticeably reacted when Molina named the target. The full impact of what he was into drove home. The anger, the frustration, the righteousness of this retaliation now seemed insufficient justification for what was about to happen. This was not the target of those he wished to harm. Castell tried to envision the effects based on recalling news coverage of bombing aftermaths. He knew reality was worse than any vision his mind could conjure. He also knew he now had no say in the matter. His role was already concluded.

Molina continued. "The plan is simple. There is a celebration scheduled for Saturday evening. Guests will start arriving about seven-thirty in the evening. A musical group is scheduled to provide entertainment. Carlos, Roberto, and Miguel will station themselves at the home of the bandleader. They will use a stolen van we have hidden away. Miguel will follow in the station wagon.

"When the other band members arrive, all three of you will enter the house. You will bind and gag everyone in the house. Their performance equipment is kept at the bandleader's home, so they will meet there. Carlos will be in charge.

"Our specially prepared speakers will be in the van. You will load the additional equipment and the musical instruments from the house. Carlos and Roberto will then leave in the van. Miguel, you will stay at the house and secure the musicians. At approximately six-thirty, Carlos and Roberto will arrive at the embassy. Your cover is that you are there to set up the musical equipment before guests arrive. Expect the van to be thoroughly searched. Victor's triggering device for the truck bomb will be concealed in a third speaker which will remain in the van.

"Carlos, you and Roberto will carry the musical equipment into the embassy. Carry your prepared false identifications. No weapons of course. Set up the equipment as we practiced. Connect all of the cabling between the amplifier, the keyboard, and the speakers. It must look normal. Before you leave, activate the switch Victor installed. The small red lights will indicate the bombs are armed.

"After you have set up the equipment, leave the embassy grounds after activating the detonating circuit for the bomb in the van. Inform the security personnel that you will be returning at midnight to disassemble the equipment. Walk off the embassy grounds and go underground as previously arranged. Burn your false papers immediately."

By underground, Molina meant retreating into their respective public lives. No contact with any of the others until he contacted each of them. Government security forces could be expected to react in the extreme in the aftermath of the bombing. That was the purpose.

"At approximately seven-thirty, I will call the embassy and inform them that the band has been delayed slightly. They should expect them to arrive approximately eight-thirty. This will allow the majority of guests to arrive. Miguel, you will also leave the bandleader's home at precisely eight-thirty. If the embassy should call before, advise them that the band is on the way and will arrive there by eight-thirty. Make sure everyone is bound securely, the telephone disconnected, the doors locked, the lights off. Drive away. Stick to the neighborhoods. Be careful to avoid security checkpoints since it will be after the curfew.

"At this same time, I will drive to a position across the street from the embassy. I have reserved a rental car to which Victor will have wired the mobile telephone. I will dial the appropriate code to detonate the bombs no later than eight-thirty-five. Any questions?"

"Why must it be the United States Embassy? Won't there be mostly innocent people killed?" Castell asked. He knew he had avoided asking this question when he first agreed to help Molina without knowing the intended target. Now this target would mostly involve other than Salvadoran military personnel. It was a futile attempt to appease his conscience.

"This is still about those in power in El Salvador, Victor. There will be high ranking Salvadoran military and government officials at the event. That is all important even though this is about the United States' involvement in El Salvador. Unfortunately noncombatants will also be killed. Just as in any war. But not necessarily innocent people. Remember, it's the Americans that facilitate the brutal excesses against the people of El Salvador. The Americans prop up the right-wing Salvadoran government. By their aid, they have chosen sides. The embassy represents their influence in El Salvador's affairs. History is full of noncombatants dying in war. Some are innocent. Some have to bear responsibility for their political support. Look at Hiroshima and Nagasaki in Japan, Hamburg, Dresden, and Cologne in Germany during World War Two. Those engaged in a just war have always been faced with this terrible dilemma.

The words were for Castell's benefit. Molina himself was not concerned with innocent blood, particularly American blood.

Castell stared at the wall and said nothing in argument or response.

"What about Victor and me?" Reyes asked.

"You will stay here with Roberto's mother until you recover. Everyone will go about their normal activities. There will be some sort of increased government retaliation. Things will become even more dangerous. I will leave El Salvador. So must Victor. Tomorrow Jose will take Victor back across the border into Honduras.

"Victor, you have a passport entrance stamp indicating your arrival in Honduras a week ago. So it will be easy to return to the United States from there. You have no entry stamp of returning to El Salvador. Besides, you were essentially expelled so you can't risk leaving from San Salvador by conventional means with the heightened security.

Castell and Reyes looked at each other.

"Patricia cannot go with you, Victor. She does not have a visa to go to the United States. Besides, she is not able to travel in her condition. Best that she recovers while you pursue getting her a visa to allow her into the United States."

Not a reassuring thought for Castell. Molina was about to bomb the U.S. Embassy. It would be some time before Salvadorans could seek visas through local U.S. diplomatic services.

"Is everyone clear on their assignments?" Molina asked.

Everyone nodded.

"Good. We will meet again tomorrow night. I will have the rental car for you to install the mobile telephone, Victor. After that, you must leave El Salvador.

"Victor, I know what you feel. We all feel it. In time you will realize the necessity. Now is the time to evoke those hatreds that brought us all to this point. To harden our resolve. We are attacking the enemy. Those that killed our loved ones. Those that kill and subjugate the common people. Most cannot, or will not resist. We however shall resist. To topple this government, military aid from the United States must be cut off."

Castell was emotionally exhausted. Regardless, it would be pointless to debate with Molina. The only recourse for him was to avoid confronting the issue. Get out of El Salvador. Put this behind him. He couldn't undo what he had already created.

With little further conversation, Molina left, leaving Castell and Reyes alone. Castell gently took her arm and guided her to the bedroom.

"Victor?"

"Yes?"

"Can you get me papers to come to the United States?"

He thought about her question. It was to be their escape. He had found Patricia in El Salvador. Somehow he had also found

this worsening nightmare. Something primitive had been uncovered deep within himself. Now things had gone appallingly
too far. But in this alien landscape he had found Patricia Reyes.

"I think so. Not sure of the best way. I'll work on it. My father may be able to help. I want us to be together, Patricia, and
away from here. Away from all this fear and death. Maybe if we
could claim we are married. Could Santiago create a false marriage certificate?"

Patricia pulled him to her. He held her carefully, mindful of
her bruised body. She kissed him first on the cheek then slowly
moved to his neck and ear lobes. Her gentle caresses progres-
sively became more demanding as she probed his neck and ears.

"We may be apart for a long time, Victor. Make love to me
before you must leave."

He undressed her gently. The moonlight was fortunately not
bright enough to display the ugly discolorations of her healing
injuries. Patricia guided him into her. Castell felt an exquisite
bond and trust as they gently made love.

At five o'clock in the afternoon on the appointed Saturday,
Cortina parked the station wagon across the street from the bandleader's home in San Salvador. The van had been parked down
the street within sight of the bandleader's home.

Perez and Salas walked toward the house and were joined by
Cortina. They knocked on the door. It was answered by a petite,
middle-aged woman. Before she could speak, Perez pushed back
the door almost knocking the woman down.

The woman's screams were cut off by Perez leveling a pistol
to her head. Her husband the bandleader came out of the bedroom upon hearing his wife's scream. Both were led to the living
room. Salas tied their hands with duct tape. Perez asked if the
other band members were expected soon. The terrified man
nodded yes.

The other members of the musical group arrived over the next half hour. All were restrained the same as the bandleader and his wife. Salas then walked back to the van and drove it up to the bandleader's house. It took twenty minutes for Salas and Cortina to load the musical instruments and amplifier equipment into the van.

Perez ordered Salas and Cortina to go outside to the van. Cortina looked puzzled.

"Santiago said I was to stay and guard them until eight-thirty."

"That is changed. Santiago gave me different orders. Now go. You're to leave with us instead, Miguel," Perez said.

After Cortina and Salas left the house, Perez reached into his pocket and extracted an eight-inch sound suppressor which he twisted and locked onto the end of a specially adapted 9mm semi-automatic. It took less than fifteen seconds to execute all the hostages by a single bullet each to the head.

Perez took the wheel of the van. Gunshots from a 9mm could not be *silenced*, only the loud crack somewhat muffled. By the sounds, Salas and Cortina knew what had taken place.

Perez locked the door to the house. Turning to his shocked colleagues he said, "It was necessary. There can be no witnesses. Santiago's orders. Your new instructions, Miguel, are to arrive at this location some distance from the embassy at precisely eight o'clock."

Perez gave Cortina a hand drawn map. Perez and Salas handed Cortina their pistols. "Roberto and I will walk to your location."

"But that entire area is heavily patrolled by police. After the curfew it will be very dangerous," Cortina said.

"Everything we do is dangerous. Arrive no earlier than eight-twenty. Stay out of sight inside the car, Miguel. Once Roberto and I arrive we will wait for the explosion. That will draw all the police to the embassy. It will be chaos for at least a short time. I have practiced escape routes out of San Salvador that wind through residential neighbors. Hopefully not patrolled by the police. If we are stopped, there are three of us. We are well armed. With luck it will be a good fight."

Cortina embraced his two comrades before leaving them to drive away in the station wagon. Perez and Salas climbed into the van and proceeded to the United States Embassy. They arrived on schedule at six-thirty in the evening.

Security was tight. Two Salvadoran National Police jeeps with mounted machine guns were positioned outside the embassy compound gates along with six heavily armed officers. The van was stopped. Perez explained that they were here to set up the equipment for the band. Waved through by the Salvadorans, the van was again stopped at the embassy gate by U.S. Marines. This security check was more thorough. Perez gave a Marine Lance Corporal a business card from the musical group. The name of the band was on the list along with the catering service. Ordered out of the van, two Marines body-searched them while another covered them with an assault rifle. The Marines thoroughly examined the musical equipment, followed by a search of the van itself, including a mirror examination of the undercarriage, before allowing them to enter the grounds. They were again challenged and the search repeated before being allowed entry to the building itself. The equipment underwent another close examination by a Marine sergeant. Perez and Salas suffered several moments of anxiety fearing by the close attention of this Marine that he might actually order the speaker housings to be opened.

It took thirty minutes for Perez and Salas to unload and set up the equipment. After connecting all of the cabling, the last thing Perez did before leaving was flip Castell's arming switch on the two speakers. The small red LED light on each speaker came on.

Carlos Perez and Roberto Salas left the embassy building at seven-thirty. Guests were beginning to arrive. Perez climbed into the back of the van and set the detonating circuit on the speaker in the back. After locking the van doors, he and Salas each lit a cigarette and walked to the security gate at the entrance to the embassy grounds. Perez explained to the Marine on duty that they would be returning at midnight to reload the musical equipment. They would leave the van. The band members should be arriving shortly. At the appointed location a mile from the embassy, Perez and Salas rendezvoused with Cortina and the car twenty minutes later.

At precisely eight-thirty, Santiago Molina drove a rented Mercedes toward the United States Embassy. Slowing to a stop just before the security checkpoint a few hundred feet before the embassy gate, he dialed the prescribed number sequence from the mobile telephone. After the last digit, he put the Mercedes in gear and pulled away from the curb in a U-turn, making use of the short time delay Castell had built into the circuit.

The explosion was so violent that the Mercedes rocked from the blast wave even though shielded from the embassy building by the distance and a two foot-thick block wall. Molina smiled, replaced the receiver, and accelerated slowly down the street. Two minutes later and now some distance away, Santiago Molina heard the secondary bomb in the van explode.

When the bomb exploded destroying the U.S. Embassy in San Salvador, Victor Castell was spending what remained of the night in Tegucigalpa, Honduras, at the same hotel he had stayed in when he arrived a week earlier after making the same reverse trek. He had a reservation for a nine o'clock morning flight to Mexico City the following day, with a connecting flight to Los Angeles.

CHAPTER 9

By eight-thirty most of the guests had arrived at the embassy. All senior embassy staff were present along with their spouses. From the Salvadoran government, there was the vice president, the foreign minister, and several colonels. The president of the republic was scheduled to arrive later, as was Army Chief of Staff, General Garcia. Colonel Benavides had diplomatically found an excuse to decline the invitation.

The occasion of the U.S. ambassador's daughter's eighteenth birthday was being made something equivalent to a coming out party. Back in their native Boston it would be just that. The elite of Salvadoran society were also in attendance. René Portillo escorted his wife Maria and his sister Alicia.

Peres and Salas had assembled the various pieces of musical equipment on a raised platform constructed for the event. The makeshift stage was at the opposite end of the large reception room to the main entrance. The room measured roughly forty by sixty feet.

By eight-thirty, there were over seventy people in the room. Music played from speakers from the embassy's sound system.

Waiters moved among the guests with hors d'oeuvres and Champagne. A bar had been set up just outside the room.

After the explosion, no one was left standing in the room. The first person to enter the ballroom after the explosion was the chief security officer for the embassy, a Marine captain. The captain had been in his office located in the rear of the building. The force of the blast had knocked him to the floor. Blood seeped from his ruptured eardrums.

Next to arrive on the scene were three Marines. They entered the building through the front door. With weapons at the ready, they moved through what had been the foyer. The foyer could not easily be distinguished from the ballroom, now. The wall separating the rooms was blown away. Furniture debris and body tissue were thrown against the opposite wall. The carnage stopped all three of the Marines abruptly.

The master sergeant ordered the two other Marines outside to get what help they could assemble. He momentarily ignored the captain who had fallen to his knees from shock and his own injuries. He needed to get to the communications room on the second floor. The main staircase leading upstairs had been torn away so it was necessary to use another toward the back of the building.

Although mostly intact, the communications equipment lay about the floor, inoperable as a result of the blast. The Marine manning the desk lay unconscious on the floor.

The sergeant took the stairs as fast as he could, and went out the front door. He needed to transmit what had happened to his superiors and he needed help, lots of help. He had been in Vietnam. He'd seen men die and torn apart by land mines. But nothing like this. Maybe because these victims were mostly civilians and women. So many.

The Marines started to help the few ambulatory injured out of the embassy.

At eight-thirty-two, the van parked outside exploded. The blast caught two Marines near the front door of the embassy as they were helping injured victims. All were hit with the ignited gasoline. The master sergeant was cut down in mid-stride as he was running to the guard shack next to the gate to make the call for outside help. Fortunately, he was unconscious as he burned to death.

Within thirty minutes of the bombing of the U.S. embassy in El Salvador, messages coded `urgent' and `top priority' flashed to every corner of the United States government. Southern Military Command based in Florida informed the Pentagon. The chiefs of staff of each branch of the military were immediately contacted. The Secretaries of State and Defense were contacted following priority procedures that insured immediate contact. The National Security Advisor, the Director of the Central Intelligence Agency, and the Director of the Federal Bureau of Investigation were informed using similar priority communications procedures.

At nine-fifty-five Washington time, the White House Chief of Staff interrupted the President's informal meeting with the Speaker of the House.

For the first two hours, things were chaotic at the embassy. Salvadoran military arrived quickly, but there was nothing left to secure. Civilian medical personnel arrived sporadically over a period of an hour after the explosion.

The carnage inside the embassy was unbelievable to those still alive or helping. Those bodies nearest the stage were radically dismembered and disemboweled. Blood, viscera, and severed limbs were everywhere. A little further from the blast center, bodies were still intact, but grotesquely damaged. Pools of blood formed around many. Further away from the blast, there was a range of injuries. The massive tearing of bodies was not as prevalent, but the effects of the ball bearing projectiles were clearly apparent. Even furthest from the origin of the blast, most survivors were severely wounded. Very few of the casualties in the ballroom would survive. Most of those that did would be irreparably maimed.

The U.S. ambassador, Lawrence Bennett, had been near the stage and the speakers at the time of the explosion. Standing next to him was his wife and his eighteen year old daughter. All were unrecognizable. Official identification of the body parts would require forensic confirmation.

Not far from the ambassador, were the bodies of René, Maria, and Alicia Portillo.

Egan Kavanagh's telephone rang at ten-twenty in the evening eastern standard time at his townhouse condominium in a suburban Maryland community outside of Washington D.C. He hated calls at home since they were usually intrusions from work or some unwanted communication with his ex-wife. Tempted to let the answering machine take the call, he answered on the fourth ring.

"Egan? Bernard. Hang onto to your seat. We've got a really bad one."

The caller was the Executive Assistant Director for the National Security Branch of the FBI.

"A little over an hour ago our embassy in San Salvador was bombed. Looks like a lot of dead. Apparently there was some big social event going on. You're to get down there immediately. We need a high profile on this, Egan."

"How bad is it, Bernie?"

"Real bad. Real fucking bad. Killed the ambassador, his wife, his daughter. Most of the senior staff. Seems the event was a coming-out party or something for his daughter's birthday. Killed maybe as many as eighty people. The military attaché, a full bird colonel, any number of diplomatic staff, U.S. Marines. Several high ranking Salvadoran officials, including their Foreign Minister and three colonels. Ranking diplomatic staff from other embassies. The Ambassador from Mexico was killed. Many influential Salvadoran civilians were killed. Surviving casualties are pretty ugly."

Kavanagh had a good working relationship with his boss Bernard Saunders. On the one hand, Saunders was the consummate professional. On the other he could be the consummate bureaucrat. Bernard Saunders was that rarest of all breeds, a highly competent public servant who knew how to play the Washington game.

The Assistant Directors for the various organizational branches actually ran operations for the Federal Bureau of Investigation. Since the days of J. Edgar Hoover, the position of Director and often the number-two position of deputy director was too often a political appointment. At the least, the Director usually lent nothing to the operational function of the agency. Frequently he was an impediment to operations because of the political nature of the job, particularly when it came to the murky world of intelligence related to national security. Bernard Saunders knew how to *manage* FBI directors.

"So the Man wants a high profile," Egan commented sarcastically.

"Egan, don't be an asshole as usual. Just because the Director sometimes misses the mark, this *is* a big deal." Managing Egan Kavanagh was a challenge for Saunders. Kavanagh was a contradictory mix of affable Irish with a pushy sharp edge.

"Okay, Bernie. What do we know about what happened?"

"Almost nothing. That's why the Director is sending in the first team. Larry Scofield will be there with his forensic people. Williams will be in charge."

Williams was Charles Williams, Assistant Director for Criminal Investigations. Larry Scofield was Chief of Forensics for the FBI.

Kavanagh respected the abilities of both Scofield, and even Williams. Scofield was an innovative genius with infinite patience. He lived in a world of microscopic materials and needles in haystacks. Scofield was odd, but likeable.

Kavanagh considered Williams on the other hand, a tight-assed, gung-ho charger. A highly competent cop, but too often a by-the-book autocrat who personally dominated high-profile investigations. Williams was chief of the Criminal Investigations Division reporting to the head of the Criminal Branch of the FBI. A cop. Williams was old-school, a product of the Hoover era. Williams preferred to be addressed as Charles, not Charlie, certainly not Chuck.

"Egan, the obvious assumption is that the bombing was executed by the rebels. You are aware of the recent assassinations of their defense minister and the secret police colonel?"

"No shit, Bernie. What the fuck do you think I do all day? Of course I know about the assassinations. Christ, the picture of that ugly fucker's severed head was in the tabloids. The Defense Minister was killed in a whorehouse, and I'm quoting the Washington Press."

Egan Kavanagh headed the FBI's Counterterrorism Division as part of the National Security Branch. Comparatively young at thirty-seven to hold that post. It was his section's function to know about all terrorist events happening in the world. He operated apart from everyday FBI criminal operations. Most of his work focused outside of the country. He typically had more contact with foreign police organizations, Interpol, and the U.S. intelligence community than with his colleagues in other branches of the Federal Bureau of Investigation.

"Don't get testy, Egan. I've just got a bad feeling about this one. This was big time. It appears the bomb was planted inside the building. That suggests a certain level of sophistication. They seized on a major opportunity when a large number of prominent people would be gathered. That suggests an intelligence capability. And, this was accomplished in a heightened security situation in a police-state. The rebel insurgency down there has never demonstrated such a capability before. Your job, Egan, is to determine if this is part of the civil war down there, or something else."

"What do you mean *something else*, Bernie?"

"I mean, is it backed by someone; Iran, Cuba, Gaddafi? Especially is it Gaddafi again? Is it from the lunatic fringe, you know like in the bad old days of the Baader-Meinhof gang, the Japanese Red Army, or Black September. Specifically, is this directed at us or at the Salvadorans?"

Kavanagh had been working the investigation of the downing of Pan Am 103 over Lockerbie, Scotland for the previous several months. He was working closely with the CIA and other foreign intelligence agencies. 189 United States nationals died in that crash. The FBI was massively assisting investigators from the United Kingdom. Fortunately the bomb exploded over land allowing for reconstruction of the aircraft debris. A twenty-inch hole in a baggage compartment eventually pointed to a bomb. Bomb related fragments were recovered along with clothing that apparently was inside a Samsonite suitcase containing the bomb. Evidence was increasingly pointing to Libya. There was concern that it might be an act of state-sponsored terrorism from the volatile and erratic Libyan dictator, Muammar Gaddafi.

"I get the picture, Bernie."

"Good. Then get down there as fast as you can. Coordinate with Williams and Scofield. Requisition a military flight. Call me tomorrow afternoon with a preliminary report."

"What about Charlie?"

Saunders knew what Kavanagh was asking. "Like I said, Williams is in charge to the extent that he will be the official contact for the FBI. You will still make your report to me. In other words, Williams is the case supervisor. This is a criminal matter at the moment. I trust you understand, Egan?" Saunders said with feigned sarcasm.

Saunders had played this mating dance with Egan Kavanagh before. Kavanagh was a challenge and could be a pain in the ass. But he was extremely effective at what he did. Kavanagh had better contacts and rapport with foreign governments and intelligence agencies than anyone Saunders knew in the U.S. government. He had cultivated an international network on a personal basis. Within the United States, he had the best relationships with the CIA and NSA of anyone in the FBI. If Kavanagh were to quit the Bureau it would mean an enormous loss in the increasingly complex demands of intelligence coordination.

Kavanagh was a senior official with the FBI, with eighteen years of service. Yet he was considered a rebel, out of sync with the system. His position put him out of the mainstream of the traditional FBI mission devoted to locating and arresting conventional criminals. Although his capabilities were highly regarded, further promotion might be questionable in an organization still operating under an archaic cultural legacy.

Even his detractors reluctantly acknowledged his effectiveness. On paper, he was an intellectual with a law degree, a master's in political science, working on his PhD. In person, he struck quite a different impression. He was confrontive with little regard for authority. Hated bureaucracy and was a master at circumventing it. His supporters found his talents invaluable. He could alternatively be charming or invective depending on the situation. Everyone acknowledged he got results.

Perhaps the greatest talent Egan Kavanagh possessed was his ability to network effectively. He took networking to a sophisticated level. Whenever he spoke with someone, no matter the reason or topic, he filed it away for future use. Beyond that he was scrupulous in cultivating contacts in every conceivable area, high or low level. It was not uncommon for Kavanagh to get calls from all sorts of government agencies looking for a contact or some piece of information. The inquiries were often made *unofficially*. He always documented such calls. All good deeds had their value. He compared his operation to a bank with the currency being the trade of information. He kept scrupulous accounts of the debits and credits.

The importance of Kavanagh's network had fallout beyond the world of international terrorism. More than once he had secured information from *unofficial* sources that assisted not only the FBI but also the CIA, DIA, NSA, DEA, ATF. The well-known hostility and isolationism between the CIA and FBI was often bridged when Egan Kavanagh was involved.

"Who else will be down there?" Kavanagh asked.

"Fuller from the State Department Bureau of Diplomatic Security is already on his way. Imagine the shit he's in. Someone from the White House is bound to show up soon. Expect someone from CIA and DIA. NCIS of course. U.S. Marines were killed. There's also a large contingent of medical personnel being assembled. They'll be flown down tomorrow in a C-130 to assist with treatment to the surviving casualties."

"Who from CIA?"

"I don't know who they've assigned yet. You call them. You're their buddy."

"I just understand them better, Bernie. They're a little twisted, sometimes psychotic, but basically fun people. They don't identify well with the buttoned-up, crew-cut cop-types in our outfit."

Kavanagh would take two agents from his section. He sent messages to their pagers. Both agents called him within minutes. After issuing instructions to his team, he packed a bag with enough clothes for a week. He took a shower. Only after he had dressed, did he call Andrews Air Force Base and arrange for a flight. He had been through this routine before. Another thirty minutes would not change the course of world events. He specifically avoided contacting FBI headquarters and coordinating transportation with his other FBI colleagues. The last thing he wanted was to share a flight with Charlie Williams and his crew of agents.

Shortly after midnight, Kavanagh and his two agents lifted off from Andrews Air Force Base in a military Lear jet. Estimated time of arrival in El Salvador was 3:40AM local time.

Colonel Benavides received the news of the bombing about ten minutes after it happened. A short time later he arrived at the site.

Benavides spent over an hour at the destroyed embassy. His only contribution was to send orders to make a warehouse available to lay out the bodies and body parts. Mostly he just contemplated the scene. It afforded him time to compose what he would recommend to his superior, General Garcia, and the President of El Salvador. He was expected at the presidential palace for a meeting in an hour.

Benavides felt sure that this was not the work of the rebels, or any known element of the opposition. It was his guess that it was the same people who carried out the Ruiz and Solorgano killings. The problem was not so much the direct threat posed by whomever this was, but restraining the government's and the military's reaction.

The massive scale of arrests after the assassinations had yielded little hard information. It was true that some irritants like the French journalist had been removed, but nothing of any real value resulted.

Case in point was the Portillo killing. The amount of problems this was causing was still growing. Protests were still coming from all quarters. Benavides was immune to such protestations, but the U.S. government was not. It was frequently the subject of his conversations with U.S. officials. Benavides was totally dissatisfied with how things were progressing. They were taking heat from the Americans for human rights abuses with overt threats concerning continued aid. No telling what the posture of the United States might now be. Benavides would be dealing with a new military attaché, perhaps not as collegial as

Colonel Taylor killed in the bombing. Thanks to Major Rivera and the entrenched practices of the Treasury Police, he had not been able to seize full control over their operations. Complaints were escalating about the curfew imposed in San Salvador. Now he was faced with the possibility of an entirely unexpected new enemy. An enemy surprisingly effective in causing real difficulties.

At the meeting with General Garcia and the President, Benavides recommended a straight forward course of action. A declaration of martial law would be declared upon the justification of national security. The curfew would be lifted. This would remove the inconveniences causing the pressure from certain influential business elements. The powers vested in the government under a declaration of martial law would expand the existing authorities for arrest. Mass arrests would be curtailed in favor of targeted opposition strategic arrests. Military tribunals would try political crimes. Benavides could sell the concept to the Americans on the basis of maintaining law and order and national security.

The second part to his plan was for reorganization of the Treasury Police. Benavides argued that the impediment to securing meaningful intelligence from the organization was the leadership within the Treasury Police. Their tactics were counterproductive. Furthermore, the excesses practiced by the Treasury Police were the prime cause of pressure from the Americans. Benavides wanted carte blanche to reorganize and re-staff the Treasury Police.

Newly elected President Alfredo Cristiani was uncertain as to what course of action to take. Benavides' plan didn't seem to offer any real risks, therefore it was politically acceptable. On the other hand, there didn't seem any proposed direct action to address the problem. He would have to sell that to those influential in his ring-wing ARENA political party and the ranking military leadership. Many of the officers within the Treasury Police were intimately connected with the ARENA party.

Having gauged the political winds, General Garcia endorsed Benavides recommendations. He had also arrived at the same conclusion as Benavides concerning the unproductive excesses of the Treasury Police. He had tested the waters among other senior military officers and found significant support. For the time being he would support Benavides. However, he would keep a close eye on developments. Control over a secret police organization held enormous powers.

The next day, President Cristiani announced a declaration of martial law on television and radio. That night, Major Rivera was shot to death along with his mistress after leaving a restaurant. Captain Jimenez and four other ranking officers of the Treasury Police were also killed by unidentified assailants later that same night. None of the killings were made public.

The Lear jet with Egan Kavanagh and his agents landed in El Salvador just before four o'clock in the morning. Much to the surprise of Egan, a Marine master sergeant was awaiting his arrival. So as not to feel too important, Egan found out that the sergeant was the official welcoming committee for U.S. government officials arriving throughout the night.

The Marine escorted him to a small rental sedan. The driver was a Marine private, part of a contingent flown in from Panama within three hours after the bombing.

On the outskirts of San Salvador, they stopped at a roadblock manned by the Salvadoran National Police. The troops were wary, covering Kavanagh's car with M16's. After showing their I.D.'s, the car was allowed to continue after one of the FBI agents addressed the Salvadorans in Spanish.

"They're real nervous after this bombing," the Marine driver said. "Helps that you can speak Spanish."

Kavanagh ignored the attempt at small talk by the young soldier. "Where are we going, Private?"

"My orders are to take you to the El Presidente Hotel, Sir. A sort of command center has been established there."

"I want to see the embassy first," Kavanagh said.

"I can't do that, Sir. My orders were clear."

"Whose orders?"

"The chief FBI guy, a Mr. Williams."

"Listen, Private, I don't give a rat's ass what Williams said. You'll take me to the embassy first."

"Sir, I don't know where the embassy is. I'm not based here. They only showed me the route to the hotel." The young Marine was noticeably flustered with these conflicting orders from some obviously important officials. Where was an officer when you needed one?

Kavanagh could see that the young soldier would take him to the embassy if he knew the way. "Very well, Private, take me to the hotel then."

Kavanagh was greeted by a Marine lieutenant at the hotel. A bellboy escorted him to a third floor suite. Two Marines in full battle dress stood guard at the door.

Kavanagh entered the suite. A large table had been set up in the center of the living room. Several men in white shirts, and four military officers were in the room. Kavanagh recognized most.

"Kavanagh, good of you to make it," Charles Williams said sarcastically. Williams made no attempt to shake hands. Neither did Kavanagh. The other men introduced themselves. Kavanagh knew several of them. Most showed the effects of a sleepless night. By contrast Kavanagh got a couple of hours sleep on his flight. He knew he would be facing little opportunity for rest the next few days.

Most of the key agencies were represented. John Fuller, head of the State Department's Bureau of Diplomatic Security, represented State. Bill Cranston and Luis Pacheco from CIA. Commander Karl Richter of the Navy's NCIS. Kavanagh didn't know the Army major from the Defense Intelligence Agency, or the Marine lieutenant colonel in camouflage fatigues. The fourth military officer was Salvadoran, a Colonel Martinez of the National Police.

"We were just reviewing arrangements for the eventual transport of the dead and mobile injured back to the United States," Williams said.

"Well you don't really need me then, Charlie. I want to see the embassy. In fact, where is Larry Scofield?" Kavanagh said.

"Scofield is at the embassy with his people. If you would have come down with us, you would have already seen the embassy."

Kavanagh ignored Williams and said to Colonel Martinez, "Can you arrange for me to get to the embassy, Colonel?"

"Listen, Kavanagh, I'm in charge of this investigation," Williams interrupted, while throwing the pen he was holding down on the table.

"Charlie, don't be an ass. Colonel?" Kavanagh said turning to the colonel.

The colonel looked first to Williams. Williams gave him what served as an affirmative gesture.

"Come with me, Señor Kavanagh, I'll arrange for someone to take you to the embassy.

It was only a short distance to the embassy. Both Salvadoran troops and U.S. Marines secured the perimeter.

As he entered the embassy compound, an odor of blood hung in the air. The scene around him was terrible devastation. Everything outside appeared scorched by fire. The covered dead were still in evidence. This was a crime scene. Inside the embassy building, things were far worse. It was difficult to imagine anyone surviving but a few had. Kavanagh found Larry Scofield huddled with two of his forensics staff. Scofield was in his late fifties, balding, horn-rimmed glasses, every bit the professorial type. In fact, he had turned down more than one prestigious offer for an academic post in forensics.

"Larry, how goes it?"

"Egan," Scofield said as he turned. "Ever seen anything like this?"

Kavanagh surveyed the scene. The front wall had partially collapsed to the outside. Part of the ceiling had fallen in. A huge crater was evident at the end of what had been a large room.

"Yes. Beirut, the Marine barracks in '83. But this looks just as bad."

The dead remained where they fell, covered with blankets. Their positions were necessary to the reconstruction of the bombing. Large pools of dried blood and fragments of body tissue were evident throughout the destruction. Actually this was worse than Beirut. There, it was an external blast that collapsed the building. Here, the victims had been hit directly by the force of the explosion.

"What've you found, Larry?"

"Hard to say yet. The explosion originated from over there obviously." Scofield pointed to the raised stage area, or what was left of it, and the crater at the end of the room. "My guess is the explosives were concealed under the temporary stage or probably in some sort of musical equipment. We've found remnants of what appears to be an amplifier. That suggests speakers. We haven't yet found speaker fragments, but we will. Somewhere in the debris. It's my guess it was the speakers. Speakers would have ample internal open space to house explosives. Besides, the van ties it to the musical equipment."

"Van? What do you mean?"

"Another bomb exploded in that burned out van outside. The van that delivered the musical equipment. Seems the bastards also rigged a delay to a second device in the van. Caught a lot of people on the grounds. Lots of gasoline ignited. More than just the gas tank volume it appears. This was some sophisticated bombing, Egan."

"What's your schedule, Larry?"

"We finished the photos about an hour ago. Next is examination of the dead. That will provide more detail on the bomb particulars. After the bodies are removed we'll start the initial phase of searching and sifting the debris. My guess is that we'll be poking around here for at least four or five more days. Personally, I'm going to get some sleep after I make sure things are under control here. One of my key people will be here in a few hours with some more of our technical people from Washington. I'll let him take over."

"What about the survivors?"

"They're at a hospital in the city. I understand there is a heavy contingent of U.S. medical personnel being flown down. There are only thirty-five wounded that survived. I've heard there were over seventy dead. Many of the wounded are also expected to die."

"How long till you know about the explosive and the detonating method, Larry?"

"Depends on what type of fragments we locate. Eventually, we'll identify enough material to tell you the type and approximate quantity of explosive. As to the detonating device, that may take longer."

Kavanagh let Scofield return to his work. He wandered the scene of the devastation trying to picture the events. It was difficult to imagine anyone surviving this explosion. Those that did must be terribly injured. The secondary explosion of the van was an insidious touch. It did not point to the methods of the leftist guerrilla movement. The rebel FMLN had never used terrorist bombings in their long-running civil war. Could of course be a new tactic. But the target here was the United States. This was more like Middle East attacks on the U.S.

The burned-out hulk of the van was still outside. Actually just the chassis remained. Scorching was evident on the stucco exterior of the embassy and the surrounding perimeter wall. There was little more for Kavanagh to see. He collected his driver and returned to the hotel leaving his two subordinates at the embassy. Dawn was breaking as Kavanagh arrived in front of the lobby. He disconnected the telephone to ensure a couple of hours of sleep.

At ten in the morning, Kavanagh was awakened by a knock at the door. The bellboy indicated that his telephone had been reported out of order. There was a message to call a Mr. Williams in suite 405. He showered, dressed, and ordered breakfast from room service. Forty minutes after the bellboy knocked on the door, Kavanagh reconnected the phone and dialed William's suite.

"Where the hell have you been, Kavanagh?" Williams said in response to Kavanagh's call.

"Listen, Charlie, I'm going to make this clear enough for even you to understand. You're in charge of FBI operations down here. Personally, I don't give a shit. I'll report to you when I damn well please, if I please. I'll meet you at eleven-thirty if you wish. If you don't, that's okay too. Am I getting through?"

"Who the hell do you think you are, Kavanagh?"

"See you shortly, Charlie." Kavanagh hung up. There was a history of bad blood between them fuelled by their equally strong personalities as well as turf conflicts between the counterintelligence and criminal branches of the FBI. Counterintelligence was increasing becoming a growing function within the FBI's portfolio. Moving on actionable intelligence sometimes meant muddying the rules of evidence required for criminal prosecution.

Kavanagh knocked on the door to suite 405. One of William's subordinates opened the door. Chairs had been assembled in a rough circle in the living room. The meeting consisted of Williams, Fuller from State, the marine colonel commanding the U.S. troops, Cranston from CIA, Richter from NSA, and Major Collins from Defense Intelligence. Colonel Benavides and the deputy foreign minister represented the Salvadoran government and military. Most looked weary from hours without sleep.

The conversation halted when Kavanagh entered the room. Williams glared at him.

"Please continue gentlemen, don't let me interrupt," Kavanagh said. He took a seat next to Don Fuller.

There was an awkward silence, broken by Fuller introducing Colonel Benavides and the deputy foreign minister to Kavanagh.

"Please continue, Colonel," Williams said.

"As I was saying, Mr. Williams," Benavides said, "It is our opinion that the murders of General Ruiz and Colonel Solorgano were perpetrated by the same people that bombed your embassy. Furthermore, we feel that contrary to the denials of the FDR-FMLN, this so called Hand of Justice is indeed a faction of the coalition of Communist opposition. While we cannot prove it yet, we also have reason to believe that there is assistance from the Cuban Dirección de Inteligencia."

Kavanagh looked around the room to gage the expressions of everyone. All the Americans had an intent but noncommittal look. He was not an expert on the political situation in El Salvador but he knew enough to detect the self-serving bullshit this colonel was spouting.

"As you gentlemen know, the Communists have been suffering ever increasing setbacks for quite some time. Continuing the present course will eventually see an elimination of their threat. This is a new tactic growing out of their desperation."

Kavanagh listened to Benavides words not for their information value but rather what Benavides was trying to accomplish. The Colonel clearly had an agenda. He noticed that Benavides always referred to the rebels as Communists. Kavanagh knew that the composition of the FDR-FMLN was politically left, made up of some Communist factions, but the situation certainly could not be considered a direct confrontation with a broader Communist movement.

Benavides continued. "Faced with mounting defeats in the field, the Communists have simply resorted to terrorism. Probably with outside assistance. It is important that we all keep the ultimate objective in mind. That objective is to deny further Communist incursions in the Americas. We cannot let our resolve falter because of the media attention to this bombing. This would be playing right into the hands of the Communists."

"I understand your concerns, Colonel. However, the people here are only concerned with the investigative aspects of the bombing of the embassy," Williams said. "The political issues are not within our purview. It is our task only to determine the methods and identify the perpetrators."

Everyone present knew that to be diplomatic nonsense. For a purely investigative function, the CIA and DIA were not necessary. This was all about broader geopolitical politics.

"Colonel, you said you were convinced that the attack on the embassy was linked to the assassinations of the two military officers. What evidence do you have to make that connection?" Kavanagh asked.

Williams immediately sat forward in his chair fearing that Kavanagh could derail the collaborative tone he had set for the meeting with Kavanagh's confrontational style.

"No direct evidence yet, Mr. Kavanagh. But it is the most probable conclusion. It would be a natural progression of events, since the Communists have reverted to tactics of terrorism with these high profile assassinations," Benavides answered.

"What evidence links the assassinations to the rebels?" Kavanagh said.

Benavides stared without expression at Kavanagh for several seconds. Williams glared at Kavanagh for disturbing the diplomatic climate he thought he had established.

"We have information obtained from arrested FMLN members, sympathizers, and captured guerrilla fighters. There is no doubt on that account Mr. Kavanagh."

"Since you feel there is a strong link between the embassy bombing and the assassinations, it is important for the U.S. government to concur with your assessment. If this is an extension of the civil war in El Salvador that is one thing. If this is a new externally backed terrorist group that is entirely another issue. After all, U.S. nationals were killed in this attack."

"I understand that your responsibility with the Federal Bureau of Investigation is counter-terrorism, Mr. Kavanagh," Benavides said.

"That is correct."

"Maybe your natural inclination is to look for international conspiracies. I assure you though this is nothing more than a new tactic from the leftist guerrillas with probable assistance of Communist Cuba. They have practiced terrorism on Salvadoran nationals, now they have turned to our allies, the Americans. This is nothing more than a carefully orchestrated political plan to attempt to drive a wedge against our two countries' continuing struggle to counter Communism in the Americas."

"Would you be willing to share your evidence with us?" Kavanagh said.

"As I said, Mr. Kavanagh, the evidence is in the form of testimony from prisoner interrogations. I will have one of my people compile summaries of the pertinent transcripts and get it to you as soon as possible. Will that be satisfactory?"

"We appreciate the cooperation, Colonel. However, we will need more than unsubstantiated information obtained under questionable means in order to conclude that this is the work of the rebel opposition. And assertions that assistance from the Cuban DGI may be involved opens up entirely other levels of concern."

"See here, Kavanagh," Williams said angrily, but was stopped by Benavides holding up his hand.

"I understand Mr. Kavanagh's need to be sure of the conclusions. Be assured gentlemen, that the government of El Salvador stands ready to assist in any way possible to determine the perpetrators of this terrible attack and bring them to justice. Now if that is all, Mr. Williams, I am required to meet with the President shortly."

Benavides did not like being challenged. This Kavanagh clearly had little regard for diplomatic niceties. Benavides rose from his chair to leave.

"I appreciate your help, Colonel," Williams said also standing then escorted Benavides and the Deputy Foreign Minister to the door.

Returning to the group, Williams lit into Kavanagh. "What the hell was that all about? Do you have to always be disruptive, Kavanagh?"

"Look, Charlie, you may be willing to sit here and listen to that fucking banana republic colonel give a political speech but I'm not. I'm here to conduct an investigation not to listen to the local party rhetoric. He as much as told us he won't give us direct access to any of this so-called evidence he has."

"We're not here to alienate the Salvadorans."

"Goddamn it, Charlie, you sound like you're running for office, or maybe an ambassadorial appointment. I don't think Benavides has any evidence on the assassinations. But you need to press him on this. As for the link to the bombing, there is absolutely nothing. The Cuban DGI thing is a red herring to promote this whole rebel thing as a Communist threat. If he had anything concrete he'd have presented it."

Kavanagh decided to soften his attack on Williams. "The fact is there is no evidence that this bombing was executed by the rebel opposition. We need to keep our objectivity and not be persuaded by Salvadoran political motives."

"You know better than that, Kavanagh. I'm doing what is necessary to maintain productive relations with the Salvadorans. I have no intention of reaching premature, or non-supported conclusions." Williams' anger subsided slightly. He had been through these confrontations with Kavanagh before. He shared Kavanagh's view on the situation but was not about to acknowledge that.

"Don, what do you think?" Kavanagh asked the head of the State Department's Bureau of Diplomatic Security.

"So far I've heard nothing of substance. I'm waiting to see what the FBI forensic people turn up." Fuller was tired and disgusted, and in no mood to get in the middle of the antagonism between Williams and Kavanagh. This debacle fell squarely into his lap. Congressional hearings would inevitably follow to pin responsibility on someone, mostly likely his department. Somebody's head would roll, probably his.

The meeting broke up with most opting to catch a few hours of sleep. Kavanagh spent the rest of his day by returning first to the embassy followed by visiting the hospital treating the victims. Of the twenty-four injured still in the hospital, only six were able to talk to him. Six had been treated and released. Five others had died of their injuries. Several more were also expected to die.

Nothing of substance was gained from the victims he interviewed, only a sense of the horror of the event. One man he interviewed had lost an arm, and would probably lose an eye. His wife would walk with a limp and suffer facial disfigurement for the rest of her life. Both had been outside, just about to enter the embassy at the time of the explosion. A Salvadoran employee of the embassy survived injuries that would leave him crippled. A Marine would require extensive reconstructive surgery to his badly burned face.

While Egan Kavanagh was at the hospital in San Salvador, Victor Castell was boarding a Mexicana flight leaving Tegucigalpa, Honduras. He would arrive in Mexico City midday to connect with a flight leaving two hours later for Los Angeles.

After landing at LAX, Castell made his way by bus to Pasadena. There he booked a room at a modest hotel. He would stay there for a least a few days while he looked for an apartment close to Caltech. He was already enrolled in a graduate program to study computer science. What happened in El Salvador must be buried.

In his hotel room, Castell listened to the continuous coverage on CNN television news describing the bombing of the U.S. embassy in El Salvador. He felt detached from the description of the carnage. The whole thing was a terrible mistake on his part but there was nothing he could do about that now. It was just more violence in El Salvador. He was now away from all of that. But there was still Patricia.

Late in the afternoon, CNN broadcast the content of a telegram just received.

To the people of the United States. The United States must cease all military aid to the fascist government of El Salvador. The destruction of the United States Embassy is the first in a series of attacks on United States targets and United States nationals. Support of right-wing dictatorships throughout the world can no longer be tolerated. The United States must come to realize its responsibilities and the consequences of its actions. Discontinuance of military aid to the government of El Salvador will prevent further attacks on the United States. We shall await your response.

The Hand of Justice

CHAPTER 10

The following day, Victor Castell called his father in San Francisco to tell him he was back in the United States.

His father answered, "Thank God you're back in the United States. Are you alright? When did you get back?" He knew his son was with his mother in El Salvador.

"Yesterday. Why?"

His father sensed from the tone of his son's voice that he did not know what had happened in El Salvador.

"Victor, you know don't you?"

"Know what, Father?"

"That terrorist bombing of the U.S. Embassy in San Salvador. Weren't you in El Salvador with your mother when it happened? It's all over the news."

There was silence for a few moments.

"My God. You should not be hearing this by telephone."

"What's going on, Father?"

There was a long silence.

"Victor, your mother was there. She was at the embassy when the bomb went off. She was killed, Victor."

Victor was stunned as if hit by a physical blow. The phone dropped from his hand as he bent over, suddenly physically ill with the horror of what he had done.

He could hear his father calling his name from the telephone lying on the floor. Eventually he was able to get hold of himself.

"You're sure of this, Father?"

"I'm afraid so. Your Uncle René and Aunt Marie were also killed. I was informed by the State Department. Once I heard of the bombing, I was frantically trying to make contact with René before I learned what happened."

Victor said nothing. What could he say?

"The funeral is to be next week. At the family's estate outside of Santa Ana of course. I am leaving the day after tomorrow. You'll come with me of course."

He continued his silence.

"Victor, I said you'll be coming with me won't you? Where are you now?"

"No, Father. I can't return to El Salvador."

"What? What do you mean? Not for your mother's funeral? What the hell happened to you down there?"

"I can't talk about it, Father. I'm sorry. I just can't go."

"What kind of son refuses to ….." but Victor disconnected the call.

Killed his mother? Horrifying, but it did not cause real emotional pain. Now that the shock of the news had subsided Castell experienced a confused sense of loss. She was his mother, but he never really *liked* her. She may have even deserved her fate along with his uncle for what they did to him and Patricia. Whatever the conflicting emotions, he was surprised that he felt little guilt.

Castell spent the rest of the day sitting in his darkened hotel room not knowing what to do. He was scared. Was he safe from arrest? And Patricia? Impossible to now enlist his father's assistance to help her enter the United States.

Nothing would be better than to immerse himself in his new studies in the fall and forget everything about El Salvador. But of course he could not forget Patricia. He was in love with her. He wanted her with him. She was still in danger there. Danger from the Salvadoran security forces. Danger from her association with Santiago Molina.

Within a week he rented a furnished apartment close to the Caltech campus using his own bank account. The account balance would cover him for a time but he would have to eventually seek financial help from his father. At some point he would tell his father about Patricia. Of how they were involved with Augustin Portillo. The grief of Augustin's and Claudia's murder. The terror of what happened to him and Patricia at the apartment. Having to leaving Patricia behind and being forced by the police to leave El Salvador. The inability therefore to return there for his mother's funeral. No mention of course of his ill-conceived participation in the embassy bombing. He would make things right with his father then request his help in finding a way to secure a visa for Patricia to come to the United States.

He had resisted calling El Salvador. The only communication link was the same cutout telephone number used before to contact Santiago Molina. He wanted nothing more to do with Molina but it was the only way to reach Patricia. So once a telephone was installed at the apartment, he made the call to El Salvador. The same voice answered. Castell gave the message for the Frenchman to *have the woman call this number.*

Patricia called the following day. After hearing she was safe and recovering steadily from her injuries, he broke the news to her. Tears ran down his cheeks but his eyes reflected hatred bred more from betrayal rather than grief.

"My mother. I killed my own mother. She was at the embassy. Santiago caused me to murder my own mother. I should never have helped him. It was only because of my stupid anger. But he betrayed me. He should have known. You must get away from him, Patricia. Christ, he even murdered those poor band members according to the news reports. Probably that psychopath Carlos did the killing. They were not the enemy. And the assassinations of those two army officers. Molina will get you killed, Patricia. He's not a revolutionary, he's a violent fanatic. Anyone is expendable if it suits his purpose. You must be done with him until I can get you to the United States."

"I'm so sorry about your mother, Victor. That was not supposed to happen. So many innocent people continue to die here. I'm sorry I got you into this. It's my fault. This is not your country. It's not your fight."

"It's not your fault. You've just been trying to stand up against this tyranny like my Uncle Augustin. But Molina has gone too far with this bombing. Doesn't matter though. I made a mistake but I'm done with all that. You need to be done with it too, Patricia. I need to get you out of El Salvador. As soon as I can arrange a visa. I promise. I have rented an apartment in Pasadena close to Caltech. Take down my telephone number and address. Write me with a return address so I can write back. Hopefully soon I'll be able to send you the necessary paperwork to get you entry into the United States."

Patricia Reyes was not as shaken by the bombing. Her sense of rebellion still burned fiercely. Her people were killed and tortured by the thousands by a regime propped up by the United States. Her own parents. Her friends. She was viciously attacked. Now they had drawn real blood against the oppressors. Victor Castell was their technician. The *engineer* that could provide them with sophisticated weapons. She had great affection for Castell, but beyond that his skills were still needed. The cause was all important. She was not done with her war.

After their conversation, Patricia Reyes contacted Santiago Molina as he instructed.

It had been days since Castell had spoken with Patricia. More difficult to reach her so he had to wait for her to call. He would not use Santiago Molina as an intermediary. To dispel his depression, he dove into the text books for classes that would begin in two weeks at Caltech.

Late in the morning there was a knock at the door. He was shocked to find it was Santiago Molina and Carlos Perez.

"What the fuck are you doing here?"

"Victor, I understand how you must feel. You must understand though, I had no way of knowing your mother would be at the embassy. She was not part of the social scene in the capital. It was only because of your Uncle René that she was there."

"Why are you here? I'm through with doing anything to help you. I made the one stupid mistake but no more."

"That's why I'm here to talk with you. It's not that simple, Victor."

"I'm not fucking going to help you. You came all this way for nothing. Find someone else to make your bombs."

"Let's talk inside, Victor," Molina said and pushed him gently back into the apartment. Placing a hand on Castell's shoulder, he forced him to sit on the sofa. Molina sat opposite on a chair while Perez stood in the background by the front door.

"I don't really expect to convince you of anything, Victor. After all, this is our fight not yours. But there are certain realities I must explain to you.

"We are at war. The people of El Salvador are at war. In war there are unpleasant things that transcend our personal feelings. I still need your technical expertise. I assure you, these will be used directly against Salvadoran army and police targets."

"No. I won't help you."

"Like I said, I assumed that would be your response. But everything has its price, Victor. I believe for you that price is Patricia Reyes."

Castell's stomach lurched at the implied threat.

"What are you saying?"

"It's very straight forward. You either help us or Patricia will come to a bad end."

Castell jumped up. Perez quickly pulled a 9mm pistol from his waistband.

"Sit back down, Victor," Molina said.

"You sonofabitch. You'd harm one of your own? How do you like that Carlos? Better watch out or you could be next."

"Like I said, war is full of unpleasant things," Molina said. "There are always casualties. Patricia would be another casualty. I wouldn't hurt her of course. That would be for the police. You see, Patricia was directly involved in the assassination of the Minister of Defense. Armed with that information, the police would apply the harshest interrogation techniques. As much as I would dread the idea of Patricia being brutally tortured, I would make that sacrifice if necessary to achieve my purpose. In the end she would be martyred for the cause."

Castell looked at Molina paralyzed by that vision. Rage clouded rational thought, but he could not physically overpower Molina and Perez.

Taking a deep breath, he countered, "Do that and I surely wouldn't help you. That's a hollow threat."

"I don't think so, Victor. There is still another lever to force your help. You are here in the United States but still at risk for what you did in El Salvador. You were responsible for the deaths of many Americans. An anonymous tip to your Federal Bureau of Investigation would lead to your arrest. I believe you could be subject to the death penalty for what you did."

"Bullshit. You do that and I'll identify you and your group."

"Obviously. But of course I will have made alternative arrangements along with Carlos here and the others. These would be just your allegations without any evidence. We were simply people you met through your Uncle Augustin. Not to be found in El Salvador. You on the other hand would be in a difficult position. I am sure that evidence could be uncovered that would incriminate you as the engineer of these bombs. You were the one who made the purchases of the electronic components. You had the training to engineer the triggering devices. I'd prefer it never came to that but if you don't help you have far more to lose than I do, Victor."

These were probably unrealistic threats. Santiago Molina would never willingly expose himself. But Castell was at considerable risk and resisting Molina would lead to some bad end. The sonofabitch killed without hesitation so he was capable of anything. All Castell could think about was Patricia's safety.

Resigned to his entrapment, he sat back down on the sofa. With elbows on his knees and hands grasping his head, "What is it you want from me?"

CHAPTER 11

The investigators from the various U.S. agencies were able to set up a command center in the undamaged residence wing of the embassy. Power, lighting, and communications were restored with the help of Corp of Engineers staff flown in along with large portable generators. Larry Scofield and his forensics team had set up a lab area to pre-process physical evidence before shipping it to the FBI laboratory at Quantico, Virginia. They had been at the tedious process of sifting even fine debris looking for remnants of the detonating device for several days. From residue samples, the explosive material was quickly identified as military grade Semtex.

"Any idea about the method of detonation, Larry?" Kavanagh said.

Scofield was looking through a microscope. "Maybe. Look at this."

Kavanagh looked at the specimen under the magnification. He had no idea what this might be. "And this is?"

"Pretty sure it's a piece of a transistor. We have some other fragments as well."

"So do you have a theory as to the means of detonation?"

"Well it could be pieces of a digital clock. Could be a timing device but we don't think so. We still need more evidence to establish not only how, but also the possible origin of the components."

"Your best guess right now?"

"I'd guess some sort of radio frequency trigger. There are fragments of capacitors and resistors that are inconsistent with a simple electronic timing circuit. But here's something of equal interest."

Scofield picked up a thumbnail piece of blackened material with tweezers and placed it under a large magnifying glass.

"It's a piece of fiberglass board about three millimeters thick. White fiberglass."

"And the significance?"

"See this small hole. Now look closely and you can see a trace of solder around the hole. This fiberglass sheet is something you'd fine at a hardware store. It's not original electronic material. The hole I would think was for the lead of an electronic component. This is not from a laminated printed circuit board. In short, this suggests it was homemade rather than a commercial device. Somebody made this. If it turns out to be a radio frequency receiver, that suggests a real level of sophistication. The guy had to know electronics well beyond a basic level."

Kavanagh conferred with Charles Williams. Williams agreed that they should press the Salvadorans to investigate sources of radio device sales. They argued about sharing Scofield's preliminary opinion that it was a sophisticated device created by a trained technician. Williams felt that the quicker they moved on that the better. Kavanagh argued that the Salvadorans might react indiscriminately and arrest anyone with electronics training. The FBI should pursue that line of investigation further before sharing with the Salvadorans. He relented when Williams pointed out they had no choice since they were not free to operate independently in El Salvador.

But Kavanagh had no illusions about the investigation proceeding objectively. The Salvadoran government and the powerful military junta were concerned with the political implications
not the truth. While the use of Semtex suggested it was not the
typical rebel choice of weapons, Colonel Benavides would counter that it represented evidence of foreign Communist support
for the rebels, probably the Cuban DGI. Kavanagh might be in
agreement about foreign involvement, maybe even the Cubans.
But he also felt that the perpetrators might not be directly affiliated with the leftist rebels of the FLMN. If so, that meant they
were something new to worry about. It made no investigative
difference other than the stupid Salvadorans would impede progress of the investigation in attempting to serve their own interests. Kavanagh wondered if this was a new international terrorist group bringing their brand of terrorism to the Americas. Everyone did agree this attack was directed at the United States. The
next target would again be the United States. In El Salvador or
another Latin American country?

The investigation became more strained over the next several
days. Kavanagh was spending most of his time on a computer
link back to Washington headquarters from the FBI's command
center in the damaged embassy. To the NSA, was there any in-
dicative signals traffic connecting El Salvador with known foreign bad guys? Feelers were put out to contacts at various intelligence agencies throughout the world looking for tracks that
might lend information about this seemingly new terrorist
group. His two staff agents from counterintelligence were in the
field with Williams' criminal investigative agents working with
the Salvadoran National Police.

Word came via an FBI agent that he was wanted for a meeting at the National Police headquarters with Agent in Charge
Williams. The Salvadorans had apparently turned up an important lead.

Colonel Benavides himself was presiding over a crowded conference room. Charles Williams sat next to Benavides. A Spanish speaking FBI agent sat next to Williams to act as interpreter. Kavanagh also brought one of his own Spanish speaking agents. The others were all Salvadoran military and police.

"Please sit down Director Kavanagh, we are about to begin," Benavides said.

"Salvadoran police immediately began investigating all possible sources for the types of electronic components used to detonate the bombs at the United States Embassy. We believe we have found that source. Bring in the witness," Benavides said to the officer by the door.

A small middle-aged man was brought in and seated in a chair. Although the room was cool, the man was sweating profusely, with dark stains evident on his shirt under his arms. His eyes darted back and forth, obviously terrified to be in the presence of all of these uniforms.

"This is Ernesto Morales," Benavides said. "He owns a television and radio shop in the city of San Miguel. That is one hundred-thirty kilometers to the east of here. Two weeks ago he sold a customer a list of electronic components. The purchase was unusual. Explain why it was unusual, Señor Morales."

"Sí, Señor. Well most of my customers come to my shop to buy televisions or radios, or for repairs. I have used televisions which can be purchased ….."

"We're not interested in your business. Tell us about the person we are interested in."

"Sí, sí. Well this man comes in and asks if I can sell him electronic components. I told him yes. What was he looking for? This man hands me a list. A long list of specific electronic items. There are capacitors, resistors, transistors, radio frequency oscillators. Radio stuff, but all different sizes. I told him if he was repairing a radio that maybe I could help if he brought it into the shop. That's when he explained."

"And he told you what, Señor Morales?"

"That he was an engineering professor at a university. Showed me his university identification. Said he was buying various components for use in his classes. Then he asked if I had an oscilloscope he could buy. That of course was very unusual. Only a person knowledgeable in electronics would need such an instrument so it was not something I would ordinarily have for sale."

"But you did sell him this piece of equipment, is that correct?"

"Yes. I had an old spare oscilloscope I was willing to sell."

"And the purpose of this oscilloscope?"

"It is used to analyze radio signals. It tells you the frequency."

The Spanish speaking agents translated for Williams and Kavanagh.

Benavides nodded to an aide who placed several photographs on the table.

"Señor Morales, come here and point out the man who came to your shop and made this purchase."

The man rose from his chair and came to the table. Picking up the photos with shaking hands, he came to the third photograph. "It was this man. The man with the foreign accent."

Looking somewhat displeased at Morales, Benavides passed the photo to Agent Williams.

"His name is Emilio Chavez," Benavides said. "Teaches electrical engineering at the Universidad Tecnológica here in San Salvador. He has been arrested. We are investigating all those with whom he is acquainted. He is undergoing questioning."

"Has he provided any information? Has he confessed?" Williams said.

"Not yet. But we are certain this is the man. He identified himself to Señor Morales. We found evidence at his home suggesting his affiliation with the rebels. Apparently he was close to Professor Augustin Portillo and his group of traitors."

That would be the late Professor Portillo that was murdered?" Kavanagh said.

"Yes."

"Can we speak to this suspect, Colonel?" Kavanagh said.

"Not yet, Director Kavanagh. This is a Salvadoran investigation."

"What about Señor Morales' comment about this man having a foreign accent?"

"We believe Señor Morales was mistaken. When we pressed him further he could not identify what kind of accent, or even what made him believe it was an accent."

Benavides said something to that effect to Morales who replied, "Yes, I probably heard wrong. It was probably nothing."

"Does the suspect have a foreign accent, Colonel?" Kavanagh said.

"No. But I am sure in your country there are many false leads and witness mistakes in any investigation."

Kavanagh and Williams met back at the embassy command center. Both were in agreement in their take on the meeting.

"That was all crap, Charles," Kavanagh said. "Maybe that shop was where the perpetrators bought the radio stuff, but this engineering professor is too pat. Makes them look good. Fortifies their claim that this is associated with the rebel left. Keep American aid coming or El Salvador will fall to a Communist-backed regime."

"I share the same conclusion, Kavanagh. But the problem is we're in a foreign country. We do not have freedom of action. We'll have to find ways to work around their incompetence."

"It's not incompetence, Charles, it's outright manipulation of the facts to suit their purpose. I don't think they have the bomb maker. The engineering professor is too convenient. That shop keeper's testimony was a put-up job. And if that professor isn't the bomb maker, then there's no lead to who's masterminding this. These terrorists are still out there. Targeting the United States."

"And just what do you expect me to do to get the Salvadorans to cooperate more?"

"Pressure the Director to pressure the White House to lean on these Salvadorans. Quit kissing their asses."

"Tell you what, Kavanagh, you can have a crack at that yourself. We're expecting the Deputy National Security Advisor, John Negroponte and State Department Undersecretary for Political Affairs, Robert Kimmitt to arrive tomorrow."

"Shit. I don't know Kimmitt, but I know Negroponte," Kavanagh said. "He's a diehard supporter of these banana republic dictatorships. Regan's right-hand man. Ready to fight Communism at all costs. Covered up human rights abuses when he was ambassador to Honduras. Had his hand in Guatemala supporting the rebels in Nicaragua. Arming the Afghanistan resistance to counter Soviet occupation. Cozy with the Salvadoran junta. Close to CIA Director Casey and all the black ops stuff they were doing in Latin America. He's totally bent to the right."

"You'd know better than I would about your pals at Langley. At any rate, Negroponte's a lame duck as deputy security advisor. He'll be moving on now that Bush is President. So he's acting the part of more Bush's envoy until Bush gets his new team in place."

"Wonderful, a lame-duck, junta-loving hawk. He'll be a great help to our investigation."

Kavanagh was right about Washington changing nothing that would assist in the investigation. But Williams was also right in his assessment, that even if the Salvadorans were more cooperative, it might not matter much. This was still a third world country. The environment in the United States and the resources the FBI could bring to bear at home were just not the same in El Salvador.

Negroponte said, "I appreciate the difficulties your investigative team is facing Mr. Williams. We will attempt to exert more pressure for more cooperation, but we are not authorized to up that pressure in the form of threats that could affect U.S. military aid as Mr. Kavanagh suggests. It's not even clear what you expect in the way of cooperation. This is still a backward place in the midst of a civil war. Meaningful police work would seem difficult at best."

Kavanagh said, "All true, Mr. Negroponte, but there's still some basics things they have failed to investigate. For example, they have no witness statements of any kind other than the radio shop owner. No witnesses from the neighborhood where the band members were murdered. Someone must have seen something, heard the gunshots. The FBI hasn't been allowed to investigate that crime scene. They haven't reported any forensic evidence from there and never will. This shopkeeper's whole story sounds like a police fabrication. This engineering professor is therefore an unfortunate stand-in for the real bomb maker. He'll be tortured by their secret police and yield either nothing or some confession that will suit the police."

"And you would like them to do what, Mr. Kavanagh?" Negroponte said.

"Allow the FBI full access to the shop keeper. He mentioned something about a foreign accent from the guy who purchased the electronic components. Access to the engineering professor with our own interrogation team. Door to door canvassing for witnesses in the area around the murdered bandleader's house. Access to witnesses and files related to the two murders of those ranking military officers.

"Right now all we know is that military grade Semtex was used as the explosive, triggered by some radio frequency control of some probable sophistication, assembled from components purchased from a radio shop, and one partial fingerprint. A fingerprint we haven't matched in any western database. Only general descriptions by four U.S. Marines of the men that delivered the musical equipment."

"In short you'd like them to get out of your way and let the FBI run the investigation," Negroponte said.

Williams tried to warn Kavanagh off by a subtle shake of his head.

"That would help. The Salvadorans are too incompetent, too corrupt to do anything credible. Remember this gentlemen, and remind President Bush, this terrorist attack on our embassy was not perpetrated by some faction of the Salvadoran rebels. It probably was of foreign origin using the civil war here as the perfect environment. An environment to launch an attack on the United States. The target is now the United States not El Salvador. And this is not the last we'll hear from these guys."

"Mr. Williams, what do you say? You're in charge of this criminal investigation."

"I'd like the same access as Mr. Kavanagh outlined, but I'm a realist. That's not going to happen here. We'll do everything we can but the results will be compromised by having to work under the constraints of this foreign government."

"Jesus, Charlie, that's self-serving crap. We help these fuckers with arms to create their police state then we don't have the balls to demand our own justice."

The State Department Undersecretary weighed in. "Mr. Kavanagh, you head up the counterterrorism division of the national security branch of the Bureau, is that correct?"

Kavanagh nodded.

"No personal criticism intended, but your group has uncovered nothing in the way of intelligence related to this terrorist group?"

"Nothing at all," Kavanagh responded. "There's nothing out there. I've been in contact with all of the western intelligence services even some that are not always the friendliest to the United States. Not a thing that would suggest a new group, or even point to some existing group. No unusual signals traffic from any of the known bad guys. Points to a new group, clever and well concealed."

Negroponte said, "Well at least your people have not found their tracks. Might all this expressed anger at the Salvadorans be a smoke screen for a failure of your counterterrorism section, Mr. Kavanagh?"

Kavanagh clinched his jaw and glared at Negroponte, wisely choosing not to respond at the provocation. It didn't matter. Two days later Kavanagh was recalled to Washington by his boss Bernie Saunders. The order came from the White House. The wording, *Director Kavanagh was not sufficiently sensitive to diplomatic circumstances to continue investigating from within El Salvador.*

The same day, Williams sent Kavanagh a message that the engineering professor was found hanging in his cell by his own belt. According to the Salvadorans, he never confessed or provided any names.

Within a month, John Negroponte was appointed Ambassador to Mexico. His replacement as Deputy National Security Advisor was Robert Gates. Gates was a former Deputy Director of Central Intelligence. Gates had a friendly history with Egan Kavanagh at the FBI. So at least Kavanagh would no longer remain persona non grata at the White House.

CHAPTER 12

"What we want is the same thing you provided last time, Victor. Remote triggering devices," Molina said in response to his question. "Like I said, for attacks on the Salvadoran military leadership. The people you hate."

"Not the United States? I thought they were the real enemy."

"They are. Because they enable the Salvadoran military junta with aid. But there are only limited United States targets in El Salvador. The U.S. Embassy was the only actual target of opportunity. The bombing made a strong statement. Continued attacks on the Salvadoran military will now have greater American attention. I have a couple of bold targets in mind. The Americans will eventually come to realize that it does not serve American interests to continue to prop up this government that is so reviled by the populous."

Castell was not sure he believed Molina intended these bombs for use back in El Salvador. Perhaps it was another United States embassy in Central American. It didn't matter. Somehow he had to maneuver out of this. He could not cause more killings whatever the targets. Was there any way to save Patricia? For that matter to save himself?

"I am saddened that I must resort to threats to obtain your help, Victor. You were once one of us. You are Salvadoran. I am truly sorry about your mother but that is now in the past. We all must do what is necessary. That means you will build control devices as before, Victor. Are we agreement?"

Looking down, Castell nodded yes.

"Very good. You know where to obtain the necessary electronic components?"

"Easy enough to find. Besides, I will not build the device from scratch as before. I will simply modify off the shelf radio frequency model airplane controls."

"Excellent. We shall begin immediately. I require two devices."

Molina explained that the plan for remote triggering of the bombs would be essentially the same as used in El Salvador.

In the telephone directory Castell located a hobby shop in Pasadena. Perez drove him and Molina. Molina stuffed several hundred dollars into Castell's hand to make the purchase. Perez entered the shop along with him to make sure he didn't bolt.

At a hardware store, he bought a soldering gun along with some hand tools, batteries, a voltmeter, duct tape, and of course the necessary latex gloves to avoid fingerprints.

Back at Castell's apartment Molina asked, "How long will this take, Victor?"

"I don't know. A few hours I guess."

"Good. You'll begin right away. Carlos, go out and get us some food."

Castell began assembling the first receiver device. It was simpler than he thought. Assembly consisted of some soldering with the components held together in a unitized ugly mass of duct tape. All he was doing was substituting the outputs of the receiver which would normally operate servo mechanisms to control the model airplane functions. For this purpose, the transmitter signal would simply close the circuit in the receiver to allow current to flow from the batteries to the blasting cap. It took longer to rig an arming circuit with a precautionary method to avoid accidental pre-detonation.

Once the first device was completed, Castell demonstrated.

From the ball of duct tape protruded a couple of lead wires, a toggle switch, and two prongs of wire from a coat hanger.

"I've attached these two red leads to the voltmeter to simulate the blasting cap circuit. The two green leads connect the battery. That's an additional precaution to the arming circuit which you will activate by this toggle switch. To arm the bomb you will simply twist the green wires together then flip the switch. The LED will come on. The bomb is armed."

"And these coat hanger wire protrusions?" Molina asked.

"For mounting integral with the plastique explosive. Just stick it into the plastique just like the blasting cap. Makes for a solid package."

"Good," Molina said. "And the control mechanism?"

"This one controller will control both bomb triggering devices. Turn the system on here. Then simply move this switch to *on*. That will close the blasting cap circuit on device number one. The second device is triggered by this second switch the same way. These control simple on-off relays at the receiver within the bomb. Ignore these larger dial controls. They're unnecessary for our purposes."

"What about interfering radio signals?" Molina asked.

"That should not be a problem. However for absolute safety, that's why I've created arming circuits just like I did in El Salvador. Until you close the arming circuit indicated by the LED light, it is completely safe. What are you housing the bombs in?"

"Luggage."

"Well, besides the arming circuit, I also left the battery wires disconnected as an additional precaution. Connect the battery wires by twisting these wires together before you're ready to place the bomb. Probably some place where you can open the luggage and access with both hands. Depending on the type of luggage, you can just reach inside and flip the arming switch at the latest possible time. Or you can connect the batteries and arm the circuit at the same time. It's still pretty safe from any accidental triggering by a stray signal."

He twisted the green battery circuit wires. "Ok, I flip the toggle switch on the receiving device. See, the red light comes on. No voltage is yet registered on the voltmeter. Now I move this switch on the remote controller to the *on* position. Notice the voltage reading indicating the closed battery circuit, simulating the blasting cap circuit."

"Very good, Victor. How long before you complete assembly of the second device?"

"Maybe an hour," Castell said. What would happen then? Would they kill him? Most likely if they were returning to El Salvador. Even though he couldn't go to the FBI without sacrificing himself, Molina would never rely on that deterrent. Then again, if Molina was planning on an attack here in the United States, he might be taken along as a hostage. Maybe he would be expected to make more devices for future bombs. These last devices were extraordinarily simple. You didn't need an electrical engineering degree to put these together like what he did in El Salvador. But most everyone seems baffled by electrical circuits.

It was close to midnight. A long exhausting day. Soon he would learn his fate. Fatalistically he wasn't sure he cared anymore. This must end. Chances were that it would end soon, most likely in a bad way.

"So now you have your remote bomb triggers, Santiago. What is to be done with me? Kill me I suppose?"

Molina shook his head slightly. "No, I'm not going to kill you. You are too useful, Victor. But I'm afraid you cannot be trusted to not do something stupid. You must come with us."

"I assume that doesn't mean to El Salvador?" Molina gave no expression. "Thought as much. You're planning this bombing in the United States. Right?"

"Of course. But once this attack is executed you are free, Victor. You will provide me with detailed instructions on how to create these triggering devices of yours. We will be gone by then. Out of the country. You cannot go to the police without sacrificing your own life. You should never again speak of this to anyone. Bury it in the past. Get on with your life. I would hope you do not do something foolish, but that is your affair."

Castell knew that Molina would never let him go. It was only a matter of time. Molina apparently wanted his expertise right up to the time of setting off these bombs. A precaution if something unexpected went wrong? Perhaps it was nothing more than just avoiding potential problems with murdering him inside his apartment. Whatever Molina's intentions, it did not make sense to argue him into a corner and force a confrontation now.

A knock on the door was answered by Perez. It was Jose Aguilar, Miguel Cortina, and Roberto Salas. Aguilar nodded to Castell but said nothing, a slight look of guilt as he turned his gaze away. Molina announced they would be leaving in the morning. Castell retreated to the bedroom. Perez and Molina held a whispered conversation. Perez then left the apartment. The others would sleep in the living room with someone always awake to guard against Castell leaving.

The drive from Los Angeles to Las Vegas was less than four hours through the Mojave Desert. Castell was in the back seat between Cortina and Salas. Molina drove with Aguilar in the passenger seat. Everyone was dressed well in fashionable sport shirts and slacks. Typical Californians setting out for a fun weekend in Las Vegas.

Perez was driving a separate rental car with the explosives. The plan was to rent a room at a motel when they arrived in Las Vegas. They would arrive midday. The bombs would be fully assembled within an hour in the motel room. Placement at their targets would be in the evening when the casinos would be at their busiest. Molina himself had been in Las Vegas a week ago to select the targets and devise the plan. Even with the heavy security at all Las Vegas hotel casinos, a bomb concealed in luggage could easily evade scrutiny. Yet the unattended luggage must not arouse suspicion. The more difficult part was placing the bombs strategically and still allowing sufficient time to get a safe distance away. This was not a suicide bombing.

Once on Interstate 15 going north, it was clear to Castell they were going to Las Vegas. He had been there one time on a drunken weekend when he turned twenty-one.

"You're going to bomb a casino aren't you, Santiago?" Castell said.

Molina looked at him in the rearview mirror.

"Obviously. Two actually. Are you familiar with Las Vegas?"

"Not really."

"You perhaps have heard of Bally's and the Tropicana?"

Castell did not reply.

"Maybe not as famous as Caesar's Palace, but they will serve our purpose. The casino areas are close to the entrance for both these hotels. Easier to get away. Caesar's is set to far back from Las Vegas Boulevard."

"You'll have a tough time getting away. There are only a couple of highways in and out of the city. They all go into the desert. They can block all escape routes within minutes."

Molina smiled in the mirror. "You sell me short, Victor. Do you think I would just try to make a run for it?"

Molina spoke with the passion of a zealot. Little doubt to Castell that he could harm Patricia if it served his purpose. No doubt that Molina would kill him soon. No reason not to. He was too much of a liability. For Castell it was a matter of finding an opportunity to attempt escape. Perhaps that opportunity might never come. Events would just have to take their course.

Aguilar was consulting a map. He advised Molina of the planned exit off the Interstate on the south side of Las Vegas. A short drive to the east put them on Las Vegas Boulevard which ran parallel to the Interstate. Bally's and the Tropicana were both located on Las Vegas Boulevard a couple of miles to the north.

The motel was a typical two story structure with a running balcony to access the upper rooms. Several cars were parked in front. Modest cars including two pickup trucks. This was part of the inexpensive working-class Vegas weekend with nickel slots and cheap buffet meals.

Perez emerged from a room on the first floor. Everyone entered except Aguilar. He would stand watch outside nervously smoking.

On the bed was an array of bricks of Semtex plastique explosive. Two rollaway suitcases were brought in from the trunk of the car and opened on the bed. These were good quality luggage since they each needed to carry thirty pounds of explosives.

Perez supervised Cortina and Salas as they assembled the explosives, shaping the pliable plastique to create a tight mass that would not shift when handled. Ball bearings were again added for increased destructive effect on people. As instructed, all wore rubber surgical gloves. In the center of the explosives mass was a cavity containing the detonating circuitry and the batteries.

Perez took over final assembly of the duct taped detonator with the four wires protruding. Once it was securely wedged tightly into place, he inserted the blasting cap. He connected the two red wires protruding from the duct tape to the blasting cap leads.

"Ok, Victor. You will complete the final wiring," Molina said.

"Do you want me to connect the battery wires now?"

"Why not? You still have to activate the toggle switch to arm the device do you not?" Molina said.

"Ok. The disconnected battery wires are just an added precaution anyway."

Before connecting the battery circuit wires, Castell made sure the toggle switch was in the off position. Once completed he said, "I still recommend only setting the arming circuit just a few minutes prior to detonation."

"We understand," Molina said.

They were ready. It was midafternoon, a few hours yet to wait. Molina had Salas walk across the street to a fast food restaurant to bring hamburgers and soft drinks.

At six-thirty Molina announced it was time. Castell wondered if he would now be killed. If not, he would probably be tied up to be killed later after the bombings. It would make more sense to Molina if his body was never discovered. So he assumed he would be killed at some remote turnoff into the desert. Shot then buried. Like something out of a gangster movie.

All afternoon Molina held a 9mm semi-automatic in his hand as a threat to Castell. Everything was removed from the room. The heavy luggage was wheeled out, one placed in each of the two cars.

"Time to go, Victor. You will come with us on this."

One of the cars had already left, apparently with Perez and Cortina. Molina got behind the wheel with Salas in the passenger seat. Castell got into the back along with Aguilar who held a gun on him.

"Do not be foolish, Victor," Aguilar said in Spanish, "I would hate to shoot you."

Molina pulled onto Las Vegas Boulevard.

"Carlos should now be at Bally's. For your benefit, Victor, this is what is going to happen. Miguel is to appear to be a guest checking into the hotel. The reservation desk overlooks a large casino floor. It should be full of people since it is a Saturday night. Miguel will activate the bomb's arming circuit in the restroom near the lobby. He will wait until we arrive. Carlos will enter the casino as a signal for Miguel to leave the suitcase at a designated location in the cocktail lounge on the casino floor."

"And the second bomb?"

"Actually it will be the first bomb which will just have been detonated at the Tropicana two miles away. That is where we are going. Same scenario as at Bally's. Roberto will activate the bomb in the restroom near the registration area and then place the luggage where it will be exposed to a large number of people. Once he exits the hotel, I will detonate the bomb and proceed directly to Bally's a few minutes away. Once Carlos sees us he will enter the casino and signal Miguel to place the bomb. After they leave, I will detonate the second bomb at Bally's."

Salas made a remark about the grandeur of the tall hotels in the distance down Las Vegas Boulevard.

"Wait until you see the casinos, Roberto."

"And how do you expect to ever get out of the city?" Castell said.

Molina smiled. "We'll not be leaving. At least not right away. We have rooms reserved at several different casino hotels. Much better places than what we just left. We shall all enjoy a few days in Las Vegas. Good food. Perhaps take in a show. I believe the expression is *until the heat cools down*. There are thousands of visitors in Las Vegas. There's no reason for us to be singled out."

Molina pulled up in front of the Tropicana. Salas got out and unloaded the suitcase from the trunk waving off the bellboy's assistance. Molina got out and told the valet attendant that he was just dropping off his friend to check in. They must return to the airport to pick up another friend. He passed a ten-dollar bill to the attendant. Could he just park here and wait until his friend checked in?

As he was having this conversation, a taxi pulled up behind. The taxi driver jumped out along with a couple in the back seat.

The taxi driver yelled to the parking attendant. "Hey, I just heard on the radio from several cabbies down at Bally's. Something happened. Big explosion. Smoke pouring out of the place. Could be something like the big fire there ten years ago."

A bewildered Salas just stood there waiting for Molina's instructions.

"Watch him. I'll be right back," Molina said to Aguilar, referring to Castell.

Molina grabbed Salas' arm and pulled him along toward the hotel entrance. Before entering the building, Molina said something to Salas who stopped and set the suitcase down on the sidewalk to the side of the entrance.

Castell watched in horror knowing what Salas was about to do. He was opening the suitcase to slip his hand in to activate the arming circuit. Castell was only two hundred feet away. At least there was another car between him and the suitcase.

Startling Aguilar, Castell crouched down to the floor of the car as best he could.

"What are you doing?"

Jose Aguilar did not survive the shattered side window glass that nearly decapitated him from the massive shock wave of the blast that blew through the car.

The car was pushed four feet sideways by the blast. Castell had been on the blast-side of the car. The force threw him up against Aguilar's corpse. It was badly mutilated from the neck up. Fortunately for Castell, the blast had carried through the car windows not only killing Aguilar but taking some of the blood and tissue away from his destroyed head. Castell was shaken by the force of the blast. He was disoriented. There seemed to be little sound. Maybe his eardrums were ruptured. His first instinct was to get out of the car.

With some difficulty, Castell forced the damaged back door of the car open, falling to his knees on the pavement. Devastation spread out in a wide arc. Bodies were evident. The taxi driver was a casualty. Further away, he could see wounded people trying to stand. Many were bloodied.

Now outside the car, his panic subsided somewhat. He must get away from the area but he had to think things through. He didn't look bad. He didn't seem to be injured. No apparent blood on his clothing. Just couldn't hear. Too many questions if he were treated at a hospital. Best to get away from the scene and melt into the growing crowd. Before leaving he had the presence of mind to wipe down any surfaces in the car he touched with his handkerchief.

He still had his wallet and a credit card. A little cash. Get a hotel room. Claim the airlines lost his luggage. Hole up right here in Las Vegas until he could assess if any of Molina's group survived. They knew where he lived in Pasadena. He would be blamed for things going wrong with the bombs. But of course they didn't go wrong. This was his doing. The bombs were deliberately rigged to explode prematurely. But he could not control where they might be detonated. Unfortunately there were still casualties other than the terrorists. Might have been better if he had been among them.

Castell was not about to be the instrument of killing hundreds of people for Molina's fanatical sense of revolution. Not again. Under the circumstances he did the best he could by rigging the bombs to kill the terrorists. Killing Santiago Molina himself made it worthwhile.

It was a simple booby trap. The radio frequency receivers had two outputs. He simply rigged one hot with the battery circuit when the arming switch was thrown. During the test, he simply attached the voltmeter such that it registered armed when activated by the transmitter signal. Once the receiver assembly was wrapped in duct tape, you could not tell where the two leads attached to the blasting cap originated. So flipping what was thought to be the arming switch actually sent the battery current directly to the blasting cap. They became suicide bombs. His best hope was for the bombs to be set off in a less populated space like inside the car before entering the casinos.

CHAPTER 13

Egan Kavanagh was enjoying a rare Saturday. He had spent the afternoon wandering through art galleries with his long-time girlfriend. A wonderful dinner out. A bottle of very good wine. Prospects for a romantic night.

Entering his house at just past ten o'clock, the telephone rang.

"Shit." Kavanagh answered the call, "Yes?"

"This is Smith at the duty desk. All senior personnel are to report immediately to the Director's conference room. How soon can you be here, Sir?"

"Forty minutes I guess at this time of night. What's going on?"

"Something has happened in Las Vegas. A bombing apparently. They didn't give me any details, Sir, only that it is something major."

Kavanagh kissed his girlfriend. She knew the drill. Grabbing his emergency suitcase, always ready with clothing and toiletries, he was out the door in five minutes.

The meeting convened at midnight at FBI headquarters. Twenty senior FBI officials were present. FBI Director William Sessions opened the meeting.

"Gentlemen. We've had a major terrorist attack in Las Vegas two hours ago. Bally's Hotel and the Tropicana Hotel were targets of at least two separate bombs. Significant casualties. But according to preliminary information, not as bad as it could have been had the bombs been more strategically placed. Before Bernard takes over to give you more details, I want to emphasize that this investigation has top priority. I know you've heard that before, but in this case I mean it. I just got off the phone with the President. Coming on the heels of the El Salvador Embassy attack we now have to consider that this may be part of a larger terrorist campaign directed at the United States. In all aspects, resources, communications, whatever, this investigation ranks priority. Pull out all the stops, gentlemen.

"In a few hours, I'll be meeting with the President and the Cabinet. The White House will be expecting not only more details but what we are doing to identify these terrorists. The lineup is like this: Bernard, as Executive Assistant Director for National Security, you will take over direct supervision of the investigation. My job will be to keep the White House off your back by taking care of PR with Congress and the media. But let me tell you, I'm going to need something soon to give the President.

"Bernard. What do we have right now?"

Bernard Saunders looked down at his scribbled notes.

"At approximately 1850 hours Pacific daylight time, a bomb was exploded inside the casino at Bally's Hotel in Las Vegas. A few minutes later, another bomb exploded outside the Tropicana Hotel & Casino. These were not car bombs. Possibly suicide bombs, but we don't think so. The first bomb was detonated in the men's restroom near the registration area at Bally's. I understand that the large casino floor is adjacent to the registration desks. Had the bomb been detonated on the casino floor, causalities might have been in the hundreds. As it was, they're reporting casualties in the dozens. The restroom walls did a lot to contain the blast effects.

"The second explosion occurred at the Tropicana Hotel & Casino two miles south of Bally's on Las Vegas Boulevard approximately ten minutes later. That explosion occurred outside the main front entrance. Casualties of course, but less than at Bally's. Most were people outside in the car drop-off, luggage unloading area. Again, not an optimum location for the terrorists to inflict maximum casualties had they detonated the bomb inside the casino."

The conference room door opened and an agent brought a folder over to Saunders. He looked at the information for only a moment before sharing the contents with his colleagues.

"Interesting information just received from the Vegas field office. It would appear they have discovered what could be a control device for detonating the bombs. Here's a photo."

He passed the photo to the Director.

"It was found on the front seat of a car in front of the Tropicana. The car was heavily damaged by the bomb blast. In the back seat was a victim. We're beginning to process his identity papers. Salvadoran passport which is interesting."

"That would also suggest these were not suicide bombers," Egan Kavanagh said. "No need for a remote control if you're just going to blow yourself up."

"Then why the poor choice of locations for maximizing damage?" Someone said.

"Poor construction of the detonation system?" Someone else said.

"In both cases?" Someone else said. "Suggests maybe a flawed design?"

"In any case we have our first piece of forensics," Saunders said. "It's on its way to the Quantico lab right now."

"What about the perpetrators? Are any among the dead?" Director Sessions said.

"Only the guy in the back seat of the car with the control device in the front seat at this time, Sir. Assuming the control is associated with the bomb not just a model airplane radio control which it appears to be," Saunders said.

"So where do we stand at the moment, Bernard?" The Director said.

"We're in the process of getting more than a hundred agents to Vegas by the end of the day. More over the next several days. The Vegas field office is securing a working area and communications links. Larry Scofield, Chief of Forensics and Egan Kavanagh, Chief of Counterterrorism will accompany me to Las Vegas within the hour. I will handle any media briefings from the Federal level.

"The crime scenes have been well secured. Road blocks and airport security checks were initiated immediately but that will be largely useless since there are no descriptions. The next step is the laborious work of sifting for more forensic evidence of bomb fragments. Parallel to this is the identification, followed by the vetting of all the causalities. Whether suicide perpetrators or unlucky bad guys, we'll find out if any are among the dead. The extra manpower will largely be focused on hundreds of interviews of witnesses."

"Any reason to believe this might be the same group that did the El Salvador Embassy bombing?" The Director asked.

"Egan?" Saunders said.

"Too early to speculate, Sir," Kavanagh said. "The dead Salvadoran makes an interesting link if he turns out to be a bad guy. However if this remote control hobby device turns out to be modified for triggering a bomb device then we have a probable similarity of bomb construction. The signature of a bomb designer lies in the detonation method. If we can find bomb fragments, that could be very important too. We'll also know better when Larry's people identify the type of explosive used. I'll say this though; the bombs were particularly well positioned for maximum effect in the El Salvador bombing. Successfully detonated remotely with the perpetrators all getting away. If it was the same group, Vegas did not come off as well for them. We'll just have to get more evidence to see if they're connected. There's always the possibility it's a badly executed copy by another group."

Victor Castell walked south on Las Vegas Boulevard to the Hacienda Hotel & Casino. To account for his somewhat disheveled appearance, he commented to the desk clerk on his bad luck. First the airline loses his luggage then Las Vegas is bombed. Airport gets shutdown. Taxis all taken. Had to walk here. Not the start of a good weekend.

If he was ever questioned, he was a graduate student with an address in Pasadena. No false name. Paid for the hotel with a credit card in his name. The only hole in his story was how he got to Las Vegas. No plane ticket record. No car. But it should never come to that. He would stay a couple of days in Las Vegas just like Molina had planned. The larger question was whether any of the group survived the rigged bombs. He might know better in a couple of days by the news reports. To be on the safe side, he would make amends with his father and stay with him in San Francisco until things became clearer.

But what about Patricia still in El Salvador? Would he ever see her again? With Molina dead, there was no way to contact her short of returning to El Salvador. That was impossible. And if he did see her, what would he tell her about what happened? Would he admit to his sabotage? She was a committed revolutionary. These were her colleagues that he killed. She had been equally committed to Santiago Molina. Not likely she would be sympathetic to what he did. She was lost to him. It had to be that way. If he was to bury the terrible events of the last several months, that meant forfeiting any hopes of ever reconnecting with Patricia Reyes.

CHAPTER 14

It had been four weeks since the Las Vegas bombings. All of the victims had been accounted for except for the remains of two men in the restroom at Bally's. Three others in the restroom at the time were identified by identification still intact on the destroyed bodies and confirmed by DNA against the list of known missing people.

At the Tropicana, the FBI had a wealth of physical evidence. The most important was a strong certainty that three of the victims of the explosion were the terrorist bombers. The dead man in the back seat of the car and another nearer to the where the bomb was detonated had Salvadoran passports. But the passports were forgeries according to Salvadoran authorities. The same for another one of the dead who held a French passport. There were no hotel registration records for any of the three. No airline tickets issued. The car with the dead man in the back seat was a Los Angeles rental. Rented by the French passport holder at LAX several days earlier. Fingerprints of the two dead suspects outside the Tropicana were found in the car with the radio control.

In addition to the bodies, the FBI also had the radio frequency control found in the front seat with the dead terrorist in the back. It was a popular control for model airplane hobbyists. There was no model airplane in the trunk adding weight to the theory that it was the radio transmitter for the bombs. By tracing back the serial number to the manufacturer, they eventually identified that it was distributed to one of four stores in the greater Los Angeles area. Based upon the radio frequency control, the detonation circuit most likely consisted of the same hobbyist RF receiving gear that would be contained within a model airplane.

The explosive material was identified as Semtex by various residue samples. Same as in the El Salvador bombing.

At FBI headquarters, Bernard Saunders chaired a meeting of various heads of the different units of his National Security Branch of the FBI. The country had resumed normality but the White House maintained continued pressure to advance the investigation. What terrorist group executed the attacks? How many got away? Who are they? Was this state-sponsored?

"Ok, Egan, what's your best guess about these terrorists?"

"Our best guess is it's the same group that did the Salvadoran embassy bombing. Same basic method using radio frequency transmission to remotely detonate military-grade explosives. Both attacks were on American targets. Residue suggests the same Semtex was used by its chemistry signature. When they took credit for the embassy bombing, they threatened further action against the U.S. And of course, we have two perps with false Salvador ID's."

"We got one print from the embassy bombing. Any match with these dead guys?" Saunders said referring to the one fingerprint recovered from a fragment of the Salvadoran bomb.

"No. No match. Most likely the print came from the guy who put these bombs together. He's probably still out there."

"So what happened?" Saunders said.

"These were not suicide bombings. So it was some careless technical mistake, or sabotage."

"Sabotage? That's quite a leap. By who?"

"No way to know. And it's just a possibility. But if it was a technical mistake, this engineer made the same mistake twice with both bombs. The circuits are not that complicated. So that would be unbelievably stupid. And yet this engineer understood electronics well enough to construct a receiver from scratch for the Salvadoran bombs. This guy's no dummy."

"And why make the receiving device from scratch in El Salvador if you can just buy this stuff in a hobby shop?"

"My guess is it might be harder to find model airplanes in a backwater like El Salvador."

"So back to your theory about sabotage."

"It's not my theory, Bernie, just a possibility that cannot be ruled out considering the evidence. But if that is what happened, you could speculate on several possible causes. Some sort of resentment? A leadership struggle? Jealousy? A woman maybe? But if in fact it was sabotage, then one thing is clear. The guy who did it is probability not among the dead. Most likely it was the bomb maker."

"And he's still out there?" Saunders said.

"That's what we think. But on a more positive note, the leader of this group may be among the dead perpetrators," Kavanagh said. "We know his real name. He's the body with the French passport. His real name is Santiago Molina. Salvadoran by birth. Seems he lived in France for a time. Fingerprints are on file with the French Police Nationale from his authentic passport. "

"And what suggests he's the leader?"

"His age. He's much older than the other dead guys in their early twenties. The Salvadorans haven't identified the other three by the way. Not likely they ever will, or if they do, it might be self-serving. The Salvadoran government will most likely offer up identities of some otherwise already dead rebels."

"Your prejudice is showing, Egan. Get to the point," Saunders said.

"Well, beyond his age, he clearly moved in different circles from others who appear to probably be just soldiers. According to French immigration records, Molina enrolled in school in France at the age of twelve. Mother reportedly died of natural causes in 1960. His father was an investment broker with ties to Europe. In fact, the young Molina was placed in the custody of one of his father's business associates in Paris.

"And here is where it gets more interesting. The Paris business associate, one Pablo Valverde, was an expatriate Salvadoran. According to the French, he had Communist leanings with suspected ties to Cuba. He was on their low-level watch list. Valverde died of natural causes in 1979. Molina took over his surrogate family's investment brokerage business. Then Molina's own father was killed by the Salvadoran Treasury Police in 1980. According to them, the senior Molina was smuggling weapons to the rebel FLMN. So this Santiago Molina had a personal history with the Salvadoran civil war.

"Lots of influences that could have led to his radicalization. Molina's international business travels would have provided excellent cover. Easy to contact whomever he partnered with for the logistical support. Could have been Libya, the IRA, the Palestinian PFLP, maybe the Basque separatist organization ETA. Maybe Cuba. Somewhere along the line, he found his engineer to design remote electronic detonating devices. The engineer and the Semtex could have come from any of these sources. The false passports on the other hand suggest more sophistication. Most likely from a state-sponsored intelligence organization. The most active in that arena are the Cubans. Since this occurred in Latin America, they're the most likely source for Molina's support."

"Like the Salvadorans suggested," Saunders said.

Kavanagh said, "Come on, Bernie. Like most bullshit there's usually some part that is true. The Cubans provide support for leftist revolutionary movements but are not known to sponsor terrorist groups. What the Salvadorans wanted to promote was an escalation of the rebel's capability with outside support, pointedly Cuban support to get our attention. They're so incompetent it was probably just a guess anyway. The FLMN didn't launch an attack on Las Vegas."

"Back to this Molina. What else?" Saunders said.

"We have inquiries out to all friendly countries to search travel entry records to see if we can get a picture of his movements. But considering his cover line of work, he could have easily obscured the trail. Still looking at the Cuban angle with the help of the CIA. Unfortunately even with all the anti-Castro expatriate sentiment in Florida, the CIA still has poor human assets in Cuba, and no one of stature inside the Cuban Dirección General de Inteligencia where any support would have originated."

"And from what you have so far, you conclude he was the probable leader?"

"Bernie, in the intelligence field what we have is compelling. Besides, it would not make sense that someone with his background would be in the trenches with the guys that placed the bombs."

"Well obviously that was what he was doing. Got himself blown to pieces. Why was he doing the field work? The bomb detonating control was in the front seat of the car. Why did he leave the car?" Saunders said.

"No way to be sure, but obviously something must have gone wrong. We've ruled out somebody prematurely detonating the Tropicana bomb with the control device, like the dead guy in the backseat, since the Bally's bomb exploded before the Tropicana bomb, and the transmitter was well out of range to trigger the Bally's bomb. Best guess is whatever happened occurred within the triggering mechanism to both bombs."

"What's next?"

"The remaining question of course is attempting to determine how many others were involved. There were three dead at the Tropicana, but we have narrowed it to only one at Bally's. That would not make sense. We think that there must have been at least one, maybe two others involved at Bally's. One of which is probably the bomb designer. We don't think Molina designed the triggering mechanism himself even with bomb-making training. The electronics in the El Salvador bombs suggested advanced knowledge in electronics. The engineer remains our greatest future threat. He's got the knowledge and the motivation. If he came on loan from another terrorist group then we'll see his work again. And of course, the White House would like to know who gave Molina his support."

CHAPTER 15

Unknown to Castell, Patricia Reyes had been in Las Vegas all this time, having arrived with Carlos Perez in the second rental car. She was now sitting in the lounge in the Bally's Casino area. She was dressed in designer jeans, black heels, and a low-cut white blouse. Her long dark hair cascaded about her shoulders. A gold chain hung low to her cleavage with matching hoop earrings. She fit in with the other attractive people in the lounge. A glass of white wine remained untouched on the small round table.

The plan called for Miguel Cortina to enter the men's restroom off the registration area adjacent to the large casino floor. He would arm the bomb and come to sit with Reyes. He would order a beer. Reyes would ask the cocktail waitress to watch their drinks and luggage while they each went to the restroom. They would both leave the casino. Perez would be watching and drive the rental car to pick them up. All of this was to happen with precise timing. As Perez would be pulling away, Santiago Molina would drive close to the entrance. The bomb would be triggered killing scores of people in the heavily populated gambling area on an early Saturday night.

Reyes looked at her watch. Cortina should show up at the table in two minutes. She was exceedingly nervous. Soon there would be thirty pounds of high explosive sitting at her feet. The bomb would be armed waiting only for the radio signal.

The explosion knocked her from her chair. The lounge was far enough away from the restrooms for the pressure wave to become non-lethal, yet still destructive. Like others in the lounge, she was knocked to the floor. The noise left her disoriented. She sat on the floor for at least a minute before attempting to rise unsteadily. What happened?

Slowly her brain began to processes what had taken place. Their bomb had gone off. Prematurely. Miguel must have done something wrong. How close had she come to being killed? She had to get to Carlos. Get away from this mess.

Reyes left as quickly as possible maneuvering around overturned tables and chairs. There were others getting up slowly from the floor while others were scrambling to escape the scene in panic. Dust wafted from the reception area. The bright lights had gone out to be replaced by emergency battery lighting. No sound of the constant clanking din of the slot machines. There was substantial devastation as she got closer to the hotel reception area. She could see people still on the floor. Once outside she looked frantically for Carlos. Suddenly he was at her arm pulling her along.

Carlos Perez had dropped into the line of cars inching toward the entrance doors to rendezvous at the designated time with Reyes and Cortina when the bomb detonated. Something had gone very wrong. All the vehicle traffic coming and going toward the front entrance to the hotel and casino came to a halt. Drivers stood beside their cars trying to understand what was going on. The premature explosion meant that both Reyes and Cortina had probably been killed. But he had to know so he proceeded to walk to the front doors.

Before he reached the doors, he saw Reyes exit the building. He quickly escorted her to the car then slowly pulled away. Police and fire sirens could be heard approaching.

"What happened?" Perez said. He could see she wasn't visibly injured.

She was still disoriented but managed to say, "I don't know. I was in the lounge waiting for Miguel. Next thing I know, I'm on the floor. He must have done something wrong. Where is Santiago?"

"I don't know. He's not here yet. But the schedule called for him to arrive several minutes from now. Best not to wait though. He'll find us at the hotel. We'll get the news of the bomb going off at the Tropicana."

She located a local AM news station on the car radio.

This is KDWN Las Vegas with breaking news. Police report an explosion at Bally's Hotel and Casino a short time ago at approximately seven o'clock this evening. This was followed by another explosion at the Tropicana Hotel just ten minutes later. Sketchy reports suggest significant casualties, with fatalities at both locations.

While the explosion at Bally's occurred inside the building, police report that the explosion at the Tropicana was outside the main entrance. An unidentified police official speaking unofficially suggested they almost certainly were bombs. Police and fire units are on site at both locations. Our Caroline Davis is in route to Bally's to provide a firsthand account of the situation from that scene while John Buckner is making his way to the Tropicana. We'll resume normal programming until further information becomes available at which time we'll interrupt with updated news on the explosions on the Strip.

"Outside? They said the bomb exploded *outside* the Tropicana, Carlos. That wasn't Santiago's plan. It went wrong too."

Perez did not respond. He drove at the speed limit north on Las Vegas Boulevard. He was headed downtown to the Union Plaza Hotel. There were three rooms reserved under a false name. Santiago Molina had a reservation at the Golden Nugget just a couple of blocks away. Perez and Reyes would wait for Molina to make contact. If the same thing happened at the Tropicana than Salas may have suffered the same fate as Cortina at Bally's. But Molina should have been in the car waiting to trigger the bomb. He would show up and tell them what to do.

Perez checked in for all three rooms using a credit card that matched his false identification. Reyes took one room but spent the next several hours waiting in Perez's room. Expecting Molina, they ordered room service not wanting to be away from the room or telephone. There was nothing new in the continual television reporting. Police were reporting that at least some of the terrorists were thought to be among the dead but forensic identification would take time. Perez and Reyes knew that Miguel Cortina was surely dead. By the reports, probably Roberto Salas as well. But what of Santiago Molina and Jose Aguilar? There were no reports of arrests. And what about Victor?

Reyes spent a sleepless night returning to Perez's room early the next morning. No contact from Santiago. Nothing new on the television. They decided to spend another day before leaving Las Vegas. They needed to make their way back to El Salvador. Perez told her it was important not to leave a trail. The false identifications on Cortina and Salas would reveal them as Salvadoran. The U.S. authorities would by now have made that connection although not released to the public. That would suggest a connection with the U.S. Embassy bombing in San Salvador. Leaving by air, even from Los Angeles, would be out of the question.

Perez had a sudden unsettling thought he now shared with Reyes. Their car had been rented at the Los Angeles International Airport. So had the other car Santiago was driving. That car would now be in police custody with the trail leading back to LAX. The FBI must be looking for any other rental cars rented by Salvadorans not only at LAX but other airports as well.

"So what are we to do, Carlos?"

"Leave the car in a parking lot of some other hotel. Take a bus south to Los Angeles. From there we take a train to San Diego. We'll walk across the border into Mexico. We'll take a flight out of Tijuana."

"Back to El Salvador?"

"No. Too soon. The Americans will be assisting the Salvadorans looking for anyone returning from the United States. Tijuana is too close to the United States. So we'll go to Mexico City. Spend a few days there before returning to El Salvador. We'll use our real names and passports in case there is something wrong with these false documents."

"Wrong? What could be wrong with them? We got into the United States using them. Why use our real names?" she said.

Perez looked at her for moment before answering. "Because there is much we do not know. Do the Americans and therefore the Salvadoran government know us by our false identities? Whatever happened to Victor? He was not one of us in Las Vegas. Only the threat of harm to you made him help us. If he was taken by the American police he knows too much about us."

"Victor knows our real names, Carlos."

Perez paused. "Yes, you're right. But we have no choice but to risk that. If the Americans know our identity there will be no escape anyway. Their reach is too long. Let us hope that Victor escaped like we did. Or that he is dead."

She was jarred by the thought that Victor might be dead. Everything had fallen apart.

Within a week Carlos Perez and Patricia Reyes were back in El Salvador. Both were uncertain as to what they would do. Santiago Molina was either dead or on the run. His terrorist group was destroyed. If he resurfaced, would Perez and Reyes rejoin him? They both talked about that. Both decided no. Both decided there were better prospects then desperate acts of terrorism for a political cause. Las Vegas changed everything.

The few days spent in Mexico City before returning to El Salvador provided some emotional relief. Perez still had lots of cash and the credit card given to him by Molina. But he realized the credit card might be compromised. So he paid cash at the hotel when he checked out leaving no paper trail other than their fake passport identities. With Mexican police incompetence, the Americans would probably never track them to Mexico City.

But those days in Mexico City led to something else. The stress and fear were pushed into the background. They were like young people anywhere ready to enjoy good food, drinks, and good times. Perez had always been attracted to Patricia Reyes. How could he not be? She was pretty with all the right curves. But of course she was the girlfriend of Victor Castell. Hard to compete against the allure of a rich, educated American. All Perez had going were his good looks and a muscular physique.

This was not lost on Reyes. She was attracted to Perez before meeting Victor. Now Victor was gone. Forever. He was a mistake. A gringo from a different social environment. A fairy tale romance. He was never part of the struggle for El Salvador. He was never one of them. It was only because of her that he joined Santiago Molina. Although only weeks, it seemed like much longer since they parted. He was already receding from her thoughts. Time to return to reality. Under the influence of a night of music and too much tequila, she laid her hand on Carlos' arm. Looking into his eyes she said, "I've had enough to drink. Let's go back to the hotel."

CHAPTER 16

It had been over four weeks since the terrorist attack in Las Vegas. The death toll was twenty-two with another thirty-four injured. Remarkably light considering the potential if the bombs had been placed and detonated as the terrorists must have intended.

Egan Kavanagh was briefing his boss Bernard Saunders and FBI Director Sessions on the status of the investigation.

"We have identified four of the dead as terrorists. Process of elimination by ruling out all the other casualties. Three had false Salvadoran identifications. They have now all been identified. The fourth terrorist, the one with the French passport was also Salvadoran by birth. Santiago Molina. We're now fairly certain he was the leader."

"What convinces you he was the leader Mr. Kavanagh?" Director Sessions said.

"His background. Father was killed by the Salvadoran government. He was raised in France by a family acquaintance with leftist ties. Those ties extended to Cuba. We believe that the technical support was from the Cuban DGI. False documents. Semtex explosives. Other leads are still being pursued.

"Molina also used credit cards in the name of his investment firm. The French have been most cooperative in investigating Molina's firm known as Central American Investments S.A. Examinations of the small corporation's books suggests non-business related funding. Since those funds did not wash through the corporation, it wasn't money laundering. Fairly clear it was funding for his terrorist cell. The source of these funds has been obscured, but one of the cutouts has a past that involves Cuba."

"Can you prove direct Cuban involvement?" Sessions said.

"Not enough for the White House to make a real stink about, Bill," Saunders said.

"Go ahead Mr. Kavanagh."

"The curious aspect of the attack was it went very wrong for the bad guys this time around."

"What makes that curious? Terrorists blow themselves up all of the time don't they?" Sessions said.

"True, Sir. But here there are some inconsistencies. The first explosion at Bally's would appear to be just that, some failure of the design that caused premature explosion. The guy was in the restroom probably to arm the bomb. Maybe he did something wrong to explode it prematurely.

"But the situation at the Tropicana raised some questions. Three terrorists died there. Why were there two of them close to the bomb when it detonated instead of just one like at Bally's? One was this Santiago Molina himself. Why does the leader expose himself like that?

"Then we have the third terrorist in the rental car. He's in the back seat yet the control transmitter is sitting in the front seat."

"How'd he die?"

"Got his head nearly taken off as the shock wave blew the side window glass of the car into his head. Since he was in the back seat and the control in the front, he would appear not to be the trigger man.

"As the leader, we believe that Molina would have been the one to trigger the bomb. In fact we believe the single control we found in the front seat of the car with the dead guy in the back was possibly to activate both bombs. It had two separate control circuits. Molina's fingerprints were on the steering wheel and the remote control. Why did he leave the car? That we don't know."

"What about others from this terrorist group? Did some get away?" Sessions asked.

"We don't know, but the short answer is probably. The Salvadorans have been largely uncooperative in pursuing an investigation in El Salvador. If it was here in the U.S. we would be talking to anyone Molina ever came into contact with. Business associates, social acquaintances, girlfriends. No help there from the Salvadorans. The best we got from them is just the identities of the other three perpetrators. The only thing we have is a questionable allegation that Molina's investment firm was a front for channeling funds to the FLMN rebels. That's according to Colonel Benavides. Problem is he has not backed it up with any tangible evidence.

"But that aside, we're pretty sure the guy that engineered these bombs is still out there. Same guy that did the embassy bombs. Probably on loan from some European or Middle Eastern group. The only way we might confirm that is by some future bomb with the same construction signature."

"Doesn't sound like he might be a credible threat after the failure in Vegas. Didn't both bombs malfunction?" Sessions said.

"That still troubles us, Sir. The embassy bombing in San Salvador worked as they planned. More than that, the radio frequency triggering mechanism was constructed from individual components. Fairly sophisticated work. The detonation circuits in the Vegas bombs were commercially available radio control devices. Wouldn't seem to be the work of someone that would make a fundamental design error. Then you have two separate incidents of the bombs detonating prematurely. That would suggest it wasn't an accident related to some error in assembly. Sabotage cannot be ruled out."

"You're suggesting the guy who put these bombs together may have sabotaged them? But you have nothing to support that other than these seeming inconsistencies, is that correct?" Sessions said.

"Yes, Sir," Kavanagh said. "Either way, it doesn't necessarily help us identify him. He's still a threat. Unfortunately we have no promising leads. This terrorist cell originated in El Salvador. That's where any useful information must come from. The Salvadorans have been an obstacle by not letting us participate in whatever investigation they're conducting, or were conducting. It's getting stale by now with the passage of so many weeks. The State Department and the Pentagon have not weighed in to push the Salvadorans. So unless something develops from El Salvador, we have nothing to really pursue at this time. The bomb maker will eventually turn up somewhere. Probably after another bomb goes off. But even with that serious loose end, this terrorist group appears to no longer exist."

PART TWO

Southern California
2014

Victor Castell opened the remote controlled gate to his large property in South Pasadena. It was a grand home constructed in the 1920's on a large lot. The home had been extensively renovated in the 1970's. Castell purchased it during the recession of 2009 when property values plummeted. He sunk another $500,000 dollars into another modernization renovation.

Things had gone well for Castell after the unfortunate detour in his life twenty-five years ago. Those wrenching memories still brought an internal shudder. It was impossible to rationalize why he could have ever veered down such a path. Could be blamed on a woman but that really didn't explain how he could have descended into killing people. From the perspective of middle-age maturity, it was totally inexplicable.

The single memory he dwelled upon was Patricia Reyes. He let thoughts of her often intrude. Thoughts of making love to her, thoughts of her flashing eyes, her passion. They had loved. What ever happened to her? He had always been too scared to try to pursue making contact. She was in El Salvador. No way to find a means of locating her. He couldn't use his cousin Hector. No one left from Molina's group. Not a good idea to telephone the one contact number he had at the restaurant used to communicate with Santiago Molina. Castell couldn't return himself to El Salvador after being deported.

It took many years to concede that he would never again see Patricia Reyes. Emotionally that was difficult. Practically he understood that was for the best. Certainly safest. She and Carlos Perez were the only people that could directly implicate him in the bombings. A lot of Americans had died because of him. He was a mass murderer. He would receive the death penalty. Ever seeing her again was just a sexual fantasy.

In solitary moments after several Scotches, Castell sometimes forced himself to revisit his escape from Santiago Molina. It had been a gamble. He got lucky. Beat the Vegas odds. His plan worked before Molina could kill him. Lucky again when he escaped the effects of the bomb exploding outside the Tropicana. Salas might have activated the sabotaged arming circuit while the bomb was still in the trunk of the car. The vision of Jose Aguilar's destroyed head still brought a disturbing memory.

A couple of days in Las Vegas allowed him to compose himself. To rehearse what would become his story for the remainder of his life. To his father he explained his inability to return to El Salvador. He had fallen in with some students through contact with his Uncle Augustin. There was a girl. There was a confrontation with Salvadoran security police. The girl was beaten. He lied by explaining she was arrested. He feared she may have been tortured, probably killed. Being an American from a prominent Salvadoran family, he was put on a plane and ordered never to return.

This occurred just prior to the embassy bombing that took the life of his mother. After the death of his mother, he could not concentrate on his graduate studies at Caltech. He needed a couple of months. His father understood and quickly wanted to help his son. For three months he stayed with his father in San

Francisco, putting some distance between himself and Pasadena until he could assess the situation.

With eventual news that the terrorist leader Santiago Molina and most of his group had died in the Las Vegas bombings, Castell felt a measure of relief. There might yet be a life if he could bury this deep enough. Of course Patricia Reyes and Carlos Perez were still out there, though probably not in the United States. If they were ever arrested, would they implicate him? No reason they should suspect he sabotaged the bombs. Hopefully they would just consider him lucky like they were to escape the failed attack. Maybe they would just stay silent. Maybe they too were now dead. If they remained in El Salvador during the early nineties, the civil war there turned increasingly ugly in its final years. Death squads affiliated with the ruling political party and condoned by the military resumed their reign of terror. The rebel FLMN retaliated often in kind. Most likely both Reyes and Perez rejoined the insurgency in some capacity.

Over the years the past gradually receded further from a tangible threat to a nagging bad memory. A memory of terrible guilt, but guilt can always be managed. It was increasingly unlikely that those terrible few months so long ago would ever intrude into his present life. If he had left any tracks, the FBI would long ago have caught up with him. Castell could never be totally comfortable, but neither was there a constant fear that the past would ever intrude.

Returning eventually to Pasadena, Victor Castell graduated from Caltech in the early nineties with a master's degree in computer science and a dual degree in mathematics. His exceptional mathematical ability put a unique bent on his approach to designing certain complex software. He took his first job with a small software firm in Santa Monica doing business with the Department of Defense. He was assigned to a project team tasked with developing encryption security. It was here that Castell found his niche in software security. He was not only able to break through the team's newly created security wall, but to also demonstrate the failed approach that was the foundation of most software security at the time. From there he successfully developed a new generation of software. His groundbreaking work led to a new project group within the firm with Castell at its head.

After a couple of years, Castell knew he could be successful on his own. He knew the market needs of the military and the government. He knew the contracting process. His name was becoming well regarded in the exploding software security field. His startup company was a success from the beginning. Each year saw double digit growth. Surprisingly he found he was both a good business man and a competent manager. He attracted first rate people and was able to keep them. The projects were challenging. He still guided the technology. Unchecked funding was awash as information technology exploded in the nineties with the advent of the Internet. Systems security was Castell's special niche. His firm had their pick of lucrative projects in both the public and private sectors.

Financial success with work he loved was only part of Victor Castell's transformation from nascent terrorist to successful entrepreneur. Married sixteen years, Eleanor Castell had the looks of a trophy wife, along with a high intellect. She was a successful attorney. They met as he was incorporating his growing business, she being the business law specialist assigned to his project by the law firm.

The marriage was successful. They had one daughter now age fifteen. Smart like her parents with inherited good looks. Eleanor continued practicing law. They enjoyed the same things. The house was full of art, an indulgence shared by both. Pasadena was not far from the theater area of downtown Los Angeles. They both enjoyed theater and the philharmonic at the Disney Concert Hall. Eleanor kept them socially engaged with an eclectic range of stimulating friends.

That was all to change on a beautiful fall day in late November. Unlike much of arid Southern California, the greater Pasadena area was blessed with a fair amount of deciduous trees that were turning colors with the approaching cooler weather.

Castell's company offices were located on a quiet tree-lined street. His personal office took in a view of a small park across the street. He was reading the Los Angeles Times at his desk. The headline read *Major Gang Arrest in Pico Union*. The article was about a major police confrontation two nights ago. Federal and local law enforcement had moved to arrest top members of the vicious MS-13 ethnically Central American gang that originated in Los Angeles. Their violent brand had spread to other American cities. Reading the caption underneath four pictures, Castell abruptly recoiled spilling some coffee from his cup.

One photo identified a Carlos Perez. A Salvadoran national. Was this the Carlos Perez he knew? Could be him. It had been a long time. The arrest photo made everyone look different. Unlike the other three pictured, the one identified as Perez did not sport the traditional MS-13 extreme tattoos on the face and neck. Yes, it could be the Carlos Perez he once knew. The more Castell studied the photograph, the more he became convinced.

Castell had hoped that Perez and Reyes were in El Salvador. What was Perez doing in the United States? And now part of this Mara Salvatrucha gang? Worse yet, Perez was in a U.S. jail. The article listed a long string of federal and state criminal charges. Would Perez's past terrorist activities be discovered?

The telephone rang. Castell answered. His administrative assistant announced, "There is a Patricia Reyes in the office asking to see you. She said it was a personal matter, Mr. Castell."

He held the telephone hand set, frozen without responding.

"Mr. Castell? Are you there? Shall I send her in?"

He felt dizzy then took a deep breath, "Yes. Send her in."

The office door opened. Patricia Reyes entered, closing the door behind her. Turning around she just looked at Victor Castell still sitting behind his desk.

"Victor. It's been a very long time."

CHAPTER 18

Patricia Reyes made her way away from the Pico Union motel on foot for a distance of close to a mile. She did not know Los Angeles. Had no idea where to go. Wanted by the police, she was confused and close to panic. How did the police know her name? Her false identification was now useless. What happened to Carlos? Arrested? Killed? Escaped? How would she get out of the United States without him?

Best to get far away from this area. The only place she knew of in Southern California was Pasadena. Victor had lived there briefly before Las Vegas. He mentioned on the phone that it was close to Los Angeles. Reyes was fortunate to hail a taxi stopped at a traffic light. The driver was probably going home. One more fare for the night, this one a pretty woman. There ensued a frustrating discussion with the Middle Eastern cab driver who struggled with both English and Spanish.

"Not safe for woman alone. Why you out walking?"

"Never mind. Take me to a hotel. In Pasadena."

"Pasadena? Where?"

"To a hotel. Any hotel. A cheap hotel. One that does not cost too much."

"Which hotel?"

"I don't know. Any hotel. Not too much money. You choose."

The driver eventually understood. Reyes marveled at all of the traffic even this late at night. Twenty minutes later the taxi drove up to a motel just south of the 210 Freeway on the east side of Pasadena.

"This motel cheapest I think," the taxi driver said.

"Gracias."

Reyes paid the fare and checked in using a fictitious name of a childhood friend. She would pay with cash so the name was not important. Perez had left a few hundred dollars in his bag. She didn't dare use the credit card in the false name that matched the false U.S. passport. The police knew that name. How was she to escape back to El Salvador with no money?

She was exhausted but sleep was fitful. In the morning her situation still looked bleak. She was wanted by the police. Alone, far from the border and escape into Mexico. Would the police be looking at the trains and buses? The cash would only sustain her for a few days.

Coming to Pasadena had been a frantic reaction to distance herself from the Pico Union neighborhood. An act of desperation only because Victor Castell might still live in Pasadena, or somewhere in the Los Angeles area. She had no other alternatives.

Over coffee at a restaurant down the street from the motel, Reyes thought about the possibility of seeing Victor again. He could provide her with money enough to get out of the United States. He would do that. Even if he felt betrayed by her never contacting him after Las Vegas. What happened to him after Las Vegas? How would she possibly find him? He might be living anywhere. This was desperation, but she had no other plan.

Back at the motel, Reyes decided to ask the young Latina desk clerk how she might locate someone. She hoped Victor might be living somewhere in Los Angeles or some city close by in this endless sea of people.

"Do you have a telephone book," Reyes asked the clerk in Spanish.

"Telephone book? I don't think there is such a thing anymore. Just call information."

"How do I do that?"

"Use your cell phone and dial 411," the clerk said giving Reyes a look that suggested she was from another planet.

"Who are you trying to call? I'll call for you."

"The name is Victor Castell."

"What city?"

"I don't know. I hoped he might live in Los Angeles. Or maybe somewhere close by. He once lived here in Pasadena."

"Lots of cities around Los Angeles. Why don't you google him?"

"What? I don't know what you mean."

The clerk shook her head. "You ever use a computer?"

"No."

The clerk thought, what an idiot. This pretty woman must be a real airhead. Dumb middle-aged Latina that didn't know how to use a cellphone or computer.

"I'll show you," the clerk said leading Reyes over to a computer reserved for guests.

Sitting down with Reyes looking over her shoulder the young woman clicked the browser icon on the screen. "So I bring up Google. That's why it's called googling. You can search for anything in the world here."

"So we'll google *Victor Castell*. How about looking at images? Maybe you'll get lucky if your guy has his picture online. You know what this guy looks like, right?"

"Yes. But it's been a very long time. Twenty-five years."

The clerk brought up images for Victor Castell in the Google search. "Here, you scroll through these and see if you recognize your guy. Wow, twenty-five years. Old boyfriend? He must look different now. Just hold the mouse like this and keep clicking down. Holler when you think you see him."

The face was only down a few rows. It looked like it *could* be Victor. Hair was different. Some age lines in the face. Still handsome though. She scrolled down further and found another photo of apparently the same man from a different angle.

Reyes said to the young woman only a few feet away at the front desk, "I think this might be his picture. Actually these two pictures. What do I do next?"

The woman came over, took the mouse, and clicked on the image Reyes pointed to. An article from the Wall Street Journal came up.

"Says here this Victor Castell is the CEO of some company. A software company. The article's about computer security. His company apparently has contracts with the federal government. Wow! Must be rich. Says here he's forty-seven. Nice looking. That the age of your guy?"

Reyes was not listening to the girl any longer as she read the article for herself. "Yes. That's about right." She found what she needed further down in the article. The company, Castell Systems, was headquartered right here in Pasadena."

"How do I find where this company is located?"

"Just go back up here and type in Castell Systems."

The Castell Systems website came up in the Google search. The clerk opened the website for her.

Getting the hang of the navigation, Reyes clicked on the history tab. There was a brief bio of the founder and CEO, Victor Castell. Electrical engineering undergraduate degree from California State Polytechnic Institute in Pomona, California. Master's degree in computer science from Caltech, Pasadena. Lived early life in Panama since his father was a senior Canal administrator. It was Victor's background. The displayed photo clearly convinced her that this was Victor. The contact tab gave her the address of his office. She wrote it down on a slip of paper.

"Want his home address?" the girl asked.

"No. I've got the company address. Can you tell me if this is far from here?"

"The girl looked at the address. Probably not. It's a Pasadena address. Don't know the street. But I'll pull up Google Maps and we'll see how far."

It was Saturday. She would have to wait until business hours on Monday. The newspaper account told her that Carlos Perez had been arrested. It also said his girlfriend was being sought. Fortunately, her displayed picture was a grainy reprint from her false passport.

CHAPTER 19

Victor Castell was speechless. The shock of his hidden past came rushing forward. Everything he had worked for was now in jeopardy. Why had Patricia Reyes sought him out after all these years?

He got up from his chair uncertain what to do.

She came around to the side of the desk. "A hug? It's been a long time, Victor."

They hugged. The touch of her breasts against him was disconcerting. She was still a beautiful woman. Age had only refined her face. Her body was still exceptional. Well defined breasts displayed in a low-cut blouse with a tight skirt and heels. Her café au lait skin tone stood out against the white of the blouse. A simple gold chain at her neck and gold earrings made for understated sexy elegance.

It was her one good outfit she packed for the trip to Los Angeles. She hoped it would have the desired effect on her old lover.

"Please sit down, Patricia. It's .....it's good to see you."

She smiled but cocked her eyebrow. "Is it, Victor? Maybe I bring back bad memories?"

"Well .....those were days of our youth. Lots of things happened."

"Yes, Victor. We were young. Bad things happened. But I remember we were in love. That I remember fondly. The other things I wish also to forget."

He cleared his throat. "I remember all that too, Patricia. How has your life been since .....since we last ....."

"Since what happened in Las Vegas?"

"Yes. You were fortunate not to have been there, Patricia. Things turned out badly. I was lucky to escape. But apparently Carlos escaped too. His arrest made the front page. Does that have something to do with you being here?"

She lowered her head for a moment before answering.

"Things were difficult after Las Vegas. Santiago was dead. All of our colleagues were dead. Only the three of us escaped. The civil war only got worse in El Salvador. Carlos took up with a rebel group again. I returned to the university but continued to spy for the FLMN.

"I missed you. But I was glad you were safely back in the United States. That was your home. You could never return to El Salvador. I could not come to live in the United States. I was in love with you but we were now lost to each other. Life goes on as I'm sure it has for you. Anyway, you know Carlos always liked me. I kind of liked him before you came along. Things just happened."

"You mean you took up with Carlos? But he's now part of this MS-13 gang. How did that happen?"

"Carlos was forced to flee El Salvador. He was able to get a visa to enter the United States as a political refugee. There's a large Central American community in Los Angeles. He had to find a way to survive. Somehow he connected with other Salvadorans that were part of this gang called the Mara Salvatrucha. Part of it was protection from other gangs. Mexicans, blacks. It was a tough part of Los Angeles. Eventually the civil war ended in El Salvador. Carlos was able to return. We naturally reconnected. Things progressed from there."

"But this gang? They're a bunch of criminals. Why did you become part of that?"

"Not sure I have a good answer. I was with Carlos. He had lots of money. It was good to be able to live a good life. I knew what he was doing was illegal. Most of their money came from the United States. There was not much the United States police could do in El Salvador after the civil war was settled. Carlos became one of the top leaders of the Maras. It was a business. Like yours, Victor."

"Bullshit. They're a gang of murderers. They're known for unbelievable brutality. Now Carlos is in jail. Probably where he should be. With the charges against him he'll be in prison for the rest of his life."

"I know that, Victor."

He now knew why she was here. "The police are looking for you too?"

"Yes."

"Why? Were you part of this gang?"

"Not really. But being with Carlos I know a lot about what went on. The organization. Moving money. How the MS-13 works with the Mexican drug cartels. Information the police would like to know."

"Shit. And you want me to help you? To get away I assume?"

"Yes, Victor. I need to return to El Salvador."

"And how do you intend to do that with the police looking for you?"

"I just need to get to Mexico. I'll just walk across the border. The United States is looking for me under a false name I was using. Once in Mexico I will use my real name to make my way back to El Salvador. I'm almost out of money. I can't use my only credit card."

"So you just want money from me?"

She smiled. "Yes, Victor. And maybe a little help to get to the border. For old times? For the love we once had for each other?"

He took a deep breath. Could he escape this and push this threat deeply into the background once again? Obviously with Carlos Perez incarcerated in the United States he was at some threat if the FBI were to ever connect Perez with the terrorist bombings. He didn't know about Patricia. If she was arrested would she bargain him away? Both him and Carlos? Probably not since she would also be implicating herself. But who knows. Might depend on circumstances. Best for him if she left the country.

"Ok. I can help. I can get you money. Easy enough to take a train to San Diego. You can easily cross over into Tijuana from there."

Patricia knew the route. She and Carlos had made the crossing into Tijuana several times to obscure the trail between the United States and El Salvador. But she wouldn't risk the train.

"I'll need to go to the bank and get cash," Castell said. "I can bring it to you around noon. Where are you staying?"

She gave him a card from the motel. "I'm in room 118. I appreciate this, Victor. I know this is difficult resurrecting old memories. But I didn't have any other choice."

He gave a pained smile. "It's ok. Glad I can help. I'll see you in a couple of hours. Here, take what little cash I have and take a taxi back to the motel."

Patricia took the money and abruptly gave him a kiss on the cheek. "Thank you, Victor."

At the bank Castell withdrew nine thousand dollars in cash. It should be enough. Below the required currency transaction reporting threshold of ten thousand dollars required by financial institutions to report to federal authorities. He would get the money to Patricia and get her on a train. Maybe at a station other than Los Angeles' Union Station. Might the police have her physical description? She was probably a high profile fugitive.

On his cell phone, he looked up the train schedules and station locations. The next closest alternative for Amtrak to San Diego was Fullerton. That was about forty-five minutes to the south of Pasadena. Better than the potential risk of Union Station. That meant he would probably have to drive her there. He didn't want her hostile toward him. Just get her the hell away from here. He would make a point of instructing her not to tell Carlos that he existed should she ever make contact with him sometime in the future. Another reason to be accommodating to her.

Castell pulled into the parking lot of the motel in his silver Mercedes. He felt a little conspicuous so he pulled into a space at the rear of the hotel away from the line of sight of the motel's front office. No one was visible outside as he knocked on the door of room 118.

Patricia opened the door after asking who was there. He entered and looked again to see if anyone was visible. He closed the door.

She put her hand on his upper arm. "Thank you for doing this, Victor. I know I'm an unwelcome surprise. You'll soon be rid of me."

He smiled weakly. "It's certainly a surprise, Patricia, but not unwelcome."

She smiled back broadly. "Then I'm not all bad news for you? I wondered what happened to you, Victor. Perhaps you thought of me as well?"

He just nodded.

She came closer. Now standing in front of him, "I thought about everything we shared for those brief weeks so long ago, Victor. Do you ever fantasize about our lovemaking?"

Castell's face tightened. All he could do was stare at her. She was wearing the same outfit from that morning. His eyes traveled down instinctively to her cleavage with the top two buttons of her blouse now unfastened. She grasped his head in both her hands and kissed him fully with her mouth wide open.

For a moment he just stood transfixed. As her kisses became more passionate, he pulled her closer. All rational thought was quickly abandoned.

Her eyes were wide with hunger as she unbuttoned his shirt. He pulled off his shoes using the opposite foot, by which time she was undoing his belt, dropping his slacks. His full erection was evident through his boxer shorts.

"That's very nice," she said in Spanish as she pulled off his underwear and pushed him back onto the bed.

She quickly undid her blouse followed by her bra. She could sense Victor's increased arousal at the sight of her breasts. Unzipping the skirt, she stepped out of it and knelt in front of him.

"Patricia ...."

She did not let him get further. Grasping his now full erection in her hand, she took it into her mouth. "I remember what you like, Victor."

For the next hour they revisited their passion from twenty-five years ago. Both were surprised by what was happening. Only partly was it the sex. He wanted her to go away quietly. She needed something more than money to escape.

While Patricia was in the bathroom, Castell thought about what had just happened. Something else to feel guilty about. Even though sex with Eleanor had lost some passion, he never fooled around. Even with ample opportunities while away on business, he always avoided any infidelity. So why this lapse with Patricia Reyes? Because he had never been able to purge her from his thoughts.

She came out with a bath towel wrapped around her. Kissing him on the cheek, she said, "Thank you for that, Victor. We were always good together."

He wanted to get beyond this as quickly as possible. It was time to move things along. This sexual encounter needed to be buried too.

"The best way to get to the border is take a train. I'll drive you to the station. I've got some money for you. Once you get to San Diego you can take a cab to the border crossing."

He handed her an envelope with the money. She looked at him with a sad expression. "Just like that, Victor? I'm once again to be out of your life?"

She let the towel drop away from her body. He could not help but to take in the sight of her body. She proceeded to dress starting first with her bra making no attempt to hide herself. She looked around to find her panties on the floor discarded when she hurriedly undressed.

With panties in hand she paused to say, "I was hoping we could spend just a little more time together, Victor. Couldn't you maybe drive me to San Diego? We could talk. For old times' sake?"

Looking at her exposed pubic hair, he was conflicted. Maybe this was necessary to appease her. To be rid of her. A convenient rationalization for this illicit sex?

"I don't know. I guess perhaps ...."

She came up and kissed him. This led to something more. To his amazement he was able to get it up again. The sex brought back memories of why he was so obsessed with her twenty-five years ago.

Patricia checked out of the motel. They were both hungry after the lovemaking. After stopping for a sandwich, it was after three o'clock in the afternoon before they were on their way to San Diego. It was a two hour drive, maybe more with rush-hour traffic. He called Eleanor's office. The receptionist said she was in a meeting. That was some relief. He left the message that he had an unexpected meeting in San Diego followed by a dinner commitment. He might spend the night there, be back in the morning. He would call her later tonight. Didn't want to interrupt by calling on her cell phone.

While driving, Castell said, "I still don't understand how you ended up with Carlos. He wouldn't seem your type. I always thought he was Santiago's muscle."

"I don't know about that. Carlos fought with the rebels. We all fought in different ways. I spied. I set up a network of students and fed intelligence to the rebels. Did other things for them. Carlos was my contact."

She knew of Carlos dangerous streak, suspecting that he had committed his share of violence. But so had she. She never told Victor the details of her participation in the killings at the brothel with Santiago.

"I was alone, Victor. Carlos was always there. Handsome like you. Things just happened."

"But the civil war ended. Carlos moved into organized crime."

"I guess I was just caught up in the adventure. Life had been so hard for so long. I'd always moved in secrecy. I conveniently ignored the criminal side of what Carlos was into. Rationalized it was still a form of combating an oppressive government. As time went on, the life style of having money was seductive. There was a sense of power to being protected by this violent group. Carlos became one of the leaders of MS-13. He had power. That can also be seductive."

"Didn't have to be exceptionally smart to lead these MS-13 psychopaths from what I hear, just crazy enough yourself. Did Carlos fit their mold?"

"Not really. Carlos is certainly smart. Santiago-like smart. He could be hard but he was good at manipulating these gang guys. They respected him. He had blood on his hands from his experience with the rebels. They respected that. He was one of the leaders organizing them away from their locally controlled violence. Carlos was organizing them into a business."

"A business? You're never going to see him again, Patricia. You know that. How's that make you feel?"

"You sound like a jealous lover, Victor. Are you?"

He did not answer.

"Let's not talk about Carlos. Ok?"

To change the subject, she asked the question that troubled her all those years. She knew Molina used him to construct these new bombs. He was never reported among the dead.

"What happened in Las Vegas, Victor? I only know what the newspapers and television said."

He wasn't about to go into the truth. No need to accuse Molina of threatening him with harm to her as a means of gaining his help. She still revered Santiago Molina. He certainly wasn't going to tell her he killed Molina and the others.

Nor was Patricia going to acknowledge her awareness of Victor's refusal to participate, much less being complicit in Molina's threat to Victor about harming her. Nor would she reveal she was actually there in Las Vegas. Lucky to have escaped being killed in the casino. But she did want to know why it had all gone so wrong.

"Did you make some mistake, Victor?"

He looked over at her wondering how she knew he designed the detonating circuits for the Las Vegas bombs. Did she suspect his sabotage?

"So you know Santiago used me to make more triggering devices?"

"Yes. I knew that was his intent. But I never knew if he convinced you, especially after what happened in El Salvador. I never knew what happened."

She almost blundered into revealing more than she intended.

"No, I didn't make a mistake. These were purchased radio frequency control devices. Not assembled from components like in El Salvador. Nothing to get wrong. They didn't even need me. Santiago could have rigged these himself had he given it some thought. It was a simple design but for the non-technical person, a bit scary when it meant attaching batteries to blasting caps imbedded in high explosives.

"My guess is they wired the arming circuit incorrectly. That might account for both bombs exploding prematurely. I labeled the leads, but I didn't assemble the triggering mechanism to the explosives. I wasn't even around whenever they did that."

"Where were you at the time, Victor?"

"I was at the Las Vegas airport. Waiting for a flight back to Los Angeles. I told Santiago I was through with this. He understood."

Patricia knew nothing different, only that Victor had balked at helping. It was troubling that she was to be used as a threat. Molina of course did not tell her that Victor must be killed once they detonated these bombs. Molina had to assume she might rebel at that no matter her devotion to the cause. In hindsight that was probably naïve of her to believe that Molina would let Victor go. But since Molina and the others died, Victor obviously escaped along with her and Carlos.

She had no reason not to believe Castell's version of events. Carlos Perez didn't know any more about what went wrong. Perez had not participated in assembling the bombs. He was to be just the driver of the other car. Perez always wondered if Castell escaped since he was not among the dead from the Tropicana bomb. By the time the victims names were published in the United States, Perez and Reyes were back in El Salvador and read only scant details in the bombings. It did not really matter. Castell would never go to the police without incriminating himself.

Molina had however told Perez that Castell was a threat. Perez understood he would be required to take care of the problem once they completed the attack on the Las Vegas casinos. There was a lot of open desert outside of Las Vegas. Perez never shared that with Reyes.

Knowing nothing about the planned fate for her lover, Molina had convinced Reyes that Victor had balked against helping them. He had no choice but to use the false threat that he would harm her. Molina expected her to put her personal feelings aside and play along. Sadly she was reconciled that she must choose between Victor, or to continue fighting for her people. Another wrenching sacrifice. But she was good soldier. Molina said he would release Victor after this last assistance. Obviously that was what happened, or at least resulted by Molina's death.

Castell found a hotel in San Ysidro close to the border crossing into Tijuana, Mexico. In the parking lot, she said to him, "I don't want to say goodbye, Victor. I'm sorry for popping up like this. Involving you. But it was still special seeing you after all these years. You're still handsome. Spend the night with me?"

"That's not a good idea, Patricia. You know that. We have such different lives."

"And you're a rich businessman while I'm a wanted fugitive."

"I didn't mean it like that, Patricia. I have a life here now. I can't throw all of that away."

She leaned over and put her head on his shoulder. "I know. I wouldn't want to ruin that for you, Victor. I've just lived in the shadows for so long it's good to see the sunlight if even for just a short time. Would you do me one more favor, Victor?"

What now?

"Let's have dinner. Somewhere nice. Our last time together. Will you?"

Shit. No way to avoid this. He assured himself he would not spend the night with her.

"Ok. But I still need to get back to Pasadena tonight. You go check in while I try to locate a restaurant on my iPhone."

Patricia kissed him and smiled broadly. While she left the car to check into the hotel, Castell searched his cell phone for something nearby, fixing on a Mexican restaurant on San Ysidro Boulevard. The photo gallery suggested a decent place with a good bar. He needed a drink. Once he returned Patricia to her hotel, he would find his own hotel. He would not be enticed to spend the night with her. This had to end tonight.

CHAPTER 20

To his dismay, Patricia had changed back into her tight skirt and heels. She looked very good. He suspected what she was doing. He was a weak sonofabitch and she knew that too.

They talked mostly about things other than their briefly shared time together long ago. It was mostly about him. His life since that fateful summer long ago. Two martinis helped.

Over dinner they shared a bottle of wine. At some point, Castell excused himself to go to the restroom. He took the opportunity to call home, speaking briefly to Eleanor. *They were still at dinner. His customer had arrived late. He was exhausted. Once he could graciously make his escape he would go to the hotel and crash.* He did not say which hotel. *He'd see her tomorrow after work. Let's plan on going out for a nice dinner.*

An after-dinner coffee made him feel falsely more capable to drive. Once he dropped Patricia off at her hotel he would stop at the first hotel off the 5 Freeway going north. The problem was going to be extricating himself from Patricia. As they left the restaurant she walked a little unsteadily because of the alcohol while clinging to his arm. He just needed to get her to bed and make his exit.

Instinctively Castell pulled into the parking on the side of the hotel. He wanted to avoid being seen by anyone if possible. Patricia Reyes was a federally wanted fugitive. She was the carrier of plague as far as Victor Castell was concerned. An awful thought suddenly intruded. What if she did not carry out her plan to cross into Mexico? What if she was arrested in Mexico and extradited back to the United States? Was she only a material witness or facing charges she had not mentioned? Her plan to find her way back to El Salvador appeared very tenuous. As long as neither she nor Perez were ever suspected of participation in those terrorist bombings, Castell was probably safe. They could never reveal his involvement without implicating themselves.

"I'm afraid it's goodbye, Patricia. I hope the best for you. Get back home and find a new life. Find a respectable man. Forget Carlos. He'll never get out of jail. Use this as an opportunity for a real life."

She kissed him. Tears rolled down her cheeks. "If it had been you, Victor, everything would have been so different for me. We might have had children."

Patricia covered her face with her hands and cried.

Now what to do? A light rain started. He got out of the car and opened her door. Helping her out of the car, he put his arm around her. "What room are you in?"

"140. Around the back."

At the door, still crying, she fumbled with the keycard. He swiped the card for her and pushed the door open, turning on the light.

She sat down on the bed. "Stay with me tonight, Victor. Please?"

"I can't, Patricia. It's better this way. I should go."

"No wait. Not just yet, Victor. Just a little while. Please? I have a bottle of tequila in my bag. Have a drink with me."

"We've both had enough to drink, Patricia. This is just making it harder."

"Please, Victor. Just a little while longer?"

Patricia grabbed the bottle of tequila and two glasses from the bathroom. She poured each glass half full. Reluctantly Castell sat down on the short two-seat sofa. Dropping down next to him, she positioned herself against him.

"To old memories, Victor."

She downed the glass of liquor. He was more measured. He knew where this was leading. She was getting amorous and a little drunk. Her hand wandered down to his crotch.

"I understand why things changed after you heard what happened to your mother."

He moved her hand. "Of course they changed. Why would I do this again? Why would I help Santiago? I was stupid in the first place. I only helped because of us. What they did to you. What they did to my Uncle Augustin. But to be the cause of my own mother's death?"

"But it was an accident, Victor. There was no way for you to know."

Patricia got up and poured herself more tequila. Now a little agitated, Castell also got up from the sofa.

"But once it happened, Molina wouldn't let me go. He threatened me. Threaten to harm you if I didn't help. You were in El Salvador. I had no way of knowing what he might do to you. I hated the sonofabitch for that."

She looked intently at him.

"It was our *cause*, Victor. We were still fighting the terrible repression in El Salvador. It was war."

"Wait a minute. This doesn't surprise you now to learn that Santiago threatened to harm you in order to force my help?"

She looked down and made no response.

"What the fuck does that mean, Patricia? You *knew*?"

"There was nothing I could do, Victor."

Castell sighed. "I suppose not. You were probably still recovering from that beating. I never did ask you about that today. Sorry."

She came over to him. Touched his arm. Kissed him on the mouth trying to arouse him. Instead he backed away and went to pour himself more tequila.

"Well Santiago didn't get away with it. Thought he was so fucking smart. The great international terrorist. Delusional with his own importance. The dumb shit couldn't even assemble a simple bomb. You'd have thought the Cubans provided better training. As for the rest of the group, all stupid sheep following the great Santiago Molina. Well they followed him straight to hell. I saw to that."

For Patricia, the fog of the liquor receded as if a curtain had been drawn back. Stupid sheep? Her included? "What do you mean, *you saw to that?*"

"I mean, Patricia, the bombs exploded prematurely because I booby-trapped them to go off. When the supposed arming circuit switch was activated, it directly closed the battery circuit instead. Boom!"

"You fucking sonofabitch! You killed all of them. You almost killed me."

Castell looked confused.

"I was there too, Victor. I was in the Bally's casino. You could have killed me too!"

"Fuck! Fuck! You were in on it with Santiago? You were in Las Vegas all the time? You stayed out of sight knowing I would do whatever to protect you? You set me up!

"You're a real piece of work, Patricia. Was I just a recruit back then? Did Santiago tell you to go sleep with me because he needed an engineer? Maybe you were fucking Santiago before that? Is that why you did anything he wanted? After that, you just happened to end up with Perez. Last guy left. A fucking gang leader. A murderer. Didn't matter to you. Just a good looking body to fuck. Dumped him when he got arrested. You needed money to get away so you took up fucking me again."

Patricia threw the glass at him catching him on the chest. She rushed at him trying to hit him with her fists. He grabbed both her arms to fend off the blows and twisted her off balance since she was still wearing her heels. Falling awkwardly to the side under her full weight, she struck her head on the sharp corner of the coffee table tearing a gaping wound at her right temple.

Blood squirted in spasms for several moments. The table had opened a major wound, apparently severing a major artery. Castell moved her onto her back. Blood continued to pulse from the wound in spasms. He rushed to the bathroom grabbing several towels. Attempting to compress the bleeding, nothing seemed to stem the flow. Patricia Reyes quickly bled out. Eventually there was no pulse. He felt her wrist, her neck, laid his hand on her chest. But his own heart was beating so rapidly maybe he wasn't detecting if a weak pulse remained. He took a makeup mirror from her purse and held it to her open mouth. No condensation of the breath. Although somewhat contained by soaking into the carpet, there was a copious amount of blood. She must be dead.

Was that better than her just being injured? Wouldn't that be an even bigger problem? Patricia in a hospital? He once loved this woman. What had he become? But all thoughts right now turned to survival.

The day had started out with a terrible shock but had now descended into something beyond all comprehension. He forced himself to sit on the bed to let the panic pass. Was his life now over? Could he once again escape involvement? He fought the urge to vomit as the surge of adrenalin washed over him. That would spill his DNA all over the place.

After some minutes, Castell started to take stock of things that needed to be done. First close the drapes. Careful to avoid stepping in any blood. He must remove anything that could place him here. There was never any thought that he would go to the police. At the least it was manslaughter. Could be charged with second degree murder. Everything would be gone. And that assumed it did not open the uglier can of worms from twenty-five years ago.

There was no way that it might be ruled an accident. People don't fall and split their head open like that even if drunk. Most of the towels were soaked in blood. Even if he were to get rid of them, why would the room be missing towels? So he could only remove any evidence implicating his presence. Wipe down everything to remove any of his prints. Make sure he didn't step in any blood. Make sure he had no blood on his clothing.

It took twenty minutes wiping every surface a second time using the one remaining clean towel. He would take the towel with him along with the glass he had used and a plastic dry cleaner bag. For a final time, he pragmatically went over the entire room again making sure nothing had been overlooked, including the keycard, her handbag, and mirror. Was he overlooking anything? Fortunately he was not in the room for very long.

Turning off the lights, he cracked the door to check if anyone was outside. Placing the *do not disturb* sign on the door handle, he closed the door quietly. At his car, there was still no one visible. Of course someone could be looking out a darkened window. No way to tell. Just get the hell away from here as soon as possible.

He slipped off his shoes and wiped them down for prints before putting them into the plastic bag, making doubly sure there was no blood on them. The bag was then wiped for prints and put into the trunk along with the towel and the glass. He would dispose of everything somewhere else in a trash dumpster. He put on a pair of running shoes from the trunk.

At least he was not expected home that night. He would check into a hotel much further north of San Diego. Take a shower, purge the alcohol from his system, and try to get some rest. Doubtful if he could sleep, but better equipped to get himself together. Was there anything he hadn't thought of?

CHAPTER 21

Egan Kavanagh now headed the National Security Branch of the FBI as an executive assistant director. It was Bernard Saunders old job. Saunders had taken a forced retirement after September 11, 2001. He was the principle FBI scapegoat who was accused of failing to connect the dots. Kavanagh escaped that purge because of his assertive style. His was the lone voice from the multi-agency United States bureaucracy that had not yet grasped the full potential of a foreign-based threat. Those fragments of unconnected intelligence had value only if interpreted from a comprehensive perspective. Kavanagh and a few others on his staff appreciated the potential ramifications of this puzzle of fragmented information. Kavanagh did connect the dots from assembled intelligence from sources of other U.S. as well as foreign agencies. His sounding of the alarm fell into bureaucratic quicksand but left a vivid audit trail that portrayed him as singularly prescient in the aftermath of 9/11.

Since the terrorist attack of the embassy in El Salvador, followed closely by the failed but still deadly attacks in Las Vegas in 1989, terrorism directed against the United States steadily increased. A decade of escalating terrorist attacks during the nineties culminated in the unprecedented attacks that brought down the Twin Towers of the World Trade Center in Manhattan.

The targets of terrorism attacks directed toward the United States had moved beyond the Middle East. Lockerbie, Scotland was followed by El Salvador, then Las Vegas. In 1993, a truck bomb detonated in the parking structure of the North Tower of the World Trade Center. In 1995, a couple of home-grown right-wing extremists detonated a fertilizer-based truck bomb in front of the federal building in Oklahoma City.

Bombs delivered in trucks became the favored method of attacking buildings where there were large numbers of Americans. In 1996, a building housing United States Air Force personnel was destroyed by a truck bomb in Khobar, Saudi Arabia. This was followed in 1998 by the devastating bombings of the United States East African embassies in Nairobi, Kenya and Dar es Salaam, Tanzania on the same day. Over 200 Americans were killed.

With the exception of the aberration of Oklahoma City, the origin of these attacks were from militant Islamic fundamentalists. For the first time, the name Osama bin Laden came to the forefront as the architect of the African embassy bombings. He soon became the highest value target for the FBI and the entire U.S. intelligence community. All that increased exponentially on September 11, 2001.

That was now history. Bin Laden had been killed three years ago. His Al Qaeda organization had metastasized across the Middle East after its centralized leadership was decimated by targeted assassination from the United States. There was now a host of Islamic terrorist organizations that posed various levels of threat to the United States. But outside of the war zones of Iraq and Afghanistan, there had been comparatively few terrorist attacks against U.S. targets. The Libyan consulate attack in Benghazi was more associated with a war zone in the turmoil following the toppling of Gaddafi. It was not a bombing.

The Boston Marathon bombing was more like the Atlanta Olympic bombing in 1996 and the Oklahoma City bombing. Even though the Boston bombers had Islamic backgrounds, they were still rooted in the United States making it more the work of home-grown radicals.

Kavanagh took some pride in his contribution to the changes since 9/11 that made America safer from foreign terrorist threats. His special relationships with the intelligence community proved fortuitous with the mandated changes in inter-departmental cooperation after the failures that allowed for 9/11. The FBI had traditionally viewed their role as law enforcement. International bad guys were often out of reach. But not for intelligence agency black operations with operations like the spectacular killing of Osama bin Laden and drone attacks. The massive communications collection by the NSA became the singularly decisive weapon. Kavanagh understood the changing role the FBI played in national security. Through his efforts he had advanced the FBI's capabilities of cataloging and mapping the fragments of intelligence to identify meaningful targets for investigation.

The Federal Bureau of Investigation was renowned for its tenacity to track down those accused of committing crimes against the United States. While many terrorist leaders had been killed or captured, there were many lower level players that were still out there with American blood on their hands. Ordinary criminals were frequently caught in the commission of some future crime resulting in being tied to some previous crime. It was no different in the murky world of international terrorism. It was a pseudo-profession with the players moving about in reaction to groups being decimated, or the political environment changing. Those with expertise such as bomb making always found other employment opportunities.

Almost all of the direct participants in past terrorist attacks had been identified. A few had yet to be killed or captured. Not so with the Santiago Molina group from 1989. The engineer of those bombs had gotten away. Possibly a couple of others. The engineer had never repeated his signature work. That investigative dead end deeply frustrated Egan Kavanagh even to this day. He could not abide the fact that someone had gotten away with mass murder.

Kavanagh was now in his sixties. He occupied a corner office with expensive mahogany cabinetry. All the trappings of bureaucratic power. Behind his large desk was a workstation with two large computer monitors. This is where he spent a good deal of his time looking at intelligence reports.

A knock on the door was followed with his executive assistant entering. Mary Cummings had been working for Kavanagh for close to thirty years. She was close to his age, matronly, efficient, and maintained Kavanagh's vast network of contacts. Cummings was Egan Kavanagh's most valued subordinate.

"Thought you'd want to see this right away, Sir."

She still called him sir even after all the years working together. With an uncharacteristically broad smile, she placed a printout of an email on his desk. It was a rather lengthy report. Before he could start to read it, she said, "It's about the El Salvador bombing. The one fingerprint. The one you always talked about."

"The guy who made the bomb?" Kavanagh said.

"Not sure about that, Sir. The fingerprint is from a woman."

Kavanagh read the report. The print matched that of a recently deceased woman in San Diego. A possible homicide. Routine check of prints with the FBI database resulted in a computer matching it to the lone print extracted from the bomb fragments from the U.S. Embassy bombing in El Salvador. Twenty-five years ago.

But a woman? Could she be the person who engineered those bombs? And therefore probably the Las Vegas bombs? Did she have the technical background? And what did it mean that she had both a Salvadoran passport and a U.S. passport under different names?

"Mary, get the agent in charge of the San Diego field office on the phone right away. Then get me on a plane to San Diego tomorrow morning."

CHAPTER 22

The agent in charge of the FBI's San Diego field office, Peter Fredericks was on hand personally with a car on the tarmac of San Diego International Airport as the Lear jet taxied to the general aviation services terminal.

"I'm Peter Fredericks, Sir. Agent in Charge of the San Diego office. Glad to meet you."

The two shook hands and got into the back seat of a Lincoln Town Car driven by another agent.

"Since we learned of this fingerprint match I've had a team working with local law enforcement. I've set up a meeting with the San Diego County Sheriff's Department Chief of Detectives, Terrence Gallagher.

"A fellow Irishman?"

"Very much so, Sir, red hair and all. I've worked with Terry for several years. Good cop. He's going to lay out what they've got."

"Excellent. How's he feeling about our intrusion into his case?"

"Well, Sir, I've developed a good relationship with Gallagher but I have to say he's not a fan of the feds. Might want to tread delicately if jurisdictional questions come up."

"Understood. I'll be on my best behavior. I'll try to cultivate our shared ethnicity. Just a couple of old time Irish cops. How old is he?"

"Not sure. Somewhere over fifty. The red hair's deceiving. But he's been around."

"So the initial report said there was a federal warrant for this woman. Connected with an MS-13 gang leader I understand?" Kavanagh said.

"Yes, Sir. At the time we were looking for her under the false name of Pilar Valverde. Wife of Manuel Valverde. Both false identities. Manuel Valverde is really Carlos Perez. High up the food chain in the Mara Salvatrucha organization. Their U.S. passports were real. Seems the real Valverdes, husband and wife, were forced into applying for passport renewals with photos of Perez and this woman who we believe is really Patricia Reyes from her Salvadoran passport found in her purse. The Valverdes are uninvolved Salvadoran immigrants living in the Central American enclave of the Pico-Union district of Las Angeles. The right ages. They knew what the MS-13 thugs were capable of doing to them or their relatives back in El Salvador if they didn't cooperate. From port of entry records, it seems Perez had been using this false identity for some time to enter into the United States coming across at Tijuana."

"And Perez was arrested in LA?"

"Right. Couple of days ago. He survived a police shootout. Reyes got away. Probably had some help."

"Any leads, witnesses?"

"Not yet."

"Is she the right age?"

"Right age?"

"To have been involved with the San Salvador bombing in 1989."

"Should be. Medical examiner puts her age towards late forties. So that's early twenties in 1989. And this fingerprint, her print, came from a bomb fragment?"

"That's right. We always thought it was probably the guy, or woman I guess, that assembled the bomb. We'll have to see if she fits that profile."

Kavanagh and Fredericks arrived at San Diego police headquarters accompanied by two of Frederick's agents. Chief of Detectives Gallagher had assembled a hands-on briefing for the federal agents. Two additional FBI agents had come down from Los Angeles. They were intimate with the raid on the Mara Salvatrucha leadership that led to the arrest of Carlos Perez.

As the formidable FBI entourage filed into the conference room, Chief Gallagher commented, "Anybody back in Washington? Should have scheduled a larger room."

Kavanagh introduced himself to Gallagher and shook hands. "Does seem like overkill, Chief, but I'll explain in a minute."

Gallagher was wondering what this was all about to bring the FBI's Executive Assistant Director of National Security to San Diego. Kavanagh was a big cheese. And national security implications? Who the hell was this dead woman?

The FBI agents settled into chairs around a conference table. Several San Diego detectives stood at the back. Another detective setup a laptop computer to a digital projector.

"Ok. I'll walk through what we've got gentlemen," Gallagher said. He introduced his detectives working the case standing at the back of the room.

"The victim we believe was Patricia Reyes. That's the name on her Salvadoran passport. But her U.S. passport was a false name so we can't be sure of this name yet. We've sent the information off to you guys in Washington to work the international angle."

"We've already routed the request not only through the State Department, but also directly to the Salvadoran authorities I'm told," Kavanagh said.

"The body was reported by a motel cleaning maid around noon on the ninth. The motel is close to the San Ysidro border crossing with Tijuana. The victim was in room 140 on the first floor. Curtains closed. Do not disturb card on the door. Lights were off.

"According to the medical examiner, cause of death was blunt trauma resulting in a penetration and tearing of the superficial temporal artery. That's in the region of the temple. Cause of death was insufficient blood volume. Bled to death. These are photos of the scene."

The detective at the computer brought up the first image. It displayed the hotel room with Reyes lying on the floor. She was fully dressed. A glass lay next to her. The detective moved to different images following Gallagher's narrative.

"The damage came from the sharp corner of the coffee table. Actually penetrated her head. You can see the pool of blood absorbed by the carpet.

"We're treating it as a homicide. I'll tell you why. First of all there were blood-soaked towels in the bathroom. The victim didn't go get them. She died on the spot. Someone tried to stop the bleeding.

"The autopsy showed a considerable amount of alcohol in the victim. Maybe to the level of legal intoxication. She might have been drunk enough to simply fall and bang her head. But somebody else was there. So it could mean she was pushed although there is no indication of a struggle."

A succession of images flashed on the screen, halting with a close-up of fingerprint powder on a door handle.

"Secondly, somebody wiped the place down. Stem to stern. We didn't even find any of Reyes' prints. The only prints were from a maid on the shower curtain."

"Any leads?"

"She had dinner with a guy apparently not too long before she died. Still food in her stomach according to the autopsy. We know the restaurant from a cocktail napkin found in her purse. Looks like she used it blot her lipstick.

"Waitress there remembers Reyes. Somehow Reyes connected the waitress as being Salvadoran, probably by an accent. They chatted a bit. The waitress described the man as late forties, good looking, dark hair with some graying at the temples. Well dressed. Sport coat. No tie. Paid with cash."

"Latin?" Kavanagh said.

"Waitress couldn't tell. The guy never said anything within her earshot. Light complexion. Definitely not a gangbanger. Certainly not MS-13 with their freaky tattoos."

"Probably not," Kavanagh said. "But from photos I've seen of her boyfriend Perez being held in Los Angeles, he doesn't sport those tattoos either. Could be someone connected with Perez operating here in the States. Maybe connected in some way with the Mexican Sinaloans. Anything else?"

"Oh yes. The more interesting piece of forensics recovered. Our woman had intercourse within the last twelve hours before she died. The medical examiner found semen in her vagina as well as on her underwear."

"Enough to type the DNA?" Kavanagh said.

"Yep. Just need to find a suspect to match it to," Gallagher said.

"Any theories why she stopped on this side of the border?" Kavanagh said. "After all she was on the run from the police. She had crossed with Perez into the United States from Mexico right here before. Obviously she intended to get back into Mexico. Why not get into Mexico where she'd be much safer from U.S. law enforcement?"

"No specific indications there. You could speculate she stopped to be with this guy. Or picked up a guy in LA to drive her to the border. Turned into a good screw, a good dinner. Lots of drinks. Might suggest that whoever was with her had some reason not to cross into Mexico. The other unexplained fact is the bed. It was still made up as it would have been by the motel housekeeper. So we don't think they probably had sex here."

"She must have known her false ID was blown," Kavanagh said. "Maybe she needed to be able to get back into the United States. Probably no U.S. visa to go along with her Salvadoran passport. It does suggest that whoever was with Reyes is still in the United States. Everything suggests she knew this guy very well."

"How so?" Gallagher said.

"Well her boyfriend Perez gets arrested. She just escaped being arrested herself. She's on the run. Probably doesn't know LA all that well. Must have been pretty desperate. Not likely she picked up somebody at a bar to give her a ride to the Mexican border. Far more likely it was someone she knew. Knew him intimately or maybe just used sex to get him to help. Got to be somebody that lives in the Los Angeles area. Probably someone connected with Perez's activities.

"I gather you being here personally, Mr. Kavanagh, suggests this has real national security implications?" Gallagher said.

"I'd say so. To the extent that this Reyes woman was clearly part of a terrorist group that killed Americans twenty-five years ago. Remember the U.S. Embassy in El Salvador? That's where her fingerprint came from. Then the same group followed with the Las Vegas bombings? Carlos Perez might even be part of that too. Not sure this woman fits the profile of the person who engineered those bombs. If not, maybe that guy is still out there. Maybe did other bombings working for a different group. I was personally involved in the Salvadoran and Las Vegas investigations. It was on my watch so to speak. I want every last one of these assholes. Especially the bomb maker."

Kavanagh would leave the follow-up investigative work in San Diego to the FBI field agents and the local police. Gallagher made it clear that he could not provide many resources to investigate what was at best a low level homicide. This was predominately a federal matter with the terrorist angle. Unless they could get some better lead about who Patricia Reyes was with the night she died, there wasn't much to go on anyway.

Kavanagh needed to pursue the only obvious connection with Reyes, Carlos Perez. Was Perez part of the same terrorist cell as Reyes? Not likely Kavanagh would be able to cut a deal with Perez. The terrorism related charges of multiple cases of murder carried the federal death sentence. Far worse than the charges Perez was currently facing. Kavanagh didn't have any real leverage even if the death penalty was off the table. Perez was already going away for life on multiple charges.

Kavanagh travelled by car to Los Angeles with the Los Angeles field agents. He was mostly interested in Perez's early background. What the FBI knew was largely Perez's criminal career with MS-13. His prior involvement with Salvadoran rebels during the civil war of the eighties was sketchy at best. The efforts of the criminal branch of the FBI ran into the same issues of investigation where the information resided in a foreign country. Law enforcement in El Salvador was still incompetent with a fair amount of corruption. Kavanagh would also be looking for information twenty-five years old.

Perez was being held in the Metropolitan Detention Center, the federal prison in downtown Los Angeles. He was in a high security area reserved for special arrestees awaiting hearings or trial. Perez was one of four Mara Salvatrucha leaders rounded up in the violent raid a week earlier in Pico-Union.

Los Angeles field office Agent in Charge, Max Fielder filled Kavanagh in on the known background of Carlos Perez. Age forty-eight. Salvadoran national. Came to the United States as a political refugee in 1992. Wanted by El Salvador for crimes committed during the civil war outside the scope of the general amnesty. Even though peace was declared, hundreds of former rebels were still under the threat of arrest. The United States attempted to take a neutral stance to fortify the end of the decade-long violence. Just like the Cuban exodus of thousands in 1980, including known criminals, the United States allowed many Salvadorans with questionable pasts into the country.

Once in the United States, Perez settled in the Pico-Union district of Los Angeles. There he connected with the Salvadoran Mara Salvatrucha. Somehow, perhaps because of his being older than most of the young gang members, perhaps because of past military exploits with the rebels in El Salvador, he became a leader. His street name is El Martillo, the Hammer. Unlike most of the rank and file, he did not adopt the extreme neck and facial tattoos.

Perez was arrested multiple times in Los Angeles, ultimately convicted only on racketeering charges in 1996. After being deported, he resumed his MS-13 affiliation with the growing number of MS-13 deportees from the U.S. returned to El Salvador. He was never arrested upon his return to El Salvador.

Over the years, Perez rose in what constituted the loose central leadership of the Mara Salvatrucha as it attempted to evolve into a formidable organized criminal enterprise. To accomplish this, control had to be exercised over the semi-autonomous individual local gangs bent on committing acts of excessively brutal violence. It was believed that Perez advanced within MS-13 by his efforts to partner with the Mexican Sinaloa drug cartel to act as their enforcement muscle. The arrangement brought in enormous money and provided a channeled outlet for the MS-13 to exercise their special brand of violence. It also provided the framework for MS-13 to spread to other U.S. cities.

Kavanagh watched the video monitor of the FBI abortive interview with Perez. It was a futile exercise. Perez had lawyered-up and maintained his refusal to say anything.

"Who's the lawyer?" Kavanagh said.

"Name is Delgado. Luis Delgado," Fielder said. "Lawyer to the scum. Represents Latin American organized crime. Those connected with Mexican drug cartels, LA street gangs, and of course MS-13. We're not sure how far he's gone with being cozy with the bad guys but he's their go-to guy. They are his only clients. Usually straightforward work. His clients are generally in deep shit with multiple charges and strong evidence against them. Delgado's task is usually to negotiate plea bargains. The work is easy. The money is very good. A thousand bucks an hour. IRS is all over Delgado's tax returns. He makes sure his fees are not sourced from obviously illicit drug profits. Probably helps them launder the money for his fees."

"And Perez and this Reyes woman?" Kavanagh said.

"Not sure. They've been together for some time. Haven't determined yet if she was involved with the rebels in El Salvador. They've used these same fake passports to enter the United States for a couple of years. Travel as husband and wife. Could pass for that. Same age. Both good looking. Probably lovers."

"Apparently not Reyes' only lover," Kavanagh said. "Does Perez know Reyes is dead?"

"Not yet. But he's about to."

Fielding turned up the volume of the conversation in the interrogation room.

"Agent Smith, you've been at this for thirty minutes. My client has nothing to discuss. Nothing has changed since he was arrested. He's exercising his constitutional rights against self-incrimination. So can we quit wasting everyone's time?" Delgado said.

"Well there is one more question, Counselor."

Delgado shook his head in an expression of frustration. Perez remained silent throughout the one-sided interview, exhibiting no emotion.

"What does Mr. Perez know about the bombing of the United States Embassy in San Salvador in 1989?"

Perez noticeably reacted to the question with his eyes but made no comment.

"What's this about, Agent Smith? Piling on to add more charges against my client? For a fishing trip, couldn't you do better than something twenty-five years ago?"

"Well we've just obtained some new evidence. Evidence that might connect your client."

"Are we through, Agent Smith?"

"Consider this. A lot of Americans died in that bombing. If Mr. Perez was involved that could mean the death penalty."

"If you had any credible evidence you'd be laying it out. You're just fishing," Delgado said. "Now are we through?"

"I guess there is just one more matter. It concerns Patricia Reyes."

"We've been over that many times, Agent Smith. Mr. Perez has nothing to add about her whereabouts."

"Not that, Counselor. We know her whereabouts. Patricia Reyes was found dead two days ago."

Perez came bolt upright out of his chair. "What the fuck are you talking about?"

Delgado tried to pull Perez back down in his chair as a second FBI agent readied himself if Perez became violent.

"Died in a fall. Hit her head. Bled to death. A real ugly mess. Big pool of blood. Might be an accident, but somebody else was there at the time."

"How do you know that?" Delgado said.

"Lots of evidence points to that. Does Mr. Perez have any idea who she might have been with?"

Perez said nothing but remained clearly agitated.

"Seems whoever he was Reyes knew him *very* well. They had dinner together. We're waiting for the autopsy results but semen in Reyes' underwear suggested they'd been fucking the same day she died. Most likely she was murdered by this guy."

CHAPTER 23

Victor Castell spent the night at the Marriott Hotel in Newport Beach. He wanted to get far away from San Diego. If he ever had to explain to his wife, he misspoke or she heard wrong about San Diego. The meeting was in San Clemente, just to the south of Newport Beach. Of course that was no alibi if it ever came to that. No way to construct an alibi now. But if that was ever required, there would be much more to worry about. It would be the end of everything.

Sleep came only in the early morning hours. He woke abruptly with the sunlight coming through the open curtains. Sometimes you woke from a dream and it took moments to grasp that the circumstances were not real. This nightmare was all too real. A surge of panic struck him. Had he left any evidence?

The shoes were thrown into a dumpster behind some strip mall miles from the motel where Patricia lay dead. He made sure to wipe them down again with the towel. Could DNA be extracted from the inside of shoes? Taking up his clothing he made another thorough examination. Nothing obvious. No blood splatters. At least he couldn't find any. Could there be microscopic droplets? Might there be fibers left in Patricia's room? Worse yet, one of his hairs?

He decided to take a shower. Calm down. Quit this obsessive rewinding of details about covering his tracks. He hadn't left any trace evidence. Keep telling himself that. Fortunately he hadn't been that long in the motel room.

As he toweled off, the thought suddenly came to him. Shit! They had made love. Twice. If he hadn't left any hairs he certainly had left his semen. Some of him was still in her. Still in her dead body. Would it be found in the autopsy that would surely be performed? Of course.

Sonofabitch. He leaned on the bathroom sink and took deep breaths. Ok. That could confirm he was with her. Had intercourse with her. Didn't mean he killed her. At worse manslaughter. Christ, he *didn't* murder her. Of course his life would be ruined. Eleanor would leave him. His business would suffer, but that would depend if he was convicted of any crime. It was an accident during an illicit sexual affair. Met her in a bar. Had a Salvadoran heritage in common. Both spoke Spanish. Satisfy the Salvadoran connection with the obvious. That's if it ever got that far.

Shit! His cell phone. It could place him in the general area of the San Diego motel even though he did not make or receive any calls. He knew the technology. He had consulted with the NSA on more than one technology project. But the thought struck him, so what? If it got that far the police wouldn't need any more evidence beyond the DNA.

Ok, ok. Think on the problem. Analyze and break down the pieces. What are the critical pitfalls? Get your story prepared. Where is the weakness in the story? Research the background details. Create the legend as they call it in the world of espionage.

All that in preparation for some unlikely contingency. The police might be able to match him to the DNA, but only if he were ever identified as a suspect? There should be nothing to connect him to Patricia Reyes.

But his biggest worry was probably irrational. Why would the police even connect Patricia with Santiago Molina's terrorist group? She was wanted because she was involved with Carlos Perez, a leader of a criminal organization engaged in drugs and murder. Her death, whether ruled a murder or accident, was just another casualty within that violent criminal environment.

Not as grim a situation once he thought about it rationally. A terrible emotional trauma, but learn to live with it. He'd learned to live with worse.

Arriving home mid-morning, he bundled his clothing from the day before into a trash bag. Before lunch, he dropped his car off at the car wash where he arranged for a complete detailing. The trash bag went into a dumpster. If there was any minute physical evidence, he would at least take every precaution. While he waited for the car across the street at a Starbuck's, he called Eleanor on his cell phone.

"How was your meeting last night?" she said.

"The usual bullshit of having to smooze with customers. But I think it was successful. The two guys were late so that made the entire evening later than it should have been. Too much alcohol. They couldn't follow most of my technical pitch but they seemed impressed anyway. I think they were already primed to award us the project. Not all that big a deal anyway. Glad I got a good night's sleep. Too much wine to make it home safely."

"You at the office?"

"Not yet. I slept in a bit. Having a coffee and a scone. That'll be my lunch. How about we go out for dinner? Maybe you can get Regina to come too."

"She probably has something else going. But you ask her. Call her. Fifteen year-old girls respond better to their fathers."

Castell would prefer to go off by himself. For days just to be alone. Retrench. Rethink. Recalibrate. But that would only make things worse. Harder to eventually rejoin his former life. He had to reset everything back to normal immediately. Make as if Patricia Reyes never happened. Immerse himself back into normality. See if he can pull it off. He did this before, why not again? Whatever moral compass he had was now so terribly flawed as to not exist. If it meant survival, any moral compromise seemed easily rationalized.

CHAPTER 24

Egan Kavanagh arrived on a commercial airline flight accompanied by six of his FBI agents, all Spanish speaking. Unlike the chilled reception of twenty-five years ago, the Americans were warmly welcomed upon their arrival at the San Salvador airport by the Attorney General himself. Along with the Attorney General was the commander of the National Civil Police.

"Señor Kavanagh, welcome to El Salvador," Attorney General Antonio Herrera said. "May I also introduce, Colonel Humberto Calderón."

Kavanagh shook hands with the two senior officials and introduced his team of agents.

The political winds had greatly changed since those days when El Salvador was still in the violent throws of its long civil war. The U.S. Embassy bombing was a distraction to the ruling government and the Salvadoran military at the time. Peace from the exhausted combatants came in 1992. Upwards of 80,000 Salvadorans had been killed during the civil war. Another 8,000 have never been accounted for. It was one of the last ugly ideological classes in the Americas. The ultra-right-wing

Salvadoran government was supported by the United States, Chile, and Argentina. The leftist FMLN rebels were supported by Cuba and Nicaragua. But even the surrogate sponsors eventually tired of the years of bloodletting.

The infamous Treasury Police and National Guard, both under command of the military, were abolished in 1992 under the peace accords. Under that prior system, the military waged war on insurgents operating in the rural areas while rogue secret police forces terrorized the urban population. The newly constituted National Police, the *Policia Nacional*, was separated from military command and became the singular police agency for the country.

Egan Kavanagh subjugated his long held feelings of anger and frustration over the lack of cooperation on the part of the Salvadoran regime twenty-five years ago. He was given to believe that the current administration and national police might be receptive to allowing the Federal Bureau of Investigation to participate in reopening the investigation. Political winds had shifted. However, this was still a backwater banana republic with questionable investigative competence. And the case was decades old.

When he chose, Kavanagh could put on a convivial Irish demeanor and become persuasively charming given the right circumstances where it might produce results. He would assume the best from these current Salvadoran police officials, at least until they tried to blow smoke up his ass.

After the obligatory social exchanges, Kavanagh was surprised by the position the Salvadorans were now expressing. Colonel Calderón's opening statements about those long ago events set a surprisingly conciliatory tone.

"Director Kavanagh, with your recent communication and request for assistance, I took the opportunity to examine the police files following that terrible tragedy. I myself only remembered that time vaguely. But not in an official capacity as part of the police. I was a young intelligence officer in the regular army at the time. I came to my police responsibilities years later.

"But to the point. I must tell you that I was astounded by the lack of any meaningful investigative records. I will not get into the politics of the time. That is part of an ugly past. At best I can only assume that the guerrilla war with the rebels in the rural areas overshadowed everything. Clearly the Government paid little attention to pursuing the terrorists that perpetrated this bombing. One can speculate that it was thought to be an American problem. After all, America was the target of the attack. However, many Salvadorans were killed so this remains of vital interest to El Salvador. Any amnesty that ended the civil war does not apply here. If there are still members of that terrorist group, we also want to see them brought to justice."

"My thanks, and my country's thanks to you, Colonel, and to you, Mr. Attorney General," Kavanagh said. "This old case remains open. Even though we are sure the perpetrators that died in the bombings in Las Vegas that followed soon after San Salvador were from the same group, we have never felt that all were accounted for. The lone fingerprint extracted from a bomb fragment of the embassy bombing never matched those dead terrorists in Las Vegas.

"Now with the positive identification that the fingerprint was that of this recently deceased woman, it further supports our suspicions there are perhaps others still unaccounted for. Specifically, we do not think the woman engineered the bombs. Based on the mishap that the terrorists suffered in Las Vegas, we think the terrorist that designed the triggering mechanism was not among the dead. He at least is still out there.

"Now this Reyes woman is linked with the Mara Salvatrucha gang leader Carlos Perez, currently in custody in the United States. We want to find out if Perez was part of this terrorist group twenty-five years ago."

"That would certainly be interesting," the Attorney General said. "We also have pending charges against Señor Perez here in El Salvador. Mara Salvatrucha is a disease here just like in the United States.

"As to your return to El Salvador this time, Director Kavanagh, I hope we can assist in effecting results that will prove helpful. I fear however, that your efforts are measurably more difficult after so many years."

Kavanagh said, "Yes, unfortunately that is true. But even with the coldest of cases, there may be some thread to be found. A thread that may lead to more tangible evidence. With Colonel Calderón's assistance we may be able to find that thread."

Kavanagh disliked the diplomatic mating dance of protocol. But it appeared his team could expect broad support from Calderón's police. How effective that might prove remained a question.

The following day Calderón convened a working meeting of several of his key officers and Kavanagh's FBI team. To Kavanagh's surprise, Calderón ran it as professionally as any police chief in the U.S. After giving a detailed summary of the FBI's body of knowledge of the El Salvador bombing, the staff from both sides began discussing an investigative plan.

There was little possibility of answering any further questions about these old terrorist bombings by further investigation in the United States. Las Vegas had yielded up all the evidence it would years ago in the form of dead terrorists and bomb fragments. The only evidence uncovered suggesting there were other terrorists unaccounted in Las Vegas was a second rental car from LAX in the name of a Salvadoran national, abandoned at a hotel in Las Vegas. It was rented under a false name but not one of those identified among the dead terrorists. It was wiped clean of fingerprints. Another reason to believe someone got away, probably the bomb maker.

The San Diego police homicide investigation into the recent death of Reyes quickly became cold. The local police would look to the FBI to unearth something related to Perez's criminal enterprises to suggest a suspect in the homicide. If in fact it was a homicide. Her death is more likely to be somehow associated with her MS-13 connection rather than her involvement in terrorism from another era. But the thread of that fingerprint is why the FBI has returned to El Salvador.

Egan Kavanagh articulated the FBI's objective. "Gentlemen, the purpose of the investigation is to determine if there were other members of Santiago Molina's terrorist organization that evaded capture. The death of Patricia Reyes confirmed that there were others. The United States Federal Bureau of Investigation believes at the least, the person who constructed the radio frequency detonation system was not one of those that died in Las Vegas. That bomb maker is still wanted for multiple homicides by both our countries. He may have been involved with some other group since the death of Molina in 1989. The Reyes woman was not the bomb engineer even though it was her fingerprint on the bomb fragment."

Kavanagh did not add that this was personal. A loose end that has always gnawed at him. It perhaps should not have this much of his personal attention but since he was the Executive Assistant Director for the National Security Branch of the FBI, rank exercised its privilege. Besides, if this guy was discovered still alive it would further the mystique that the FBI would eventually find anyone no matter how long it took.

Kavanagh continued, "With the assistance of the Policia Nacional, we would like to start interviewing relatives and known associates of all the dead terrorists. We realize that there may well be reluctance to provide information, but that is no different than interrogating reluctant suspects. We need to press any potential information sources aggressively."

His senior agent smiled slightly. Kavanagh was also thinking that down here they beat or tortured suspects to get information. At least they used to. That was their idea of being aggressive.

"My agents are all fluent in Spanish and experienced interrogators. Teamed with Colonel Calderón's officers I'm confident that we'll learn more than we know right now. All we need is another piece of the puzzle, just like Reyes' fingerprint, to open up new possibilities."

"Anticipating how we might proceed, my staff has prepared dossiers on all of the known terrorists. In English," Calderón said as one of his officers passed out folders to everyone. "Unfortunately, the material is somewhat limited beyond the identification of family members and other background facts from civil records. I again must apologize for the poor police procedures that followed the deaths of these terrorists in the United States. It was prematurely treated as a closed case here in El Salvador. There was no further investigation to determine if there were others. Matters associated with the continuing civil war took priority. Much opportunity has been lost in twenty-five years."

Kavanagh's FBI team proceeded to scan the data. To establish a working rapport with their Salvadoran counterparts they started asking questions, in Spanish. His team was diplomatically good. They were careful to avoid a posture of being in charge, or superior as the FBI was too often accused, even within the United States. Initial ideas for commencing the investigation specifics were jointly suggested. Without direction from either superior officer, both teams developed working protocols to divide the investigative tasks.

Calderón was correct about the background materials being thin. Only Santiago Molina's dossier was thick. Most of that material consisted of FBI reports shared with El Salvador at the time. These were the results of the international aspects of the

FBI's investigation into Molina, conducted after Las Vegas in 1989.

There was scant information about Molina's life in El Salvador other than his front business enterprise. No known business dealings listed. No relatives. No identified associations. No social connections. Obviously he wasn't a recluse. Certainly opportunities existed to flesh him out even after so many years.

For Patricia Reyes there was the brother and sister-in-law she lived with. As a university student she was known to be a follower of the outspoken opposition academic Professor Augustin Portillo. Again no names of her social group were documented.

Carlos Perez was identified as fighting with the rebels. Ultimately amnestied in 1992, but there's still some question about outstanding charges beyond the scope of the general amnesty. Came to the United States as a political refugee in 1992. Extensive criminal record in the U.S. Deported back to El Salvador from the United States. Known association with MS-13. Thought to occupy a high-ranking leadership position. Intelligence, mostly provided by U.S. law enforcement, suggested he was associated with the Mexican Sinaloa drug cartel. But other than his romantic association with Reyes for many years, there was no evidence of involvement with Molina's terrorist group.

Jose Aguilar was the guy who died in the back seat of the car in Las Vegas by the premature detonation of the Tropicana bomb. Former student. Parents and several siblings still residing in San Salvador. Same university as Patricia Reyes. Also believed associated with Professor Portillo.

"Colonel, this Professor Augustin Portillo? Opposition critic to the government at the time?" Kavanagh said.

"Yes. A very vocal critic. He was able get away with his public anti-government attacks because of his stature in the international academic community and his reputation with foreign journalists."

"Is he still active in politics?"

"No. Eventually he became too much of a threat to the military and ruling party. He was a victim of a death squad killing in 1989. His death might have become a larger public relations problem had it not been for the U.S. Embassy bombing following soon after his death," Calderón said.

"Could he have been associated with Molina?"

"Possibly. But unlikely that Portillo would have supported terrorism. Especially Molina's brand of violence with the spectacular assassinations of those military officers, followed by the embassy bombing. I remember Portillo from that time. He was sympathetic to the rebel movement, maybe even their political face, but he still advocated against violence. However, Molina was not a known terrorist. He operated in the open as a business man. So they might have known each other."

As for the other two dead terrorists, Miguel Cortina and Roberto Salas, there was a list of relatives but little more. Their occupations were listed as mechanic and truck driver respectively.

Kavanagh let his team work the investigation with their Salvadoran counterparts. He was briefed each evening. Based in an office at the U.S. Embassy, he took care of his broader responsibilities dealing with more immediate threats to the United States. Those responsibilities would demand his return to Washington within a matter of days. This old case would have to be left to his team.

On the fourth day in El Salvador, a joint meeting of all the investigators convened at the National Police headquarters. Those relatives and associates that could be located had all been questioned. Old police and civil records were researched. No breakthrough discovery was made, only some additional leads to pursue.

After reviewing all of the investigative details, the senior FBI team leader summarized those remaining areas to be investigated.

"We discovered that the house Santiago Molina occupied in 1989 was owned by a woman named Martha Rodriguez. A high school teacher. Here's her picture," the agent said.

"Pretty woman. Molina's girlfriend?" Kavanagh said.'

"We think so. Former neighbors said she lived there. But we haven't located her yet. She sold the house in 1989 after the embassy bombing. Left her teaching job then apparently left El Salvador. There's a record of her leaving on a flight to Mexico City. The FBI liaison office there has been requested to pursue her whereabouts with Mexican authorities.

"Of course none of the relatives questioned knew anything. Claimed to have never known about any involvement with terrorists. All claimed to have had no connection with the FMLN rebels during that time. All loyal citizens.

"Except for one. Roberto Salas' mother. An elderly woman dying of terminal cancer. She was interviewed in a hospital in the city of San Miguel to the east of San Salvador. Feisty old lady. She made no bones about where her politics lay. Virulently anti-government both then and now. Accused them of killing her husband. Running death squads. Got off on a rant about the murder of her beloved Archbishop Romero. Challenged us to torture a dying old lady. But there wasn't much else about her son Roberto who died at the Tropicana. His siblings did not offer anything helpful. They lived elsewhere and had infrequent contact. Roberto lived with his mother. He drove a truck for an agricultural transport company."

"What about Perez? Anything to link him to Molina beyond Reyes?" Kavanagh said.

"Nothing yet. But Perez had a certain amount of notoriety when he fought with the rebels. That was both before the 1989 bombings and later until the peace in 1992. A lot of his past came to light with the amnesty that ended the civil war. Seems he had reputation for liking to kill. Reported to have personally tortured and executed prisoners. That's why he fled to the United States. Just the kind of skills he could put to use with the Mara Salvatrucha.

"All sorts of people to talk to about Augustin Portillo. A very public figure. Prominent opponent to the ruling party and military during the period of the civil war as Colonel Calderón said. We're still working through a long list of people to locate and interview."

"I can perhaps offer something there," Calderón said. "His nephew, Hector Portillo is our Economics Minister. However, they certainly were not close. On opposite sides politically. After the murder of Augustin Portillo, Hector's own father and mother, along with an aunt, were killed in the bombing of the U.S. Embassy."

"I'll offer to talk to him personally. Could you arrange that, Colonel?" Kavanagh said.

CHAPTER 25

The news of Patricia Reyes' death effected Carlos Perez like nothing ever before. Reyes was his woman. They'd been together for sixteen years. At first it was the sex. Reyes was a passionate lover with a great body. But it became much more than the physical attraction. Shit, he'd not even been with another woman since the first time with Reyes in Mexico City. Even though frequently tempted, he knew she would somehow know. She was that kind of woman.

Now she was gone. But that other part, that's what disturbed him. She'd been fucked before she died. The effect was almost physical pain. It blotted everything else out. Some other man had been inside her. He couldn't shake the vision. Who? Did the guy kill her? The fucking police enjoyed telling him.

Once the initial shock passed, Perez's thoughts turned to who did this? No one in the Mara Salvatrucha would dare this. Even other ranking leaders. The Mexicans? What reason? No reason they should target her. But she was a very attractive woman. The Sinaloa big shots had practically come in their pants when they met her. Certainly possible with Perez now being out of the way.

But this happened within days of his arrest. Was she raped? The police implied it wasn't rape but they might be lying. If it wasn't rape, who and why? What the hell was she doing with another man?

At first it was just a vague speculation. Too many years have passed, too implausible. As he probed the idea further it might not be that farfetched. Did she panic and somehow find Victor Castell? Did he even live here? How did she find him? But Castell was the only possibility that could fit. They were once lovers, why not again?

After Las Vegas, Perez and Reyes talked a lot about Castell. Why did the bombs explode prematurely? Did Castell get away? They never read that he was arrested for the bombings. How did he get away? Where was Castell when Molina died at the Tropicana? Was he among the dead victims killed? How did Reyes feel about Castell? But once they became real lovers, Perez didn't ever want to hear about Castell again.

Above all else, any contact with Castell could be dangerous. He and Reyes needed to bury their terrorist past just as Castell must have done if he survived Las Vegas. Perez still harbored some expectation of a reasonable prison sentence. Maybe deportation again after serving a few years. He was facing charges of accessory to murder, drug trafficking, racketeering, conspiracy, and money laundering. Serious enough charges but still defendable with always the possibility of a plea bargain. The mass murders of the bombings would however mean a certain death sentence in U.S. Federal Court.

Perez was sitting in the Metropolitan Detention Center. Bail denied. His trial was months away. The only outside contact was with his lawyer. But even locked away, Perez still had resources. He needed to know more of the details about Patricia Reyes' death. He'd find the guy that screwed her and then killed her. He would have his revenge. Perez had a small army of sociopaths still under his control even from jail. Money could buy him the information. He passed a note to the prison officials that he needed to see his lawyer.

Luis Delgado was seated in one of the jail's attorney-client conference rooms when Perez was brought in.

"What's on your mind, Mr. Perez?"

"I need your help."

"I'm your lawyer. That's what I've been doing. But you have to understand ….."

"It's not about my case. I need something investigated. Do you know someone?"

"Investigated? Such as what?"

"The murder of my woman. I want the fucker that did it. I want his balls shoved into his mouth."

"The police haven't even called it a murder yet."

"I don't give a fuck. I want the guy. Do you have someone who can do this kind of work? It's worth a lot of money. For you too."

Delgado rubbed his chin and said nothing for a few moments. He could stall but in the end he'd do it. If he said he didn't know anybody, word would get around that he wasn't all that powerful an attorney. Outright refusal was out of the question. Both career and life limiting. Perez's street name, El Martillo was well earned.

"I may have somebody that could help with this kind of work. A bail bondsman. Hunts down bail fugitives all the time. A bounty hunter. How much?"

"I'll put up fifty thousand. You pay out what you need to get the information, keep the rest."

Delgado eyes widened at the mention of the amount and nodded affirmatively. "Ok. You got any idea where my guy starts?"

"No. First of all he needs to find out what the police know."

"If the police have little to go on my man maybe isn't going to fare any better."

"The police have other crimes to investigate. I expect your guy to be more motivated. But there is one piece of information I want him to check out. Something the police don't have. Find someone named Victor Castell. Late forties. Has a college degree in electrical engineering. Used to live in Pasadena twenty-five years ago."

"American?"

"Yeah. An American. Speaks Spanish though."

"Who is he?"

"Somebody I knew from a long time ago."

Frank Torres was in his fifties. Physically fit. He could handle himself in most any altercation. His parents were Mexican immigrants. Ran a small restaurant in Alhambra all their lives. The two daughters and their husbands now ran the business. Early on, Frank the eldest son made it known that he wasn't interested. At the first chance he joined the Army. He had ideas about getting into some elite special operations unit but soon found he wasn't that gung-ho. Not willing to endure continual physical training until you dropped. Settled instead for two enlistments in the military police.

Leaving the Army, Torres had thoughts about getting into law enforcement. An uncle enticed him to join his bail bond business instead. Located in downtown Los Angeles, the business catered to Mexican and Central Americans. There was no shortage of clients. The uncle needed someone to help with tracking down the frequent bail jumpers. His nephew had the right attributes. Strong and aggressive. Able to physically handle himself. Knew weapons. Knew police and investigative procedures from his military experience.

Torres thrived in his new job. It paid better than regular police work. Best of all he didn't have to operate within a bureaucracy. There were surprisingly few constraints placed on fugitive apprehension so he could make his own rules. Virtually no such thing as excessive use of force. Torres quickly established a reputation for rough treatment on those he found. The intention was to send a message to prospective bail clients, *do not try skipping out of appearing in court. The consequences were worse.*

Torres was so good that he expanded his services to other bail bondsmen to recover fugitives. By now, he ran his uncle's bail bond business. He had a team of three experienced bounty hunters, often contracting to other bail bond office assignments to apprehend bail jumpers for a percentage of the bond amount at risk. The most lucrative work was the worst offenders with the largest bonds. Torres even reached into Mexico to recover his fugitives.

"Frank, how are things, amigo?" Luis Delgado said as Torres answered the telephone. They knew each other well. The attorney provided Torres the occasional lucrative assignment to locate someone for one of his criminal clients.

"Can't complain. What's up?"

"A job. A good paying job. Need to find somebody. Just to locate him, nothing more."

"How much?"

"Twenty-five grand plus expenses."

That got Torres attention. "Who's paying?"

"A client. All you need to do is find a guy for my client."

"And this guy, what'd he do?"

"May have murdered my client's woman."

"So the police are investigating?"

"Yes."

"So why does he need my services? Expect me to find something the police missed?"

"Not necessarily. It's a low level homicide if even that. I've looked into it. The police are not going to devote manpower to this. He wants to find this guy quickly. So are you in?"

"Of course, for twenty-five plus and no need to break any legs, why wouldn't I be?"

"Be in my office in an hour. I'll give you the particulars and the money. Like I said, my client is in a real hurry."

Delgado occupied an office in a modest building a few blocks from the criminal courts building in downtown Los Angeles. The office itself was expensively furnished. His clientele were the more successful criminals. These guys often lived high. They respected power. Delgado wanted them to feel their attorney was worth the high fees he charged.

Delgado gave Torres an envelope. The contents consisted of a San Diego newspaper clipping from page three about the death of woman in a local motel. It mentioned only that the police had evidence she was not alone when she died from a blow to her head. There were vague references to possibly some domestic argument. There was a photo of a pretty woman provided by someone connected to Carlos Perez, and a separate photo of Victor Castell taken from his company's website.

"The woman was the girlfriend of my client. Longtime girlfriend. Not sure about the connection to this businessman, or how my client knows him, but he wants to know if it was him. The police claim she had sex before she died. Not sure if that was true. Could be the FBI just wanted to taunt my client. Might be this guy, might not. If not, you find out who it was."

"FBI? How are they involved? Who is your client?"

"Carlos Perez."

"Jesus Christ. That MS-13 big shot they captured in that Pico Union shootout a couple of weeks ago?"

"That's the guy. Perez thinks it could be this guy. Name's Victor Castell. Businessman. Owns a high-tech company in Pasadena. Computer systems stuff. Consulting. Lots of government contracting according to the Internet. Here's his company's website. That's where I got this picture. The police don't know about this guy."

Torres said, "Since Perez is facing a long list of federal charges, he's going away for a long time. Want's to finger the guy that was dicking his old lady. Then he'll set his MS-13 psychopaths loose. Hate to be in this poor bastard's shoes. So you're acting as Perez's bag man, right, Luis?"

"You want this job or not, Torres?"

That was never in question. Frank Torres didn't really have any qualms about trading a life for money. "Ok. How's Perez know this guy?"

"Wouldn't say. If I had to guess it was someone he knew from a long time ago. Someone this Reyes woman also knew. I'd further speculate that it might be the woman's former lover."

"Seems a little farfetched that a gangland asshole like Perez would be sharing a woman with an American businessman."

"Who knows? I didn't come up with this guy's name, Perez did. So there's some connection."

"Ok. What do the police know?"

"Christ, Torres, that's your job to find out. The San Diego police aren't about to share details of an ongoing investigation with an unconnected defense attorney."

If this guy Castell turned out to be the idiot that fucked the girlfriend of an MS-13 top guy, than Torres' job was easy. The thought struck him as what did it matter? The woman was dead. If he could construct a plausible case for it being Castell, Perez would buy it. Tough deal for this Castell guy.

The newspaper article offered little information. Torres first had to find out what the police knew. He had long ago determined that locating bail fugitives was a case of access to information. Relatives, associations, girlfriends of those he needed to find. The police databases were the best source of fundamental information already documented. So how to tap into this font of information? A source within the police department. More than one source even better. Frank Torres had cultivated multiple sources within the various Southern California police agencies. LAPD, LA Sherriff's Department, and the San Diego agencies. He even had sources within Mexico, the Tijuana Police and the Policía Federal.

Torres' sources risked little and he paid well. So it was a quick call to a sergeant with the San Diego Sherriff's Department to get him current with the Reyes case. The deputy called back an hour later providing the details of the crime scene, the autopsy results, and the only witness testimony obtained. A restaurant waitress had identified Reyes from a photograph. Police had canvased an area within a radius of the motel where the body was found. The witness said Reyes had dinner with a well-dressed man. The autopsy revealed semen from recent intercourse. The police sergeant commented on the unusual aspect that it was the FBI doing the real leg-work investigation of what otherwise would be a routine homicide investigation under state jurisdiction. The police reports didn't say why the Feds were interested.

Armed with this information, Torres called the restaurant. The waitress would be on duty that evening starting at six. Dressed in a sport coat with a handgun visible in a holster, Torres was there to meet her. He identified himself as a San Diego Sheriff's Department detective, quickly showing her a badge in a leather case. Close scrutiny would have revealed the badge to read *fugitive recovery officer*, not a law enforcement officer.

"Could I speak with you a moment, Ms Flores. I just have a couple of questions," Torres said as they stood to the side of the entry lobby.

"Is it about that poor woman that died? The police didn't say that when they asked me questions, but I heard it on the news the next day."

"That's right. This was the woman you waited on that night?" Torres handed her a picture of Patricia Reyes.

"Yes, that's her. Pretty woman. Too bad what happened."

Torres handed the waitress the picture of Victor Castell. "And was this the guy she was with that night?"

The waitress took a moment looking at the picture. "Yes. That looks like him. Good looking guy. But the other policeman didn't show me this picture."

"I know. That's how investigations progress. That's why I came back to get your help. Tell me, were they having a good time, or were they arguing?"

"Well I didn't listen in on what they were talking about, but I'd say they weren't arguing. The woman had her hand on his hand a lot. Looked like they liked each other."

The easiest twenty-five grand Torres ever made. That prick lawyer Delgado could have almost done this himself. Too bad for this poor bastard Castell. The MS-13 was the most violent gang in Los Angeles. Even the other gangs avoided tangling with them. Fucking this big shot Perez's woman would surely get your balls wacked off before those crazy assholes literally wacked off your head. But that wasn't Frank Torres' problem.

CHAPTER 26

The investigation continued to progress with good cooperation from the Salvadoran National Police. However that didn't change the difficulties of looking for information from twenty-five years ago. Nor did it change the fact that this wasn't the United States. Record keeping was inconsistent. Everything resided in paper files. The entire security apparatus had changed in the intervening decades. And the Salvadoran police simply did not possess the level of expertise required. Not that long ago, suspects were just beaten to obtain dubious confessions as the standard operating procedure.

Colonel Calderón resurrected old files on the extensively investigated assassinations of the two senior military officers prior to the U.S. Embassy bombing. Several witnesses from that time subsequently identified Molina as the male suspect in the General Ruiz murder. With the passage of so many years, the same witnesses could not conclusively identify his female companion as either his girlfriend Martha Rodriguez, or Patricia Reyes.

However, the prior kidnapping and murder of Colonel Solorgano suggested Carlos Perez might have been involved. He had the most experience with weapons from his participation with the FMLN rebels. From two of Perez's cousins, there was a reputation for violence. Of all the others within Molina's group, he would have been the most capable of decapitating the Colonel, assuming he was even part of the group. The only link was his subsequent involvement with Reyes. The murders of the band members prior to the bombing may have been his doing but there was no evidence to link him to that crime either. Therefore, these would not be new charges faced by Perez if he was ever deported back to El Salvador.

The first breakthrough came by locating Martha Rodriguez. She was living in Guatemala, teaching school. Still using her real name. She had moved there in 1989. The FBI made a formal request to Guatemala to be allowed to interrogate her. Two of Kavanagh's Spanish-speaking agents flew to Guatemala City where Rodriguez was being held.

Martha Rodriguez was scared to death fearing what might happen if she was returned to El Salvador. By the time the FBI agents arrived she was distraught, having spent two days in custody. Her newfound life with a husband may now all be destroyed. Before even being asked any questions, she claimed she was never involved with Santiago Molina's plan to attack the United States with bombs.

"Why did you leave El Salvador, Señora?"

"Because I knew it was Santiago that did those things."

"I thought you said you did not know about the bombs?"

"I .....I didn't. I knew Santiago was helping the rebels. Helping them to get weapons. He was using his company to arrange those things. But I knew something was wrong. He left the house two weeks before the embassy bombing. He took most of his clothing. He said he was coming back but he'd be away for some time. When news came of the bombing I just suspected he was involved. Later when I learned of his death in the bombing in the United States, I feared I might be implicated. So I left El Salvador."

"But you were never part of this terrorist group?"

"No. Never."

"That is hard to believe, Señora. Molina lived with you. You were lovers. You expect us to believe that you knew nothing?"

"But I didn't. Santiago talked politics. Anti-government politics, but never that he was going to do such a thing."

"Señora, understand what I am about to tell you. Many Salvadorans were killed by Santiago Molina. You will be deported back to El Salvador to face trial. At the least you will be charged as an accomplice. With that many people murdered, I would think your sentence will be harsh."

Martha Rodriguez wept. The agents let her fear sink in.

"Please don't send me back. I'll tell you everything I know. Just don't send me back to El Salvador."

"Then you must not only convince us but give us some useful information."

"Yes. Anything."

"Did you know a Carlos Perez?"

"Oh yes. A strong, good looking young man. He came to the house often. Santiago said he worked for his company."

"What about a young woman named Patricia Reyes?"

"Yes. She came by often. A student of Professor Portillo. Santiago and the Professor knew each other well. Patricia talked politics with Santiago. She was committed to overthrowing the military-ruled government. Always thought she had a crush on Santiago, however one time she brought a young man to the house. An American, but he spoke Spanish fluently. Apparently lived in Panama much of his life. Turned out that he was a nephew of Professor Portillo. That's how they met."

"His name?"

"Victor Castell."

"What else do you know about him?"

"Well, I only met him once. But he was more than just a friend to Patricia. The whole time she had her hand on him. Kissed him often. Because of the curfew it became too late for them leave. So they spent the night. In the same bed. They were lovers. Santiago and I heard them making love that night."

"What else do you know about this Victor Castell?"

"Well, he was educated in the United States. Patricia said he was some sort of engineer. I forget the specifics. She was very proud of that."

The agents relayed the information to Egan Kavanagh in San Salvador. After first calling Washington to provide information on Victor Castell, he telephoned Colonel Calderón. Would the Colonel arrange a meeting with the Economics Minister Hector Portillo?

This was an intriguing development. Augustin Portillo was an outspoken critic of the ruling government in 1989. Molina knew the Professor. The Professor's nephew was now the Economics Minister. Another nephew, this Victor Castell, was involved with Reyes and Molina. Add to this the fact that among the dead in the U.S. Embassy bombing was René Portillo and his wife Maria, and another Portillo sister, Alicia Portillo Castell. Victor Castell's mother? How did Castell fit into this tangle of violent death?

Within the hour a flood of information about Victor Castell came to Kavanagh's secure computer in his temporary embassy office in San Salvador.

The following afternoon, Kavanagh met Hector Portillo in Portillo's office. After an exchange of pleasantries, Portillo said he was aware of the United States FBI reopening the investigation after so many years.

"Not exactly reopening, Mr. Minister. It was never closed. We always assumed there were at least a couple of others unaccounted for among Santiago Molina's group that died in the

Las Vegas bombings. The identification of this Reyes woman from the single fingerprint recovered from the embassy bombing opened up new avenues for investigation. We have always felt that the bomb maker also got away."

"I too would like to see him caught. He murdered my parents and my aunt. How can I be of help?"

"It's about your cousin, Victor Castell. What can you tell me about him?"

"Victor? Well not much. I never knew him well back then. Even less since then. I've not seen him since that terrible time in 1989. I always assumed that the loss of his mother and his terrible experience when he visited El Salvador that year affected him deeply. Understandable how he would have been embittered. Probably wished to avoid anything that would recall those terrible memories. You know he was never able to attend his mother's funeral?"

"Why's that?"

Portillo sighed before answering. "You must understand the political environment here at that time. The civil war still raged. Those final years of the conflict saw some of the worse violence."

"Yes. Like the reemergence of the right-wing death squads? I believe they were responsible for the murder of your uncle Augusin Portillo."

Portillo revealed a slight scowl. "There was terrible violence, atrocities committed by both sides. That's why peace could only be secured through a general amnesty.

"As for my Uncle Augustin, well let's say I never agreed with his left-wing politics. He would have seen El Salvador devolve into a Cuban-like socialistic state. The entire family disavowed his politics. He was outcast like the Osama bin Laden of our family."

"Yet your cousin Victor apparently saw his Uncle Augustin during his visit here the summer of 1989."

"Yes, the family became aware of that. It created quite an argument. You see he was visiting here with his mother, my Aunt Alicia. She had recently separated from her husband, Victor's father. Victor had just graduated from his American university. He planned on resuming graduate studies in the fall back in the United States. Victor and his mother were staying at my father's estate near Santa Ana. Our family has large holdings in coffee and other agriculture."

"You mentioned some kind of trouble that occurred that prevented Victor Castell attending his mother's funeral. What was that?"

Portillo gave another sigh of resignation. "I never knew all of the details, only what I was told by my father. Apparently Victor and some girl had a violent encounter with the security forces. The girl was beaten. Victor was apparently not seriously hurt. His identity as a nephew of René Portillo somehow became known. As a result, he was immediately deported. My father never told me how he learned that."

"And this was when?"

"Probably a couple of weeks before the embassy bombing."

"And the girl? What happened to her?"

"I was never told. I assumed she was arrested. Perhaps something worse given those times."

"Do you know her name?"

"No."

Kavanagh reviewed Hector Portillo's description of events with the background record of Victor Castell. Passport records confirmed Castell had exited the United States on a flight bound for El Salvador in late May of 1989. He would crosscheck this with the old Salvadoran immigration control records. U.S. records showed his reentry into the United States in August of the same year. That was only days after the U.S. Embassy bombing but before the Las Vegas bombings. But if he was in fact deported from El Salvador before the embassy bombing, where did he go during those intervening weeks?

It took some doing but eventually the old paper immigration entry records were recovered. Castell did enter El Salvador in May, 1989. However, there was no record of him being deported, nor any exit record of him taking a flight from San Salvador. Calderón explained that if the Minister was correct about what happened, then it was probably an extrajudicial action to be rid of a problem American. After all, he was a relative of an influential citizen.

Could Castell be the bomb maker? He had the right credentials. Might he have been the person who bought the electronic components for the radio frequency control circuit? The one the shopkeeper said had a foreign accent? But if Castell were suddenly forced to leave the country, how did he assemble the bombs? Of course the timing was not known. Had he already assembled the detonation circuits before being deported?

Still no compelling evidence. Not even a totally convincing set of circumstantial evidence. Castell could be a red herring. Much might be explained convincingly by Castell.

There was probably little left to find in El Salvador. He would keep his team here however until they exhausted all possibilities. If there was anything to probe more deeply it was any record that might exist in the United States for the period following Castell's return to the United States and the Las Vegas bombings. Could they place him in Las Vegas at the time of the two casino bombings?

He would return to Washington. There was still a world of active terrorists looking to harm the United States. This old case had to be put into proper perspective. It had become too personal. But then again, the FBI was committed to never giving up on a cold case.

There was another wild card. If Castell could be tied to Patricia Reyes' death, might it prove as leverage to learning more about twenty-five years ago? Assuming he was the guy she had intercourse with, then a DNA match would place him squarely under the State of California's investigation into a possible homicide. But how would they get a DNA sample from Castell? Kavanagh was not yet ready to alert Castell that they were investigating him as a suspected terrorist on multiple counts of murder.

CHAPTER 27

"So it was Castell," Perez said to his attorney Luis Delgado. Delgado had few scruples but he felt decidedly uneasy giving Carlos Perez the confirmation that Victor Castell had been with his woman. Probably the guy she had sex with. Maybe he even killed her. At the least, Castell was undoubtedly the guy that was there when she died. Tried to stem the flow of blood with towels apparently. Probably wasn't murder. Maybe an argument? Whatever happened, Castell was a walking dead man. Perez would unleash his psychopathic Maras to butcher the guy.

But Delgado rationalized that he was only communicating information. He couldn't stop it. So why not take the money and chalk it up to just the bad shit in life? That's how he made his living.

Perez remained silent for several minutes. Delgado tried to engage Perez in a discussion about his case.

"Not now, Delgado. This is more important. I'll tell you what I want you to do. Give me a piece of paper and pen."

After scribbling a message, Perez signed with a special symbol. It looked like one of the Mara Salvatrucha's tattoo symbols.

"You're to go see my man, Emilio again. Give him this. He'll give you some more money. A lot of money. Once you have it I want you ...."

"Carlos, no. I know what you want. But I'm a lawyer. I can't be a part of that."

"What the fuck you talking about? You're a fucking lawyer alright. My lawyer. I'm the one who pays you. You make a fucking lot of money off me. So I expect you to do what I ask. If I could get another messenger I would. But I can't, so you're it. Now shut the fuck up and do as I say."

Delgado said nothing. He knew he had little choice if he wanted to continue living. Serves him right for taking on this Mara Salvatrucha big shot as a client. They were all crazy. Except for Perez, the rank and file MS-13 pieces of shit had tattoos all over their bodies, often their necks and faces. The worst of the gangbangers. This Emilio he was to see looked like some freak from a carnival show. The problem was their love for violence. Extreme violence. They would kill over the slightest perceived provocation. That's why the Mexicans hired them for muscle. Delgado swore to stick with Mexican drug cartel clients in the future.

"What do you want me to do?" Delgado said.

"It's not so bad, Delgado. You talk to this bounty hunter guy. I want him to set up Castell. Find out his habits. Pick a place for my people to snatch him. That's it. He leaves. Nothing violent on his part. He doesn't even participate. Makes a lot of money."

"My guy's not stupid. He'll still be an accomplice to murder. What if he won't do it?"

"You saying he might not be up for this? Emilio's going to give you a hundred grand in cash. Think that'll buy your fucking bounty hunter?"

"Why don't you just have your own people do this? Why do you need the bounty hunter?" Delgado said although the staggering amount of money had his interest. "I'll give Emilio all the info on Castell."

Perez glared at Delgado. "Listen you dumb shit. Castell runs in neighborhoods where my guys would stand out. They can snatch Castell but they can't conduct surveillance on where and how to do it. Your guy snatches people for a living. He knows how to do this thing. And I'll bet he doesn't have tattoos on his neck."

Once back at his office, Delgado poured himself a whiskey from a liquor cabinet. An hour later, Frank Torres was sharing a drink and sitting across Delgado's desk listening to Delgado lay-out the proposal.

Torres' first instinct was to tell Delgado to go to hell. That changed when he heard his fee would be fifty thousand dollars. Like Delgado, Torres' morality was cost-based. It sounded like a simple task. Castell would not be expecting to be kidnapped. He didn't have security. All Torres would have to do is set it up. He knew what would happen to Castell. But shit happens.

"So who would do the actual snatching of this guy?" Torres said.

"Some MS-13 guys."

"Fuck. You ever seen those assholes? Tattoos all over their fucking faces. How am I going to keep them under wraps without attracting attention?"

"Christ, Torres, that's your problem. That's why you're being paid all this money. Besides, isn't that what you do? Stakeout people so you can take them down?"

"Tell you what, Luis, I'll do some research on this guy to see how easy it's going to be and get back to you."

"Bullshit, Torres. Be back here in my office first thing tomorrow. I'll have the money. You have your goddamn plan. I expect you're in on this, so don't let me down. I already committed to Perez. You wouldn't want me to tell that crazy fucker that you won't do it, would you, Frank?"

Torres had already considered that. Not sure it wasn't a Delgado tactic but it was still a disturbing thought. At eight-thirty the following morning, he was waiting for Luis Delgado in his office reception area.

"So?" Delgado said.

"I'm in," Torres said.

Delgado opened his briefcase and took out an envelope which he tossed to Torres.

"Fifty thousand. Now the other thing. This needs to be done soon. A few days at most."

"Ok. I think I have a plan worked out. First of all I'll ...."

Delgado cut him off. "Shit, I don't want to know the details. Nothing about it. Just get it done. Quickly. In the envelope is how you can contact a guy called Emilio."

"How will he know me? You expect me to just walk up to this guy in some shithole in Pico Union?"

"Christ no, Frank. I told him to expect you within a couple of days. Told him you'd be the big guy that looks like a fucking cop."

"Alright, alright. How do I recognize this Emilio?"

Delgado smiled. "That's easy, Frank. Apart from all sorts of tattoos on his neck he's got this solid dark tattoo covering his whole nose. Comes out from the nose and curls up each cheek," Delgado said as he traced his fingers along his own face. "Even amongst these weirdoes, Emilio is the ugliest fucker of the bunch."

CHAPTER 28

Frank Torres spent the next three days researching Victor Castell and his movements. Wife Eleanor was an attorney. Age forty-five. Works at a law firm located in downtown Los Angeles, a thirty-minute drive with rush hour traffic from Pasadena. Daughter, Regina, age fifteen. A sophomore at South Pasadena High School. Victor Castell, CEO of Castell Systems, Inc., Pasadena. Majority shareholder. According to their website the company provides information technology services to large corporations and governments. They were even licensed for top security clearance work. Castell was forty-seven. Degrees in electrical engineering from Cal Poly and an advanced degree in computer engineering from Caltech.

Torres checked out Castell's residence in South Pasadena. The address was on a tree-lined street with expensive older homes on large lots. Castell's was an elegant old mansion dating from the 1920's. The house set well back from the street on several acres with a long drive. The perimeter was surrounded by an eight-foot high ornate metal fence with a gate. The property value would be well into seven figures.

This was a successful, wealthy, smart guy. Wife was a real looker. Hard to figure why he was screwing some low-life Mara Salvatrucha's woman. But not all together surprising in Torres line of work. Lots of fucked-up people. Even those with money.

According to DMV records which Torres had the ability to access, Castell and his wife had matching silver Mercedes S class sedans. He also had a three hundred thousand dollar red Aston Martin sports car.

To avoid suspicion while watching Castell's home, Torres used a white service van labelled *Southland Construction, Plumbing Contractor* on the side, complete with a logo. He also wore a white jumpsuit with the same name and a fake work order on a clipboard. The disguise was one of his standard props. It was not inconceivable that while loitering on the street he could attract a police patrol in this sort of neighborhood. Delgado was right about a bunch of tattooed Mara Salvatruchas sticking out like a bad advertisement in this part of the city.

Staking out the house on three consecutive week days revealed that Castell left his house around eight-thirty in the morning. It was about a twenty-five minute drive to his company's office building including his usual stop at a Starbuck's Coffee. Each of those days Castell drove the red Aston Martin. Torres took a number of photos. Easy enough to follow even for these MS-13 gang bangers.

Castell's company was not far from the Caltech campus. It occupied a three story office building adjacent to a private parking structure. Torres walked the parking structure by climbing a rear stairway thereby avoiding the attendant manning the vehicle entrance. Except for visitor allocated spaces, each space was identified by a reserved sign with a number. Castell's red Aston Martin was parked in the space labelled *Castell Systems #1.*

Torres needed a plan to capture Castell that was simple to execute and allow for a bunch of guys with facial tattoos to get close enough without attracting public attention.

The necessity to do this job on short notice with people he didn't know meant that the plan had to be extremely simple. These people were also violent thugs, not Torres' own experienced crew. So that meant only three options; Castell's house, on the way to his office, or at the office.

The best option was clearly at the office. More specifically the office parking structure. The house had too many unknowns beginning with a wife and daughter. If these MS-13 guys killed all three, the public outcry would be extreme. No telling where that might lead. Trying to run Castell off the street by using a vehicle could attract all sorts of attention. It would also take some real driving skills. Even if these gang bangers could pull it off, they'd be exposed and easily identified by their tattoos. So the parking structure was clearly the best option.

There were two sets of stairways to the parking structure upper levels, and a single elevator toward the front. The rear stairway offered the possibility for the Mara Salvatruchas to enter without being seen from the street. The rear of the parking structure also faced toward the rear of a string of retail buildings on the next street. The Maras with their distinctive tattoos still had to get into the area, park their vehicle, and make their way to the stairway. This access alley would afford some measure of relative concealment in the early morning.

Those goddamn MS tattoos were the biggest problem. When he meets this Emilio character he will try to convince him to use guys without freaky facial tattoos. It was a four-man job. One driver, with three guys to take Castell. Besides guys with minimal tattoos, they'd have to dress like normal people from this more affluent area, not the tough Latin ghetto. No white sleeveless T shirts and baggy pants.

The plan couldn't be much simpler. The kidnappers would access the rear stairway to the parking structure by driving their vehicle to a place by the dumpsters behind the retail buildings. If they used a vehicle with tinted windows they would be able to park for a brief time without attracting attention. He would draw them a simple map. Once inside the parking structure, they would go to the second level. He would draw a map of that as well, showing Castell's parking space. They could conceal themselves behind cars already parked. Castell typically arrived about nine o'clock after stopping at Starbuck's.

Simple yet with one seemingly serious flaw. There was no way to ensure there would not be other people also parking their cars. But of course Torres didn't give a shit if the kidnapping was seen. Any bystanders would pull back when the Maras brandished guns. Castell would turn up dead anyway soon enough. So his fate wouldn't be a secret for long. If witnesses identified the perpetrators as MS-13 gang members, Torres didn't much care. He wasn't going to be with them.

Torres concluded his planning on a Tuesday. The next morning he would see this Emilio character. Assuming Emilio could put together the crew to do this, they'd plan it for Thursday morning.

Frank Torres drove one of his older surveillance cars to the meeting with Emilio. No sport coat, no gun. Dressed in working class clothes, baseball cap, and dark glasses, Torres did not want to stand out. Better if nobody could describe him well. He parked in a lot next to a Salvadoran hole-in-the-wall restaurant. As instructed, he sat down at a table. A heavyset woman came over to take his order.

In Spanish, Torres ordered a coffee and plate of eggs. "I was told to meet Emilio here. I was told you would call him and give him my cell phone number."

The woman took the slip of paper. She returned to pour Torres coffee as his cell phone rang.

"You're Torres?" the caller said.

"Yes. Emilio?"

"Stay where you are. Have something to eat. Fifteen minutes." The call disconnected.

Torres had just started on his eggs when Emilio entered the restaurant with two others. By Delgado's description, this could only be Emilio with his elaborate nose tattoo. He took a seat at Torres' table while the other two took another table. Two other patrons hurriedly paid up and left their unfinished breakfasts.

"You look like a fucking peasant, Torres, not some hotshot investigator."

"Well I didn't want to stand out."

"You mean like me, Torres?"

Torres ignored the taunt. "Let's get down to business, Emilio. Here's the plan."

"What if I don't like your plan, Mister Hotshot? What if I do this my fucking way?"

"All the same to me. I was paid to get the information on your target and set this thing up. You want to do it some different way, go for it."

Emilio just grinned. "Easy, Mister Hotshot, I'm just fucking with you. Tell me about this plan of yours."

"Ok. You need four guys. One driver. Three to make the capture. They need to be dressed like they fit in. No hoodies, no baggies. No offense, but can you get four guys with less ....."

"Tattoos? You don't like tattoos? You maybe don't think I'm pretty?"

"Listen, Emilio. If your guys are even seen driving in Pasadena they'll be pulled over. This is rich gringo territory. Can you find four guys that at least don't have facial tattoos?"

Emilio stared at Torres for a moment before responding. "I have four guys. So what's the plan?"

Torres handed Emilio the hand drawn map of the area and the parking structure.

"I'll follow Castell when he leaves for work. Usually about eight-thirty. He stops for coffee. Arrives at his office around nine o'clock. I'll give your guys a call on a cell phone when Castell is about to pull into the parking structure. That's his parking space marked on the drawing. Second level. Can you get your hands on an SUV? One with tinted windows?"

Emilio nodded.

"Ok. At a quarter to nine, your guys pull behind these buildings here. Driver stays with the SUV, engine running. The other three go up these rear stairs here. They'll hide behind cars already parked. Usually a lot of cars are already parked by the time Castell arrives. He'll walk toward these stairs toward the front to go to his office."

Emilio nodded again. "When?"

"Tomorrow. Once I confirm that Castell will be at his office first thing in the morning I will call you. Can you be ready?"

Emilio nodded again and started to get up from the table.

"Tell me something, Emilio. Why don't you just shoot this Castell and be done with it?"

Emilio no longer smiled. "That is not our way, Mister Hotshot. This Victor Castell has done things he must pay for. How he pays is not your concern."

Torres called Castell's office on the pretext that he was an attorney for one of Castell Systems' customers. He needed to courier a critical document requiring Mr. Castell's signature first thing Thursday morning. Was Mr. Castell expected to be in the office? The receptionist checked the boss' schedule. *Yes, Sir. I expect him at nine o'clock.*

On Thursday morning Frank Torres pulled in with his non-descript Ford Crown Victoria behind the red Aston Martin as Victor Castell left his house. As typical, Castell stopped at his favorite Starbuck's Coffee. As he was leaving the coffee shop, Torres rang a cell number for Emilio's crew.

"Five minutes," Torres said. The call was disconnected with no reply.

As Castell proceeded to enter the parking structure, Torres turned onto the perpendicular street. He parked and looked down the alley behind the retail shops. A large black SUV was parked next to a dumpster. It was facing toward the street.

Several minutes later, three guys came running down the rear stairs of the parking structure and jumped into the SUV. The SUV accelerated out the alley taking the turn onto the street with screeching tires. Castell was not with them. Torres heard no gun shots. What the fuck happened?

CHAPTER 29

Castell pulled into the parking structure and inserted his card to raise the barrier. Most of the first level was allocated to handicapped parking and visitor spaces. He eased the sports car into the right hand turn up the ramp to the next level. His designated parking space was toward the front of the structure. As he eased forward he noticed a man in his rearview mirror. He was dressed in a jacket and jeans not unlike some of his younger staff. Except this guy had a shaved head with his collar turned up. Not a computer techie look.

Castell pulled into his parking space and watched the man approach through the rearview mirror. Coming straight toward the car. Suddenly there was a shout. The man walking turned away from Castell's car. Castell abruptly turned in his seat. There were now three men. They had handguns drawn. A bystander was making his way toward the stairs as one of the assailants yelled for the man to get down on his knees. The other two turned back toward Castell. He clearly seemed to be the target.

Castell put the sports car into reverse and executed a ninety-degree turn, slamming the brakes as he shifted into first gear.

The two guys with guns were almost upon him when they had to jump to either side to avoid being hit as he reversed. Staring at him through the windshield, they were only thirty feet away. They could easily shoot him at this range. One was now close enough for Castell to see what looked like tattoos on the guy's neck.

Castell would not go down like a sheep. Careful not to stall the engine in his panic, he let out the clutch and depressed the accelerator. He would take these guys with him.

But no shots were fired. Nor did Castell hit any of the three. The two closest to his car again jumped out of the way. The third guy looked at him as he passed, still with his gun trained on the poor bystander now on his knees.

Castell took the turn down the ramp with screaming tires. Wasting no time on inserting his parking pass into the slot to open the gate, he slowed only slightly, hitting the toll barrier. The gate arm was torn off its mount doing considerable damage to the front of his car. Once onto the street, he raced down the street four blocks before pulling into another parking lot. Steam was pouring from the hood from the damaged radiator.

Within minutes, a continuous stream of police cars began converging on the office parking structure with sirens and lights.

Castell has badly shaken. Mild shock was setting in. He was dizzy and nauseous. After throwing up the scone he had earlier at the coffee shop, he sat back in the car seat for some time with the door open. The cool morning air felt therapeutic as beads of sweat materialized on his forehead.

Being a short distance away from the developing police spectacle allowed Castell a brief period to compose himself before the inevitable confrontation with the police. He had the disturbing thought that this must be connected to Patricia. Did Carlos Perez somehow know? That one image of the tattoo on the neck of one of the assailants made him wonder if these thugs were MS-13. If so, then it had to be Perez. But if not, if they were just out for robbery, why didn't they shoot? If nothing more than to scare him and that poor other guy. Shit, maybe they did shoot the guy. The only thing to do was to walk back to the chaotic scene at the office parking structure. Along the way, he rehearsed his script for what he would tell the police.

At Pasadena Police Headquarters, the interrogation was more grueling then he expected. Things like this just didn't happen in Pasadena. A senior detective, Lieutenant Walt Tominski, was in charge of the case. After three hours of repeating his story to several detectives and looking at mug shots, Tominski was about ready to wrap things up.

"The other witness, Mr. Johnson, said these guys seemed to be targeting you. Your own description of events supports that. Yet you claim you know of no reason why someone would try to harm you."

"That's not true. I only said there was no business related reason I could think of. I don't make enemies in my line of work, Lieutenant. Certainly no personal reason. I said my guess was a botched robbery. Scarier yet, a botched kidnapping. Anybody could find out that I probably had money. Driving my red Aston Martin maybe advertised me as a target. Why is that not the logical explanation, Lieutenant?"

"Because, Mr. Castell, that's not the style of these Latin gangs. And our best guess is that the perpetrators were gang members. They run drugs. They're not into kidnapping wealthy white guys. And they don't operate here in Pasadena. This was in broad daylight. Poorly planned. If they were a bunch of crazies and you were just a target of opportunity, why didn't they shoot you, especially after you tried to run them over?

"Mr. Johnson said these guys looked Mexican. Shaved heads. One guy had a big tattoo on his neck. But you say you don't know what ethnicity they might be, Mr. Castell."

"I don't. I can tell you they weren't black. Beyond that I have no idea. They weren't particularly dark complexioned. Could be

Middle Eastern. Might be Mexican, but Mexicans don't look a certain way. My mother was Salvadoran, my father of Spanish descent, but I don't think you could determine that heritage from my looks. Beyond the shaved heads, I'm not sure I could describe them. From all those mug shots I was shown of guys with shaved heads, frankly it could be any number of them. The shaved heads make everyone look alike if you only see them briefly."

"What about this guy with the tattoo?" Tominski said.

"I didn't see any tattoo so I can't say. Look, Lieutenant, I'm exhausted. I expect an emotional scene later when I have to tell my family. I'd like to leave now. I've been over everything again and again."

CHAPTER 30

"Director Kavanagh. I am calling because we have uncovered some important information," Colonel Calderón said via telephone to Kavanagh in his Washington D.C. office. "I believe we have firmly established that the bomb maker was this Victor Castell. The same name provided by Santiago Molina's girlfriend. The cousin of our Economics Minister Hector Portillo."

"Extraordinary. What have you uncovered, Colonel?"

"Two things actually, Director. Do you recall a man named Ernesto Morales when you were involved with the bombing investigation in 1989? He was the owner of the San Miguel radio shop that sold the electronic components used in the triggering circuit of the bombs."

"Yes. He identified some instructor at the university. The guy conveniently died in jail as I recall. Supposedly hanged himself," Kavanagh said with pronounced sarcasm.

Calderón said he too agreed that the engineering professor was not the bomb maker. "One of my more able investigators, Captain Gutiérrez, finally located Morales. I believe you met the Captain when you were here recently. Speaks good English. Morales son took over the business when the father became ill a few years ago. The son sold the shop and apparently immigrated to the United States. We recently located a daughter with whom we believed the old man was living.

"Ernesto Morales is in ill health. Apparently advanced emphysema from years of smoking. Breathes with the assistance of an oxygen bottle. However his mind is still alert. Like you, Director Kavanagh, Gutiérrez did not necessarily believe the man that purchased the electronic components from his shop was this engineering professor. The professor's arrest was based solely on the shop keeper's statement about the identification the person used when purchasing the electronics. Morales supposedly confirmed it was this professor after being shown his photograph. No other evidence is recorded to suggest why this professor came to the attention of the police."

"The reason is understandable, Colonel. The poor guy was picked to be a scapegoat on the basis of his name being used. It wasn't real police work."

"That would appear to be the case based upon what Captain Gutiérrez found," Calderón acknowledged. "Morales was terrified that this old event was being resurrected. He was terrified back then also. But Captain Gutiérrez is a gifted interrogator as you will see when I get to my second piece of news. After convincing Morales there was nothing to fear, he showed Morales ten photographs of men in their early twenties from that time. The engineering professor and the early photo you provided of Victor Castell were among the pictures. Morales conclusively identified Castell. When Gutiérrez asked why he identified the professor, Morales simply said that he was shown only that one picture. Morales also added, *"Besides, you were not from that time, Captain."*

"Excellent work, Colonel. Please commend Captain Gutiérrez for me."

"There is more. The enterprising Captain discovered something even more conclusive. It concerns the mother of one of the dead terrorists, Roberto Salas. You will recall she still harbors strong anti-government views when she was interviewed by our investigators during your recent visit. Like Morales, she is also terminally ill with cancer in a hospital in San Miguel. Apparently the disease has substantially advanced. Death is imminent. The doctor informed Señora Salas' daughter that her mother had perhaps as little as a few days to live.

"The daughter tearfully informed her mother of her deteriorated condition. According to our source, the old woman was not as scared of her impending death as she was of her stature in the afterlife. She confided to her daughter that she knew more of her son Roberto's involvement in the old bombing than she had told the police when they questioned her. She even confided to the daughter that she herself had helped this terrorist leader, Santiago Molina. *I have carried my own terrible guilt all these years, Mija.* She said to the daughter."

Kavanagh interrupted, "This source, Colonel, who was that?"

"A nurse. She was standing on the other side of the curtain drawn around the old woman's bed. She reported it to the police whom she recalled questioned the old woman weeks before."

"And why would this nurse be so helpful? Why become involved?"

"Politics. Old history. Everyone carries scars from the civil war. The nurse was a young girl during that time. She lost two brothers in the Army to the FMLN rebels. Grew up in a household not necessarily pro-government, but certainly anti-rebel. A chance to strike her own blow for past injustice? Who really knows?"

"Did the old woman reveal anything specific to her daughter?"

"Not specifics. But Captain Gutiérrez learned of the nurse's information. Gutiérrez is creative. With what he did, I can't say his methods don't trouble me, although they proved effective. You can judge for yourself, Director Kavanagh."

Christ, what did Gutiérrez do? Torture an old dying woman? "Ok, tell me, Colonel."

"Captain Gutiérrez created an innovative subterfuge. Without my permission you understand. But with the information he obtained, I will say no more about his methods. While disturbing, the Captain did obtain results.

"To put it bluntly, Director Kavanagh, Captain Gutiérrez impersonated a priest. He heard the dying woman's confession."

Kavanagh was stunned. As an Irish lad he was raised Roman Catholic although his parents only attended mass occasionally, mostly weddings and funerals. Kavanagh himself had only ambiguous religious feelings. However, the Church still served a larger cultural influence that was still part of Kavanagh. The thought of someone invading the sanctity of the confessional by impersonating a priest to extract information from a dying old woman made him decidedly uncomfortable.

But the deed had been done. Kavanagh withheld his personal feelings. "And what did he learn from the Salas woman, Colonel?"

"Molina's group encamped at Isabel Salas' rural home outside of San Miguel. Apparently to prepare the bombs used in the U.S. Embassy bombing in 1989. She named all of the participants. That includes Carlos Perez now in custody in Los Angeles, Patricia Reyes, and all the others that died later in Las Vegas. She also identified this Victor Castell that you have been interested in.

"She talked of the Reyes woman suffering injuries from being badly beaten by security forces. Isabel Salas nursed Reyes back to health. Victor Castell had apparently become her lover. Reyes told Salas about how she met Castell through Castell's uncle, Augustin Portillo. How Castell was blinded by rage looking for revenge both for his uncle's murder as well as the confrontation where they beat Reyes and deported him."

"His cousin, your Economics Minister alluded to something like that. But if he was deported, what was his role in the bombing?"

"According to Salas, he returned back to El Salvador. Castell made his way back by covertly returning to El Salvador by way of Honduras with the help of Santiago Molina. After Castell arrived at her house she said he was clearly bent on revenge. Reyes boasted that Castell was an engineer. Came from a wealthy family but he was on the side of the people. Castell had promised to help Molina devise a mechanism for remotely detonating the bombs. Reyes said they would strike a major blow against the government and the military. "

"Did this Salas woman actually see Castell working on the bombs?"

"She never says, but she makes several references to Castell being the engineer who devised the method of detonating the bombs remotely. Besides learning of this from Reyes, she also makes reference to her son Roberto talking about Castell's role. And she confessed the bombs were assembled at her house. She regarded Castell was the bomb maker."

"Well, Colonel, that is truly something. Not sure we can use it as evidence in the United States, but at least it resolves the questions."

"Perhaps that may be different in El Salvador, Director Kavanagh. We shall have to see. Our rules of evidence may permit seeking charges against this Victor Castell. He murdered many Salvadorans."

"You would have to seek his extradition from the United States, Colonel. That's a high hurdle for a U.S. court to grant extradition of an American citizen to a foreign country."

Kavanagh could have added that it was almost impossible for a banana republic with a checkered past. Adding that the suspect was wealthy, probably well connected, and could therefore mount a defense with the best attorneys available, it would be virtually impossible. If the same evidence could not produce an indictment in the United States, why would a federal court grant extradition to a more lax judicial process in a foreign country?

"One more thing, Director Kavanagh. I just provided you with a summary of what Isabel Salas said. Captain Gutiérrez extracted additional details. He secretly recorded everything the woman said. My staff can send both the audio recording and a transcript electronically to you."

Kavanagh thanked the Colonel. It took several minutes to consider this new information. And it was just information not really evidence. It did establish that Perez and Castell were the only remaining terrorists from Molina's group. But he still had no compelling evidence to make a case against either one.

With some ethical discomfort, Kavanagh read a translation of the transcript of the contrived confession of Isabel Salas. Most disturbing was Captain Gutiérrez's closing benediction of absolution while masquerading as a priest. But no matter how acquired, Kavanagh would still use the information if he could find a way.

CHAPTER 31

Victor Castell knew what this was about. It had to be. This wasn't a robbery. He had seen the tattoo on the neck of one of the would-be assailants. He couldn't be sure but it probably suggested MS-13. The other witness said they spoke in Spanish. If they were just crazies maybe high on drugs, why didn't they shot him when he tried to run them down? *Because they intended to kidnap him.*

What the hell was going on? Had to be Perez's doing. He would have learned of Patricia Reyes' death. Could he have somehow connected him? Not inconceivable. Perez knew Reyes was on the run from the police after escaping arrest. But for her to look him up after all these years? Just a wild guess by Perez? Still, it appeared to be the only answer. Perez had to be the one to set these thugs after him. Pasadena didn't have daylight armed robberies or carjackings.

It was one o'clock in the afternoon when Castell returned home. He was emotionally and physically spent after answering police questions for three hours. His stomach churned after too many cups of burnt police station coffee. He took a couple of antacid tablets with a glass of milk. It would be a long afternoon of trying to rationally determine what to do. It would be an even longer evening rehashing the day's events to his wife.

He had been home less than an hour when the gate intercom buzzed.

"Yes?"

"Is this Victor Castell?

"Who's asking?"

"Pasadena Police Department. Lieutenant Tominski, Mr. Castell."

"What is it now, Lieutenant? I've told you all I know about what happened."

"Ah, this is about something different, Mr. Castell. I have a court order, Sir. Please open the gate."

"A court order? What for?"

"The gate, Mr. Castell. I'll explain after you let us in."

Castell let Tominski and another plainclothes officer into the foyer of the house.

"The court order is to obtain your fingerprints and a DNA sample, Mr. Castell. It was issued by a judge in San Diego County. It's in connection with a homicide investigation. If you'll please come with us this won't take long."

"I need to call my lawyer."

"Once we're at the police station that can be arranged, Sir. You are not under arrest. This is simply a court order to obtain a DNA sample and fingerprints. Once that is accomplished, we will return you to your residence."

Castell was shaken. Everything was unraveling. Distressed, he accompanied the detectives to Pasadena Police Headquarters. At least he was not handcuffed. The day was becoming an unfolding nightmare of even more terrible things to come. Of course this was Perez's doing. He was the only one able to connect him to Reyes. Somehow Perez had fed the police information that it might be Castell's DNA from the semen that would have been found in an autopsy of Reyes.

He certainly needed to call his lawyer. He'd need his corporate lawyer to find a good criminal lawyer. Would his DNA be enough to charge him in connection with Reyes' death? Whatever the outcome, he'd have to eventually tell his wife. Tell her that he had a one-night stand with an old girlfriend? Who died in an accidental fall? He couldn't help her so he did his best to remove any evidence then snuck away. Except for the one item of evidence he couldn't remove.

He knew Eleanor. She wouldn't forgive him. It wasn't some affair with a younger woman. Eleanor was not only very attractive, but younger than this old girlfriend. Why this woman after twenty-five years? And someone wanted by the police? The girlfriend of a vicious gang leader now in jail. No, she would assume he must have been seeing her more than just this one time. Some old shared attachment. Castell couldn't exactly explain the potential of an even greater threat as the reason he agreed to see Patricia Reyes.

The police returned him to his home at three o'clock in the afternoon. His daughter would be home soon. His wife probably by six o'clock. He dreaded the prospect of recounting the hijacking episode. That's the word he would use regardless what the police called it. These guys were out to steal money, the Aston Martin, or maybe even to kidnap him. That would be a difficult couple of hours. After the emotions were exhausted then would come the logic-based discussion. His wife was an attorney. Sometimes she acted that way in her personal life. Why you? What did the police think? Was this something personal? Could it be related to some of the classified government work performed by Castell Systems? He would have to carefully stay on script. Now this new development would soon expose his involvement with Patricia Reyes. An illicit affair. Manslaughter? Even there he must conceal the much worse truth of these connected events to the past.

Worse yet, Castell suspected the real reason for the attempted attack. That now meant that Eleanor and Regina might very
well be in danger. Perez might try getting to him through hurting them. That also meant he would have to find some way to
safeguard them without telling them the real truth. But what ra-
tionale could he fictionalize to get them to go somewhere for at
least a couple of weeks while he tried to construct a more permanent solution? The labyrinth of lies was propagating at an un-
controllable rate.

Eleanor Castell came in from the garage right at five-thirty.

"You're home early, dear. That's nice," she said and kissed
him as she took off her coat. It was a chilly early December day.
"Is Regina home?"

"No. Not yet."

"Well she should be along soon. She had debate practice this
afternoon. Her friend Shirley's mom is bringing her home. They
probably stopped somewhere."

"Ok. Sit down, Eleanor. I've got to tell you about what happened today."

For the next hour Castell recounted the attempted hijacking
and aftermath. As expected, once Eleanor got beyond the initial
shock, she reverted to the professional question-asker. Castell
couldn't put up with the stress any longer.

"Enough, Eleanor. I don't have the answers. There's no reason anyone should want to harm me other than for money. I've
been through this for hours with the police. But I tell you, since
it's so unusual for something like this to happen here in Pasadena, we should take precautions. Maybe I am being targeted for
some unknown reason. I suppose it could be connected with
some of the classified work we do."

"Are you suggesting foreign agents might be behind this?"

"No, no. That would seem farfetched. But since we don't
know, we should take prudent precautions."

"So what kind of precautions are you suggesting, Victor?"

"Perhaps you and Regina might consider visiting dad in San Francisco. Make a long early Christmas holiday. You like San Francisco. Lots of things you and Regina could do. I'll come up when I can. Regina would only miss a week of school before the regular Christmas break."

"Speaking of Regina, where is she?" Eleanor said.

"Well just call her."

That's when Victor Castell's predicament became even more dreadful.

There was no answer when they called Regina's cell number. Over the next fifteen minutes they tried three more times, all unsuccessful, leaving messages.

"Call her girlfriend's mother. The one that was to bring her home," Castell said. There was an edge of fear to his voice.

He followed Eleanor's conversation up to when she yelled *what?*, accompanied by an expression of wide-eyed alarm.

"Put it on speaker."

According to the friend's mother, Regina had apparently left school at lunch. Didn't say anything to her daughter but she wasn't at her first class of the afternoon. Regina missed debate practice. The teacher didn't know why she wasn't there. Is everything all right?

Eleanor hurriedly got rid of the call with a promise to have Regina call the woman's daughter as soon as she got home. Must be some problem with her cell phone.

For the next hour Eleanor argued with her husband about calling the police. He was torn. Bringing in the police would obviously raise their interest in all of these collective events involving Castell. This court order for a DNA sample might even come up. But was he endangering his daughter?

After another hour, Castell had reached the point where he felt he had no choice but to call the police. Eleanor had become nearly distraught. He still expected his daughter to call or walk into the house with some perfectly logical explanation.

Before he took that next step to call in the police, events took an ominous turn.

The text message tone sounded on Castell's cell phone. Expecting it was finally his daughter, the message instead brought a new terror. *We have your daughter. Do not call the police. Will call you in five minutes.*

More disturbing was an accompanying brief video attached to the text message. A terrified Regina Castell with tears streaming down her face was being held by someone not visible to the camera. A tattooed hand cupped one of her naked breasts.

Eleanor Castell gasped as her husband showed her the message and video. "No!"

Castell's cell phone rang a few minutes later.

"Shut-up and listen, Castell," the caller said in Spanish. "If you want to see your daughter unharmed, do as I say."

Castell yelled in frustration, "Don't touch her you sonofabitch! What the hell do you want?"

"Watch what you say motherfucker. Just shut-up and listen. You come alone tomorrow night after dark. Eight o'clock. Ernest Debs Park. East of the 110. Know it?"

"I'll find it. Where exactly?"

You come up the road from the gate on the east side off Monterey Road. The gate will be closed but the locked chain will be cut. Close the gate and secure the chain after you enter. Come up the road to the picnic area. Park and wait there. We'll see if you're alone. If so we let your daughter go.

"Now to business, motherfucker. You bring a hundred thousand dollars. Small bills. Nothing bigger than fifties. Used bills. No consecutive serial numbers. No fucking dye or any of that clever police shit. You do this right, your daughter lives."

"I can't get that kind of cash on short notice."

"Bullshit. You've got twenty-four hours. You're a big shot rich guy. Use your clout with your bank."

Castell needed a better deal if he hoped to get his daughter back. This wasn't about the money. These assholes wanted him. Carlos Perez wanted him. He knew his life was forfeited with this new threat. But so was his daughter's if he met them unprotected at night in some desolate park. They wouldn't let her go.

"Well, mister big shot? You still there? What's it to be?"

"No deal. Not that way. No reason you will let me and my daughter leave after I hand over the money. So here's my counter. I'll get you the money. I'll bring it to you in this park. But you bring my daughter back to her house. She calls me on my cell phone that she is safe. Verified by my wife. Only after that do I hand over the money."

"Fuck you, mister big shot. You think we're stupid or what? What's to stop you from just leaving once your daughter is returned?"

"I'll be in the park, in my car. You'll be able to see me. Once she is safely returned home, I'll hand over the money."

There was a pause on the other end.

"Ok, motherfucker. But no bullshit. No cops. You better have the money. Try to fuck with us in any way and your little girl gets fucked. Really fucked. Fucked by a lot of big-dicked guys. Then we'll start cutting off pieces of her. She'll be a long time dying. You think about that. Be in the park at eight tomorrow night. Don't be late."

The caller disconnected.

Eleanor Castell had said nothing during her husband's exchange with the kidnappers. Now a flood of questions poured out. Her husband told her to calm down and just listen as he recounted the kidnappers' demands.

"You can't do this, Victor. They'll kill you. They'll somehow attack you before Regina is returned. We've got to call the police."

"No! That will put Regina in more danger. This way there'll be no uncontrolled exchange. Regina will be safe before they're able to get the money. That's the condition I set."

"Victor, you can't go out there. We've got to get police help."

"I'm telling you, Eleanor it's safer for Regina this way."

"And what about you? You expect me to wait for your safe return from meeting these extortionists in some dark place by yourself? And why are they after you? These must be the same guys that tried to hijack you this morning? Why is this happening? What's this about, Victor?"

Castell rubbed his temples trying to relieve the near-blinding stress. "I can't tell you right now, Eleanor. I'm not even sure myself. But I think it may have something to do with El Salvador."

"El Salvador? I don't understand."

"I was there a long time ago. When the civil war was still going on. The same time my mother died in the U.S. Embassy bombing."

"So what does that mean, Victor? That was twenty-five years ago. What happened? And what's that got to do with all this?"

Castell wasn't going to go into even his fictionalized version of events in El Salvador right now. He had to focus on getting his daughter returned. Nothing else mattered. Events were rapidly slipping beyond his control. If he were somehow able to escape Perez's thugs, everything else would still unravel. He would probably face criminal charges related to Patricia Reyes' death. Even if he beat that with a good lawyer, his marriage would be ended. Eleanor would not forgive the infidelity. All that mattered was getting Regina back.

"Victor, this is stupid. You're jeopardizing Regina not to mention yourself. You can't trust these monsters. For all you know they'll just kill both of you immediately when you get to the rendezvous. You don't even own a gun. You've got to let me call the police. I won't let you do this."

"I'm telling you no, Eleanor. Don't do it. You do it and I won't cooperate with the police. Only I know how and where I'm to deliver the money. I'm not about to let the police screw it up. The deal is for her to be delivered back here. Christ we can't have the police here when that happens. They'll insist on that. Something else to possibly go wrong if they're seen by the kidnappers."

His wife glared at him. "You sonofabitch. You arrogant stupid sonofabitch. You're not even considering what I think. This isn't just your goddamn decision alone. You think you always know best. You'd better goddamn be right on this, Victor."

The arguing went well into the night. Eventually exhausted, they both dosed fitfully for a couple of hours before being roused by the sunrise. Castell made coffee and retreated into his study. He couldn't just go to the park and expect to escape if the kidnappers tried to take him before returning Regina. Just staying in his car in the park afforded no assurance they would return Regina. After a couple of hours a plan had formed. It certainly wasn't foolproof but it was the best he could devise.

Castell called his banking account manager on the banker's cell phone at eight o'clock in the morning.

"You know the bank is required to report this?" the banker said.

"I know. That's ok. By then it won't matter."

"Victor, I don't mean to pry, but if this is a police matter I can perhaps be of help."

"I appreciate that. But I have things under control. I just need the cash. Can you get it ready for me by closing time today?"

"I'll need to pull some strings but I'll get it. Be at the bank at four."

Eleanor was an emotional wreck. What was her husband up to? The unrelenting fear for her daughter caused her to vomit up the continual cups of coffee she was using to sustain herself.

Castell left mid-morning after assuring her that arrangements for the money were being made. There were other things he had to do to prepare for tonight. What contrived explanation would he tell her? What would be his last words to her?

Castell could not tell his wife that he did not expect to survive the encounter with Perez's gang. The hijacking at the parking structure wasn't about money. They weren't going to hold him for ransom. So this taking of his daughter wasn't about money either. The hundred thousand dollars was just a masquerade to get him to a secluded place. Worse yet, it wasn't about just killing him. They could do that in a drive-by shooting. No, they wanted something far uglier. Carlos Perez wanted revenge. It had to be about Patricia. Castell had read about how the Mara Salvatrucha exacted brutal revenge that included the most bestial forms of torture. He was not about to be taken by these animals.

The gun store opened at ten in the morning.

"Can I help you, Sir?"

"Yeah. I just bought a cabin up in the Sierras. Beautiful setting but pretty remote. I'm told there are bears in the area. Plus I'd feel more comfortable with some protection being that far away from any police. Don't want a handgun. Too dangerous for having accidents. Thought maybe a shotgun would satisfy all those needs. What do you think?" Castell said.

"Absolutely. Shotgun might not kill a bear, but it sure as hell will do plenty of damage. As for intruders, well a shotgun will scare the hell out of any bad guy. I'd recommend a twelve gauge. Anything less is just too light for anything but bird shooting and skeet."

Reaching behind to a rack of shotguns, the clerk selected two.

"This Remington and Ithaca are both medium priced good firearms. Now, there's both pump action and semi-automatic. With the semi-automatic you just repeatedly squeeze the trigger and another round is chambered and fired. With the pump you move the slide to chamber a new round."

"I think I like the semi-automatic feature."

Castell spent only a few minutes selecting a particular model. "And for ammunition?"

"Well for your purpose, clearly 00 buck. That's larger sized, fewer pellets. You still have a pattern but each pellet has a hell of a wallop. Good against any bear. As for an intruder, well, let's just say that it would stop any NFL lineman dead. Literally. You can also use a three-inch shell in this model gun. More pellet load and powder in the longer round. You can still load four and one."

"What does that mean," Castell said.

"Four in the magazine and one in the chamber. Five rounds in all."

Castell bought six boxes of shotgun shells telling the clerk he intended to do some practice shooting. Before returning home, he stopped at a hardware store for other items on his list.

CHAPTER 32

Frank Torres was parked on a perpendicular street to the alley where the MS-13 gang's black SUV was waiting behind the retail stores. He saw what appeared to be three men scramble down the parking structure stairs to make their escape with the SUV accelerating and sliding into the turn onto the street. Castell was not with them. Maybe they had killed him right there? Something happened. Sirens could be heard in the distance. Torres drove off. Ten minutes later he got a call from Emilio.

"Your fucking plan was shit, asshole."

"What happened?"

"My guys tried to take this fucker but there was a witness that messed everything up. The rich guy got away."

"Got away? How'd that happen?"

"Because your stupid plan was shit!"

"Well why didn't they just waste the witness and the rich guy? They had guns didn't they?"

"Because this was to be a snatch, not a hit."

"Well I'm sorry it didn't work out, *compadre*. Shit happens. The snatch was your problem."

"Not my fault, motherfucker. My boss will hear it differently. You got paid a lot for this I hear. You fucked up with this bull-shit plan. Just easy money for you. No risk to you. My boss is gonna be plenty pissed. You gotta make it right, *pendejo*."

Torres thought, *make it right?* How the hell could he do that? But he did take fifty grand for this. Even though it was Perez's people who fucked this up, no telling how Perez might react. Emilio was scared. He would make it out to Perez that it was all Torres' fault. Torres might end up on a morgue slab as a dead scapegoat alongside Emilio.

Torres had pulled into a parking place to listen to Emilio's ranting. Was there any way now to get to Castell? Castell would know this was about him fucking Perez's woman. He had to know. Castell would now be overly cautious. Probably leave town.

Castell would be vulnerable through his family, but he'd move to protect them quickly. He'd certainly get them out of town. And he'd do it soon. But not *immediately* was the thought that occurred to Torres. Castell would be occupied with the po-lice for probably hours. If Torres could move quickly he might be able to remedy this fiasco before Castell had the opportunity to circle his wagons.

The key was Castell's daughter. Hard to judge how devoted he might be to the wife since he was screwing around. But no question about a daughter. Castell's daughter was also nearby at her high school, the wife in a law office in downtown Los Ange-les. Should be easy to grab the daughter. The problem was he would have to involve himself directly. He couldn't use Emilio's tattooed monkeys in Pasadena. That meant a risk that he could be identified later.

Torres called Emilio.

"This is Torres. Listen up. I have an idea how you can get to this guy. Even make some money in the process. Those dick-heads that fucked up still available with that black SUV?"

Torres laid out his plan. Again it was simple. Emilio still act-ed the tough guy but listened. He was in a jam because of this bungled job and grasped at a way out.

"Thirty minutes," Torres said. "And for Christsakes tell them not to get out of the SUV. Not until it's time. You got that?"

At five minutes before one o'clock students started to reenter South Pasadena High School after the lunch break. Torres had been sitting in front of the main entrance on Freemont Avenue for half an hour. From his research into Victor Castell he ob-tained a picture of the daughter and her cell phone number. He wanted to catch her on her lunch break. Get her outside hopeful-ly without her telling anyone, but at least not having to explain to a teacher while in class.

"Is this Regina Castell?"

"Yes. Who's this?"

"Detective Smith, Pasadena Police Department. I'm afraid there's been an accident. A shooting actually. Your father has been shot."

"Oh my god! How bad is he?"

"I'm not sure, Miss. He's been taken to Huntington Memori-al. I was told to find you and take you there. Your mother's al-ready there I'm told. Just come out onto Freemont Avenue. You'll see me. Big guy, dark hair. I'm wearing a navy blazer, striped tie, dark glasses. I'll be holding my badge up so you can see it. But please hurry, Miss Castell."

Torres spotted Regina Castell running toward the street. He held up his arm holding his official-looking fugitive apprehen-sion badge in a leather folder. He made sure to slightly exposure his holstered handgun to complete the impression of a police officer.

"Miss Castell? This way please."

Castell took her arm lightly and lead her to his Crown Victo-ria with its plain wheels, parked on the other side of the street. It was the ubiquitous unmarked police-type vehicle he used when he found it convenient to impersonate a cop. The car was parked directly behind a black SUV with tinted windows.

As Torres opened the passenger door facing the sidewalk, two guys jumped out of the SUV and pointed pistols into Regina Castell's face. In accented English they told her not to scream. One guy pressed his gun into the side of her head while the other secured her wrists with a large plastic tie-wrap. Within less than a minute she had been shoved into the backseat. Torres saw them place a black hood over her head before they closed the door and pulled away.

Now this was up to Emilio and his thugs. They had the ultimate leverage over Castell. All they had to do was get him to some remote place where they could take him. A place of their choice. Make a shitpot of money to boot. Good for them. He didn't even want a cut of the ransom. Just get it done, get it behind him. This was a stupid contract. In the future he would know better.

Torres shuddered as he visualized what was going to happen to this young woman. His only instruction to Emilio was to take care of both Castell and the daughter. The girl saw his face. But he suspected these assholes would have some fun with her before they killed her.

CHAPTER 33

Castell returned home at midday. His wife was still in her robe curled up on the family room sofa, hair uncombed, eyes red from crying.

"Where have you been, Victor?"

"Getting some things."

"What are you doing, Victor? Are you planning something crazy? Please, let's call the police. Please?"

"No, Eleanor. It's arranged. They'll bring her to the house. That's my insurance."

"Insurance? What's to stop them from just shooting you, taking the money, and ….." she said trailing off not wanting to articulate what might happen to her daughter. She looked at her husband who revealed nothing by way of expression.

"That's what you've been doing isn't it? You're planning something stupid. I can't let you do this. You and Regina will both be killed. I can't take this any longer. We've got to get help."

His wife moved toward the telephone. Castell grabbed her gently. "No, Eleanor, please. You've got to trust me. We call the police and there's no telling what might happen to Regina. These guys that have her are the worst?"

"What guys? You know who they are? Goddamn it, what's going on? What aren't you telling me, Victor?"

"Later, Eleanor. I'll tell you what I know, but later. Right now let me handle this."

She returned to the sofa and held her face in her hands, crying quietly. Castell placed a call to his banker. He was assured the cash would ready at four o'clock.

"I stopped and picked up some sandwiches. They're in the kitchen. Try to eat something. I need to do some things in the garage."

He had only the most basic hand tools in his garage but he wouldn't need much to assemble what he needed for the confrontation that night. Eleanor was right. He had to protect himself sufficiently to get the kidnappers to return Regina. If they got to him before, then she was dead. After she was safe, he wasn't sure he cared anymore. At least about dying. Only not a protracted death by torture.

From the trunk of his car he took out that morning's purchases, placing them on his workbench. The shotgun was the first modification. He would need to conceal it. It would be a chilly evening therefore a trench coat would appear normal. Using a high speed Dremel electric hand tool, he was eventually able to cut through the hardened steel barrel to reduce the overall length of the shotgun to about thirty-four inches. Short enough to conceal under a trench coat if he rigged it right.

The next defense was to assemble a small bomb. The irony was not lost on Castell. Unlike using a shotgun, at least in that area he had some working knowledge.

The explosive part was simple. It was to be a pipe bomb containing gunpowder from the extra shotgun shells he purchased. He could have bought reloading powder in bulk, but that would have raised suspicions with the gun store clerk since he didn't know anything about reloading ammunition. Better to stick with his plausible story and spend the time prying open several boxes of shotgun shells.

The bomb would consist of a twelve-inch long galvanized pipe threaded on both ends. The gun powder would be packed inside with each end closed off by a threaded cap. Through one cap, he would drill a hole for the wires to the ignition device imbedded in the gunpowder charge.

The detonating mechanism would be a makeshift bridge wire detonator. For this he would use a small Christmas light bulb with the glass tip removed to expose the fine filament wire. The design called for sending a much larger current from a nine-volt battery through the wire causing it to instantly vaporize with sufficient temperature to ignite the gunpowder.

Just like in the past, he would use a remote radio signal mechanism to close the battery circuit from a modest distance. For the relay, Castell removed the circuit board from his remote garage door opener. He could activate the bomb from no more than a hundred feet using his garage door control.

The finished bomb components would be held in place in a small box bound with duct tape. It would sit atop the hundred thousand dollars in a gym bag.

All good theory and simple engineering, but he had to be sure the device would work. He first prepared several of the small lights by carefully scoring the tiny glass with a file and breaking off the glass tip. He would actually use two in the final bomb assembly for redundancy. To test the ability to ignite the charge, he performed several test ignitions using cotton swabs soaked in alcohol. It worked remarkably well.

Next was a test of virtually a mini-bomb. To test ignition of even a minute quantity of gunpowder, he needed some distance. The test would also test the triggering circuit with the garage door opener control.

The test would be conducted as far away from the house as possible in the large back yard, shielded behind a large tree. There were no neighbors to the rear of his property which sat on a hill sloping down to a street below. Far enough from the house for Eleanor not to be alerted.

Castell placed half a teaspoon of gunpowder in a plastic bottle, taping the Christmas light so that the exposed filament was imbedded in the gunpowder. He ran three feet of wire so that the radio frequency relay circuit would not be damaged in the test. If this worked with the increased voltage drop of the longer wire, the real assembly would surely work.

The sound was muffled by the plastic bottle but more powerful than he expected. The volume of explosive within the iron pipe would be lethal. Maybe even for him. He would have to be close enough for the remote control to work.

Promptly at four o'clock, Castell entered his branch bank. His banker was waiting for him in the manager's office. Once again the banker tried to dissuade him from doing whatever he was intending with the cash. Whatever the reason, it was ill advised.

Arriving home, Castell found his wife asleep on the sofa allowing him to return to the garage to finish his preparations. Once the bomb was completed, he placed it in the trunk of his Mercedes. The battery circuit was not connected as a precaution. The only thing left was rigging the shotgun so it was hidden but could be brought to bear in a matter of seconds from under his coat.

He experimented with a couple of ideas before settling on the simplest setup. A length of nylon cord was tied to the narrow part of the shotgun stock and looped around his shoulder. The weapon would hang somewhat under his right arm with the butt of the stock behind his shoulder. It was now short enough to be concealed within the length of his coat. The cord was tied with a large bow knot that he could easily pull loose with his left hand. So as not appearing to be concealing a gun in his pocket, he could walk with both hands free until he was ready to act. Then he could thrust his right hand into the coat pocket which had been cut away inside, grab the shotgun, release it from his shoulder by untying the cord with his left hand, and bring the weapon out. A couple of seconds at most. Five shots that could be fired in a couple of seconds. It represented fearsome firepower especially if the bad guys were not expecting the attack.

Castell had no illusions about what he was getting into. As long as he secured the release of his daughter, nothing else mattered. He had no illusions about surviving the encounter. Just don't be taken alive. With the right provocation that should be easy with these natural born killers. He didn't especially want to die, but it was the best way out. Life could never be the same now. Events were converging that might reveal his past participation in terrorist bombings. Murder. Mass murders. Somewhere there was evidence out there that would implicate him once the police knew he was involved. Then of course there still was Carlos Perez. Perez couldn't implicate him without implicating himself, but who knows how Perez might react to the criminal charges he was facing. He might not be rational about Patricia Reyes. Might Perez cut a deal offering up Victor Castell?

But Castell wasn't going into this trap defenseless. And it certainly was a trap. If it was about the ransom, they would not have gone along with returning Regina to the house. They wouldn't be expecting a shotgun, much less the ransom bag rigged with a bomb. A desperate move but one that would end the confrontation with finality. He would not be taken alive. Too bad Carlos Perez himself wouldn't be there.

CHAPTER 34

A t the same time on Thursday afternoon that Victor Castell
was concluding the police questioning after the failed attack in the parking structure, Egan Kavanagh had convened a
meeting with the Justice Department's head of the criminal division, Clarence Atkins, at the latter's office on Pennsylvania Avenue in Washington D.C. It was a small meeting including only a
couple of senior aides for Kavanagh and Atkins.

"I've read your report, Director Kavanagh. Even had my
staff examine the backup material in detail to see if there was
anything more there. Clearly this Victor Castell and probably the
gang leader Carlos Perez participated in the U.S Embassy bombing in San Salvador, and probably the follow-up bombings in
Las Vegas. But I think you know the conclusion by your waffling
summary conclusion," Atkins said.

"Not sure I'd call it waffling. I intended it to mean that constructing a viable case against Castell still had difficulties?"

"Difficulties? Come on, Director. You have a circumstantial
case and not an especially strong one I might add. Of course you
have this old woman's declaration. Obtained through a subter-

fuge involving the impersonation of a priest hearing confession? Is that correct?"

Kavanagh sighed. "I'm afraid so. Not our doing, Sir. But we can't undo it. Neither can we ignore it."

"You believe it?"

"Yes, Sir. Everything the old woman said fits with other things we uncovered in El Salvador."

"Beyond the fact she is now dead, you know as well as I do, Director, that it would never be admissible as evidence."

"Of course. However, I've been informed that the Salvadoran government is considering bringing their own charges. After all, quite a number of Salvadorans were also killed in the embassy bombing. In your opinion, what are the chances of the Salvadorans prevailing in U.S. court to having Castell extradited?"

"Just as much of a problem with the circumstantial nature of the evidence. Castell's a U.S. citizen so the extradition evidentiary bar is not much different than bringing the same charges in a U.S. court. Not to mention that Castell has resources. He can afford the best legal defense. Extradition will never happen, Director Kavanagh. But I'm also sure you would rather have him tried here in the U.S. He'd face the death penalty here, maximum of life in El Salvador. But you would already know that, correct?"

"Yes, I'm aware of that. But we want Castell any way we can. He's evaded justice for too many years."

"How personal is this, Director? You investigated the embassy and Vegas bombings. A loose end that keeps gnawing?"

"Maybe. But Castell is the sonofabitch who made those bombs. Killed a lot of Americans. All the others from Santiago Molina's group are dead. Perez we already have. He's already facing a life term on existing charges. But Castell got away. Living a life of privilege all these years. I'd certainly say he should be the subject of some special attention."

"Probably would agree with that, Director Kavanagh. What about any state charges related to the death of this Reyes woman?"

"The San Diego County DA's office is struggling with much the same issues. The evidence clearly points to Castell being involved, but they can't convincingly place him at the scene of her death at the motel. Beyond that, her death may have been accidental. At best it's a pressure point we might be able to exploit against Castell. However it's a better pressure tool against Perez. He's locked away and his girlfriend of sixteen years shacks up with an old boyfriend, perhaps a romantic rival back when they all knew each other. She ends up dead. It's got to be eating at Perez."

"Any competent lawyer will argue that Perez was an equal accomplice to Castell. Even if Perez did testify against Castell, it would have limited weight without corroboration. It could also be persuasively argued that his testimony was tainted by this romantic triangle with Reyes."

Kavanagh had few options. Push the Salvadorans to seek charges and continue to pressure Perez. The old woman directly identified Perez as part of Molina's group. Maybe Perez will do something stupid that will help the case against Castell. It was Castell that Kavanagh especially wanted. That Friday evening Kavanagh got his wish.

Kavanagh had decided to back off from his intense involvement in the reopening of the old bombing case. After the recent breakthrough, the frustrations were maddening. The plan was for a long weekend somewhere in the country with his longtime girlfriend. But this weekend was not to be rest and relaxation for Egan Kavanagh. The call came just as he arrived home.

"Catch this, Boss. Our Mr. Castell was involved in a failed carjacking only a few hours ago. Maybe an attempted kidnapping. Just got off the phone with the LA Agent in Charge, John McIntyre."

"What's the read on this by local law enforcement?"

"Skeptical according to McIntyre. The perpetrators are believed to be Latin American. A witness heard them yell something in Spanish. Caught a glimpse of a tattoo."

"A tattoo? MS-13?"

"Could be but a lot of Latin gang members like their tattoos."

"Where'd this happen?"

"That's what makes this interesting. It wasn't a random drive-by. It occurred in the parking structure next to Castell's office building in Pasadena. Castell was clearly the target. He got away. Drove right through the ticket barrier in his expensive sports car and raced down the street to get away. The perps had guns but no shots were fired. Three of them. Looks like they wanted to take Castell."

"Saddle up. You and I are going to LA tomorrow," Kavanagh said.

CHAPTER 35

Waiting for nightfall was a trial on Castell's nerves. This was a desperate move. Would it save his daughter? Was she ok? Would she recover emotionally from the ordeal? Should he have called the police instead?

Eleanor remained sullen and withdrawn. Castell secluded himself to avoid further confrontation. The point of no return for calling the police passed.

He had tested the relay function from the garage door closer establishing the maximum distance that it would operate from the hand-held control. Anything more than one hundred feet was erratic in response. He knew electrical circuits but nothing about explosives. He had to assume at only hundred feet, he would be vulnerable to the shrapnel of the exploding pipe. But he had no idea what kind of explosion would result from the gunpowder charge. The thought of a quick death may have had appeal, but that probably would not be the result of the pipe-bomb. But then again, he first intended this to be a gunfight. When he turned the shotgun on these guys, all hell would break loose. For all he knew, he'd be cut down before he could ever detonate the bomb. It was to be his doomsday weapon to avoid a protracted death under torture.

Nightfall came early in December. Total darkness by eight o'clock. He would allow twenty minutes to reach the park. A dry run that morning all the way up the hill to the parking area provided an understanding of the grounds in daylight. A last check of the bomb and the shotgun in the trunk. For safety, the battery circuit remained unconnected. The pair of wires would be twisted together just before he removed the gym bag from the trunk. The control was in his left pocket of the trench coat. The shotgun was loaded with five rounds. Once secured under his coat, the safety would be set to off.

Castell held few allusions about this turning out well. At least for him personally. The only real objective was getting Regina returned unharmed.

"Eleanor, I've got to go."

With tears streaming down her face, his wife desperately tried pleading a last time. "Please don't, Victor. I have a bad feeling about this. I'm going to lose Regina and you too. I can feel that. Please, please let me call the police."

"We've been over this so many times, Eleanor. Trust me. This is the best way. Besides, it's too late now." It was only thirty minutes to the rendezvous time.

"One last thing. In my desk drawer is a printout of everything you'll need to do if .....if things go badly. Remember though, nothing will happen until Regina is safely back here and you confirm that by calling me. You keep the door locked until Regina comes home. When you call, if everything is ok, say *the princess has returned*. Then I'll know she is ok. That you're both ok."

"What do you mean if everything is *ok*? You're not suggesting these kidnappers might come into the house are you."

"No, Eleanor. It's just a precaution. I'll be taking my own precautions. I don't intend for them to kidnap me either."

"How? What are you planning? You bought a gun didn't you?"

"I don't have time to go into that. But it's me they're after. I'm absolutely sure of that. Regina was just a way to get at me."

"But why, Victor? You know don't you?"

"There's no time now, Eleanor. I'll tell you later. I love you."

With that he kissed her, embraced her for a moment, then left.

Castell arrived at Ernest E. Debs Regional Park five minutes before the appointed time. There was no traffic on Monterey Road at this time of night. A sign said the park closed at dusk. Trespassing at night violated municipal code. The gate chain was cut.

He drove slowly up the winding park road easing over the severe speed bumps. Perez's thugs were probably already concealed somewhere in the picnic area. It was a moon-less night. No other vehicles were visible but a service road with another gate exited the far end of the large parking area so another vehicle might be concealed there. His headlights illuminated picnic benches and a restroom building.

Initially Castell had planned to wait in the car with the engine idling until he received the call on his cellphone. After reconsidering his vulnerability if attacked while still sitting in the car before receiving the call, his only option would be to try to drive off. These thugs were stupid enough to try that. The deal would be blown. No telling what might happen to Regina.

So he must put himself in a better defensive position. Once parked, he exited the car. To aid in concealing his preparations, Castell had removed the trunk light bulb. Opening the trunk, he twisted the battery circuit wires, arming his bomb using a small penlight. The bomb was placed on top of the cash in the gym bag. Hoping that the open lid to the trunk shielded him from view of the assailants wherever they were secluded, he looped the cord sling holding the shotgun over his right shoulder. He quickly put on his trench coat, checking for the garage door control in his left pocket.

Although terrified, he was not paralyzed by fear. This was about rescuing Regina. He was fatalistic about his own survival but that made him all the more dangerous. He wasn't going to take all these guys out with the shotgun. They would be too heavily armed. They were killers. But Castell thought somewhat ironically, so was he. His trump card was the bomb. Ever since Patricia reappeared, his stable life had disintegrated. The convergence of events twenty-five years ago would soon destroy him. Time for all of this to end.

Castell walked purposefully up the hill to the first picnic table he saw. His right hand was inside the coat pocket gripping the shotgun. He set the gym bag on the concrete picnic table then backed away a few feet.

In Spanish someone said, "The money is in the bag?"

"Yes. But it's rigged with lighter fluid. I'll burn it all unless I hear that my daughter has been returned home. Follow the deal." Castell flicked a flame on a butane lighter.

"You're fucking crazy, Castell. You'd burn a hundred thousand dollars?" the voice said in Spanish. After a pause, "Maybe there's no money in the bag. You wouldn't be that dumb would you, Castell?"

Castell returned to the gym bag and carefully extracted a bound pack of cash.

"Your money's right here."

He held it up to be seen then dropped it on the picnic table. Reaching into the bag, he took out a can of grill lighter fluid. A squirted stream of the flammable fluid wetted the outside of the gym bag.

Holding up the lighter and flicking a flame, "Believe me, I'll do it if you try to get to it before my daughter is safely back home. The money's not important to me, only my daughter. I'm waiting on that call."

Nothing happened for an agonizing couple of minutes. Castell held the lighter in one hand his cell phone now in the other. He wasn't all that sure now that his plan would work. They might just shoot him from a distance, take the money, and then kill Regina too. But he was sure it was him they wanted. Taken alive. Regina was only a means. Hopefully the money had importance even if this was more about getting to him. All his chips were on that bet.

His cell phone rang, answered on the first ring as his home phone number displayed.

"Victor, Regina's home! Terrified and crying, but she's all right. They dropped her off on the street two blocks away. We're alone. Locked securely in the house. I'm going to call 911 now."

"And what else, Eleanor?" he had to be sure his wife didn't have a gun to her head.

"Oh my god! Yes, yes, I forgot. The *princess has returned*. Yes, *the princess has returned*! You come back too, Victor. Where are you? Are you ....."

"I love you." He disconnected.

Things would now start to happen quickly. He started to back away toward his car. The lighter was transferred to his left hand. His right hand returned to grasp the shotgun through the coat pocket. If they were to take him it would be any time. But the thought struck him that perhaps they might be lying in wait back at his car. He would then be too far away to detonate the bomb. They would get their money and kill him if he didn't do something. The bomb was to be his secondary weapon. The last resort if he couldn't fend them off with the shotgun.

So Castell moved to one side into a nearby clump of bushes. His defenses only worked if he could see his adversaries. He was also still within range to detonate the bomb.

From the direction of his car the same voice called out, "What's this Castell? Your daughter has been returned. You think you can protect your money? Is that why you do not leave?"

Castell said nothing. He undid the slip knot of the sling holding the shotgun. Holding it in his right hand, he still kept it under his coat in case they could make him out in the darkness. The weapon would be effective only if he could maintain surprise.

Although there was no moon with the cloud overcast, the distant city lights allowed enough illumination to still see the gym bag on the picnic table. Enough illumination to see someone moving to retrieve the bag. Enough to see the guy was carrying what looked to be an assault rifle.

The guy would undoubtedly open the bag to see if it contained all the money. When that happened he would see what clearly was a bomb sitting on top of the money. Castell had actually brought the entire amount of money knowing it would be sacrificed. In case all his planning went to hell, he didn't want to be empty handed and cause something to happen to Regina as a reaction because he failed to bring the cash. But it now appeared to be a waste of a hundred thousand dollars.

What to do? Only the one guy was visible. Where were the others? This was not going according to his envisioned scenario, however vague that had been, but it mattered far less now that Regina was safe.

Castell lay flat on the ground on a gradually descending slope of the ground, concealed within a stand of bushes. The shotgun lay across his arms. The garage door control was in his left hand. He had no choice now. Best to take out at least the one guy and go on the offensive. Provoke the fight on his terms. As the guy unzipped the bag, Castell depressed the garage door control button.

The sound was deafening. Castell heard the zip of what must be pipe shrapnel ripping through the brush over his head. Yelling in Spanish came from the direction of his car. A moment later, somebody was rushing directly toward him in the dark firing an automatic weapon. The guy knew where Castell was concealed.

Castell could make out only the vague outline of the assailant in the dim light, but he could see the muzzle flashes now only twenty yards away. Remembering what the gun store clerk said about the recoil of the shotgun and keeping the butt tight to his shoulder, Castell fired a round at the muzzle flash. The twelve-gauge bucked upward. He settled the sight back to where he thought the target to be and fired a second round.

For several moments it remained quiet. Castell got up cautiously from his concealed position. He started to take a circuitous route back toward the car when more shots rang out, spraying the ground near him. His left leg felt like someone had delivered a hammer blow to his thigh sending him to the ground. In response, he fired off two more shotgun rounds in the direction of this other assailant.

Again there was silence. Attuned to any sound, Castell could hear what sounded like a moan and some muted Spanish. Several minutes passed. Castell knew he had been shot in the thigh. But reaching inside his coat he also felt his shirt soaking with blood. He'd been hit at least a second time somewhere in the abdomen. For some reason it was this second realization that accelerated the effects of shock setting in as the surge of adrenalin began to take effect. Fighting consciousness he focused his thoughts on not allowing himself to be taken alive. The Mara Salvatrucha did terrible things to their victims. He was sure he still had one round in the shotgun. Should he exercise that final option now?

As sirens sounded in the distance, Victor Castell passed into unconsciousness in the damp grass.

CHAPTER 36

Eleanor Castell called 911 immediately after the return of her daughter. She was frantic but she didn't know where her husband was making the ransom exchange. The 911 dispatcher told her to lock her doors, police were on their way.

She followed with a call to Larry Siegel, corporate counsel to Castell Systems and a longtime personal friend as well as a professional associate. Siegel promised to be at her house in thirty minutes to help her with the police.

Two Los Angeles County Sheriff's patrol cars arrived at the park shortly after the shooting began. On routine patrol, they received a dispatch call of reports of gunfire in the park. Pulling up to the closed gate, the first deputy got out of his patrol car. His flashlight revealed the gate chain had been cut. He opened the gate and got back into his car and drove slowly up the entrance road followed by the second patrol car. A minute later, they faced headlights coming straight down the park road. The first patrol car turned to the left to block the width of the road. The second patrol car pulled in behind. Both deputies got out of their cars training their service weapons on the oncoming SUV.

The black SUV came to a sliding halt on the slight down-grade.

Repeated yelling for the driver to get out with his hands visible accomplished nothing over the next several minutes. The two deputies eventually moved cautiously to either side of the SUV at a distance of fifty feet and out of the glare of the headlights. Sirens from backup were close. The deputies waited for reinforcements before attempting to extract the SUV occupants.

After a total of eight police officers surrounded the SUV, two officers armed with shotguns approached the driver side. Eventually the door opened slowly. A single hand was raised.

"Let me see both hands. Now!" one officer yelled.

"I can't. I'm wounded. I'm unarmed." The driver said. Stepping out of the vehicle, he fell to his knees.

The officers approached cautiously. The man was bleeding profusely from his damaged left arm. They laid him on his back careful with the damaged arm.

"Jesus Christ. What an ugly sonofabitch," one officer said. "Who gets a solid tattoo covering your whole nose?"

"He's MS-13. LA gang. Crazy-ass nasty fuckers. They like their facial tattoos.

"Got another one here," another officer said as he carefully opened the backdoor to the SUV. "Shot in the lower abdomen. Looks pretty bad. Got an assault rifle on the floor."

"Got a 9mm on the front seat," another officer said.

The sergeant in charge said, "EMT's are on the way." He designated three of the officers to stay with the two wounded suspects. "These guys look like they got the worse of it. Let's see where this gunfight took place. Watch your step. More backup is on the way."

Two patrol cars inched their way up the park road past the SUV. The road wound up the hill for half a mile to the parking area. The patrol cars stopped some distance from a silver Mercedes. After determining there was no one inside the Mercedes, they began canvasing the large picnic area with flashlights. Several minutes later they came upon a body. Same sort of tattoos as the SUV occupants. Dead from a massive wound to the torso.

Some minutes later, "Over here, Sarg. This guy's looks to be still alive. Still breathing. Fuck all. This the guy that did the shooting? That's a twelve gauge shotgun. He's not a gangbanger. Looks like a gringo."

Before the sergeant could examine the wounded Victor Castell, another deputy called out, "Sarg, over here. You gotta see this."

Paper currency was blown all over the area. Next to a partially destroyed picnic table was another body. A badly mangled body. The face was totally destroyed, an unrecognizable bloody mass. The torso had been eviscerated. In the cool night air, a pile of still steaming intestines had spilled out of the torn abdomen and lay coiled next to the body.

"What the hell happened here?"

Kavanagh arrived in Los Angeles earlier that day. He was taking a break by relaxing with a drink at the hotel bar with Agent McIntyre when McIntyre's cell phone buzzed.

After a couple of minutes back and forth, McIntyre hung up and said to Kavanagh, "The plot does thicken. That was Tominski, Pasadena PD. Seems there was a massive shootout just west of Pasadena a short time ago. Bunch of MS-13 guys got wasted in a Los Angeles park. But catch this. Looks like it was our Mr. Castell that did it."

"Victor Castell? Are they sure?"

"Seems so. Castell was seriously wounded. He's at Huntington Memorial going into surgery right now. Tominski also mentioned a report about Castell's daughter allegedly being kidnapped, but apparently returned. They haven't sorted that out yet. Tominski said to join him at his office right away and he'll fill in the details. But get this. This is the best part. Looks like Castell detonated a bomb."

Egan Kavanagh spent a long night with Special Agent McIntyre, Lieutenant Tominski, and Los Angeles County detectives. These seemingly bizarre incidents were bringing things into focus. Eventually getting to bed at three in the morning, Kavanagh had developed a rough plan for using these recent events to possibly close his case on Victor Castell.

The ugly tattooed Mara Salvatrucha lieutenant, Emilio, surprised everyone by singing his heart out. Seems he was more afraid of what would happen to him in jail for having fucked up twice. Carlos Perez welded a lot of power. And this thing about his woman being screwed by this Castell guy who then killed her had blinded Perez with rage. Especially since he was on the inside and had to rely on others. Emilio was promised incarceration at a location safe from Perez if he talked.

With the extra federal charges now piling onto Perez, Kavanagh might have some leverage. He would even add the multiple murder charges for the terrorist bombings even though there wasn't sufficient evidence. The sheer weight of charges for murder, attempted murder, money laundering, racketeering, and terrorism would send Perez to the deepest high-security federal lockup, ADX Florence. Although a modern facility, the psychological and even physiological impact on the inmate was something from the nineteenth century. The inmates were either the most dangerous or those the United States wanted most to punish. Kavanagh didn't have a strong prospect for the threat of the death penalty since that would apply only to the terrorist bombings where it would be hard to prove Perez's involvement. But it was still a possibility, and a throwaway for a plea deal. ADX Florence might prove more effective. It was the next worse thing to a death sentence.

At the federal detention center, Kavanagh, McIntyre, and Detective Tominski arranged an interview with Carlos Perez.

"Good morning, Mr. Perez. Hope we're not interfering with your attending church services this fine Sunday morning," Kavanagh said.

"Fuck you. I'm not talking to you assholes without my lawyer."

"You haven't heard what we've got to say, Carlos. Besides, Mr. Delgado has his own legal problems right now. Let's just say he's not available to confer with his client at this time. Did you hear what happened last night?"

Perez said nothing while slouching back in his chair.

"Well your boys fucked up, Carlos. For a second time it seems. First on Thursday they tried to kidnap Victor Castell. You know Castell don't you from the old days in El Salvador? Patricia Reyes' old boyfriend. Apparently still some sparks there. He's the one screwing her before she died. But of course you knew all that didn't you? That's why you had your slimeball mouthpiece Delgado contract with a lowlife bail bondsman bounty hunter named Torres to setup a kidnapping of Castell. You were going to have him tortured and killed as you Maras like to do.

"But they screwed that up, Carlos. Let Castell get away. This Torres guy got nervous that you might come after him so he thinks up this idea to grab Castell's daughter. Your boy Emilio is desperate too so he goes along with Torres' dumbass plan using the same monkeys that botched the first attempt to grab Castell. Emilio thought he could not only rectify the first screw-up, but make some real money in the process. Redeem himself by grabbing Castell and pocket a hundred thousand dollars to pay for his trouble. Real independent thinker this Emilio.

"Well Emilio isn't all that bright. Fucked that up too. Got two of his guys killed, another badly wounded. Even got shot himself. Seems Victor Castell came to the gunfight better prepared. Rigged an ambush for your guys. And something you can appreciate, Castell brought a bomb. Blew the shit out of one of your guys.

"Now poor Emilio is headed for jail. But he's thinking these stupid failures might not sit well with Mara Salvatrucha big shot Carlos Perez. Emilio wonders how long he'll last inside. So Emilio decides to save his own ass by giving up big shot Carlos Perez."

Perez continued to say nothing but his posture had changed. He sat straight up in his chair, elbows on the table.

"Emilio's testimony is not your only new trouble, Carlos. We've got new evidence from El Salvador. Enough to place you as part of Santiago Molina's terrorist cell. Enough to convict you of multiple murders in the United States for both the U.S. Embassy bombing and the Las Vegas bombings in 1989. That'll mean the death sentence."

"Bullshit. I wasn't part of any terrorist group. From 1989? You're fishing."

"We'll see about that, Carlos. But now you've got these kidnapping charges to add to all the other shit you'll be charged with in federal court. So let me paint a picture for, Carlos. Forget the death penalty for a moment. Even without that, you'll be headed for maybe even a worse place. Ever heard of a place called ADX?"

Perez did not respond.

"It's in Colorado but you'll never know that once you're inside. ADX is the federal version of what states call their super-max prisons. Except ADX is so much worse. Think of ADX as a cleaner version of hell. The cell is eight by ten. No furniture. Concrete desk. Concrete stool. Concrete bed. Image that. And a combination toilet, sink, and drinking fountain. Can't image what that's like. Some sort of shower rig in the room. And one window. But the window is only four inches wide looking out onto a courtyard. No sky. You can't even see into the cellblock hallway. Your cell is a concrete crypt. A little black and white television but all you'll see is educational crap, closed-circuit classes, and religious stuff. No telecommunication with the outside world. You spend twenty-three hours a day in your cell by yourself. One hour exercise a day but it's in an indoor concrete pit, again just you alone. Meals are brought to your room. Closest thing to being thrown into a hole I can image.

"So you'll either be at Terre Haute, Indiana awaiting your death sentence to be carried out, or live the rest of your miserable natural life at spa ADX.

"So here's the offer, Carlos. Give us testimony on Victor Castell's participation in Molina's terrorist group. We'll take the death penalty off the table. With all the other stuff you're charged with, you're going away for life anyway. Give testimony against Castell and the U.S. attorney will agree not only to a life sentence but to serve that time in a conventional federal maximum security prison, not a hell-hole like ADX."

Perez continued to remain silent.

"Think it over, Carlos. But be quick. We're putting together a strong case against Castell without your testimony. Your testimony just seals it. Wait too long and you'll miss your one chance. You're fucked, Carlos no matter what. All you can do now is take the best option."

CHAPTER 37

Victor Castell survived his injuries with a prognosis for an eventual full recovery. He was seriously wounded but no major organs had been damaged. The round that hit his left thigh just missed the femur, and more importantly the femoral artery. The muscle and tendon damage was however severe. On the left side of the abdomen the bullet had again done a lot of tissue damage and had slightly nicked the small intestine. The prognosis was for a full recovery although the leg wound would mean walking with crutches for weeks.

It was three days since the encounter. Eleanor and Regina had remained at the hospital for most of that time. Castell's aging father had come to Pasadena visiting his son briefly each day.

The media had besieged the hospital waiting for news as to Castell's condition. This was the dominate story in the country and sure to push all other stories aside once a full accounting of the incident became public. The hospital made special arrangements to allow Castell's family to enter by a staff entrance. Larry Siegel and his wife remained at the family's side with Siegel assuming the role as spokesman for the family. At Siegel's insistence, Castell's doctors did not allow him to be interviewed by the police for those first couple of days.

Once the effects of the pain medication were manageable, Siegel had to relent to the inevitable. Pasadena Detective Lieutenant Tominski introduced LA Sherriff Detective Lieutenant Alvarado, FBI Special Agent McIntyre, and FBI Assistant Director Kavanagh. They were standing around Castell's bed along with Eleanor, Regina, and Larry Siegel.

"Mrs. Castell, Mr. Siegel, if I might ask you to leave us alone with Mr. Castell. We have some questions we need to ask privately."

"Go ahead, Eleanor," Siegel said. "Take Regina and go get some lunch. I'll handle this. I'm Mr. Castell's attorney, gentlemen. So I'll stay."

"Very well, Mr. Siegel," Tominski said.

Once Eleanor and Regina had left the room, Siegel said, "Before we start, is Mr. Castell being charged with any criminal offense in connection with the events of Saturday night?"

"Not at this time, Counselor. But that will be up to the District Attorney. Or the U.S. District Attorney for that matter. Mr. Castell not only killed two people, but he detonated an explosive device."

"In self-defense. Self-defense to save his kidnapped daughter. Faced with armed assailants he defended himself. May have even been the same assailants that attempted to kidnap him a couple of days before," Siegel said.

"We're all aware of these circumstances, Counselor. That's why we're here to get a fuller picture. I was simply answering your question," Tominski said. "However, as a formality, I'll read Mr. Castell his rights against self-incrimination."

"One more thing before we begin," Siegel said. "Why is an assistant director of the Federal Bureau of Investigation involved? And what branch are you in charge of Director Kavanagh?"

"My precise title is Executive Assistant Director for National Security. As to why I am here, I am sure Mr. Castell knows. It concerns certain events from twenty-five years ago."

Siegel looked at Castell who remained expressionless.

"Very well. But I suggest you proceed very cautiously with this questioning. I may even terminate the interview until Mr. Castell can be represented by counsel more experienced in criminal matters. Under that condition, go ahead with your questions."

"I'll be recording what you say, Mr. Castell. Let's start with what sequence of events brought you to the Ernest Debs Park on Saturday night?" Lieutenant Alvarado said.

Castell recounted receiving the text message with the terrifying video image of his daughter, the subsequent phone call, arranging for the money exchange, and devising a plan.

"I wasn't about to meet these kidnappers carrying only the money. I had to assume these were the same guys that tried to kidnap me a few days before at my office. So they know I have money. They get a hundred thousand dollars to start with then kidnap me for my wife to pay an even bigger ransom. She would do anything with both her husband and daughter being held. No reason they would ever return my daughter. Or me for that matter. So I made sure that wasn't going to happen."

"Why the bomb? Pretty extreme wasn't it?" Agent McIntyre said.

"Maybe. I didn't know firearms. I had to assume I would be shot before I could use the shotgun. Might not even get a chance to use it. But I could finalize everything with the bomb. Just press a button."

"And kill yourself too?"

"If necessary. But that wasn't my plan. I intended to place the gym bag at some height. That way I could fall to the ground and maybe miss the blast effects. It was a park. I was hoping for a picnic table to serve that purpose."

"How is it you know about bombs, Mr. Castell?" Kavanagh said.

"I don't. I rigged this from simply looking up the subject on the Internet."

"And the triggering mechanism?"

"That too. The means in this case was a very simple electrical circuit. After all, I have a degree in electrical engineering so understanding the effects of connecting a nine-volt battery to send a high current through the high resistance filament of a Christmas light bulb causing it to vaporize, was just basic electrical knowledge."

"Do you know a Carlos Perez?"

"No."

"He's a Salvadoran just like you, Mr. Castell."

"My mother was Salvadoran if that's what you mean."

"Yes. I'm aware of that. Died in a bombing in El Salvador in 1989, I believe."

"What the hell are ....." Castell began to say but was cut off by Larry Siegel.

"Never mind, Victor. And just what are you implying, Director Kavanagh?" Siegel said.

"I'll get back to that in a moment. But let me tell you what we know about Mr. Castell and Mr. Perez. "

"Who's Carlos Perez?" Siegel said.

"Perez is a top leader of the Salvadoran gang known as MS-13. Stands for Mara Salvatrucha. Started here in Los Angeles by Salvadoran immigrants. Perez was a charter member. But before that, Perez was associated with a terrorist named Santiago Molina. Also associated with Molina was a woman by the name of Patricia Reyes. Mr. Castell knows Patricia Reyes very well don't you, Mr. Castell?"

"Don't answer that, Victor."

"No matter. But the story becomes more tangled. Mr. Castell and Patricia Reyes were lovers when he was in El Salvador for

one summer. The summer of 1989. The same year the U.S. Embassy was bombed in San Salvador. The work of Santiago Molina. Molina followed this attack with the bombings a few weeks
later in Las Vegas. Turned out badly for Molina and most of his
terrorist cell. They died in a botched attempt by their own
bombs. All except Carlos Perez and Patricia Reyes. We only discovered their involvement recently.

"With the terrorist cell wiped out, Perez found a new career
with the Mara Salvatrucha. He helped them expand to become
contracted muscle for Mexican drug cartels. MS-13 is now active
in many cities in the United States, moving their own drugs. A
real business success story.

"Seems as though Patricia Reyes hitched herself to Perez.
He's a good looking guy. Avoided the freakish tattoos that his
soldiers favor. Anyway, Perez got arrested. Here in Los Angeles
not too long ago. He's awaiting trial on a raft of charges while in
jail without bond. Reyes was with him at the time of his arrest
but escaped being arrested herself. Desperate to get out of the
United States, we believe she looked up her old boyfriend Victor
Castell. The assailants that were involved in the incident at the
park are all MS-13. They don't pull this sort of thing in Pasadena.
Castell was a target. It was a personal matter between Carlos Perez and Mr. Castell."

"That's a ridiculous speculation, Kavanagh," Siegel said.

"No it's not, Counselor. You see Patricia Reyes died in a motel in San Diego a few weeks ago. The autopsy revealed she had
recently had sexual intercourse. DNA was recovered. We obtained a court order for your client's DNA. That recovered DNA
from the body of Patricia Reyes matches Victor Castell's. Perez
apparently found this out according to one of the perpetrators.
This wasn't about a kidnapping, it was revenge. A personal matter. Perez wanted to kill Mr. Castell for having sex with his
woman, and maybe even killing her. On that account, you were
very lucky, Mr. Castell. The Maras are particularly noted for sa-

distically torturing their victims before killing and then dismembering them."

Siegel was dumbfounded and speechless for a moment. "Tell you what, gentlemen. This interview is over. I'm advising my client to answer no further questions about anything until such time as he can arrange for appropriate legal representation. Am I to assume there are no charges currently being filed against Mr. Castell, either federal or state?"

"Not at this time," Alvarado said. "But I'd advise Mr. Castell not to leave California."

"No federal charges have been filed either," Kavanagh said. "But we are still early into more than one investigation involving your client. Undoubtedly we will have further reason to question Mr. Castell. Your advice about retaining a criminal defense attorney, Mr. Siegel is sound legal advice."

Once the law enforcement officers left, Siegel said to Castell, "I don't know what this is all about, Victor. It's obviously something more than a random event of bad luck. As to this woman they mentioned, I won't say anything to anyone. You'll have to deal with that in your own way. But I suggest you deal with it promptly. My guess is that it will become public. If the police know, then the media will find out. They'll be looking into every detail of your life. Lots of news hours to fill with content. You're now the number one nationwide news story. Businessman rescues daughter and kills gang assailants.

"And one last thing, Victor. By what I just heard, you need a criminal attorney. A damn good one. I won't press you, but I suspect you know exactly what this is all about. My advice is to be forthright with your criminal attorney. Hide anything and it could destroy you."

"I'm sorry to have dragged you into this, Larry. You're right about everything. I'll tell you the whole story in due time. Obviously I need to explain things to Eleanor. It's not just some casual affair with an old lover the way they made it sound. It's far more complicated."

Siegel held up his hand. "Just do the right thing and explain to Eleanor. Things are going to get rough when details become public. You owe it to her."

"I will, Larry. And one more thing I need you to do. Get me that criminal defense attorney. A really good one."

CHAPTER 38

Castell was well aware of the media storm swirling around him. It was the riveting banner story each evening because of all that was not known, and the intriguing inconsistencies. Why was the vicious MS-13 Central American gang involved with a wealthy high-tech business man? Yet the businessman was Latin too. Salvadoran on his mother's side. Mother was killed in a bombing in El Salvador in 1989? The businessman used a makeshift bomb to kill the kidnappers of his daughter? Money scattered all over a gruesome scene of violence in a quiet Southern California park? Was it even about kidnapping for ransom, or something else?

There were the endless commentaries about the vigilante prevailing over the bad guys. And the Mara Salvatruchas were certainly poster examples of very bad guys. It wasn't good business for a criminal enterprise to receive such unrelenting publicity. And the MS-13 with their bizarre facial tattoos made great visual copy in every form of media. To many, Victor Castell was a hero. Someone who stood up against the lowest of scum and fought back, beating them in spectacular fashion. It was the stuff of action movies and video games.

Castell knew that it would only get worse. The media's thirst for copy could only be fulfilled with every possible detail of his life. That life as he knew it was now over. But he could never imagine confessing to making those bombs. Keep to the lie to the end. Even though he was forever haunted by causing the death of so many people as a reaction to his person tragedy, confession would resolve nothing. He had fallen prey to Santiago Molina's persuasive arguments. Fallen prey to Patricia Reyes' charms. Followed a woman to his doom like something out of a novel. Fueled by the impetuous stupidity of youth. The aftermath of a confession would be worse than a quick death.

But he had tried to remedy the situation. After all, he had been the instrument of death for Santiago Molina and most of the terrorists. Unfortunately, additional innocent people had died. But what else could he have done? He was a victim himself. A captive at the time. What he did was the only means of escape short of suicide.

Did he feel guilt for the El Salvador bombing? Las Vegas? Certainly. But what form did that guilt take? He wasn't religious. Confession would not cleanse his soul. Sitting in a prison cell for the rest of his life would not provide some solace of atonement. Like an injury, scare tissue eventually developed to conceal the wound while still acting as a constant reminder. The guilt was manageable. He never delved too deeply into the metaphysics of his dealing with the circumstances. His was more the pragmatic view of an engineer and programmer. A survivor.

Castell rehearsed the details of his fictionalized account of what happened in 1989. It was generally the truth except for the omissions of his involvement with Santiago Molina. This was the story he would stick to with the police. Even to his own attorney. And of course to his wife. Unfortunately there was no way to lie about Patricia Reyes.

Of all his stupid reactionary actions in 1989, having sex with Patricia after twenty-five years was unconscionable. That ultimately led to all this. He loved Eleanor. Why had he allowed Patricia to seduce him? Was he that shallow and weak willed? Of course he was. Was he that afraid of what she might do if he rejected her? He could have deflected the sexual liaison and simply got her to the Mexican border. Now he feared it would cost him Eleanor.

That confrontation with that part of the truth followed the next day after the confrontation with the police. Eleanor could be put off no longer. Castell was still in his hospital bed. Eleanor had pulled up a chair. They were alone. She told her husband that she had made his father stay at the house with Regina. She needed to have a private discussion with her husband.

"Ok, Victor. Tell me what's been going on."

"Let me first say that I love you deeply, Eleanor. I'm so sorry that my past has come back to haunt me and jeopardize you and Regina.

"This is about 1989. I'd just finished school by getting my bachelor's in electrical engineering. I was taking the summer off. Planning on attending graduate school that fall at Caltech. My parents were separated. Mother returned to El Salvador and was staying with her brother René. Big landowner. Beautiful plantation in the highlands of western El Salvador. Been there as a kid many times. I was going to spend that summer down there."

"I know all that, Victor. She and her brother and her sister-in-law were all killed in the U.S. Embassy bombing. You told me that when we first met."

"Yes. But I never told you that I was in El Salvador at that time. I never told you that I did not attend my own mother's funeral. Or the reason I couldn't.

"It started with looking up my Uncle Augustin. He was a leading opposition figure to the military junta backed right-wing government. Remember in 1989, El Salvador was still gripped in a long-running nasty civil war. On the other side of that political divide was my Uncle René. Needless to say, the two brothers were virtual enemies.

"My rebellious youth made me clandestinely look up Uncle Augustin. He was a professor at the university. I had met him only once when I was younger. Met my new Aunt Claudia, his second wife, for the first time. Wonderful people. I took to them immediately. Instinctively I hated the police-state of the Salvadoran government after hearing Uncle Augustin speak of the repression, the torture, the sanctioned murder by the military. In contrast, my Uncle René was part of the moneyed caste that supported this brutal regime. My mother infuriated me with her affectations of being part of an imagined Salvadoran aristocracy.

"Unfortunately, both Uncle Augustin and Aunt Claudia were killed. Murdered by the right-wing government sponsored death squads. My uncle had become too much of a political threat.

"Now this brings me to something even more painful, and more immediate. It's why all this has been happening, Eleanor. It has to do with a woman I met in El Salvador in 1989. She was a student of my uncle's. Part of my uncle's opposition activist group. Left-leaning politics. We were attracted to each other. For a brief time we became lovers that summer."

"And what happened to this woman?" Eleanor said anticipating that there would be some further painful revelation from her husband.

"I'm getting to that. Her name was Patricia Reyes. We knew each other for only a couple of months. First my uncle and aunt were murdered. Then Patricia and I had a fateful encounter with the Salvadoran security forces. Without going into the details, Patricia was badly beaten. I would have been too except the security thugs knew that I was the nephew of the powerful René Portillo. So I was forced to watch her being beaten and threatened with rape. She avoided being raped only because they beat her unconscious. As for me, I was escorted to a plane leaving for Mexico City and immediately deported."

"And what happened to this woman, Victor?"

"I'm so sorry, Eleanor. It was an accident, a moment of weakness. I love you. Out of the blue she contacts me and ...."

"And you're going to tell me something happened. This old girlfriend comes back into your life. You're going to tell me you jumped into bed with her for old times' sake. Am I right?"

"It wasn't like that, Eleanor."

"No? What was it like then? You did have sex with her didn't you?"

"Yes. Just the one time. A stupid mistake."

"Oh, just once? But aside from your marital infidelity, is she the cause of whatever it was that happened this last week? Regina's kidnapping?"

"Unfortunately, yes. Apparently she became involved with a dangerous Salvadoran gang leader. He's in jail awaiting trial on all sorts of charges. Somehow he learned ....."

Eleanor cut him off, "That you were screwing his woman. Christ, Victor, you're having an affair with the mistress of some Central American drug kingpin? Of course the guy comes after you, failing that, he kidnaps Regina. And you like something out of an action movie script, get into a gunfight.

"And what happened to this woman?"

"She died. How I don't know."

"Are you sure, Victor? Are you telling me you were not involved in her death?"

"I didn't have anything to do with how she died. The police said it was possibly an accident. Some sort of fall. But the difficult part for me, why the police are so interested, is that it happened in San Diego after I drove her there. She wanted to escape being arrested here in the United States by walking across into Mexico. I just wanted her gone. Apparently something happened after I dropped her off at a motel close to the border."

"You sonofabitch, Victor. You have a one-night stand and drag me and Regina into your sordid past. Do you have any idea what we're going through? I've pulled Regina out of school. The managing partner at my firm has made indirect references concerning the implications of this national notoriety on my professional work. You think any prospective client will want me working on their account? And to make this even worse, if that's even possible, the media feeding frenzy is just heating up. Every night I listen to the news talk-shows. The speculation is all over the map. There are reporters staked out at our front gate. We're on the national news every night. They'll be sticking their noses into every aspect of our past.

"To be honest, Victor I don't believe you're telling me the whole story. The media talks about unconfirmed reports that even the FBI is conducting an investigation into you. It's too much. It was until death do us part, not this shit. So I'm leaving, Victor. I'm taking Regina and going to my sister's in New York. I can't live with this. Not sure I want to live with you any longer either."

Eleanor got up and left the hospital room ignoring her husband's plea not to leave.

"Goodbye, Victor"

CHAPTER 39

Egan Kavanagh was obsessively frustrated as never before. So close yet so far away. The bombings of 1989 were continually on his mind. It was the unresolved nature of the investigation. Namely, the engineer who rigged the bombs got away. Did he sabotage the Las Vegas bombs? And if so why? Did he have a subsequent career as a bomb maker? He now knew the identity of the bomb engineer; Victor Castell. But he could not assemble sufficient evidence to make a case. Maybe never be able to do that. His last hope was for Carlos Perez to turn states-evidence in a plea deal. That was a longshot. It might allow for an indictment of Castell, but even then it would be a difficult case to get to a guilty verdict.

There was no physical evidence linking Victor Castell to the bombings. The only witnesses that had implicated Castell would never be able to appear in an American courtroom. Isabel Salas who had the most expansive knowledge of Castell's involvement died of cancer. Only her recorded testimony questionably obtained under a sham confessional remained. The San Miguel radio shop owner was gravely ill. He too would probably die before Castell could ever be brought to trial. The only potential witness was Carlos Perez.

It had only been a matter of days since Kavanagh returned to Washington. Special Agent McIntyre informed him that Castell had indeed lawyered-up big time by retaining one of the most successful criminal defense attorneys in the country. Even if they could convince the Justice Department to file charges, it was going to prove to be a tough process to get a conviction. And with the unprecedented media attention, it would take agreement from the Attorney General himself in order to proceed.

With that already gloomy perspective, news came that would perhaps put any case against Castell out of reach. Carlos Perez was dead. Murdered in the exercise yard of the Los Angeles Metropolitan Detention Center. A makeshift knife from a piece of plastic stabbed into Perez's jugular vein. The wound was massive enough to cause Perez to bleed to death before medical assistance arrived. McIntyre said there were no suspects in custody. None of the inmates were talking. The word in the lockup is Perez was killed by his own, the Mara Salvatrucha. Ordered by the other leadership. Perez had become a liability. He had jeopardized all MS-13 operations by this unwanted publicity for his own personal reasons. And worse yet, he had failed. Anybody in Perez's position would have enemies. Easy to see how they would capitalize on these events.

Kavanagh now realized that there probably never would be any additional evidence implicating Victor Castell in acts of terrorism. Perez was the last person that could testify as a first hand witness to Castell's involvement. And it was the terrorism charges, the mass murders that Kavanagh wanted Castell to pay for. The other criminal charges Castell might be facing were trivial. Proving any level of homicide in Reyes' death was becoming unlikely for the State of California. Federal charges for possessing and detonating an explosive device might gain some traction, but since Castell could argue he was defending himself and his daughter, not a good bet for conviction from a jury.

The thought that Castell would never be held accountable was intolerable to Egan Kavanagh. He had been in law enforcement long enough to understand that justice did not always prevail. Foreign conflicts saw all manner of mass murder where no one was ever brought to trial. But this was an American citizen that literally might get away with the indiscriminate murders of so many of his fellow citizens. It just wasn't right.

Kavanagh brooded for days. He had poured over the evidence repeatedly with his team closest to the case. No matter how they summarized the body of evidence, it was weak at best. Everyone including Kavanagh knew the Justice Department would not seek an indictment on what they had. It had all the pitfalls of repeating the disastrous implications of the failed investigations publically targeting Richard Jewell for the Atlanta Olympics bombing in 1996, or Dr. Wen Ho Lee for espionage at Los Alamos in 1999. He was also mindful of the Wen Ho Lee civil suit settled in 2006 for the government's leaking of Lee's name before filing charges against him. Kavanagh was contemplating doing exactly that in this case.

Castell might eventually crack under the intense pressure, but that was probably unlikely. What Kavanagh was planning was simply justice. Castell was clearly guilty of terrible crimes. Society should not tolerate his crimes of mass murder.

Kavanagh had always been close to the intelligence community. He had many close relationships at the Central Intelligence Agency. He would now use that to inflict a form of vigilante justice on Victor Castell. Kavanagh rationalized that Castell was no different than a terrorist captured in Afghanistan or Yemen. The CIA did that all the time. The Guantanamo prison was full of people that would never be tried for their supposed crimes because there was insufficient evidence to present in a judicial process. While some at Guantanamo might not be guilty of anything

worse than being associated with enemies of America, Castell
was undoubtedly guilty of mass murder. No different than Tim-
othy McVeigh in the bombing of the Federal Building in Oklahoma City. McVeigh paid with his own life. Unfortunately, society would not be able to inflict that punishment on Victor Castell. But Egan Kavanagh would insure that he paid in other
ways.

The only weapon at Kavanagh's disposal was the media.
Castell's violent confrontation with these kidnappers continued
to be the foremost news story. The media was thirsting for more
details to fill the hours of continual broadcasting. If they were to
find out about Castell's past in El Salvador, this could lead to his
association with Patricia Reyes and the salacious details of sex,
drug gangs, and violence. With that sustained media interest in
Castell, Kavanagh planned to find a way to introduce the terrorism angle of the 1989 bombings. Who knows, enough media attention might even lead to indictments. But Kavanagh would
have to proceed very carefully so that the source of these leaks
could not be traced back to him. Castell's lawyer would not hesitate in filing a civil litigation against the government.

The first precaution was to limit involvement with any others. None of his staff could be involved. No compromising records, notes, emails, or telephone conversations would exist. The
key as to how to accomplish the destruction of Victor Castell was
El Salvador. The origin of the leaks needed to be from there with
no trail leading back to the United States government.

Once Egan Kavanagh made up his mind he telephoned
Colonel Calderón requesting a meeting to include the El Salvador Attorney General, Antonio Herrera. He wished to explore
how to proceed to bring legal charges against Victor Castell for
the bombing of the U.S. Embassy in San Salvador.

Kavanagh made the trip to El Salvador alone. Ostensibly it
was a follow-up to determine the status of what was an ongoing
investigation by El Salvador into the old terrorism case. He had

never documented the information about Isabel Salas' confession. He would let that contaminated piece of information be *discovered* by the tabloid press.

The meeting with Calderón and Herrera went according to Kavanagh's plan. Even better. Herrera had already been considering filing charges against Castell. He felt there was sufficient evidence to make a case for multiple charges of murder in El Salvador.

"I appreciate the difficulties in U.S. court," Herrera said. "The Salas testimony would be inadmissible. Morales might not live long enough so his affidavit might not be admissible as I understand your evidentiary rules.

"However, it's unlikely that El Salvador will prevail in seeking extradition in U.S. federal court. Those same evidentiary hurdles will apply in being granted extradition, especially to a U.S. citizen. And one with the means to hire the best legal defense possible. Am I assessing that correctly, Director Kavanagh?"

"You are correct, Mr. Attorney General. However, those legal processes of bringing charges here in El Salvador and seeking extradition will allow for my agency to formally investigate those charges against Victor Castell for acts of terrorism. Otherwise, if his name was used and we were never able to bring indictments, then under our laws the government could be subject to civil penalties. Worse yet, that would serve to deflect the charges in favor of Castell's innocence. And at the bottom of this, the clearly established fact is that he is guilty. Guilty of scores of murders, both Salvadoran and American."

"Very well, Director Kavanagh, we will move swiftly on this. Once charges are filed here we will formally petition the United States for his extradition. Hopefully new evidence may be discovered sufficient to bring charges in the United States. I understand Castell would be subject to the death penalty in your country. In El Salvador, only life imprisonment is possible."

"We would prefer that outcome but the chances of new evidence surfacing after twenty-five years are remote. With the death of Carlos Perez and Patricia Reyes, all of the known members of Santiago Molina's terrorist cell are dead. Except for Victor Castell. We can only hope that there might be more people, perhaps here in El Salvador, which might come forward with new information. To keep that possibility alive, there is something else I'd like to suggest we pursue. It is outside the boundaries of our legal processes, but in this case of violent international terrorism, I feel it is justified."

Kavanagh explained his plan.

Colonel Calderón nodded understandingly as Kavanagh explained about leaking the details of the evidence against Castell using Captain Gutierrez. After all, it was Gutierrez that firmly established Castell's identity as the bomb maker with his impersonation of a priest to extract the confession of Isabel Salas. What better source to tout his own ingenuity to the tabloid press. After that, the mainstream press will pursue the story, especially with the current media interest. At that time, the government of El Salvador would openly comment on their charges against Victor Castell, and their efforts to extradite him to stand trial for multiple murders in the bombing of the U.S. Embassy in 1989.

The Attorney General was not as enthusiastic as his police commander. "I don't know, Director Kavanagh. Not sure that I should be a party to that .....whatever the term is."

"Unorthodox I admit, Mr. Attorney General. But that is the nature of fighting terrorism in today's world. As you are aware, I head the branch of the Federal Bureau of Investigation charged with national security matters. In that post I work closely with the intelligence community. We are confronted daily with dealing with terrorists and those assisting them. Unfortunately, that requires using all means necessary to thwart these people. Often extrajudicial means. Victor Castell is one of those people. He may otherwise escape justice. We can't allow that to happen."

Herrera reluctantly nodded his agreement. "Very well. I'll leave it to you and Colonel Calderón to do what is necessary. I would rather not know the particulars."

Calderón and Kavanagh left Herrera's office. In the hallway, Kavanagh gave Calderón a slip of paper. On it was printed a name, address, and telephone number.

"This is a reporter for a Salvadoran newspaper. He's been known to have contact with a reporter for the New York Post. The Post is a tabloid that pays for sensational stories like this. Suggest that your enterprising Captain Gutierrez should negotiate a share of any money the Post might payout.

"And just one more thing, Colonel. This meeting we just had never took place."

CHAPTER 40

Two weeks later the New York Post splashed the headline, *Hero or Terrorist?* over a large photo of Victor Castell. The story cited an unidentified source that had new information on terrorist bombings twenty-five years ago on the U.S. Embassy in El Salvador, and subsequent bombings by the same group at casinos in Las Vegas. The hero who single-handedly thwarted a kidnapping, killing two vicious gang members recently, was identified as being under investigation for allegedly being part of that former terrorist group.

The story went on to explain that the information newly surfaced through a contrived confession from the dying mother of one of the terrorists that was killed in the Las Vegas bombings. That provoked its own set of media debates about the ethics of such tactics.

The broadcast news talk shows switched the tone of their continued preoccupation with the Victor Castell saga to this new strain of speculation. The mainstream press was not far behind the tabloid shock-value headlines with their own continuing serialization of the ever widening story. Additional details emerged almost daily. Foreign correspondents besieged the Salvadoran Ministry of Justice. Both Herrera and Calderón gave repeated press conferences and interviews.

The Attorney General of the United States was forced to address the Salvadoran accusations about Victor Castell being a former terrorist. He even had to defend why the FBI lagged behind a small Central American country in uncovering evidence enough to bring criminal charges. The Attorney General thought Egan Kavanagh would find that ironic.

For Victor Castell his former life had now truly ended. Eleanor and Regina had left. The press had somehow even found them in New York and was subjecting them to constant confrontation outside Eleanor's sister's Manhattan apartment building. For Castell it was worse. Reporters congregated outside his driveway gate. Pasadena police prohibited film crews from parking their vans in the street, but the scene became intolerable each time anyone came or went to the residence. So Castell left to stay at the Langham Huntington Hotel in Pasadena under a room arranged by Larry Siegel, and billed to his law firm, allowing Castell to remain incognito. But the five-star hotel was nothing more than a well-appointed prison with good food.

Hiding out was not a way to weather the storm. It would never blow over. It would only get worse. With the mounting pressure for answers around the public accusations raised by the government of El Salvador, Castell feared the U.S. government might file their own charges at any time. His lawyer was confident that if they did, the government's case would be very problematic. But it would still be an unbearable ordeal that could last years.

With his criminal defense attorney and Larry Siegel, Castell stuck to the same sanitized story he told to his wife. The whole episode in El Salvador had to do with getting involved with opposition politics through his Uncle Augustin. Then the romance with Reyes. The only admission was having met this Santiago Molina one time at a party. He was introduced through Reyes. If

Reyes was a terrorist he never knew that. Yes there was a violent confrontation with Salvadoran police. Reyes was badly beaten. He was recognized as the nephew of an important person and thrown out of the country. He was never sure what happened to Reyes. Prison? Death? Lots of people turned up missing at that time in El Salvador. No way for him to make contact once he was expelled from El Salvador.

This radio shop owner that sold the electronics used in the bombs was mistaken. After all, it was twenty-five years ago. Castell was supposedly identified through just a group of photographs by questionable Salvadoran investigators. The same investigators that impersonated clergy to con a dying woman. He did not know a Roberto Salas or his mother, Isabel Salas. Apparently Patricia Reyes did. Perhaps a senile dying old woman had confused her own son's activities with Reyes' talk about her boyfriend from the United States. Perhaps the Salvadoran police tricked the old woman by suggesting his name. Who knows? And the woman is now conveniently dead.

Why did he help Reyes when she came to him in Los Angeles? Afraid it would get out that he had a previous intimate relationship with the girlfriend of a vicious Central American gang. What would she do if he didn't help her? It could result in damaging publicity for his firm. A difficult explanation to his wife. Yes he succumbed to Reyes sexual advances. He had once had a very sexual relationship with Patricia Reyes. She was still a very attractive woman. She initiated the sexual encounter although admittedly he did not resist. A dumb mistake. He left her at the motel in San Diego. She had a lot to drink. Probably just fell. A freak accident. He was not the one that tried to help her before she died. He wasn't there.

The story was solid. According to Castell's defense attorney, unless some new and compelling evidence surfaced, there was no case for federal charges other than the use of an explosives device and aiding a fugitive. The attorney could argue the explosive device was a means of self-defense. No innocent people were injured. Aiding a fugitive wanted only for questioning was a questionable charge. Any state charges against Castell related to Reyes death were unlikely by now.

Victor Castell had beaten his past. But at what cost? Maybe this was his punishment. He would have to sell his company. His wife was gone. Even if she could forgive the infidelity, she could not live a life of notoriety. Could he? He would need to abandon seeing his daughter to shield her from the same notoriety. What the hell would he do with his life? Where could he go without being recognized?

Yet he had done this once before. Covered his mistakes. Buried everything. Not well enough it seems, but only because of factors beyond his control. While those old events resurfaced, they could not legally connect him to these crimes. Terrible as though crimes were, he had no intention to confess now that he had once again survived.

It had been two weeks since Castell had been in hiding. His only contacts were Larry Siegel and his defense attorney. They typically met at the hotel. Castell had made his decision about moving on. He planned on moving to the Bay area. Close to his aging father. Close to the center of digital high-tech work. That's all he knew, all he cared to do. Perhaps he could contribute on project work. Under a different name of course. Larry Siegel was exploring how to quietly have his name changed legally. The next thing was to sell Castell Systems.

Except for senior managers, Siegel made arrangements to send all Castell Systems staff home on a Friday afternoon. Joining the Company's management was an investment broker that would take Castell Systems to market. Castell was officially resigning as CEO and named his senior vice president of technology as interim CEO. Castell wanted to insure his key people that it was his intention to get top-dollar for the company so that everyone fared well with their stock ownership. He also wanted to insure them that he was seeking a buyer that would allow their group to remain intact to the extent possible within a different corporate structure. To that end, everyone was incentivized to help in promoting the sale to perspective buyers. Castell would arrive at one o'clock to talk with everybody. He'd give a brief explanation to events that had brought on this crisis and his assurances for getting a good deal for all of them in selling the company.

Reporters had since given up their vigils at Castell's residence and office. So Castell drove into the parking structure in his red Aston Martin, parking in his designated space. As he exited his car and walked to the stairway, a man came up the stairs.

Castell stopped abruptly. He was riveted looking at the man in a hooded sweatshirt. He had never seen a face so grotesquely disfigured. The entire left side of the man's face was not only a mass of scar tissue, but the whole geometry of his face was distorted.

"Did I frighten you? Sorry. My face does that. Pretty horrible isn't it?"

"Ah, I'm sorry, I didn't mean to stare. Forgive me."

"Quite all right, Mr. Castell. You are Mr. Victor Castell aren't you?"

Castell hesitated. Who the hell was this guy? A reporter? Not likely with a face like that. "Yes. I'm Victor Castell. And you are?"

"My name's not important. We've never met. Up until a few weeks ago I never knew you existed. Or what you had done. You see I got this way because of something that happened a long time ago. An explosion followed by a fire. Happened in El Salvador in 1989. You were there too. In fact I now know you're the cause of this. Would have been better if I had died with my fellow Marines that day. Life has not been as good for me as it apparently has been for you, Castell. Semper Fi."

With that the former U.S. Marine lance corporal assigned to the diplomatic protection detail at the U.S. Embassy in San Salvador in 1989, withdrew his old service semi-automatic, a Colt M1911 .45 caliber, and fired the entire seven-round magazine into Victor Castell.

www.ingramcontent.com/pod-product-compliance
Lightning Source LLC
Chambersburg PA
CBHW030349030726
47497CB00002B/254